PRAISE FOR

The Swift and the Harrier

'This well-researched, atmospheric tale is as gripping as any of her thrillers' — *Good Housekeeping*

'A cleverly crafted combination of romance and adventure story' — *Sunday Times*

'The author best known for her crime fiction sets this enthralling tender love story against the brutal background of the English Civil War' — *The i*

'Minette Walters, a stalwart of crime fiction, is excellent on the horrors of civil war in Dorset, and Swift is a memorable and spirited heroine' — *The Times*

'Both gripping and fascinating. The civil war in Dorset is evoked brilliantly, the characters are real and intriguing and the love story tender.' — Elizabeth Buchan, bestselling author of *The New Mrs Clifton*

'A sweeping historical romance with a very appealing central character … a great story well told' — Andrew Taylor, bestselling author of *The Ashes of London*

'This is historical fiction at its finest … Jayne is a fantastic character, a woman very much in a man's world, living and working to bring succour to those in need' — *Belfast Telegraph*

'I have loved every moment of this brilliantly evocative saga of struggle, love and danger set against the horrors of civil war' — S W Perry, bestselling author of *The Jackdaw Mysteries*

PRAISE FOR

The Turn of Midnight

'Walters writes a mean historical drama…compelling' — *Daily Telegraph*

'A mammoth tale' — *BBC History Magazine*

'Stunning' — *Daily Express*

'This intriguing read makes excellent use of outstanding historical detail and depth…an impressive literary adventure' — *Canberra Weekly*

'Vividly readable…Walters' transition away from crime is complete, bringing her a wealth of new fans' — *Herald Sun*

The Players

MINETTE WALTERS

ALLEN&UNWIN

First published in trade paperback in Australia in 2024 by Allen & Unwin

First published in hardback in Great Britain in 2025 by Allen & Unwin,
an imprint of Atlantic Books Ltd

10 9 8 7 6 5 4 3 2 1

A CIP catalogue record for this book is available from the British Library.

Hardback ISBN: 978 1 80546 315 3
Trade paperback ISBN: 978 1 80546 316 0
E-book ISBN: 978 1 80546 317 7

Printed and bound by CPI (UK) Ltd, Croydon CR0 4YY

Allen & Unwin
An imprint of Atlantic Books Ltd
Ormond House
26–27 Boswell Street
London
WC1N 3JZ

www.atlantic-books.co.uk

MIX
Paper | Supporting
responsible forestry
FSC® C171272

For Jenny, Ricky, Matt and Jane

All the world's a stage, and all the men and women merely players. They have their exits and their entrances; and one man in his time plays many parts.

WILLIAM SHAKESPEARE, *AS YOU LIKE IT*

Faber est quisque fortunae suae.
(Every man is the architect of his own fortune.)

APPIUS CLAUDIUS CAECUS

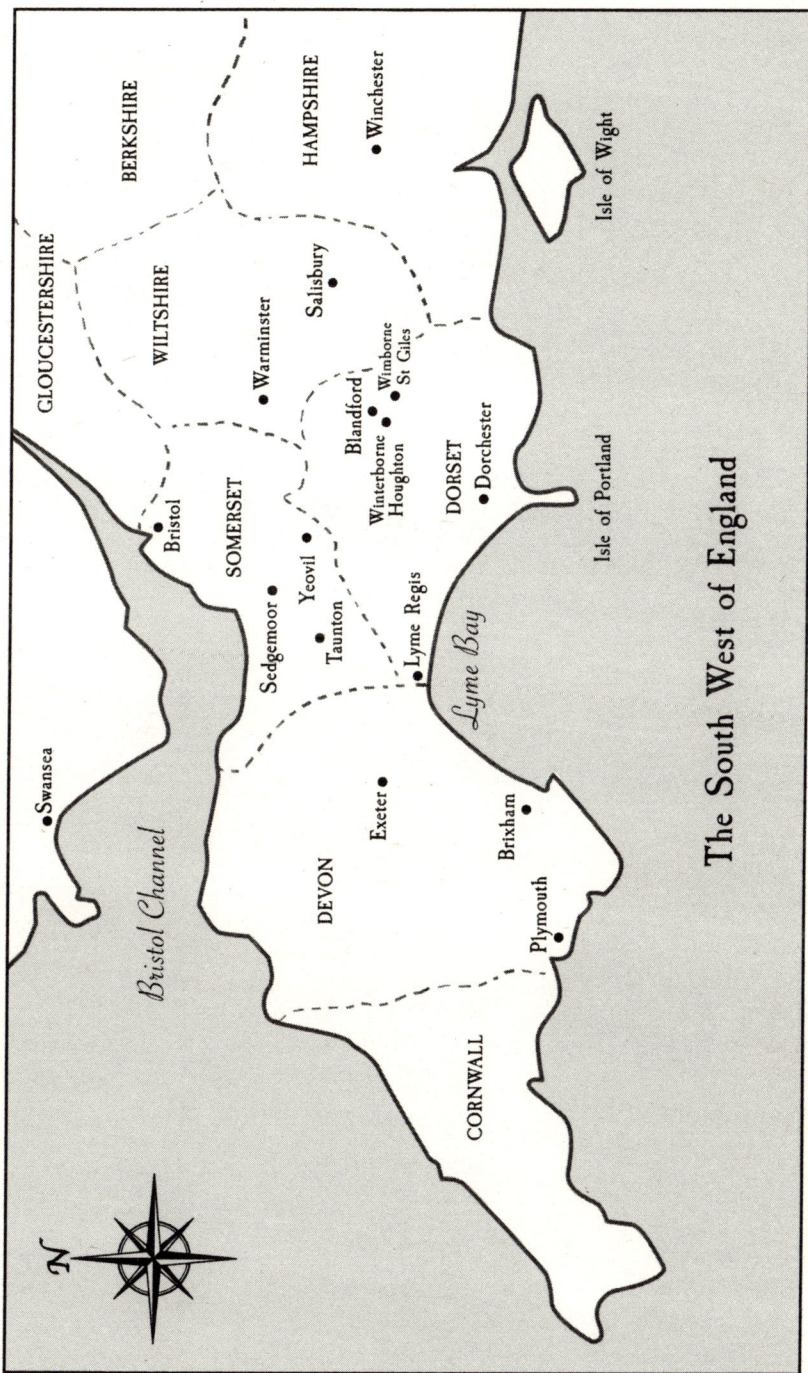

The South West of England

Map labels:
- BERKSHIRE
- HAMPSHIRE
- Winchester
- GLOUCESTERSHIRE
- WILTSHIRE
- Salisbury
- Warminster
- Wimborne St Giles
- Blandford
- Winterborne Houghton
- DORSET
- Dorchester
- Bristol
- SOMERSET
- Yeovil
- Sedgemoor
- Taunton
- Lyme Regis
- Lyme Bay
- Isle of Wight
- Isle of Portland
- Swansea
- Bristol Channel
- Exeter
- DEVON
- Brixham
- Plymouth
- CORNWALL
- N

THE AFTERMATH OF THE ENGLISH CIVIL WAR

IN THE TEN TURBULENT YEARS that followed the brutal Civil War between Parliament and the King, which ended in victory for Parliament and the execution of Charles I in 1649, only five delivered stable government. These were under the leadership of the Lord Protector, Oliver Cromwell, whose control of the New Model Army imposed order, albeit through a military dictatorship. A king in all but name, Cromwell filled the void left by the empty throne, but his early death in 1658 threatened to plunge the country into turmoil once again.

With no strong figurehead emerging from its own ranks, Parliament voted to restore the monarchy, and Charles I's heir, his eldest son, was invited to return as King in 1660. Dubbed 'the Merry Monarch', Charles II was likeable, good-humoured and charming. He reigned for twenty-five years and, by steering a more intelligent course than his father, never lost the loyalty of his subjects. His single failure was his inability to produce a legitimate heir with his wife, Catherine of Braganza, although he was known to have twelve illegitimate children by his many mistresses, the eldest being the Duke of Monmouth.

On Charles II's death in February 1685, the only successor with a legal claim to the throne was his brother James, Duke of York, younger son of Charles I. However, James's conversion to Catholicism in 1669 had set many against him, and voices of discontent were heard across England, warning that a Catholic king would once again subject his country to the tyranny of Rome.

The Players

PROLOGUE

The Hague, Holland, April 1685

IT WAS A FAVOURABLE NIGHT to stand unseen in the shadows of an alleyway. The sickle moon was obscured by clouds and a cool mist rolled off the sea, shrouding The Hague in fog. The watcher eased his position occasionally to relieve an aching muscle, but his movements were slight. Dressed in black, with a wide-brimmed hat pulled low over his face, he escaped notice in the darkness that surrounded him.

The alleyway led off a street of tall, elegantly gabled buildings and, despite the mist, the watcher had a clear view of the Duke of Monmouth's house. In contrast to the muted glow of candles in the upper chambers of its neighbours, flaring lanterns hung from brackets along the facade, throwing light across the cobbles. The watcher had known where Monmouth lived from previous visits to The Hague, but even if he hadn't, the duke's penchant for flying his standard from a pole above his front door made his whereabouts obvious to anyone with an interest in his activities.

In the three hours since the watcher had taken up position in the alleyway, eight men had presented themselves at the door and not one had attempted to hide his face. Rather, they had seemed to revel in drawing attention to themselves, pounding on the panels and announcing themselves loudly in English to the servant who answered. The watcher had been certain of only four names before he arrived. Now, he knew them all and questioned their foolishness in making their conspiracy so obvious. Were they ignorant or careless of the spies that haunted The Hague and reported everything they saw and heard to the court of King James?

He judged it to be close to midnight when the guests emerged again, and he counted them off as they left. The last to leave was the Earl of Argyll, and his annoyance was evident as he stepped onto the street and rebuked Monmouth's servant for being dilatory in handing him a lantern. At fifty-six Argyll was the oldest of the plotters and the least content to be living in exile in Holland, a fact he made clear in every letter he wrote. The watcher listened to his footsteps disappearing into the night and was unsurprised to see a cloaked figure follow behind him a few moments later.

Conscious that there might be others, he remained where he was, and his patience was rewarded within five minutes when a second figure passed in front of the guttering lanterns on Monmouth's house. Shortly afterwards, the servant appeared from the side of the building to quench the flames with a candle snuffer, and the thoroughfare was plunged into darkness. Even so, the watcher waited on, listening for the scuff of shoes or boots on stones, but when nothing disturbed the stillness of the night, he slipped from the alleyway and trod softly across the cobbles.

He found the narrow alley from which Monmouth's servant had emerged more by feel than sight, but once inside a glow at the far end of the right-hand wall led him forward. As he'd hoped, the light was coming from the kitchen quarters, and a glance through the narrow window showed him that Monmouth's valet was the only occupant of the room. Relieved not to have to explain himself to a Dutch maid, he rounded the corner of the house and used the light from a larger window to locate the door. Aware that his sudden appearance would shock the valet, he removed his hat before lifting the latch and stepping inside.

He smiled in recognition as he crossed the floor and stationed himself in front of the fire. The man was an old soldier who had been serving Monmouth for nearly twenty years. 'Good evening, John. I trust you're well.'

The valet clapped his hand to his heart. 'Mercy me! Is that you, my lord?'

'As I live and breathe.' He tucked his hat beneath his arm, removed his gloves and began to unbutton his coat.

The elderly valet's expression was easy to read, for he was clearly suspicious of the visitor's motives in coming. He knew well that his master had enemies in England, from where he guessed the visitor had travelled, though his chances of learning anything from the other's expression were negligible; the younger man was too well-schooled in the art of deception.

'May I ask what you're doing here, my lord?'

'Trying not to be seen,' came the amiable response. 'The Hague is awash with men keen to record the names of your master's guests. It seemed safer to enter through the kitchen quarters.'

'I meant, what are you doing in the master's house, my lord? Is he expecting you?'

'Not at all, John. My intention is to surprise him, in the hope that he'll listen to me. He appears to be keeping dangerous company.'

The valet looked for weapons as he relieved the visitor of his hat and gloves and assisted him out of his fog-saturated coat, but if the visitor was hiding anything it wasn't obvious. Clad in tight-fitting shirt, waistcoat and britches, anything deadly would have been visible.

Reassured, he answered honestly. 'I'm forbidden from commenting, my lord, but you'll have no argument from me if you've come to remonstrate with him. He's been in need of good advice since his father died, but he rejects mine in favour of the whisperings of schemers.'

'Has he retired to bed?'

John draped the coat over the back of a chair and angled it towards the fire to dry. 'Not yet, sir. He sits in the parlour with a bottle of cognac staring at his father's portrait. It's most unhealthy. Do you wish me to announce you?'

'No need. Just tell me which door to enter.'

'The second on the left, my lord.' The valet opened a cupboard and removed a glass. 'You'll need this if you're to partake of the cognac. The master will be insensible within thirty minutes if you leave him to drink the bottle alone.'

'Has he eaten?'

'Not since breakfast. He lives on his nerves these days.'

'Is there food in the pantry?'

'Only raw mutton for tomorrow. This evening's guests ate the last of the bread and cheese.'

4

The visitor reached down to extract ten guilders from his coat pocket and exchanged them for the glass. 'Buy what you can at this hour, keep some for yourself and bring the rest to the parlour. I'll be insensible myself if cognac is all that enters my stomach. I haven't eaten since leaving England at dawn yesterday and lost most of what I consumed into the sea.'

John's gaze was sympathetic. 'A rough crossing, sir?'

'Rough and long,' came the wry response. 'It's not a journey I'd wish on anyone, least of all your master.'

'Be sure to tell him that, sir. He has a fanciful notion that his return to England will be as calm as when he left it two years ago.'

Rumour had it that Monmouth was selling everything he had of value, and his reduced circumstances showed in the modest furniture of the parlour. There was no uniformity to the chairs, donated by well-wishers, which stood about the rough-hewn table at the centre. The room was warm enough, being small and benefiting from glowing embers in the hearth, but to the visitor's eyes the single candle and the dark oak panelling on the walls gave it more the look of a monk's cubicle than the drinking chamber of a future king. The only adornment was a portrait above the mantel of the fireplace—a representation of Charles II in the style of Sir Peter Lely—which took the place of a crucified Christ in this gloomy cell.

'Leave me be,' muttered Monmouth when he heard the creak of the door behind him. 'I'm wearied of your scolding, old man.'

'I've a mere two years on you, James, and you've yet to hear me scold you.'

Monmouth turned his head from contemplation of the portrait. 'Goddamn it!' he cried. 'Are you real?'

The visitor placed his glass on the table and stepped forward to grip Monmouth's hand. 'As real as you.' He assessed the duke's face in the flickering light of the candle and thought him barely changed from when they had first met twenty-two years ago. He still had the same boyish good looks and charming smile of the fourteen-year-old who had captured the hearts of his father's people. 'My mother sends her regards and wishes you to know that she shares your grief,' he said, drawing out a chair and lowering himself to the seat. 'As do I. Your father's death was most sudden and unexpected.'

'He was poisoned,' Monmouth declared bitterly, filling the visitor's glass with cognac and passing it to him with an unsteady hand. 'Join me in drinking to the death of his murderer.'

'Gladly. What name does he go by?'

The words came out in a slur. 'King James of England . . . hated uncle . . . hated namesake . . . Catholic traitor . . . enemy of Protestants . . . vile slayer of his brother.'

The visitor shook his head. 'I can't drink to a lie, James. Let's toast your father's memory instead.' He touched his glass to Monmouth's. 'To our Merry Monarch, a man much loved and mourned by his people—and by none so much as his first-born son.' He took a swallow of brandy, welcoming the heat it generated in his throat and belly.

Tears sprang into Monmouth's eyes. 'He was taken before I could reconcile with him. He died believing me capable of killing him.'

The reference was to the Rye House Plot of two years previously, when members of the Whig party in Parliament had devised a plan to assassinate King Charles and his brother in order to ensure that a Protestant succeeded to the throne of England. The attempt was never made, but the names of the conspirators were revealed when one of their number turned informer. Amongst those cited were the Duke of Monmouth and the Earl of Argyll.

'Your father wouldn't have let you flee to Holland if he thought you as culpable as the ringleaders,' the visitor said matter-of-factly. 'You'd have suffered the same fate as Lord Russell and the eleven others who were executed.'

Monmouth couldn't have been as drunk as he seemed because his response was immediate and fluent. 'But I had no culpability in the plot,' he protested. 'I never participated in it, and those who said I did were lying. They hoped to save their own skins by implicating me.'

The denial was so practised that the visitor wondered if Monmouth had succeeded in persuading himself of his own innocence. He took a second sup of brandy and responded with a falsehood of his own. 'I believe you, my friend. You've more sense than to involve yourself in treason.' He chose the word deliberately, but Monmouth's only reaction was to shed more tears.

'Why could my father not see that?'

'He would have done in time.'

Monmouth raised his gaze to the portrait again. 'It's too late. Did he speak of me before he died?'

'I don't know. He had a seizure on the second of February and, despite the efforts of his doctors, passed from life four days later.'

Monmouth's tears dried abruptly. 'Men of fifty-four don't have seizures for no reason.'

The visitor shook his head. 'My mother would disagree with you. One of the attending physicians sent her a copy of his notes, and from the symptoms he described, she believes the King's heart and lungs failed him. His health had been deteriorating for months, causing pain from near-constant gout, ulcers and breathlessness, and she's of the view that these were the outward symptoms of inner disease. For that reason, she urges you to ignore the rumours of poisoning, and says further that if anything hastened his death, it was the unremitting purges and bloodletting performed by the royal physicians.'

Predictably, Monmouth seized on the single phrase that suited him. 'The rumours of poisoning must be rife in England if your mother has heard them.'

'They are, but only the most ardent Catholic-haters give them credence. Wiser heads ask what your uncle had to gain by having his brother killed.'

'The throne.'

'But why now?' the visitor asked reasonably. 'Why not next year or the year after? He's younger than your father and could have waited a decade if necessary. He's too aware of how the English view his conversion to Catholicism to show impatience to become king.'

Monmouth's eyes narrowed. 'Have you come at his request? You seem mighty keen to play the advocate for him.'

'You know me better than that, James. I'm here as your friend to give you more honest advice than the discontents who mutter in your ear.'

'Which discontents?'

'Argyll for one. You're being used by a practised deceiver. His promises to deliver Scotland for you are as false as his stories of poisoning.'

The glass in Monmouth's hands quivered violently. 'What can you possibly know of Argyll's business?'

The visitor gave a low laugh. 'The same that King James and his advisers know. Argyll's letters are regularly intercepted and he's criminally loose-lipped about your plans for rebellion.'

The duke rose to his feet and leant against the mantel, presenting his back to his guest. 'I'm not responsible for what he writes.'

'But you're party to his plan, James. Every meeting you've had with him and your fellow conspirators has been witnessed and reported by men in the pay of your uncle. The King knows the names of everyone involved.'

No answer.

'If you need better evidence, I've been watching your house since sunset and I wasn't alone in doing so. Two spies, as well-hidden as I, followed Argyll after he left. I'm ignorant of whether they were Dutch or English—perhaps one of each—but be in no doubt that your intrigues are as well known here at the court of Prince William as they are in London.'

A stifled groan issued from Monmouth's mouth. 'What other claims are being made about me?'

'That you're soliciting your supporters for money, particularly those in the south-west. Your letters are intercepted as frequently as Argyll's, and you press your need for capital funds in all of them.'

'My father's death has left me wanting.'

'Yet you've recently pawned your jewellery and silver for three thousand pounds, and the mother of your mistress has promised you another three thousand.'

Monmouth kicked a burning ember. 'Where did you learn that?'

'From a source in Prince William's court. I cannot emphasise enough that you have no secrets, James. You and Argyll have raised less than twenty thousand pounds between you, and that sum is insufficient to purchase the ships, troops and weapons needed for a successful invasion of England and Scotland. The King's army totals above ten thousand, and there are many more thousands of local militiamen who are sworn to his service. Tell me how you expect to defeat them without troops of similar numbers and experience.'

The silence that followed this question was interrupted by John, who entered the room with a platter of food. 'You forget the love the people have for my master, sir,' he said, placing the plate on the table. 'Lord Argyll assures him that every able-bodied Protestant in the British Isles will rally to his standard once he sets foot ashore.'

Monmouth rounded on him angrily. 'Cease your damned meddling!'

The elderly valet stood his ground. 'Lord Argyll says, too, that the master can land anywhere and walk to London with naught but a stick in his hand. The people will follow him wherever he goes.'

'Out!'

The valet searched the visitor's face. 'Is there anything else I can do for you, sir?'

The visitor smiled. 'No, thank you, John. You've provided me with everything I need.' He waited until the valet left, then spooned pickled herring onto a hunk of bread. 'Will you eat with me, James? Honest Dutch food will do more for your health and temper than a diet of cognac.'

With another petulant kick at the embers, Monmouth resumed his seat and selected a wedge of edam. 'As long as you end your lecturing. Do you think me such a fool that I take everything Argyll says on trust?'

Since Monmouth's recklessness was matched only by his poor judgement, that was precisely what his guest thought, but he avoided an answer by chewing on the bread and pickled herring.

'And you shouldn't believe anything John says,' Monmouth continued. 'His mind is so addled he forgets his own name. He'll have forgotten yours by tomorrow. He picks up snippets from the other side of the door and weaves them into nonsense.'

The visitor piled more herring onto bread. 'My ship sails at dawn, so I can't stay beyond another hour if I'm to reach the harbour without being seen. Is there any news I can give you about your acquaintances in England?'

Monmouth frowned. 'Why the haste to leave?'

'I can't afford to be linked with you, James. I'm too fond of my head to lose it over an ill-judged plot that can't succeed. The Civil War is still strong in people's memories and they won't willingly engage in conflict again.'

'A peaceful rebellion needn't involve war.'

The visitor shook his head at his friend's naivety. 'In your fantasies, perhaps, but not in reality. From the moment you set foot on English soil, you will be committing an act of high treason. Your uncle may be as bad as you paint him, but he's your father's only legitimate heir and has Parliament's authority to defend England against all usurpers. He will send his army against you whether his subjects want him to or not.'

Monmouth stared into his glass. 'Many believe my claim to be as valid as his.'

'Not in Parliament, where it matters. A son born out of wedlock cannot succeed to his father's throne.'

A twisted smile formed on Monmouth's lips. 'But a Catholic brother can.'

The visitor nodded. 'The arguments haven't changed, James.'

'And if the people decide differently?'

'The choice isn't theirs to make, and any who are foolish enough to take up arms on your behalf will be condemned as traitors. Your uncle has a long reach and his justice will be harsh. Remember that before you encourage others to join a venture that is doomed to failure.'

There was only the slightest of hesitations before Monmouth answered. 'You concern yourself unnecessarily,' he said lightly. 'I made clear to Argyll this evening that his plans are his own, and I'm neither so foolish nor so rash as to engage with them. He left in anger, which you will know if you watched his departure.'

The visitor acknowledged the point with a tilt of his glass, but he disbelieved the rest of what Monmouth had said. Lies had always tripped off his hot-headed friend's tongue more easily than truth.

He fingered the small paper sack of white arsenic in his waist-coat pocket. It would be a simple sleight of hand to drop the contents into Monmouth's brandy glass, but he foresaw more problems than solutions if murder was suspected. Legitimate or not, Monmouth was of royal blood, and King James needed no better excuse to break his treaties with Holland than the killing of his nephew on Dutch soil.

The visitor made his way back to the harbour along lanes he knew well from previous visits. As King Charles II's personal envoy, he had crossed the Channel regularly, carrying letters from the King to his nephew Prince William of Orange, Stadtholder of staunchly Protestant Holland. Prince William was the son of Charles and James's sister, placing him fourth in the line of succession to the English throne, and the sensitive nature of the correspondence between the two men had necessitated secrecy. For this reason, the envoy had grown more accustomed to moving at night than during the day.

The Anglo-Dutch wars, fought sporadically for twenty years as each country battled for trade dominance around the globe, had ended in victory for Holland in 1674. The settlement that followed had held, but distrust had lingered on both sides. The same was true across Europe as old alliances fractured and new ones formed. The legacy of the Continent's thirty years of religious wars had led to France under Louis XIV becoming the leading power in Europe, and animosity towards French imperialism was rife.

Holland had strongly resisted Louis XIV's attempts at invasion, but Prince William, ever suspicious of Catholic France, saw merit in cementing peace with Protestant England. To that end, he had petitioned King Charles to approve his marriage to Mary, the eldest daughter of Charles's brother James and second to James in the line of succession. The negotiations had taken time, not least because James opposed the match. As a Catholic, he believed it was against God's law for first cousins to marry, though sceptics thought his objections owed more to the risk that William and Mary posed to his own succession, both being Protestant and with near equal claims to the English throne.

In the interests of peaceful cooperation, King Charles had overruled his brother, and the cousins had wed in 1677. Thereafter, the only matter of personal interest that had concerned the two heads of state had been the Duke of Monmouth's exile to Holland in 1683. Neither had wanted him to create problems for themselves or their governments, and while King Charles lived, there had been little to report; on his death, the warnings of an imminent rebellion began.

King James, unwilling to engage in secret or open correspondence with his son-in-law, dismissed his brother's envoy and employed an army of spies to inform him of Monmouth's plans. In contrast, Prince William drew the envoy closer and used his own spies to intercept and read the reports sent to King James.

The envoy's route took him to Vissershaven, the fishing port, where light from the ever-open taverns spilt onto the cobbled quay. He stood there for several minutes in thought, then retrieved the sack from his waistcoat pocket. His intended target had been Argyll, but his chances of gaining access to the earl had always been slim. With only minor regret at his failure—murder would have troubled his conscience—he dropped the sack into the water and turned towards the lights.

The door of De Drie Vissen was open and he cast around for his Dutch counterpart. Spotting him in a darkened corner, conversing earnestly with a man whose profile bore a strong resemblance to the second spy to follow Argyll, he withdrew to the opposite corner and prepared to wait.

Jan Hendriksen joined him some quarter-hour later, slapping two filled tankards on the table between them. He spoke in English, being less understandable to eavesdroppers. 'If I didn't know you so well, I'd call you a liar if you said you met with Monmouth. My informant watched the street for five hours, and named or described every man he saw—whether they entered the duke's house or not—and you were not amongst them.'

The envoy grinned. 'But I saw him well enough. He showed himself minutes after the King's man who was dogging Argyll.' He touched his tankard to Jan's and took a swallow of frothy beer. 'I have only bad news for Prince William. Monmouth is in too deep to stop now. He claimed he's broken ties with Argyll, but he was lying. They had words, but I would guess the argument was more about timing than whether or not to proceed. My best advice for Prince William is to honour his treaties with England and keep a healthy distance from his cousin. Any hint of collusion with Monmouth will give King James an excuse to name his daughter and son-in-law as conspirators in the rebellion.'

'All of Holland, too, no doubt.'

'Indeed. Do you know when Argyll is due to sail?'

'In a couple of weeks. They plan to wait in the Zuider Zee for a favourable wind.'

'And Monmouth?'

Jan took a swallow from his own tankard. 'He'll not be ready before June. He's acquired three ships but little else. I'm told he lacks the necessary funds to purchase muskets, let alone field guns. To date, he's mustered a mere five dozen mercenaries to support his campaign, and Prince William wonders if we shouldn't incarcerate him for his own safety. He seems completely ignorant of the strength of the force that will be sent against him.'

The envoy steadied a drunken sailor who stumbled against him. '*Wees dankbaar dat ik een vergevingsgezinde man ben,*' he said. '*Doe het nog een keer en ik gooi je de straat op.*'*

---

* Be thankful I'm a forgiving man. Do it again and I'll toss you into the street.

The sailor muttered an apology and staggered back the way he had come. The noise in the tavern was loud enough to cover their conversation, but the envoy waited until the sailor was out of earshot before continuing. 'Argyll has convinced Monmouth that England is rife with anti-Catholic feeling and that so many will rally to his cause he'll march to London without a shot being fired.'

'Only a fool would believe that. With his meagre army, he'll be routed within days.'

'Indeed, but Monmouth needs to believe it. His entire wealth is invested in the venture. To withdraw now will bankrupt him. He's a gambler and always has been. He'll continue whatever the risks and hope to charm his uncle into exiling him back to Holland if he fails.'

'Will that work?'

The envoy shook his head. 'Argyll is right about the anti-Catholic feeling. King James will make an example of Monmouth, if only to deter future rebellions.' He drained his tankard. 'I'll write my report aboard the ship. The captain is pledged to delay our departure until it's finished.'

'How long?'

'Two hours at most. Tell your man to look for the *Kent Maiden*.' He reached over to grasp Jan's hand. '*Vaarwel, mijn vriend.** I'm guessing it won't be too long before we see each other again.'

Jan returned his grip. 'What will bring you back?'

'King James's intemperance,' the envoy answered, rising to his feet. 'He'll earn his country's hatred if he demands that

---

*   Farewell, my friend.

Monmouth's followers pay the same price as their leader. Even if their numbers are limited by a quick defeat, there'll be no loyalty to a Catholic king who orders the mass execution of Protestants.'

REBELLION

Summer 1685

A PAMPHLET PRINTED AND DISTRIBUTED THROUGHOUT DORSET
ON THE EVENING OF 11 JUNE 1685 (AUTHORSHIP UNKNOWN).

A Strange Arrival by Sea

A man of Royal descent stepped ashore this day in our fair
port of Lyme Regis. Handsomely attired, he declared himself
to be the Duke of Monmouth, come from Holland to claim
his rightful place as King of England. A multitude lined the
shores and streets to see him, and many more hastened in
from outlying villages as word spread that the son of our late,
lamented King Charles was amongst us. He delivered a speech
on the defence and vindication of the Protestant religion,
advising the crowd of his intention to liberate the Kingdom
from the tyranny of Catholicism. Rousing cheers greeted his
words, but this writer noted that the fervour came from the
younger members of our community while older, wiser heads
stayed silent.

Those who lived through the brutal Civil War that
ravaged our country forty years ago viewed the Duke of
Monmouth's pitiful fleet of 3 small ships, his abject army
of 82 souls, and derisory weaponry of 4 light field guns and
1500 muskets with alarm. The cause of Protestantism is a
worthy one, but such a paltry force is insufficient to mount
a rebellion against King James. This writer urges every reader
to resist the Duke of Monmouth's call to arms.

You have been warned.

**THE PENALTY FOR HIGH TREASON IS DEATH BY
HANGING, DRAWING AND QUARTERING**

ONE

Wimborne St Giles, Dorset, 8 July 1685

WORD THAT THE DUKE OF Monmouth's short-lived rebellion had ended in defeat at Sedgemoor in Somerset reached the neighbouring county of Dorset within hours. Few doubted the truth of the news, for the uprising had been doomed once the siren voices that had lured the duke from exile fell silent under threats of punishment for high treason. It was said that he had been promised an army of trained militiamen, but only labourers and artisans armed with pitchforks and clubs had rallied to his standard. It mattered not that many in the south-west had sympathy with his cause; England's quarrelsome history of the last half-century meant people were wary of making their allegiances known.

Hard on the heels of the reports of King James's victory came rumours that Monmouth and several of his aides had fled the field of battle in a bid to escape capture. Some claimed he was making his way west to Wales, others that he was heading south-east towards the Dorsetshire coast in the hope of paying a fisherman to give him passage back to Holland. Whatever the truth, no one who lived and worked on the Earl of Shaftesbury's estate, some thirty miles north of the nearest port, expected to find themselves at the centre of the search for him.

As dusk fell on 7 July, a regiment of soldiers under the command of Lord Lumley and another of militiamen led by Sir William Portman encircled part of the estate, claiming to have tracked him to this very place. Acting on information supplied by a peasant woman who alleged that she had seen two strangers cross a hedge into a pea field, Sir William set his company to searching the cultivated land while Lord Lumley's men tramped the area of scrubland beyond. Nevertheless, despite moving in serried rows and beating the vegetation with their musket stocks, the efforts of both companies proved fruitless.

Lanterns were commandeered from the many bystanders, who had been drawn by curiosity to see if there was any truth in the rumour that the fugitive had chosen their estate as a hiding place, and as Sir William's militiamen began a second search some shouted that it would make better sense to set fire to the crops and burn the duke out. Sir William, unwilling to pay reparation to Lord Shaftesbury for such wanton destruction, refused, but his irritability grew as midnight came and went without success. His militia consisted of Somerset men, mustered in Taunton where he was the Member for Parliament, and none had any knowledge of the area they were searching. If they had, they would have known of the water-filled ditches beneath the hedgerows and would have tramped those as diligently as the fields.

A message came shortly after dawn on 8 July that a Dutchman had been taken prisoner by another militia some three miles away. Under brutal questioning, he had confessed to being one of the strangers the peasant woman had seen, claiming to have made his escape before Lumley's and Portman's cordons had been fully established. He further confessed to leaving his companion, the Duke of Monmouth, behind, saying the duke had been too exhausted to walk. Upon hearing this, Sir William instructed his men to renew their efforts, reminding them that a bounty of five thousand pounds had been placed on the fugitive's head.

The sun had been up two hours when cries for help echoed across the pea field which the peasant woman had first identified. The shouter was Henry Parkin, and when his fellows ran to his aid he pointed to a patch of brown fabric showing through a straggle of ferns and brambles at the bottom of a ditch. In darkness, it had been invisible; in daylight, it contrasted strongly with the green vegetation above it. Even so, a command to 'stand and show yourself' brought no response. Either the garment had been abandoned or whoever wore it was deaf, asleep or dead.

Parkin seized a sword from one of his companions and prepared to thrust the tip into the fabric, but a tall bystander, dressed in black with the white lace bands of a parson about his throat, stepped forward and took hold of his right arm. 'Piercing him with a blade will not cure his weakness, sir. Allow me to enter the ditch to assist him.'

'As long as you recognise that the find was mine and will testify the same to Sir William Portman.'

'I do and will,' said the parson, easing himself down the bank and pulling aside the ferns and brambles with gloved hands. 'I have no interest in the bounty.'

The sight he exposed was a sorry one: a human shape, wrapped in a saturated, threadbare cloak, lying on his front in the damp mud of the ditch with his face resting on folded arms and the hood of the cloak covering his head. With no signs of life, the parson stooped to turn the body onto its back, causing the arms to unfold and the hood to fall away, revealing a shaven head and a gaunt, colourless face torn by brambles.

Parkin gave a grunt of disappointment. 'It's not him,' he said. 'This man's too old.'

'Is he dead?' asked another.

The parson removed a glove and touched his fingers to the unfortunate's neck. 'I fear so. There's no warmth in him. I'll need your help if we're to lift his body from the ditch.'

The request was met with shrugs of indifference, as if none thought it worth the trouble. The Duke of Monmouth had been described to them as a man of thirty-five who bore a strong resemblance to his father King Charles II, while the emaciated creature in the mud looked more like a starving vagrant than a pretender to the throne of England. They would have returned to their searching and left the parson to deal with the corpse alone had Sir William not seen their gathering from a hundred yards distant. He arrived at a canter and demanded to know why they were idle.

Parkin gestured behind him. 'I saw a cloak beneath the ferns, sir, but the man who wears it is too old to be the duke . . . and dead also, by the looks of him.'

Sir William dismounted and pushed through the group to stare down at the upturned face. 'It must be Monmouth. The Dutchman named him as his companion.' He raised his gaze to the parson. 'What attempts have you made to revive him?'

'None. You reached us as these gentlemen were about to help me lift him onto dry ground. If he's alive, he'll need to be warmed and fed before he can speak or stand.'

Sir William drew his own sword with a contemptuous laugh. 'I don't have your soft heart, Reverend. Let's see what a few pricks to the groin can achieve.'

With a sigh, the parson deflected the thrusted blade with his gloved hand, causing the tip to embed itself in the bank. 'I can't in good conscience allow you to do that, sir. Whoever this man is, and whether he's insensible or dead, you'll be torturing him to no purpose. We can all see that he's incapable of rising out of this ditch of his own accord.'

'Do you doubt it's Monmouth?'

'I do, sir, for he looks nothing like the description you gave your men. Are you so well acquainted with him that you don't have doubts yourself?'

'Who else can it be?'

The parson knelt on one knee to search a pocket of the cloak. 'A destitute in search of food?' he suggested, pulling out a handful of raw peas and displaying them on his palm. 'It's not uncommon for such people to make their beds in ditches. I buried a woman six months ago who was found in similar circumstances.'

Sir William sheathed his sword with unnecessary force. 'You're trying my patience, sir. Your name and reason for being here?'

'Reverend Houghton. I have business in Ringwood but paused out of curiosity to discover why so many men were drawn to search these fields.' The parson discarded the peas and replaced his glove. 'Unless you intend to leave this man in an unmarked grave, I suggest you instruct your soldiers to assist me in lifting him up the bank.'

It is truly said that the margins between success and failure are very thin. Had the 'corpse' remained insensible, the parson might have been able to perpetuate the pretence of death; as it was, rough handling caused a sigh of pain to escape the man's lips, and once he was laid upon the ground a kick from Sir William Portman's boot brought another.

'It seems he's not as dead as you thought, Reverend.'

The parson removed his long black coat. 'God be praised,' he murmured, dropping to his knees and bending his head in prayer before laying the coat across the body and speaking clearly. 'I am a man of the cloth, my friend. My name is Reverend Houghton and I will give you what succour I can while the many gentlemen who surround you question you about your presence here. I seek only to help you and will remain at your side for as long as is necessary. Are they right to think you're the Duke of Monmouth? If so, you will suffer less by admitting it than subjecting yourself to the same brutal interrogation that a Dutch prisoner endured six hours ago.'

A slow tremor began in Monmouth's eyelids, but a minute passed before they opened. The parson looked for recognition in the gaze that stared up at him and was relieved when he saw it.

Monmouth moistened his lips with his tongue. 'Can I rely on your promises, Reverend?' he asked in a whisper.

'You can, my friend.'

'Then you may tell my captors that I am James Scott, first Duke of Monmouth, eldest son of King Charles II and rightful heir to the Protestant throne of England.'

∼

The parson was obliged to use his fists to prevent the captive being dragged by his arms to a cart on the other side of the field. His long service as a soldier and his well-aimed punches left Henry Parkin and one of his comrades with bloody noses, and his obvious ability to deliver the same to anyone else who stepped forward dissuaded others from trying. Sir William Portman, red in the face with fury, threatened him with a horsewhipping if he didn't stand aside, but the parson apologised and said he could not.

'My promise to assist this man was not rendered invalid by learning his name, sir. He needs food and water before he can stand, and I have both in my saddle pack.' He nodded to a dark bay mare tethered to a birch sapling some thirty yards distant. 'Oblige me by asking one of your men to bring the pack.'

Sir William placed his hand on the hilt of his sword. 'You're treading a dangerous path, Reverend. There'll be no quarter given to anyone suspected of collusion with Monmouth. The man's a traitor to his King and country.'

'That may be so, sir, but I doubt King James will want him delivered to London so broken in body and spirit that he's incapable of facing his accusers. If you think otherwise, continue with your cruelty . . . if not, send a man to my horse.'

It was a battle of wills that should have been won by Sir William, who was supported by a growing number of his militia, but the parson, alone and unarmed, was unyielding. Tall, lean and clad entirely in black apart from the white bands about his neck, with his dark hair falling naturally to his shoulders, he stood his ground fearlessly and cut a more impressive figure than stout Sir William, whose extravagantly curled wig sat askew atop his sweating, rubicund face.

With an abrupt nod, Sir William dispatched a man to fetch the saddle pack. 'Do you have a personal interest in Monmouth, Reverend?'

'No more than in you and your soldiers, sir. It's thirsty, hungry work searching through the night, and you all look in need of food, water and rest. Shall we forget our differences for thirty minutes and share what we have? With so many men guarding him, your prisoner cannot escape again.'

Sir William's expression said differently, though his suspicion was centred on the parson rather than the man at his feet. It was known that Monmouth had exchanged his clothes with a shepherd the day before in a bid to pass unnoticed, but a more effective and useful disguise would have been to become a man of the cloth with ownership of a horse. Indeed, had Sir William not thought the idea too absurd to countenance, since Monmouth would have been long gone if he'd had a horse beneath him, he would have said the men had switched places already. The parson was the right age to be Monmouth and showed all the confidence of a pretender to the throne.

'You must forgive my distrust, Reverend Houghton,' he murmured, taking the saddle pack when his man returned with it, 'but I'm curious about the contents of your bag.' He unbuckled the flap. 'You're very handy with your fists for a clergyman, and I wouldn't want a loaded pistol held to my head.'

'I forgive you readily, sir, and urge you to take all the time you need to satisfy yourself that my intentions are charitable. Meanwhile, if you care to hand me the chalice and the stoppered flagon, I'll make a start on reviving your prisoner.'

Sir William removed an earthenware bottle. 'Is it wine?'

'No, simple water.' The parson took the bottle and held out his other hand. 'The chalice, too, please. The prisoner will find it easier to drink from a cup.'

'Some would say it's sacrilege to use a holy vessel for such a purpose.'

'Which purpose, sir? Giving drink to a thirsty man?'

'Giving drink to a traitor.'

A flicker of amusement appeared in the parson's eyes. 'Well, at least God won't be offended. Jesus would not have allowed Judas to join him at the Last Supper if traitors are beyond forgiveness.'

With a sour smile Sir William handed over the silver chalice and watched with his men as the parson drew the cork from the bottle with his teeth, half-filled the bowl with water and then knelt to raise Monmouth's head. He spoke quiet words of encouragement as he held the rim of the cup to the duke's lips, but his bent head and lowered voice meant that not everything he said was heard. Certainly, none of the observers realised that short phrases in Dutch were being seeded amongst the English.

'Take as much as you need, there is more in the flagon. *Vergeet niet wie je bent.** Recall your Bible and know that Jesus said, "If any man thirst, let him come to me and drink." *Vind je moed.*† Your strength will come back to you quickly once you've eaten. *Nederige mannen zijn voor u gestorven.*‡ Nod, when you're able to sit and I will raise you up. *Geef ze nu waardigheid door uw acties.*§ Do you hear me, my friend?'

'I hear you, Reverend.' With a small groan, Monmouth pulled himself into a sitting position and addressed Sir William Portman. 'If you'll allow me a little food, I shall endeavour to give a better account of myself. My belly is knotted with cramps through being empty for nigh on a week.'

---

*   Do not forget who you are.
†   Find your courage.
‡   Humble men have died for you.
§   Dignify them by your actions now.

'It's only a day and a half since you fled the field of battle at Sedgemoor.'

'And it would have pleased me greatly to eat before it, sir, but meals and rest have been in short supply since I arrived in England.'

'Through your own fault. Your treachery has cost you dear, and you'll pay the full price when your head is removed.'

A faint smile lifted Monmouth's lips. 'Without your mercy, I'll be dead of starvation before I ever reach London, sir.' He lifted a thin hand to his emaciated face. 'If my altered appearance doesn't persuade you that I'm in the last extremities of hunger and fatigue, my death most certainly will.'

Sir William must have seen the truth of this, because he pulled a muslin-bound bundle from the saddle pack and handed it to the parson. 'Assist him to eat, Reverend, but know that I will hold you responsible if he attempts to escape once his strength returns.'

Ignoring him, the parson unwrapped the bundle and tore bread from the half-loaf inside. He gave it to Monmouth with a slice of cheese. 'Eat slowly, my friend, or you'll make your cramps worse.' He refilled the chalice. 'I have water when you need it.'

'*Geen schrik hebben. Ik ben weer mezelf.*'*

'Repeat that in English, please. If it's Dutch you're speaking, it's not a language I know.'

'Forgive me, Reverend. When I'm weary, I revert to the tongue of my childhood. I was thanking you for your kindness. It takes courage to show friendship to one such as I.'

---

*   Have no fear. I am myself again.

'I had no choice once God placed you in my way. Console yourself that He has not abandoned you, however dire your circumstances may seem.'

Thereafter, conversation between them ceased until Monmouth declared himself replete. 'I doubt I've enjoyed a meal so much, Reverend, and with your assistance, I believe I can stand. It's past time I looked these gentlemen in the eyes rather than stare at their boots.'

The parson removed his coat from Monmouth's lap to avoid it becoming tangled about his feet and then offered his hand. The duke's answering grip was stronger than he had expected and it took but a single heave to pull him upright, though Monmouth begged the continued support of his arm while he sought his balance. A bitter east wind bit through his threadbare clothing and, with every joint and muscle aching from having lain in the saturated ditch all night, his pain was obvious. He closed his eyes and muttered to himself in Dutch, seemingly to strengthen his resolve—*Je hebt genoeg gedaan. Verlaat me nu. Je wekt argwaan als je blijft**—before stepping away from the parson and addressing Sir William.

'May I know your name, sir?'

'Sir William Portman, Member of Parliament for Taunton.'

'Then I am at your service, Sir William. How do you wish to proceed?'

In his shepherd's smock and cloak, both wet and stained with mud, he made a comical figure. The garments were too short

---

* You've done enough. Now leave me. You'll rouse suspicion if you stay.

for a man of his height and exposed the trembling of his knees through the tattered britches.

Sir William barked a laugh and turned to the parson. 'Does your charity run to giving this traitor your coat, Reverend? You're of similar height and your long skirts will hide his fear.'

'I'd rather lend it, sir,' the parson answered, lifting the garment from the ground. 'I'm not so wealthy that I can afford to purchase a new one whenever the occasion demands.' He moved alongside Monmouth and asked his permission to remove the shepherd's cloak before helping him to feed his arms into the coat sleeves and buttoning the front. 'You'll find a folded woollen chaperon at the bottom of my pack, Sir William,' he said as he inserted the duke's hands into the gloves. 'I'll lend that also, since your prisoner will shiver less once his head is warm.'

Grudgingly, Sir William handed him the hood. 'How do you expect to retrieve these items, Reverend?'

'Through your courtesy when you've acquired suitable clothes for him, sir. Lord Shaftesbury allows me to minister to his household, so a package addressed to me here at Wimborne St Giles will be safeguarded until my next visit.'

'It's not my responsibility to find suitable attire.'

'You might be wise to try, however,' said the parson, pulling the hood over Monmouth's head and tucking the ends inside the coat collar. 'You'll need a warrant to make this arrest lawful, and I doubt you'll persuade a local magistrate you've captured the Duke of Monmouth if you present him in peasant's garb and a borrowed coat.'

'He confessed to being Monmouth before witnesses.'

'As would a vagrant if it meant the possibility of food. A magistrate will demand more compelling evidence than a muttered declaration to authorise this man's transportation to London.'

Sir William scowled, foreseeing endless delays. 'What do you suggest?'

The parson gestured towards the bystanders. 'If the story these people have told me about a shepherd exchanging clothes with a well-dressed gentleman yesterday at Woodyates Inn is true, then you should search out the shepherd. In doing so, you will kill two birds with one stone. Not only will the shepherd still have the gentleman's clothes, but he will also be able to tell the magistrate whether this is the person with whom he traded. It won't prove the gentleman is Monmouth, but it will prove your prisoner is not a vagrant.'

'Where's the nearest magistrate?'

'One mile away at Holt Lodge. His name is Anthony Ettrick.'

'Will you take us to him?'

'Happily, as long as you don't expect your prisoner to walk. You can see for yourself that he's incapable of taking more than a step without collapsing.'

'You're a demanding man, Reverend. You'll insist next that I lend him a horse.'

'There's no reason why not if you ask for his parole first, sir.'

Sir William saw merit in accepting the parole but not in allowing his prisoner to ride. Instead, he gave orders for the cart to be brought from the other side of the field, permitting his prisoner to sit on the parson's saddle pack until it arrived. He also saw merit in the parson's suggestion to seek out the shepherd and offered payment to any bystander willing to take two of his men to where the shepherd could be found. A youth agreed on the promise of half a crown, saying he would never make such easy money again.

Meanwhile, the news that a man had been captured was spreading, and it wasn't long before it reached the soldiers who were beating the heathland beyond the cultivated fields. The parson, who knew them to be recruits in Lord Lumley's Regiment of Horse, watched with pretended idleness as one by one they paused in their work. It hadn't escaped his notice that Sir William had failed to send word of Monmouth's discovery to Lord Lumley, and his gaze strayed towards the handsomely dressed man sitting astride a black horse to the right of the searchers. Lumley was said to have a temper, and the parson doubted his reaction to learning of the duke's capture at second-hand would be pretty, since he had pursued the fugitive with even more diligence than Sir William.

The aim of both men was to win approval from the King and Parliament by being credited with the arrest, and the parson was ready to wager money that Lumley would be the victor in the ensuing argument. He was younger and fitter than Portman, and had brought considerably more energy to the search than his stout, red-faced competitor. In addition, he had the advantage of having joined his regiment with the Earl of Feversham's on the battlefield at Sedgemoor, and would claim to have been present not only at Monmouth's defeat but also at his arrest.

The parson had learnt these details from talking with one of Lumley's soldiers the previous evening. The man was complaining that he'd had no sleep since the battle the day before and would have none that night unless the traitor was found quickly. The parson had expressed doubt that Monmouth was in this part of Dorset, but the soldier had laughed and said the traitor had left a trail from Sedgemoor that a blind man could have followed. Had he and the aides who fled with him been better acquainted with the country, they would have moved quietly along footpaths and bridleways. As it was, they had ridden the populated highways at a gallop, and their flight had been witnessed and reported.

The soldier went on to say that Monmouth's comrades were deserting him faster than rats a sinking ship. They had abandoned their horses and were fleeing on foot in different directions, but two had been seized already and Lord Lumley's scouts were confident of finding the others. He predicted the duke would be entirely friendless by the time he was discovered, and this view seemed to be shared by the ten militiamen who had been ordered to guard Monmouth while Sir William waited on the road for the shepherd.

'What sort of a leader loses all his supporters?'

'A poor one. He should hang his head in shame to be so abandoned.'

'Perhaps they hoped he'd die if they left him in a ditch.'

'He would have done if Parkin hadn't spotted him. You did him no favours, Henry. He'll suffer worse when the executioner's axe falls.'

Parkin spat on the ground. 'I could wish the same for the reverend. It's not right to give a man a bloody nose for following orders.'

The parson, who stood a pace from Monmouth's side, gave an involuntary laugh. 'But it was such a large and enticing target, my friend,' he teased. 'A horse would be proud to own it.' He watched Parkin bunch his fists in anger. 'Nonetheless, allow me to apologise. I made the mistake of assuming you and your fellows were better fighters than you are. Had I realised you were ill-equipped to defend yourself, I would have boxed your ears instead.'

'You're either mighty brave or mighty foolish to insult us, Reverend,' said another.

'I'll settle for compassionate, sir. This man is one and you are many. In your own eyes, you may feel your worth is increased by abusing him, but not in mine. I have a great dislike of hired bullies who delight in tormenting the weak.'

'You're overly keen to protect him, Reverend. Could it be you're closer acquainted with him than you pretend?'

'I'm as closely acquainted with him as I am with you, sir. I can't give your name, but by the ingrained soot in the creases of your face and the calluses on your hands, I would hazard a guess you're a farrier or a blacksmith. Are you indebted to Sir William that you must forsake your work whenever he demands it?'

'He owns the mortgage on my smithy. I repay him through service in his militia.'

The parson nodded. 'A fair bargain, and considerably improved when your service is rewarded with bounty. You must be praying the magistrate decides this man is Monmouth.'

The blacksmith grinned. 'No prayers are needed, Reverend. It's only you who has doubts.'

'Meaning you believe him to be the son of King Charles?'

'We do.'

'Then why insult him? Was his father hated in Taunton?'

A frown creased the blacksmith's brow. 'By no means. The town regained its prosperity under King Charles and we mourn his passing deeply.'

'As does his son, no doubt. It's painful to lose a father.'

Henry Parkin launched more spittle at the ground. 'His mother was a harlot. There's no saying who his father was.'

The parson studied him curiously. 'You must be a papist, Mister Parkin. I've only ever heard that slur mouthed by Catholics.'

The remark was deliberately provocative and brought the required reaction. Parkin lowered his head and charged like a bull, for even now, a century and a half after the Protestant Reformation of England and forty years since the religious divisions of the Civil War, hatred of Catholicism remained strong. Though perhaps *blind* hatred was a better description, the parson thought, as he sidestepped Parkin's forward rush and sent him sprawling with a neatly placed foot beneath his trailing leg.

'You should look where you're going,' he murmured. 'It's never wise to blunder about with your eyes closed.' He reached down to assist Parkin to his feet. 'Dare I suggest you resign from the militia? You can hardly uphold your sacred oath to serve and protect King James if you have such a violent dislike of Catholics.'

Parkin smacked his hand away. 'I made my pledge when King Charles was alive.'

'It makes no difference. Your oath of allegiance was to His Majesty, his heirs and successors, and presumably you don't dispute that King James is his brother's successor?'

The blacksmith answered when Parkin stayed silent. 'We had no say in the matter, Reverend. The succession was sanctioned by Parliament and we must accept what we're given.'

'I imagine the Duke of Monmouth would disagree with you. He wouldn't have brought rebellion to our shores if he thought everyone so ready to accept Parliament's decision.' He watched Parkin push himself to his knees. 'Had the rebels won at Sedgemoor, your oaths of allegiance would have been as applicable to King Charles's son as to his brother.'

The blacksmith shrugged. 'But he didn't win and is now con-demned as a traitor.'

The parson acknowledged the point with a nod. 'Such is the nature of war. The spoils go to the victor. King James is fortunate that England's soldiers and militias remained loyal. He would not be so ready to accuse his nephew of treason if men such as you disagreed with him.'

The blacksmith repeated his earlier statement. 'We have no say in the matter. We must do whatever our commanders tell us to do.'

'But not by aping their ill manners, my friend. There's no requirement to abuse a man when your only order is to guard him.'

The blacksmith jerked his chin towards Lord Lumley, who was riding at full gallop towards them. 'Save your sermons for him, Reverend. He'll skin the duke alive if it suits him and then turn his wrath on Sir William for trying to cheat him out of his prize.'

The parson took advantage of the response of Monmouth's guards to the furious tussle of words between Lumley and Portman, who had hastened back to his prisoner. Led by the blacksmith, they formed a tight circle around the parson and Monmouth with the clear intention of protecting their interest in the five-thousand-pound bounty, and since the voices of their leaders were loud enough to cover a whispered conversation, the parson took the opportunity to kneel at Monmouth's side and speak into his ear. His single purpose was to remind the duke that he carried more lives than his own in his hands.

'You have a responsibility to those who took up arms for you, James. Argyll was beheaded eight days ago and, to his credit, spent his last hours petitioning for mercy on behalf of his followers. You must do the same. Do you understand?'

Monmouth's reply was lost beneath an angry demand from Lord Lumley to see the prisoner. He pushed his way through the guards and stared at the parson who was holding the chalice to Monmouth's lips. 'Who are *you*?' he snapped.

'Reverend Houghton, sir,' came the amiable reply. 'Sir William gave me leave to assist this man.'

'He overstepped his authority. The prisoner is mine.'

'With respect, sir, he's no one's prisoner until his arrest is sanctioned by a magistrate. Shouldn't you wait for Mister Ettrick's verdict before you engage in further brawling with Sir William?'

'How dare you speak to me in such a fashion? Do you know who I am?'

The parson rose to his feet. 'I'm afraid not, sir. My parish is local and doesn't stretch to acquaintanceship with Somerset folk.'

This seemed to enrage Lord Lumley more. 'Do I sound like a Somerset man? I am Viscount Lumley of Durham County in the north.'

The parson ducked his head in a bow. 'My apologies, sir. I meant no disrespect by suggesting you were from Somerset. I'm sure your own part of England is as pretty.'

The viscount gobbled like a turkey cock. 'You're insufferably impertinent, Reverend. Step aside.'

'I will not, my lord, for I cannot in good conscience abandon this gentleman to one as violently disposed as you.'

'He's no gentleman. He's the son of a whore.'

With a lazy smile, the parson rolled up his sleeves. 'I grow bored of that Catholic slur. Whatever the Duke of Monmouth's beginnings, he is of higher rank than you, sir. A duke always takes precedence over a viscount.'

Before Lumley could respond, the blacksmith moved forward to align himself with the parson. 'Begging your pardon, sir, but you'd be unwise to test the reverend's ability to defend the prisoner. He considers it his Christian duty to protect the weak.' He gestured towards his companions. 'As do we, since we are the men who discovered him and it's only fair he remains in our charge until the magistrate gives his ruling.' He turned to Monmouth. 'Are you agreeable to that, my lord? Be assured we will treat you with civility.'

Monmouth, who was known to share his father's impish humour, acknowledged the words with an amused nod. 'Thank you, my friend. You're most generous.' He nodded towards Sir William, who stood a few paces apart. 'Allow me to give my formal surrender to your commander so there can be no doubt about which militia should receive the reward.'

'You'll surrender to me,' snarled Lord Lumley.

Monmouth rose to his feet. This time, with the parson's coat adding breadth and elegance to his frame and the chaperon hood restoring some colour to his face, he had more the appearance of a pretender to the throne. 'Even in Holland, you're known to be a Catholic, Lord Lumley. A hypocrite also, since your single reason for professing allegiance to the English Church was to take your seat in the House of Lords.'

'My faith is not in question here.'

'It is when it involves me. I'll yield to honest Protestants but not to a treacherous papist whose beliefs are bought as easily as yours.'

Hot blood suffused Lumley's face. 'You dare accuse *me* of treachery!'

A smile twitched at the corner of Monmouth's mouth. 'Would you prefer me to accuse your mother of being a whore? You must wonder which of the many men she lay with bequeathed you your unfortunate face.'

Lumley reached for his sword. 'I'll have your heart for that.'

'Enough!' Sir William barked, thrusting himself between them. 'This is most unseemly. The parson is correct. We must let the magistrate decide the rights of the matter. The prisoner has already given me his sworn parole, so I suggest you allow my men to escort him in the cart while you and your regiment follow behind, Lord Lumley. You'll lose nothing by doing so, since we will both present the duke to Mister Ettrick for examination. Do you agree?'

'It seems I have no choice.'

Sir William turned to the parson. 'Are you still willing to lead us to the magistrate, Reverend? It will solve the matter of your coat, gloves and hood. I'm told the shepherd will arrive shortly with the Duke of Monmouth's clothes, and once he's shown them to the magistrate and given evidence of yesterday's transaction, the duke can dress in his own attire again.'

The parson nodded in agreement. 'My business in Ringwood is not so pressing that it cannot be delayed for an hour or two. Will it help if I ride ahead when we're in sight of the house in order to prepare Mister Ettrick for your arrival? He may be alarmed to see an army advancing up his drive.'

His offer was accepted more readily than he had expected, and with bows to both Sir William and Lord Lumley, he stooped to retrieve his saddle pack, chalice and bottle. As he made his way to his horse, one of the female bystanders called to him. 'These soldiers tell us that Monmouth and his rebels were too cowardly to fight at Sedgemoor, but none of us believes them. Do you know the truth of it, sir?'

'The truth is whatever the King's soldiers say it is, mistress,' the parson answered, releasing his mare's tether and swinging into the saddle. 'Remember that before you express your sympathy so obviously again.'

Whispered rebukes broke out behind him as the bystanders berated the woman for her foolishness, and the parson hoped they had taken his warning to heart. He had received word the previous morning that King James had ordered his Lord Chief Justice to travel to the West Country with a mandate to ferret out anyone suspected of collusion in his nephew's rebellion. In a postscript to his letter, the parson's correspondent had issued a chilling caution: the King's subjects would be required to inform on their neighbours or face being tried for sedition themselves.

The parson considered Monmouth's character as he led the convoy towards Holt Lodge. The duke would take pride in the length of his rebellion—seven weeks against the few days that most had predicted—and Dorset's chances of escaping the King's wrath were slim as a result. Rumour had it that some two thousand Dorset men had answered Monmouth's call to arms, and their only hope of escaping punishment was a pardon. But would Monmouth match Argyll's courage by petitioning for them?

The parson doubted it. His flight from Sedgemoor with his Dutch aides suggested he intended to leave responsibility for the English to the English. Or, in the case of the Dorset men, to a Dorset man.

In view of the scale of the task, the parson regretted not using the arsenic.

TWO

ANTHONY ETTRICK WAS EATING BREAKFAST when his footman announced Reverend Houghton. Ettrick had a sense that he'd met the parson before, but he couldn't recall where or when, and nothing in his memory conjured up the patronym Houghton. 'Do I know you, sir?' he asked, before spooning scrambled egg into his mouth.

'I believe we chanced upon each other once in the company of Lord Shaftesbury,' the parson told him. 'He allows me to minister to his outside workers and I was there in that capacity when you called upon him.' He made a gesture of apology. 'I wish this meeting could be as pleasant, sir, but sadly it is business that brings me to your door at this ungodly hour. A small army, led by Viscount Lumley and Sir William Portman, will arrive shortly with a man they believe to be the Duke of Monmouth. They seek your authority to transport him to London.'

Ettrick had no recollection of being introduced to a handsome young parson at Wimborne St Giles, but he put that down to the Earl of Shaftesbury's lack of social graces rather than a deliberate untruth on the part of the reverend. 'We heard that

45

searches were being conducted in the area, but not that anyone had been found. Are they right to think he's Monmouth?'

'He says he is, sir, but his words belie his looks. The soldiers took him for a starving vagrant when they found him face down in a ditch, and they would have left him there if he hadn't declared himself to be the young pretender. I question if it wasn't food he was after.'

Ettrick pushed his plate aside. 'Tell me what you know.'

The parson gave an honest description of the morning's events, ending with his postponing of his visit to Ringwood to escort Monmouth's captors to the magistrate. 'I don't envy you this decision, Mister Ettrick. I'm minded that anyone can say he's the Duke of Monmouth to those who've never met him.'

'Indeed, but who would want to? Every person in the land knows that to associate with him is punishable by death.'

The parson, who'd thought they were alone in the room, was startled when a woman's voice answered. Turning towards the sound, he saw it came from a high-backed chair that faced the blazing hearth. 'You might as well ask why people rallied to his cause at all, Papa, since, by your logic, the King's threats should have kept them at home.'

Ettrick gave a grunt of amusement. 'You must show yourself if you wish to engage with us, daughter. I doubt Reverend Houghton is as accustomed as I to addressing thin air.'

A slender hand reached for a railing that ran out from the hearth and by dint of a strong push caused the chair to turn. It was arguable which of them was the more startled. The parson to see that the chair was mounted on wheels, or the seated woman to be faced with a man whose appearance clearly surprised her.

Ettrick bestowed a fond smile on her. 'Allow me to introduce my daughter Althea, sir. She's the joy of my life when she's not reprimanding me for small infractions of law, logic or philosophy.'

The parson walked forward to lift her hand to his lips. 'Your servant, Mistress Ettrick.'

She studied him closely with piercing blue eyes. 'I was led to believe that Lord Shaftesbury's minister is an elderly man with a large girth, sir. The words used to describe him were "old and fat", yet neither adjective would seem to apply to you.'

'May I ask who spoke them, ma'am?'

'Lord Shaftesbury's son. He rides over every Friday afternoon for three hours of tuition in philosophy. The subject interests him, but not when he has to discuss it with his father's minister. Or so he tells me.'

The parson released her hand with a laugh. 'I imagine anyone over the age of thirty looks old to a fourteen-year-old, ma'am, but I think you'll find Anthony was referring to Reverend Hughes, who attends upon the household. My duty is to the outside workers.'

He could see that she didn't believe him, but she let the matter go and turned to her father. 'You're bound by Parliament's Act of Attainder against Monmouth, Papa, so you cannot recuse yourself from this decision. Nevertheless, I advise you to reach a conclusion quickly or you may be cited for assisting the duke to escape. The obvious reason for an impostor to claim to be Monmouth is to divert attention to himself, and the longer he can confuse you about who he is, the better will be the real duke's chances of reaching safety.'

Ettrick gave his jaw a thoughtful scratch. 'What questions would you advise me to ask, daughter?'

'Factual ones, Papa. Would you like me to prepare them for you? We have pamphlets in the library, dating from when King Charles acknowledged Monmouth as his son, which give details of his titles, marriage, service in the army and the births of his children. If the prisoner is an impostor, he'll attempt to answer every question in the hope of prolonging the confusion, but few of his responses will be correct.'

'And if he's Monmouth?'

'He'll refuse to speak at all, for to do so will be to recognise your right to sit in judgement on him. Certainly, I wouldn't answer if I were in his shoes.'

'But you have wisdom, my dear, and to judge by Monmouth's foolish rebellion he does not. If I push you to the library, can you have questions for me inside a quarter-hour?' He rose from his chair and moved around the table, plucking his wig from a stand and tugging it over his balding head.

The parson stepped in front of him. 'With your daughter's permission, may I do the honours instead, Mister Ettrick? I hear hooves on your driveway, and you're better qualified than I to delay the start of these proceedings.'

'Do you give it, daughter?'

Althea nodded. 'But don't be too generous with your hospitality, Papa. There's no requirement to invite an entire army into our house when a dozen men are perfectly capable of guarding a single prisoner.' She gestured to the parson to move behind her. 'We must cross the hall at speed if we're not to be seen by the visitors, sir, so don't be timid in your pushing.'

The chair moved easily and she directed him to the door of the library and thence to a shelf of pamphlets. She selected those she needed before asking him to propel the chair towards a desk.

'I shall be poor company for the next fifteen minutes,' she said, taking a piece of paper from a drawer and a quill from an inkwell. 'May I suggest that you join my father and his visitors in the salon?'

'Will it disturb you if I explore your library in silence, ma'am?'

'Not in the least. If different religions appeal to you, you'll find them two shelves above you to your right. The most interesting is the Alcoran of Mohammed, which was translated from French by King Charles I's chaplain.'

Thereafter she ignored him, and the parson moved quietly along the shelves, marvelling at the wealth of knowledge displayed upon them. Bound books, being expensive, were usually the preserve of universities and the rich, but he estimated that upwards of two hundred were gathered in this room. And that number was swelled by piles of pamphlets, gazettes and news-sheets, stacked according to subject on the wider lower shelves.

He made a point of never staring overtly in Mistress Ettrick's direction, but he surveyed her nonetheless by the simple expedient of selecting different books and turning towards the light from the window behind the desk in order to read the title pages. He knew young Anthony Ashley-Cooper well, and he wondered why the boy had never mentioned a philosophy tutor, particularly one as unusual-looking as Althea Ettrick. From there, it was a small step to questioning whether Lord Shaftesbury knew of his son's Friday visits. The parson decided not. Shaftesbury was too much of a conformist to approve of so unorthodox a woman.

If a maid had had a hand in dressing her, it wasn't obvious. Her black hair resembled an untamed briar bush, and her leather bodice, which looked like a man's jerkin, was so irregularly buttoned that her cream shift bulged through the gaps. A brown woollen skirt covered her legs but her feet were bare of both stockings and shoes. The parson had noticed in the breakfast parlour that one was withered and crooked, but she had made no attempt to hide it, and his first assumption was that she didn't feel the need for propriety in her father's company. Nevertheless, since there was nothing wrong with her hands and she could have smoothed out her skirt to cover her affliction, he thought now that her flaunting of her crippled foot was a deliberate challenge to anyone who saw it. As, indeed, was her unkempt appearance.

With a satisfied sigh, she replaced her quill in the inkwell and folded back two pamphlets, one to expose an etching of a young King Charles II and the other an etching of the Duke of Monmouth. She then used her good foot to manoeuvre her chair towards a large brass gong in the corner of the chamber. 'I have time for you now, sir,' she said, striking the gong three times with the side of her right fist. 'Ask me whatever you like, though I imagine your first question will be whether Lord Shaftesbury knows of Anthony's visits to me.'

The parson gave a nod of acknowledgement. 'I've already decided he doesn't, ma'am, but perhaps you'll surprise me.'

She employed her foot again to pull herself back to the desk. 'It depends how far you're willing to believe a fourteen-year-old in search of novelty. Anthony assures me he has his father's permission, but I think it unlikely.'

'Why do you allow him to come?'

'Because he has a good mind and I enjoy teaching him.'

The parson gestured to the shelves. 'And a fine library to assist you both. I haven't seen so many volumes on different subjects outside a university. Do you acquire them in Dorset?'

She subjected him to an intense scrutiny, as if assessing whether he deserved an explanation. 'I have two older brothers who live and work in London. They seek out books which they know will interest me. My father compensates them for the cost when they cannot meet it themselves.'

'You're fortunate.'

'Indeed. The men in my life are both kind and generous.' She looked past him as the latch lifted on the door. 'I need you to take these papers to Papa, Adam,' she told the young footman who entered, squaring the pages and passing them to him. 'Will we be eaten out of house and home by these visitors?'

The footman grinned. 'Not if Elizabeth has her way, Miss Althea. She closed the door once twenty were inside and is offering them only water by way of refreshment.' He gestured to her chair. 'Do you wish to join the proceedings?'

'No, but I'm sure Reverend Houghton would.' She turned to the parson. 'It has been a pleasure meeting you, sir. I trust the verdict doesn't disappoint you.'

The parson accepted his dismissal with a bow, aware that the footman would usher him out whether he wanted to leave or not. 'The pleasure has been mine, Mistress Ettrick.'

She smiled distractedly as if conversational niceties bored her, then resumed her study of the pamphlets.

⌐

The parson remained at the back of the salon while the footman took the pages to Mister Ettrick. The magistrate sat behind a table at the far end of the room, transcribing a record of the proceedings in a ledger. Monmouth, under the guard of the blacksmith and his companions, stood to the right of the table and Lord Lumley,

Sir William and various of their officers to the left. The centre of the salon was occupied by a man who was clearly the shepherd, since he was dressed similarly to Monmouth. He was relating the story of how he had exchanged clothes with a gentleman the day before, but, since he spoke in the lilting burr of Dorsetshire, it was doubtful that any but Mister Ettrick and the parson understood him.

He was arguing that only a fool would turn down a set of finely made attire in exchange for rags, but swore that he was quite ignorant of who the gentleman was. His intention had been to sell the clothes at market, but he assured the magistrate he would have refused to take them had he guessed their owner was the leader of a rebellion against the King. He then said he couldn't be sure the prisoner was the same man.

'This 'un looks aged and bent, zurr. My gent'man were tall and 'ad 'air.'

Anthony Ettrick touched the clothes which the shepherd had placed on the table in front of him, then turned to Lumley and Portman. 'Do either of you object to the prisoner being taken to my breakfast parlour for the purpose of being dressed in these garments? The witness might find him easier to recognise if he's clad in the same attire as yesterday.'

'As long as he remains under guard,' said Lumley.

'That's for you to manage, sir. In addition, I suggest that you or one of your officers lends him a wig, since the witness remembers a tall man with hair.' He turned to the footman. 'Will you show the prisoner and those who wish to accompany him to the parlour, Adam?'

This led to some unseemly jostling as Lord Lumley and his officers tried to elbow Sir William and his guards out of the way.

Mister Ettrick watched them leave and then, much as his daughter had done, dismissed his visitors from mind and bent his head to study the etchings and questions she'd compiled for him. The shepherd, left alone in the middle of the room, cast a cautious glance at the magistrate and then began a retreat towards the open door.

The parson moved to intercept him. 'Don't do anything foolish, my friend,' he whispered in his ear. 'You'll be accused of having sympathy with traitors if you run away.'

'They soldiers be ready to accuse me of that anyway, zurr.'

The parson shook his head. 'Mister Ettrick's a fair magistrate. As long as you stand by your story that you didn't know who the stranger was, he'll not hold you culpable for giving him your clothes.'

'Them others might.'

'They're set on taking their prisoner to London and will forget you as soon as you've given your testimony.'

The shepherd shuffled his feet in distress. 'But I don't wish to 'ave 'is death on my conscience, zurr.'

'Then console yourself that Mister Ettrick will carry that burden. You have only to confirm that the prisoner is the gentleman you met yesterday, and the magistrate will decide whether he is also the Duke of Monmouth.'

'And if I say 'e's not the same gent'man?'

The parson gave a warning shake of his head. 'You'll open yourself to a charge of perjury. Never forget that he was wearing your clothes when he was captured. Be wise. Answer Mister Ettrick's questions honestly and leave him to decide the prisoner's fate.'

'Do you feel no pity for the duke, zurr? 'E be Protestant, same as you.'

'Not enough to imperil my life on his behalf,' the parson answered. 'The King's justice operates as well in Dorset as it does in London, and anyone suspected of assisting his nephew will be tried for treason.' He glanced behind him as the door to the breakfast parlour opened. 'Be wary of adding yourself to that list, my friend,' he murmured before withdrawing quietly to his previous position against the rear wall of the salon.

He questioned if the shepherd's testimony was necessary, since Mister Ettrick's expression of surprised recognition when the prisoner was brought before him again suggested he had little doubt he was looking at the Duke of Monmouth. Dressed in burgundy red britches and a matching knee-length coat with lace bands at his throat and wearing a dark brown wig, the captive's resemblance to his late father was clear to anyone who had ever seen a likeness of King Charles II.

Nonetheless, the magistrate followed procedure as the law demanded, drawing the ledger forward and taking up his quill again. He questioned the shepherd and accepted his acknowledgement that the much-transformed prisoner was indeed the gentleman with whom he'd switched clothes. He then turned his attention to Monmouth.

'I am tasked with deciding whether you're the Duke of Monmouth, recent leader of a failed rebellion against England and her Sovereign. To that end, you will take this Bible in your hand'—he lifted a book from the table and offered it to the prisoner—'and swear by God to answer my questions honestly.'

'I will do neither,' said Monmouth. 'You have no jurisdiction over me.'

Ettrick examined the prisoner's face. 'You bear a strong resemblance to our late King. Do you deny that you're his son?'

'I refuse to answer your questions.'

'Yet I understand you've already admitted to being James Scott, first Duke of Monmouth. Was that a truthful statement?'

'That is for you to decide, sir.'

'Indeed.' Ettrick ran his finger down his daughter's prompts and paused against one. 'It's said that the Duke of Monmouth is a brave and resourceful man, but I understand you were discovered trembling with fear at the bottom of a ditch.'

It was a clever question, for—all too predictably—Monmouth's pride got the better of him. 'There was no fear,' he snapped. 'The tremors came from lying in cold water for twelve hours. Had the soldiers not chanced upon the field so quickly, I would have made my escape.'

The magistrate's finger moved to another prompt. 'How and to where, sir? You were dressed as a peasant, hadn't eaten in days and were without the money to buy what you needed. Did you have expectations that someone local would supply you with the means to return to Holland?'

'I refuse to answer.'

Lord Lumley intervened. 'The traitor knows as well as you that he was captured on the Shaftesbury estate, Mister Ettrick. Ask him why he was there if not to seek succour from the son of the previous earl—a man so reviled by Parliament for championing the succession of a bastard son over a legitimate brother that he was forced into exile.'

Ettrick studied the viscount thoughtfully. 'Your question presumes a great deal, my lord, not least that the present earl shares his father's views on the matter of the succession.' He turned his attention to Monmouth again. 'Do you have a reply for Lord Lumley? Can you explain why you were on Shaftesbury's land?'

'Ill-fortune,' Monmouth answered. 'I'm disappointed to learn we never travelled beyond Dorset. I hoped we'd ridden hard enough to be close to a fishing port on the Hampshire coast.'

'From where you hoped to hire a boat to Holland?'

'Your logic is faultless, sir.'

Ettrick gave an involuntary smile. 'In your shoes, any man would find Amsterdam more appealing than London . . . though perhaps I should say The Hague, since I believe that's where you've been living with your mistress these last two years?'

'I reserve my right to remain silent on that subject.'

'As you wish.' Ettrick folded his hands and assessed the prisoner for several long moments. 'Purely to satisfy my own curiosity, what would you do if I ordered your release?'

Monmouth's eyes lit with sudden humour. 'Providing you give me a horse, I'll ride through the ranks of soldiers outside and defy them to catch me again.'

'Then your reputation for valour is well-deserved, and I trust it serves you well in the days to come. My ruling is that you *are* the Duke of Monmouth and must be taken to London forthwith to answer the Act of Attainder against you. You are not obliged to agree with my verdict, but I invite you to do so in honour of the men who have fought and died for you.'

Monmouth acknowledged the point with a nod. 'Then transcribe my words accurately, Mister Ettrick; I would like them recorded so that others may read them.'

'I will.'

'Thank you.' The duke paused to collect his thoughts. 'Your ruling is correct. I am the Duke of Monmouth and I stand alone in committing high treason against the King. My followers bear no responsibility for the decisions I made, because the plans were prepared in Holland and the men of the south-west who rallied to my side were never party to them. They fought in defence of Protestantism, which I persuaded them was under threat, and I beg the King to consider whether love for the Church of England is so heinous a crime that it deserves punishment. In the spirit of Christian forgiveness, I ask that my followers be pardoned.'

Lord Lumley gave a snort of derision. 'This man's hubris knows no bounds. He's a traitor and in no position to beg for anything.'

Ettrick ignored him. 'Your requests have been noted, Lord Monmouth, and will be made available to anyone who asks. That leaves only the matter of who should receive the five-thousand-pound reward for your capture.' He turned to Sir William Portman. 'Am I correct in believing that the prisoner surrendered to you, Sir William?'

'You are, sir, for it was my militia that found him.' He gestured to Henry Parkin and his friends. 'These ten men are pledged to guard the duke until they're relieved of their duty by the Constable of the Tower of London.'

Ettrick asked for their names and listed them in his ledger. 'Since the reward is not in my gift, I cannot promise you'll receive the money, but you may tell whomever it concerns that Magistrate Ettrick of Holt Lodge has adjudicated in your favour. To assist you, I shall state the same on the arrest warrant.' He wrote on a separate page for several minutes, added his signature and seal, and then offered the document to Sir William Portman, who stepped forward to receive it.

Lord Lumley gave another derisive snort and addressed his officers. 'Tell our men that the judgement of a Dorset magistrate will carry no weight in London. I have the ear of the King and he will render the money to my regiment as soon as I gain an audience with him.'

Ettrick laid aside his quill and closed his ledger. 'You're worryingly selective in which judgements you're prepared to accept, my lord,' he murmured. 'I trust the King has a better understanding of the law, or his subjects may come to regret that the army supported him and not his nephew.'

'You could be charged with treason yourself for such a state-ment, sir.'

Ettrick cast him a withering glance. 'Your slender knowledge of the statutes that govern our lives alarms me, sir. As a Member of the House of Lords, I would expect you to be better informed.' He rose to his feet and addressed the other people in the room. 'These proceedings are now concluded, gentlemen. When I've left the room, my footman will show you out.'

The crowd parted to allow him passage, and as soon as he'd crossed the hall to the breakfast parlour, Sir William Portman instructed his militiamen to escort the prisoner to the front door. With a muttered imprecation about 'jumped-up lawyers', Lumley ordered his officers to follow. The only pause in the otherwise rapid exodus was when the parson stepped forward to take his leave of the prisoner.

'May God go with you, my friend.'

Monmouth searched his face. 'You've been most kind to me, Reverend. Will I see you again?'

The parson shook his head. 'My place is here.'

'Then pray for me as you would someone dear to you.'

The parson ducked his head in a bow. 'You have my word on it, sir.'

—

Once the room was empty of soldiers, the shepherd approached the parson and entreated him to ask the magistrate to restore his clothes to him. It was hardly fair that he lose his spare garments as well as those he'd been obliged to return to the duke. The parson took him by the arm and urged him towards a window overlooking the forecourt. 'Your clothes will be with Mister Ettrick in the parlour, so we'll watch and wait for these men to be on their way before we cross the hall. I have no desire for another encounter with Lord Lumley.'

'Nor the prisoner either, zurr? It pained you to say goodbye to 'im, I think.'

'It pains me to see any man go to his death through fool-ishness,' said the parson, watching Monmouth emerge onto the forecourt with his guards. For the moment, he was bearing himself with dignity, but the parson knew it wouldn't last. There was too much of the tempestuous child in Monmouth to accept his fate as calmly as Argyll had done.

'Eez of royal blood, zurr. Do you blame 'im for trying?'

'I do, and so will every man and woman in Dorset when the treason trials begin.'

'You seem overly sure that King James wants vengeance, zurr.'

'Believe it, my friend. He will make such an example of the south-west that there will be no further talk of Protestant rebellion in England.' The sound of the front door's heavy iron latch drop-ping into place echoed in the salon. 'I think we're safe to seek out Mister Ettrick now.'

The shepherd nodded towards the table where his cloak was bundled in a heap. 'Am I permitted to take that? It's a mite ragged but it still gives warmth.'

The parson crossed the room to collect it, then led the way across the hall. He tapped on the door to the parlour, asking leave to enter, and was surprised when it was opened by a middle-aged matron. She eyed him with disapproval. 'Why are you still here? You should be gone already. The front door is to your left.'

'Forgive us, mistress, but the prisoner was wearing items of our clothing when he was brought here. In the shepherd's case, a tunic and britches—in mine, a woollen coat, gloves and a chaperon hood. With Mister Ettrick's permission, we'd like to retrieve them before we depart.'

'Let them in, Elizabeth,' called Mister Ettrick. 'Both are Dorset men, so you have no quarrel with them.'

The matron stood aside to let them enter. 'That remains to be seen, sir.'

Ettrick, seated by the fireplace, beckoned the parson and shepherd forward. 'My housekeeper is annoyed that men from other counties feel they have the right to demand a judgement free of charge,' he explained.

'My annoyance runs rather deeper than that, Mister Ettrick.' Elizabeth gestured to the window. 'Have you seen the damage their horses are doing to my herb garden? And will you find it as humorous when the viscount commandeers your favourite mare in the name of the King? He has sent two of his officers to inspect your stables for that reason.'

'Why do they need a horse?'

'From what I heard of Lord Lumley's exchange with Sir William, neither sees sense in transporting the prisoner to London in a cart which can only move at walking pace. They would rather acquire a mount for him and are looking to you to supply one.'

'Damned impudence!'

Elizabeth nodded, seemingly unoffended by her master's cursing. 'Indeed, and you should confront them on the matter, sir. Without compensation, the cost of replacing the animal will fall to you.'

Her proposal was met with a sigh. 'It's not worth the effort, Elizabeth. The viscount will instruct me to lodge a claim at the Court of Chancery, and the financial burden of travelling to and from London to plead the case will exceed the value of the horse.'

Elizabeth's resigned expression suggested she was used to being told that actions weren't worth the effort. 'Do you say the same about my herb garden, sir? Or the mud that's been trampled into your floors? Shall we leave them as they are rather than bother with restoring them to prettiness?'

Ettrick's amiable face took on a hunted look, and the parson guessed that such disputes were common in this house. He stepped forward with a bow. 'Allow me to bear the loss, sir, since I'm responsible for bringing these men to your door. My mare is tethered to the railing at the side of your forecourt, and sweet-natured animal though she is, I'll not miss her. She's one of three that were left to me in my father's will, and I find it near impossible to maintain them all on a parson's stipend. I ask only for my saddle pack to be removed because it contains my chalice, paten and Bible.'

Ettrick's response was to shake his head. 'I can't let you do that, Reverend.'

His daughter spoke from the open doorway. 'Of course you can, Papa. Reverend Houghton wouldn't have made the offer if he didn't mean it.'

She used her good foot to pull herself across the threshold, then came to an abrupt halt when she saw the shepherd. It was arguable which of them was the more alarmed: Mistress Ettrick to be presented with someone she wasn't expecting, or the shepherd to be staring at a half-dressed cripple in a chair on wheels. Both made attempts to retreat.

With an audible tut, Elizabeth moved behind Althea's chair and pushed her to sit alongside her father in front of the fireplace. She then addressed the parson, clearly intent on forcing Mister Ettrick to accept his offer. 'Do you wish to inform Lord Lumley of your decision in person, sir, or shall I send Adam to do it? If the latter, I will instruct him to remove your saddle pack and bring it to you here.'

The parson smiled. 'Lord Lumley's unlikely to accept a gift horse without explanation, so I wonder if you aren't the best person to perform the task, mistress. He'll question me thoroughly about my motives for giving him what he needs, but I doubt he'll dare question you. Certainly, *I* wouldn't.'

He was rewarded by a tiny curl at the corner of her mouth. 'I shall tell him you expect Sir William's militiamen to return the animal on their way back to Taunton, sir. If there's an honest man amongst them, it may happen.'

The parson waited for her to leave the room, then nodded to a pile of clothes beneath the window. 'I believe those belong to us, Mister Ettrick. Are we at liberty to reclaim them along with this cloak that I retrieved from the table in the salon? I presume you no longer need them as evidence.'

Ettrick gave his consent readily. 'Take them, by all means. The only thing they prove is that pride comes before a fall. If that foolish young man had ever considered the consequences of failure, he would not have left Holland.'

'Undeniably,' said the parson, handing the cloak to the shepherd and moving to sort his coat from the tunic and britches. He thrust his arms into the sleeves and then folded the shepherd's garments neatly. 'Here, my friend. There's a deal of mud on them, but I trust they'll keep serving you well after they're washed.'

The shepherd snatched the bundle in his keenness to be gone. 'Can we leave now?'

The parson turned with a bow for the magistrate. 'Sir.'

'How will you get home without a horse?' Ettrick asked. 'Is it far?'

'Not so far that I can't walk, sir.'

Althea raised her head. 'Are you happy to abandon your business in Ringwood, Reverend Houghton?'

Travel to the town had been the excuse the parson had given Mister Ettrick for being present at Monmouth's capture, but the scepticism in his daughter's eyes suggested she knew it to be a ruse. 'Sadly, I must, Mistress Ettrick, but the matter can wait until another day.'

'I'm pleased to hear that. The inclusion of your chalice, paten and Bible in your saddle pack suggested otherwise. I'm told Lord Shaftesbury's minister takes his from his church only when the sick and dying require the Eucharist in their homes, and I would hate to think your generous donation of your horse will deprive the needy of your services.'

'My business in Ringwood is secular, not spiritual, Mistress Ettrick, and since the chalice and paten are my own private possessions, I carry them with me wherever I go. Communion with God should be open to everyone in whatever situation I find them.'

'Such as in a ditch?' she suggested.

'Such as in a ditch,' he agreed solemnly, tucking his chaperon hood and gloves into his pocket. He bent his head again to Mister Ettrick. 'You've tolerated our presence long enough, sir. My friend and I will await Elizabeth's return in the hall so as not to disturb you further.'

'It's been a pleasure to meet you, Reverend.'

'The pleasure is mine, sir.' He turned to Althea. 'God be with you, Mistress Ettrick.'

'And with you, sir.' She held his gaze. 'Where should I send word if the Taunton militiamen return your horse? Wimborne St Giles or Winterborne Houghton?'

The parson hid his surprise well. Blandness of expression was a deceiver's best friend. 'Wimborne St Giles, ma'am. Lord Shaftesbury's chamberlain will inform me of it the next time I attend upon his workers.' He addressed the shepherd. 'Is there anything you wish to say, my friend?'

The man shook his head and retreated towards the door. Once in the hall, he scurried for the front entrance. 'I'm off, zurr. That be a witch in there.'

The parson's long legs overtook him easily. 'You can't leave this way,' he said firmly. 'When the housekeeper brings my pack, we'll exit together through the kitchen quarter.'

'What's to fear on this side?'

'Bored and weary soldiers in search of information.'

'I'll not speak to them.'

'They'll treat you roughly until you do. I know the breed.'

'What can I tell them except that the prisoner be Monmouth?'

'The same bald-faced lie you just told me: that Mistress Ettrick is a witch.'

The shepherd smiled sourly. 'You've seen her, zurr. Do you say it's natural to look into a man's soul and have claws for feet?'

The parson, a head and a half taller, moved forward to stare down at him. 'You'll give her talons for hands and a beak for a nose next. Has she wronged you in some way that you want her condemned as a witch?'

The shepherd took an uneasy step backwards. 'You're accusing me of things I haven't done, zurr.'

'Not yet, perhaps, but you will when you're questioned about why you exchanged clothes with a traitor. It's the nature of frightened men to fabricate falsehoods about others to deflect interest from themselves.'

The shepherd retreated further. 'I won't, zurr.'

'Do you swear that by God?'

'I do, zurr.'

The parson eyed him thoughtfully. 'That's a solemn pledge, my friend. You'll answer to me first and God second if you break it.'

The shepherd closed his eyes in a kind of agony. 'I'll not speak of this day again, zurr. I wish only to return to my sheep and live my life in peace.'

Nothing further passed between them, and a few minutes later Elizabeth entered through the front door and handed the parson his saddle pack. 'I spoke with Sir William Portman, Reverend. He thanks you for this further example of charity to the prisoner, and says he will endeavour to return the horse before the month is out. I hope that meets with your approval.'

'It does, mistress, but may I ask why Sir William thought I was acting on behalf of the Duke of Monmouth rather than Mister Ettrick?'

A smile curled the corners of her mouth again. 'I told him you were kind enough to offer your docile mare for the duke's use when the master informed you of Grizelda's habit of throwing her rider, sir. Even the fittest of men would struggle to stay in Grizelda's saddle all the way to London, and the duke's weakened condition would make him vulnerable each time she shied.'

The parson gave an involuntary laugh. 'You spin a better story than I, mistress.' He slung the pack across his shoulder. 'My friend and I would prefer to make our way across the fields at the back. Will you oblige us by showing us out through your kitchen?'

'I am at your service, sir. Would you care for some refreshment before you go?'

His gaze was teasing. 'We haven't the courage to put you to so much trouble, mistress. Simple guidance through the kitchen will suffice.'

Elizabeth was surprised by a sudden sense of familiarity. She had the strangest feeling that she had met this man before . . . or someone very like him.

THREE

Curiosity drew the young footman to Elizabeth's side as she stood at the back door, observing the progress of the parson and the shepherd across the first field. The shepherd had seemed frightened of his tall companion when they walked through the kitchen, and his dragging steps suggested he still was.

Adam seemed to read her thoughts. 'The reverend scared him witless.'

'How do you know?'

'I listened to their conversation in the hall.'

'How many times have I told you not to eavesdrop?'

'It wasn't eavesdropping,' Adam protested. 'I was tidying the salon, and the reverend was so intent on putting the fear of God into the shepherd that his voice carried through the open door. I couldn't help but hear him.'

'What had the shepherd done?'

'Called Miss Althea a witch.' He described the exchange between the two men. 'The reverend was mighty frightening. I'd have been scared, too, if I'd been in the shepherd's place.'

Elizabeth watched the pair disappear into woodland. 'Reverend Houghton is either a saint or very rich,' she murmured. 'Lord Shaftesbury's minister enjoys one of the most generous benefices in Dorset, but he wouldn't give up his horse for anyone.'

'Or put himself out to defend Miss Althea,' said Adam.

The lad was yet to turn sixteen and had been in the post a bare four months, so Elizabeth was surprised by his perceptiveness. 'Reverend Hughes expected to bury Miss Althea with her mother, and would have done so if the physician hadn't worked so hard to keep her alive.'

'She says it was you who saved her, ma'am.'

Elizabeth shook her head. 'That took someone with a deal more skill than I,' she answered, closing the door and shooing him back to work.

⌇

Althea raised her head when Elizabeth entered the library some two hours later. 'You look dreadfully stern,' she said. 'What's troubling you?'

'Your father tells me you mentioned Winterborne Houghton as one of the places you should send word if the parson's mare is returned. May I ask why?'

Althea turned an opened pamphlet towards Elizabeth and tapped an engraving of Monmouth, dressed in the uniform of His Majesty's Troop of Horse Guards. Beside him stood a taller man, similarly clad, and the inscription beneath the engraving read: *Dukes of the Realm, Brothers in Arms.*

'This was published in July 1679 and celebrates Monmouth's defeat of the Scottish Covenanters at Bothwell Bridge. The account names the officer on the left as the Duke of Granville and his estate as Winterborne Houghton in Dorset. His likeness to the parson is striking, don't you think? Not many men wear their hair naturally as he does.'

Elizabeth moved to the desk and bent to study the engraving. 'What else does the account say about him?'

'That he and Monmouth served together in the Anglo-Dutch wars, and that Granville inherited the title on his father's death in 1678. There's a report in a later pamphlet of a speech he made in the House of Lords in support of King James's accession to the throne, but nothing to say he left soldiering to enter the Church.'

Elizabeth glanced at the other pamphlets spread across the desk and then at the dates and names Althea had listed on a piece of paper. 'You never show yourself to visitors,' she remarked. 'Why make an exception for the parson?'

'I couldn't escape without him seeing me, and he lied to Papa. It made me curious.'

'Why are you so intent on proving that he's the Duke of Granville?'

Althea propped her chin on her hands. 'Because I like to be right. Houghton was an interesting choice of surname, don't you think?'

Elizabeth straightened. 'What lie did he tell your father?'

'It was more of a half-truth. He needed to explain why Papa recognised him when he first arrived, so he claimed Lord Shaftesbury employs him to minister to his outside workers. He said he'd met Papa in that capacity. I'm sure he was being honest about their meeting in the earl's house—I imagine he's closely acquainted with Shaftesbury, if his knowledge of young Anthony is any guide—but the rest was a falsehood.'

'How do you know?'

Althea shrugged. 'Anthony keeps me informed about every-thing that happens at Wimborne St Giles. If there were a younger and more approachable parson than Reverend Hughes, he'd have told me.' She lowered her hands to clear pamphlets from a map of Dorset. 'Assuming this is correctly scaled, Winterborne Houghton is a mere twelve miles across country from here. At a gallop, he could have made the journey in thirty minutes once word reached him that Monmouth had been tracked to Lord Shaftesbury's estate.'

'Why would he want to?'

'It depends on whether he's a friend or an enemy. A friend would try to thwart his capture, an enemy would do all he could to assist it.'

'Which is he?'

Althea gestured towards the engraving. 'A brother in arms. Papa never tires of telling me that men who serve together under-stand loyalty in a way that others do not. He tried to persuade Papa that the captive was a starving vagrant in the minutes before the column arrived, and according to Adam he promised to pray for Monmouth as someone dear to him when they made their farewells. Both suggest friendship.'

Elizabeth took another look at the list Althea was compiling. 'Have you discussed these ideas with your father?'

Althea thought she heard a note of concern in the older woman's tone. 'No. My only comment was that the parson's patronym would be common in and around Winterborne Houghton, just as Giles is here.' She watched Elizabeth's eyes close in relief. 'What aren't you telling me?'

'Do you remember Tom, my late husband? He was your father's coachman.'

Althea nodded. 'He found a pony for me and taught me to ride through my good leg. I was sad when he died—we all were.'

Elizabeth reached for her hand. 'I know, my dear. We cried for days afterwards.' She gave Althea's fingers a gentle squeeze and then released them. 'The sweetest letter of condolence came from the present Duke of Granville's father. He wrote to me as soon as he heard the news. He was the most considerate of men and his words about Tom comforted me more than I can say.'

Althea was surprised. 'Tom knew the previous Duke of Granville?'

'He served under him during the Civil War. They stood together in defence of Lyme Regis for Parliament, and Tom never had a bad word to say about him, nor about Mistress Jayne Swift, the woman who became the duke's wife. She had charge of the hospital at Lyme during the eight-week siege and treated Tom and many others for sword and musket-shot wounds, saving lives through her skill and dedication.'

'Is she the present duke's mother?'

'Yes. I recall her telling me her son was ten at the time of your birth, which would make him the right age for the parson—thirty-eight, if my sums are correct.'

'You've met her?'

Elizabeth smiled. 'So have you, though you won't remember her. Tom rode to Winterborne Houghton to fetch her when your mama went into premature labour and began bleeding. The best the midwife could do was wring her hands and wail, and it fell to me to assist Lady Harrier in her efforts to keep you and your mother alive. Sadly, your poor mama had lost too much blood to survive, but she lingered long enough to hold you in her arms and cover your little face in kisses.'

'Lady Harrier being the Mistress Swift who ran the hospital in Lyme?'

'The same.'

'Why not the Duchess of Granville?'

'She never placed much importance on the title. Everyone in this house, even your father, called her Miss Jayne.'

'What about her husband? Did he place importance on it?'

Elizabeth shook her head. 'His soldiers knew him as Sir William Harrier. He was a general in the New Model Army. Tom joined his regiment towards the end of the Civil War and said he was the best commander he ever had.'

'Did he die in battle?'

Another shake of the head. 'Your father told me he went the same way as Tom. His heart failed him. He was alive one moment and dead the next. Had it been otherwise, Miss Jayne would have saved him.'

Althea found that hard to believe. She'd had dealings with only one physician and had realised very quickly that he was an ignorant charlatan. 'She didn't save my mother.'

'She saved you, Althea. I still have the instructions she wrote for me on the importance of keeping your tiny body warm and how to feed you the wet nurse's milk by spoon until you learnt to suckle.'

Althea wondered if Elizabeth expected her to be grateful to this unknown woman. 'And what advice did she give you on bringing up a cripple?'

'That you would fight me all the way. She said your left leg might not have developed as it should but your endless curiosity suggested a strong intelligence. She made regular visits to see you until you were four years old, and would have continued had your father's new wife not dispensed with her services.'

Abruptly, Althea closed the pamphlet to obscure the engraving of the Duke of Granville. 'Why haven't you told me this before?'

'Because you needed no further reason to dislike your step-mother. Had your health deteriorated, I would have asked your father to summon Lady Harrier to tend you, but you progressed exactly as she predicted: strong in body and strong in mind.'

'You admire her.'

'I do,' Elizabeth agreed. 'I came to know her well at the time of your birth, and it would grieve me greatly if idle talk meant her son was suspected of helping a traitor. You have nothing to confirm your doubts about the parson, but I fear your father's position as a Justice of the Peace will oblige him to report your guesses to the High Sheriff.'

Althea couldn't recall Elizabeth ever making such a heartfelt plea on behalf of another before. She was more used to hearing her criticise people than praise them. 'Is Lady Harrier still alive?'

'I believe so. Her husband converted part of their house to a hospital, and the last I heard she was still treating patients there. Some can't afford to pay, but she never refuses them care.'

A twitch of cynicism lifted the corner of Althea's mouth. 'Are you sure you haven't invented her, Elizabeth? She sounds too good to be true.'

The housekeeper's face assumed its familiar look of disap-proval. 'There's nothing to stop you finding out for yourself,' she said tartly. 'Your crutches and boot are in the chest in the parlour and you know where your father's carriage is.'

'Henry will refuse to drive me. He hasn't forgiven himself since I slipped off the step and fell on my face in mud.'

Elizabeth gave an impatient click of her tongue. 'That was seven years ago and you've used it as an excuse to remain hidden in this house ever since.' She began to turn away, then changed her mind. 'Books can't teach you everything, my girl. It's time you learnt to confront your fears instead of pretending they don't exist.'

FOUR

LADY HARRIER LOOKED UP FROM her hospital ledger with a smile when her son entered her office by the outside door and bent to kiss the top of her head. She was recording the treatments she had given a patient with the early signs of consumption, but laid her quill aside in order to study Elias.

His resemblance to his father grew stronger by the day, and she wondered sometimes if there was anything of her in him. She had no complaints about it. William's looks and character had enchanted her from the first time she met him, and it pleased her that Elias had inherited both. A son who flaunted his status to avoid having to prove himself through his actions would have disappointed them both.

'I expected you sooner,' she said. 'Word reached us at noon that Monmouth had been captured.'

Elias, still clad in his coat and with his saddle pack across his shoulder, pulled forward a chair. 'I walked home,' he said, sinking onto the seat and lowering the pack to the floor. He grinned at his mother's expression. 'I need feeding before I tell the story, Mama. Not a morsel has passed my lips since I left this house yesterday.'

Jayne rang a handbell. 'At least tell me you spoke with James.'

'I did, though there was little opportunity for more than a few muttered words. I urged him to petition for mercy on behalf of his followers, but whether his resolve will last beyond today, I don't know. He was shockingly weak when the soldiers found him.'

One of her nurses came to the door and Jayne asked her to request some food from the kitchen for Master Elias, the name the household still used for her adult son. 'As speedily as possible, please, Maggie. He hasn't eaten for twenty-four hours and is refusing to give me news until his belly is full.'

Maggie, who had grown sons of her own, chuckled. 'Will cold stew do, Master Elias? There's some left in the cauldron from lunch. I can ask Cook to heat it, but you'll be waiting a good half-hour if she does.'

'Bring me cold stew and a spoon, and I'll marry you tomorrow, Maggie.'

As the nurse's footsteps and laughter vanished towards the kitchen, Elias stood to unbutton his coat and drape it across the back of his chair. He resumed his seat and loosened the white bands at his throat.

'Did you make a convincing parson?' Jayne asked.

'For the most part. One of the people I met suspected me of deceit.'

'Will he endanger you?'

'It was a she, Mama, and in answer to your question, I don't know. She reminded me of you.'

'Why?'

Elias scratched his stubble. 'She's an unusual woman. She has upwards of two hundred books, and her interests appear to range across the world's philosophies and religions, various branches of science and political thinking. She's also better versed in the law than the idiot commanders who have charge of Monmouth.'

'Who is she?'

Elias listened to Maggie's footsteps returning. 'The daughter of a magistrate on the Shaftesbury estate.'

Ten minutes of silence followed while he devoured the bowl of congealed stew and washed it down with a tankard of ale. Jayne used the time to move to a cupboard in the corner which contained her ledgers from when she started working as a physician. She sought out those that covered the years 1655–1660 and began flicking through the pages.

'What are you looking for?' Elias asked, wiping his mouth on a napkin.

'A patient I treated more than a quarter-century ago.' She placed her finger halfway down a page. 'Here we are—Althea Ettrick, born September the second, 1657. She was delivered two months before her time, weighed just above three pounds, and her mother died of catastrophic blood loss eight hours later.' She looked up. 'I do hope she's your unusual woman, Elias. I visited her on and off for the next four years and she was quite the most intelligent child I've ever met. Her father employed a tutor to teach her older brothers, and because she was such a quiet little thing the tutor thought her mute and backward and allowed her to sit in the room while they studied. Imagine his astonishment when the daughter, yet to reach five, solved mathematical equations which the sons, aged eight and ten, barely understood.'

'Why did you stop visiting her?'

'Her father remarried and his new wife persuaded him that my services were no longer required.' She thought back. 'It was my fault. I couldn't suppress my irritation with the stupid creature.'

'What had she done?'

'Exploited her husband's absences to deny Althea companion-ship. His work as a lawyer took him away for weeks at a time, and she insisted on having full authority inside the house. The tutor was dismissed, the sons were sent to study in Oxford and Althea was confined to her chamber on the pretext of protecting her from other people's curiosity. She was born with palsy of the left leg.'

'And the stepmother thought it reflected on her?'

Jayne nodded. 'She was everything I dislike in a woman— spiteful, sneering and shallow-minded. Appearance, particularly her own, was all she thought about, and it pained her to be associated with a cripple.'

Elias laughed. 'If you said the same to her, I'm not surprised she barred you from the house. And, yes, Mister Ettrick named my unusual woman as his daughter Althea, but there was no mention of another Mistress Ettrick. If the stepmother was in residence, I didn't meet her. The person who appeared to be running the household was a fiery matron called Elizabeth.'

'I remember her well. Without her help, I couldn't have kept Althea alive. She had no children of her own and dedicated herself to the baby.'

'Then I'm puzzled, Mama. Her father seemed extraordinarily fond of his daughter. Why would he and Elizabeth have allowed the stepmother to keep her secluded?'

Jayne returned the ledgers to the cupboard and seated herself once more at her desk. 'I would guess because Althea preferred it. There's no law that says a child has to like her stepmother, and Elizabeth assured me that her father spent as much time with her as he did with his wife.' She leant forward. 'Tell me the story,' she urged. 'I'm intrigued to learn why you were in Mister Ettrick's house.'

Elias had had long practice in delivering concise and fluent reports. His mother interrupted him once or twice, but only to elicit further details on Monmouth's condition and state of mind. He had visited Winterborne Houghton several times when Elias had served with him in His Majesty's Troop of Horse Guards, and though Jayne had found him likeable, she had always suspected the charm was a learnt quality. He presented the confident image he thought appropriate for the son of a king, but underneath lay a turmoil of emotion which revealed itself in erratic and fool-hardy behaviour.

Elias put Monmouth's rashness down to his ambition to prove himself, but Jayne thought his disordered upbringing the more likely cause. At seven years old, he had been taken from his mother in Holland, transported to Paris to be placed in the care of a stranger, and then sent to England at thirteen to meet his father, the King. Few adults would cope well with being ignored for thirteen years only to be feted with titles and wealth, and Jayne could only imagine how confusing it had been for a child.

Monmouth's life had never been his to control. At fourteen, he had been married to a rich heiress—the twelve-year-old Duchess of Buccleuch. At sixteen, he was sent to serve in the English fleet, and at nineteen was promoted to the rank of colonel in His Majesty's Troop of Horse Guards. He had barely reached twenty when Jayne first met him, and she was struck by how closely he copied the behaviour and opinions of her son. She sensed that he modelled himself on whomever was closest at the time, and wondered how long it would be before men of malign intent exercised influence over him.

She responded sceptically when Elias repeated Monmouth's plea on behalf of his followers. 'That was for your benefit, my dear. There was no point making the plea to the magistrate when it needs to be made to the King.'

'Give him some credit, Mama—he went further than I thought he would.'

'Only because you were in the room,' said Jayne. 'If you'd remained outside, he wouldn't have made the plea at all. We heard this morning that he fled Sedgemoor an hour before the battle was lost, which suggests he places no value at all on the lives of his followers.'

Elias nodded. 'I heard the same story from Lumley's troops last night. They were ordered to follow him as soon as Feversham realised he'd gone, and they couldn't believe how easy it was to pick up his trail. For all of five minutes, when the militiamen thought him dead, I toyed with removing him in order to put some fire in his belly. He'd have made a better fist of petitioning for his followers if he'd surrendered on his own terms.'

'Or begged you to hide him. He may even have come this way with that intention.'

'Possibly, but I think he spoke the truth when he said he thought he was in Hampshire. You should pity him, Mama. His escape was as ill-planned as his rebellion.'

'I'd pity him more if he'd had the courage to stand with his army. It's what your father would have done.'

'Sir William wouldn't have needed to. He was too clever to involve himself in such a harebrained enterprise.' Elias described the remaining events in Mister Ettrick's house, ending with his and the shepherd's departure. 'I fear he's another whose resolve may weaken as the days go by.'

Jayne eyed him curiously. 'I'm surprised at his ignorance. Palsied limbs aren't so uncommon that he won't have seen one before. Why would he associate a twisted foot with witchcraft?'

Elias gave his jaw another thoughtful scratch. 'I was a little abstemious in my portrait of your erstwhile patient.'

'In what way?'

'Her appearance startled me as much as it did the shepherd. At a rough guess, I'd say she hasn't left her father's house in years, has forgotten or doesn't care that it's polite to be fully dressed before visitors, has misplaced or never had a hairbrush and doesn't believe in covering her feet, both of which were extremely dirty. In addition, she has incredibly blue eyes and a *very* penetrating gaze. I felt every secret I have was known to her by the time I left and, were I prone to superstition, I, too, might have thought her a witch.'

Jayne wondered that he'd noticed so much. 'I always thought her a sweet-faced child,' she said lightly. 'Has she grown ugly over the years?'

'Nothing that a maid couldn't fix in five minutes. In fairness, she and her father weren't expecting visitors, and I doubt I'd have seen her at all if she hadn't been in the breakfast parlour when I entered it. She hid in the library when Monmouth was brought in and only emerged again when she thought the house was empty. I had the impression that she's unused to meeting people.'

'Yet enjoys young Anthony Ashley Cooper's company.'

'He'll enjoy hers more. It would be hard to find anyone more different from straitlaced Shaftesbury than Althea Ettrick. Only one in three of the buttons of her jerkin were fastened, and I'll wager Anthony spends more time peeking at her shift than he does learning philosophy.'

Jayne couldn't remember him describing a woman in such detail before. Pretty daughters of marriageable age were regularly placed in his way by ambitious mothers, but few impressed him enough even to remember their names. 'She couldn't possibly have known who you were simply by looking at you. The only reason she linked you with Winterborne Houghton was your choice of patronym.'

Elias nodded. 'I should have chosen another. She was suspicious from the moment I acknowledged her father's recognition of me. If I'd known she was in the room and had a connection with Anthony, I'd not have been so honest about where Mister Ettrick and I met.'

'If he accepted the explanation, why didn't she?'

'My guess would be that I didn't conform to any description Anthony's given her of a parson at Wimborne St Giles.'

'Are you worried she'll inform on you?'

'Why make mention of Winterborne Houghton if she doesn't intend to use the knowledge?'

'To amuse herself?' Jayne suggested. 'Imagine how frustrating it must be to have a clever mind, and only a father and a handful of servants to appreciate it. She was the same as a child. She loved to impress me with her ability to solve equations.'

'Well, she certainly impressed me,' said Elias, reaching for his pack and standing up. 'I spent the whole way home worrying that an army of bailiffs would have arrived before I did.' He pulled his coat from the back of his chair. 'I need my bed, Mama. If such an army does come calling, keep them entertained until I'm so bewigged and extravagantly dressed that they'll believe Mistress Ettrick to be in error. Whatever else she thought me to be, she didn't take me for a smirking fop.'

Jayne smiled to herself as she took up her quill again and returned to her notes. If Elias had serious concerns about Althea Ettrick informing on him, he had an odd way of showing it.

⁓

The following days brought letters from Monmouth's friends and supporters, urging the Duke of Granville to add his name to the many petitions for mercy that were being presented to King James. The tenor of all the requests was that Monmouth's only crime was ignorance. He had been lured into the conspiracy on promises that his late father's subjects were begging him to accede to the throne and had realised too late that the promises were false. His single wish now was to beg his uncle's pardon, swear allegiance to him as sovereign and then exile himself once more in Holland, the country of his birth.

Elias passed one of the letters to his mother. 'This is the most honest.'

'Who sent it?'

'George Legge, Constable of the Tower. Monmouth and I became acquainted with him during the Dutch wars and I wrote two days ago to find out how Monmouth was faring.'

My dear Granville,

In answer to your question: not well. Our mutual friend is consumed with self-pity and blames everyone but himself *for his predicament. He begs the King daily for an audience and is pledged to convert to Catholicism if His Majesty is willing to pardon him. He makes no attempt to petition on behalf of those who rallied to his standard, seeming convinced that they are as complicit in his misfortune as his co-conspirators.*

Be wary of lending him your name. His Majesty is irritated beyond endurance by Monmouth's desire to save himself at the expense of his religion. Dare I say that I share the King's disgust? I expected better of Monmouth than the abject behaviour he is currently displaying.

Yours in regret,
Legge, Baron Dartmouth, Constable of the Tower

Jayne lowered the letter to her lap. 'What a wretched business it is. I wonder if the silly boy even understood the consequences of failure.'

'I couldn't have made them clearer, Mama.'

Jayne glanced at the letter again. 'He'll betray his followers if he sells his soul to the Devil.'

Elias's mouth twitched. 'Walls have ears, Mama. I doubt it's wise to call His Majesty the Devil.'

She laughed. 'I was referring to Monmouth's willingness to abandon his religion at the first sign of difficulty.'

'If you say so.'

Jayne pondered for a moment. 'I wonder if the Constable is right to suggest the ploy will fail. The King might think a public conversion to Catholicism more valuable than making another royal martyr. He won't have forgotten how the country was divided over his father's execution.'

Elias shook his head. 'If he pardons the leader, he'll have to pardon the followers, and he can't do that. The Scots will be rightly angered if their people are punished but the English aren't. For all Argyll's faults, he's shown a deal more courage than Monmouth.'

Jayne glanced at the other letters requesting Elias's help, which lay on the bench between them. 'What will you do with these?'

He gathered them into his hands. 'Burn them.' He retrieved the page from his mother's lap. 'This, too, since I doubt George is any more desirous than I to have his words read by spies.'

'Don't you trust our people?'

He cast her a fond smile as he rose to his feet. 'You have a kind heart, Mama; strangers wait outside your hospital every day for your services, and you never doubt their motives in coming. But Maggie tells me she found a peculiarly healthy one wandering our corridors just three days ago. He hastened out the front door when she threatened to thwack him across the buttocks with her broom, and the last she saw of him he was running hotfoot towards the highway.'

'He sounds more like a thief than a spy. Maggie should have searched his pockets for spoons.'

'Maybe so, but a little caution wouldn't go amiss. I'm told the Lord Chief Justice has as many informants as His Majesty.'

A second letter from George Legge reached Winterborne Houghton on 16 July, dated the day before.

My dear Granville,

I write to inform you that Monmouth was executed at noon. His Majesty granted him an audience yesterday but was unpersuaded by his pleas for clemency. Nevertheless, be assured that once he knew death was inevitable, Monmouth met his end with courage and dignity. He walked strongly to the stage and placed his neck unhesitatingly upon the block.

I regret to add that he suffered appallingly at the hands of his executioner, Jack Ketch. The man is a butcher and not

worthy of his fee. His axe was blunt, his blows misplaced,
and it took eight strokes and a saw-bladed knife to remove
Monmouth's head. The crowd groaned prodigiously to see
such cruelty.

Less than one hour ago, I received word that Lord Chief
Justice Jeffreys has begun his preparations for the Western
Assizes. As yet, this is rumour, but if my source is correct,
the trials of those involved in the rebellion will start in six
weeks' time.

Yours in friendship,

Legge, Baron Dartmouth, Constable of the Tower

Three days later, an unmarked carriage drew up on the forecourt
in front of Winterborne Houghton House. On a halter behind it
was a dark bay mare. The coachman instructed a groom to hold
his lead horse's chinstrap, before dropping to the ground and
moving to the rear of the carriage to untie the mare's halter. He led
the animal to the front and asked the groom if he recognised her.

The youngster nodded. 'She belongs to Master Elias.'

'Not the Duke of Granville?'

The question was greeted with a smile. 'They're one and the
same. Master Elias never uses his title in his house.'

The coachman cast around for a halter rail and spotted one
to the right of the front entrance. Ignoring the groom's questions
about why he was in possession of the mare, he took her to the
rail and knotted the rope around it. Next, he opened the carriage
door and removed a saddle and bridle, laying them on the ground
behind the groom.

'Tell your master that my mistress sends her compliments and hopes he's pleased to have his mount returned,' he said, climbing back onto the driving seat and nodding to the lad to release the chinstrap.

'What's your mistress's name?'

The coachman gathered up the reins. 'Your master knows it,' he said, turning the horses towards the driveway and clicking his tongue to set them in motion.

Elias was informed of this strange event when he returned from a visit to William Lewis, the High Sheriff of Dorset. Elias's intent had been to discover what he could about the plans for the approaching Assizes, but Lewis had been less than forthcoming. The two men were acquaintances of long standing and, though Lewis's welcome had been warm, he was noticeably hesitant to talk about the Chief Justice or any instructions he had received on the conduct of the trials. He was more open about his success in arresting rebels. To date, some hundred were housed in Dorchester gaol and informants were coming forward daily to name others, albeit on spurious evidence.

Elias was left with the impression that Lewis was acting more out of fear of Lord Jeffreys, whose reputation for harshness was well known, than a desire to see justice done, and he was despondent when he entered his stable and handed his mount to his head groom. His mood turned to one of pleased surprise when Timothy pointed out his dark bay mare in her familiar stall and told Elias she had been abandoned on the forecourt by an unknown coachman.

'With no explanation?'

'I understand the coachman said that his mistress sends her compliments and hopes you're pleased to have her returned.'

'Who told you that?'

'Steven. The coachman asked him if he recognised the mare as yours, and he said he did. Your saddle and bridle were also returned.'

Elias stooped to unbuckle the girths on his mount. 'I think the coachman's mistress has made her point well, Timothy.'

'What point would that be, Master Elias?'

Elias looked up with a grin. 'No equation is too difficult for her.'

FIVE

ADAM ENTERED THE LIBRARY AND shut the door firmly behind him. 'A lady and gentleman want to know if you're at home, Miss Althea. They await your answer by their carriage.'

She looked at him in alarm. 'I am *never* at home.'

'I told them that, Miss Althea, but they don't believe me.'

'Who are they?'

'The gentleman is the parson, Miss Althea, and he said names and explanations were unnecessary after your instructions to your coachman two days ago.'

'Oh dear God! Is there a crest on the carriage door?'

Adam shook his head. 'It doesn't have a door or a roof. Will you let me push you outside so that you can see it? By my reckoning, it's built for speed, so you'll not have seen the like of it before.'

Althea's refusal was immediate. 'I can't. Tell them I don't receive visitors when Papa's away from the house. Find Elizabeth and ask her to talk to them.'

'She's with them already, Miss Althea. She greeted the lady as Miss Jayne and I've never seen her so happy to see anyone.'

He moved further into the room. 'You'll like her, too, I think. She refused to let Elizabeth curtsey to her.'

'I'll disappoint her. She'll wonder why she wasted her time on me.'

'Only an ignorant person would think you a waste of time, Miss Althea.' Adam produced a tentative smile. 'If you button your jerkin correctly and allow me to bring you some slippers and a loose bonnet to cover your hair, you'll have no reason to feel uncomfortable. The lady's dressed in simple homespun and the gentleman looks the same as he did a week ago, but without the parson's bands at his neck.'

Althea glared at him. 'I don't know how to behave with strangers. If I simper sweetly, they'll take me for a halfwit.'

'Then don't simper,' he responded reasonably. 'The parson didn't expect it last time, so why should he now?' Despite his young age, Adam had a good understanding of why his mistress was so reluctant to leave the house. 'I promise to keep you safe, Miss Althea. I'm strong and the forecourt is free of stones. I'll not let the chair tip.'

Althea wondered whether to be mortified or impressed that a novice fifteen-year-old footman could read her mind so well. She was able to manage her fear of ridicule inside her father's house because her wheeled chair gave her a means of escape, but the same was not true outside. Elizabeth might think she had seized on the excuse of falling from the coach to become a recluse, but it was the cruel laughter that followed the fall that had made up her mind. Passers-by had sniggered behind their hands as she tumbled face down into the mud of a street in Blandford, and but for their coachman and an elderly gentleman lifting her back into the carriage, she would have remained there. It mattered not that with the help of a crutch she had never lost her footing in public before. The shame of that one humiliating incident had destroyed every particle of confidence she had about displaying herself in public.

Not that she had had much confidence to begin with. She had only ever agreed to leave the house under pressure from Elizabeth to discover for herself if people were as unkind as her stepmother had claimed. She had learnt that they were, and now preferred the sanctuary of her library, resisting all attempts to prise her out of it.

She studied Adam thoughtfully. 'Fetch the shoes and bonnet,' she told him—then, raising a hand to prevent him turning away, said, 'I haven't finished. Do you know the Latin phrase *quid pro quo*?'

He shook his head.

'It means if I do something for you, you must do something for me.'

'Nothing would please me more, Miss Althea.'

'Then the *quid pro quo* for my speaking to these visitors is that you will present yourself in this room every day for one hour and accept whatever lectures I give you.'

The young footman was disconcerted. 'I meant no offence in what I said, Miss Althea.'

'None taken,' she said, reaching for the first of her errant buttons. 'You have an insightful mind, Adam. The lectures will be in philosophy.'

꘠

The carriage was as strange as Adam had described. 'Flimsy' was the word that came to Althea's mind when she emerged from the front door and saw how insubstantial it was. A seat wide enough for two was situated centrally on a slender metal base, with three-foot diameter wheels at each corner. The two horses that pulled it were positioned one behind the other, and the only protection for the rider and his passenger were low wickerwork panels around the seat.

Althea, who knew from what Elizabeth had told her that Lady Harrier must be close to seventy years of age, wondered how so elderly a woman dared ride in such a dangerous vehicle. From there, she doubted that the person conversing on the forecourt with Elizabeth could be Lady Harrier. She was taller than the housekeeper, had only a smattering of grey in her brown hair, and held herself as upright as the parson who stood at his lead horse's head.

Her doubt gave way to surprise when the woman turned at the sound of chair wheels on the impacted ground. 'Oh my goodness!' she declared. 'I *do* remember you! We used to watch from the window as you galloped down our driveway. Papa sucked his teeth because you rode astride, but Elizabeth and I thought it wonderful and clapped our hands.'

Lady Harrier smiled. 'You promised to do the same when you were older.' She walked forward to take both of Althea's hands in hers. 'Did you succeed?'

Shyly, Althea returned the pressure of her fingers. 'For a short period when Elizabeth's husband was alive. I lost heart after he died.'

Elizabeth contradicted her. 'It was the coachman your stepmother chose to replace Tom who made you lose heart, Miss Althea. He was a beastly young man and had no patience with you.'

Unwilling to discuss the coachman's cruelty—he had taken joy in thwacking her weak leg with his crop—Althea answered lightly. 'His impatience was directed more at my stepmother,' she told Lady Harrier, releasing her fingers. 'She expected him to carry water and cloths on every journey in order to wash the sides of the carriage when they reached their destination.'

'To what purpose?'

'Gertrude favoured wide skirts and didn't want them dirtied by mud when she alighted.'

'Wouldn't a cloak have served the purpose as well?'

Althea made no answer, being as disinclined to discuss Gertrude's stupidity as the coachman's callousness. Bitter words rarely achieved anything.

Lady Harrier spoke again. 'Elizabeth tells me your stepmother died twelve years ago, my dear. I was shocked to hear it. She can't have been above forty.'

'We were all shocked, milady.'

'There's no need to use my title, Althea. You called me Miss Jayne as a child—will you not do so again? We were the closest of friends once.'

This time the ensuing silence was uncomfortable, and Elizabeth wished she had had the sense to warn Lady Harrier of Althea's deeply held conviction that expressions of sentiment were invariably false. Elias intervened to draw Althea's attention to himself.

'Since we share an interest in wheeled vehicles, Miss Althea, what do you make of my carriage?'

'Is it your invention, sir?'

'It is.'

'Then I admire your mother for agreeing to travel in it.'

He smiled. 'As do I.'

It seemed brief answers pleased him as much as they did Althea, but curiosity was consuming Adam. Against all Elizabeth's patient training in how to behave, he blurted out a question.

'What's to prevent you being thrown to the ground when you hit a bump, my lord?'

'Leather straps are anchored into the corners of the seat panels which we buckle about our waists, and the metal frame to which the seat is bolted is mounted on leaf springs. They're of French design and allow the seat to remain level whatever the wheels encounter.'

Adam leant forward to peer at them. 'But the springs are made of metal, my lord. How can something so hard flatten?'

'Through the work of a master blacksmith who knows how to forge a thin but strong curve from high-quality iron. If Mister Ettrick allows it, you may come to the smithy at Winterborne Houghton to see how it's done.'

Elizabeth shook her head at Adam's excitement. 'Not yet,' she warned. 'First, we will have to explain how you came by such an invitation.'

Althea was looking at Elias. 'It's a mercy Father's absent today or we'd be making that explanation now,' she said. 'Were you aware that he had business in Blandford?'

Elias nodded. 'I rode over last night, and your coachman, Henry, was kind enough to alert me to the fact. We would not have come otherwise. I have no desire to embarrass you or your father, Miss Althea.'

Althea glanced at Elizabeth, wondering if Henry had informed her of this nocturnal visit, and guessed from her determined looking away that he had. 'Why come at all?' she asked bluntly. 'Was your mare not returned in the condition you expected?'

Lady Harrier spoke before her son could. 'You must blame me,' she said. 'Elias's description of his meeting with you made me curious. I wanted to see for myself that you had proved me right and your stepmother wrong.'

'About what?'

'Your intelligence. We fell out on the matter and she banned me from the house.'

'What did you say to her?'

'A great deal more than I should have done. She had no choice but to ban me.'

Unexpectedly, Elizabeth laughed. 'Miss Jayne lost patience with her after trying for three hours to persuade her to allow you downstairs to meet visitors, Miss Althea. She told Mistress Ettrick that a four-year-old with a palsied limb had a better intellect than she did, and that given the choice of sitting with the clever child or the ignorant stepmother, visitors would choose the child every time.'

Althea wondered how truthful Elizabeth was being. 'Three hours is a long time to keep patience with someone as stubborn as Gertrude.'

'It seemed longer,' said Lady Harrier. 'She was extraordinarily opposed to changing her mind.'

'Especially when it came to you, Miss Jayne,' Elizabeth observed. 'Mister Ettrick wanted to summon you when her sickness worsened, but she responded so violently to the idea that he worried for your safety if you came. She was always ill-tempered, but her rages became ungovernable in the last month of her life.'

Lady Harrier frowned. 'Rages?'

'There's no other word to describe what we had to endure, milady. The attending physician had none of your ability. He left the mistress to die in agony.'

Lady Harrier turned to Althea. 'What cause did he give for her death?'

'Apoplectic stroke due to extreme agitation. She was screaming at her maid when she collapsed.' Althea thought back. 'She complained of near-constant pain in her head, persistent nausea, worsening eyesight and difficulty keeping her balance. Do you know of a condition that would cause such symptoms?'

'What diagnosis did her physician offer?'

'Drunkenness. He blamed everything on her consumption of alcohol. She developed a prodigious appetite for brandy, which exacerbated her anger rather than calmed it.'

'It usually does, but it's as likely she drank to numb the pain in her head as that the brandy caused it. Did she have seizures before the stroke that killed her?'

'Two. Both in the last week. Her physician thought it was the beginnings of epilepsy.'

Lady Harrier shook her head. 'A better guess would be a growth in the neck or on the brain,' she said. 'Epilepsy wouldn't have affected her so quickly or so drastically.'

'What kind of growth?'

'A cancer.'

Althea searched her face. 'Might you have diagnosed that while she was alive? Her own physician never considered it.'

'Her altered moods would have alerted me to the possibility, but I wouldn't have known for certain. Tumours are easily diagnosed when they can be felt beneath the skin—as in the breast—but not when they're hidden. It's a vile disease with no cure, so there's nothing the physician could have done. The only remedy is to try to mitigate the pain, and from what you've told me, Gertrude found her own way to do that.'

Althea felt a small sense of triumph because her own research had led her to the same diagnosis. 'I had guessed at a cancer myself. Her symptoms were similar to those described by an Italian doctor who lived in Florence in the fifteenth century. The Hospital of Santa Maria Nuova permitted the dissection of hanged felons for the better understanding of human anatomy, and the doctor was assigned a murderer who killed his wife in a frenzied rage. The man's brothers swore he had been kind and generous until he experienced headaches and nausea, and Doctor della Torre opened the skull to discover the reason.'

'What did he find?'

'An unnatural growth on the frontal lobe. He called it "*karkinoma*", the same name Hippocrates used in a treatise he wrote on cancer half a century before Christ was born, and Doctor della Torre concluded that the cost of the execution had been wasted when the man was close to death anyway. I translated the piece for Gertrude's physician, but he dismissed it as nonsense and told my father I'd invented the story to draw attention to myself.'

Lady Harrier studied her with amusement. 'I trust you took that as a compliment. He had no other way to excuse his own inadequacy than by denigrating you.' She paused. 'You sought my endorsement of a cancer before you told me your own theory. Would you like me to write the same in a letter to show this physician?'

Althea shook her head. 'I gave up trying to persuade ignorant people that a palsied leg does not indicate a palsied mind a long time ago. Papa believed I was right and that was all that mattered. He was better able to keep his patience with his wife once he accepted that disease was the cause of her behaviour.'

'Did they have children?'

'No.'

Elizabeth moved to Althea's side. 'Mistress Ettrick was the foremost of the ignorant people Miss Althea referred to, Miss Jayne. She barred her door to her husband rather than chance giving birth to an imbecile.'

Elias, who had been listening in silence, greeted this statement with a laugh. 'Was she deaf as well as ignorant?' he asked. 'Anyone who listens to Miss Althea for half a minute can see how clever she is.' He turned to her. 'If my sums are correct, you were fifteen at the time of her death.'

'I was.'

'Then I'm put to shame. I like to think I have fluency in three languages—French, Dutch and Spanish—but even now I'm not so proficient in any of them that I could read, understand and translate the detailed dissection of a corpse. May I ask who taught you Italian to that level?'

Certain that he would question her ability if she told him, Althea stayed silent.

'Miss Althea taught herself,' said Elizabeth. 'She has mastery of five languages other than English.'

Elias was surprised. 'Is that true?'

Althea shook her head. 'Elizabeth flatters me. I can read French, German, Italian, ancient Greek and Latin, but cannot speak them because I don't know how the words are pronounced. I imagine your own fluency comes from your time as a soldier abroad, and

I envy you that opportunity. Listening to people talk is a better way to absorb language than through the comparison of texts.'

'Which texts did you compare?'

'Translations of the Bible. There's a beautiful logic to using one book as the foundation for five different vocabularies.'

Elias ducked his head in respect, before straightening with a teasing look in his eye. 'I stand ready to be corrected, but I don't recall *karkinoma* being mentioned in the Bible.'

The briefest of smiles transformed her face. 'Foundations form the base of a construction. It takes time, effort and a multitude of bricks to create the whole. My father purchased a Greek glossary for our library, and I discovered that *karkinoma* derives from *karkinos*, meaning crab. Hippocrates saw similarities between crabs and the shape of tumours, and chose *karkinoma* to describe them. Is that explanation enough?'

'So much so that I wonder you aren't a physician yourself, Miss Althea. Have you considered making medicine your profession?'

He saw immediately that he'd said the wrong thing. Her smile vanished and she instructed Adam to take her back inside. 'Milady, Your Grace,' she said, making perfunctory bows to each. 'It has been a pleasure meeting you. I wish you good day.'

Elias waited until she was inside. 'Which part of my suggestion offended her?' he asked Elizabeth. 'The idea that she should consider a profession or that the profession should be medicine?'

Elizabeth sighed. 'I believe she thought you were mocking her, sir.'

'In what way?'

'By feigning confidence in her abilities.'

'Does she distrust all compliments or just mine?'

'All, sir, excepting those her father pays her. She knows those to be true because he's heavily reliant on her knowledge of the law. There isn't a statute she hasn't read or an example of case law that she doesn't understand.'

'Is that the profession she would choose if she were able?'

'I'm too fond of her to jeopardise our relationship by asking, my lord, but her father says she's the most competent lawyer he's ever met. She can apply her mind to anything, but cannot conceive of a single situation outside her father's house where a cripple might earn respect.'

Elias eyed her thoughtfully. 'The only person I know who can rightly call himself a cripple is the smith who fashions my leaf springs. He walks on stumps because both his legs were amputated below the knees.'

'Miss Althea isn't interested in comparisons, sir.'

'Nor should she be.' He ducked his head. 'You've been most kind, Elizabeth. Please thank her for agreeing to talk to us. I trust she won't have difficulty explaining this visit to her father.'

'I doubt she'll try, sir. She'll ask him about the cases he's heard today in Blandford and leave explanations for another day.'

Lady Harrier moved alongside the woman. 'Thank her for me also, my dear,' she said, taking Elizabeth's hand. 'You've done well. Her mind is as sharp as I hoped it would be.'

'Maybe so, Miss Jayne, but I should have worked harder to prevent her becoming a recluse.'

Lady Harrier shook her head. 'You'd have worn yourself out to no purpose. She's intelligent enough to decide for herself how to live her life.' She released Elizabeth's hand and mounted the step to the carriage seat without assistance. 'The only pity is she uses such an inappropriate word to describe herself; scholar would be more apt than cripple.'

Althea had instructed Adam to take her into the salon so that she could watch the visitors' departure through a window. To accomplish this, she pulled herself upright by grasping the edges of the sill and standing on her good leg. Because the July day was sunny and warm, most of the panes were open, and she heard the entirety of the conversation on the forecourt—as did Adam, who stood behind her.

'Lady Harrier's braver than I am,' he said as the carriage set off at a fast pace down the driveway. 'I'd be too afeared to travel in anything so light.'

Althea asked him to push her chair closer. 'You're a poor liar,' she responded, lowering herself to the seat again. 'You'd find the speed so thrilling you'd beg His Grace to give you a position in his stable.'

'I'd never leave you, Miss Althea.'

'Well, you should. Even to my ears, lessons from a smith who walks on stumps and forges leaf springs sound a great deal more exciting than scholarly lectures on philosophy.'

Adam drew her backwards in order to turn her towards the door. 'You're taking their remarks wrongly, Miss Althea. They were praising you not criticising you.' He pushed her across the floor. 'Mind, I wouldn't call you a scholar myself—it's a dry sort of word—but the lady was right about you not being a cripple.'

'What would you call me?'

'A lawyer, same as your father,' said Adam cheerfully, pushing her through the door. 'It's what you do best.'

A letter from Mister Hugh Milton, attorney at law, to William
Lewis Esquire, High Sheriff of Dorset, dated 24 July 1685:

Dear sir,

*Please excuse my writing to you without introduction, but
I believe I can be of service to you during these costly times
for your region. I reside in London but retain strong ties to
Dorset, which was the county of my birth.*

*Acquaintances there tell me that Dorchester gaol is filling
with rebels, and that many of the prisoners are vehemently
disclaiming any association with the Duke of Monmouth.
For that reason, you may wish to employ me as an impartial
arbiter of the charges against them.*

*The Assizes draw close, and to present Lord Chief Justice
Jeffreys with a multitude of prisoners, one-quarter of whom
may be able to prove their innocence, would be a mistake.
You will be aware from your dealings with him that he is
irascible and impatient. These traits are exacerbated when
he is obliged to travel long distances between the different
cities on the Assize Circuits. This is particularly true of the
Western Circuit, which is extensive in area, and to force him
to sit through hours of testimony from alleged rebels who
should never have been brought before him will provoke him
beyond endurance.*

*As arbiter, I will examine individual cases and advise
you on whether to release or hold the prisoners for trial. My
advice will be communicated by letter, which will allow you
to decide at leisure whether to reject or accept it. In simple
terms, a man who has been arrested on the word of a jealous*

rival is not worth Lord Jeffreys' time, while one who bears the wounds of battle is.

If you consent to this offer, I shall require the names and addresses of the accused, the charges that have been laid against them and the defence each man intends to cite in court. The latter objective is best achieved if pen and paper are made available to the prisoners and they are permitted to seal their communications afterwards. As a general rule, words written in confidence are more honest than those spoken to gaolers.

My fees are nominal, and are paid by those whom I adjudge to be suitable for release. All correspondence should be directed to Hugh Milton Esquire at Middle Temple, Middle Temple Lane, London, where it will receive my immediate attention.

In conclusion, I attach letters of accreditation from colleagues and clients, attesting to my unblemished character and peerless record as a practitioner of law.

Your servant,
Hugh Milton

SIX

DORCHESTER GAOL WAS A SPRAWLING, rectangular building which normally housed a few dozen common criminals. Now, with in excess of three hundred men and a handful of women awaiting trial for treason, the conditions were cramped and squalid.

Lady Harrier was permitted to visit the gaol once a month to tend to the medical needs of the inmates. It was a charitable duty she had been performing since the end of the Civil War in 1649 when two Royalist soldiers, caught stealing food, had spread camp fever through the prison population. No other physician had been willing to enter, and the then High Sheriff, a close friend of her husband, had entreated Lady Harrier to cure and eradicate the disease. Her treatments had proved successful, but the price she had demanded for the service had been continued and unfettered access to the prison. Her shock at the filthy, emaciated state of the incarcerated men and women had been profound, and her visits had involved the dispensing of food as much as medicine.

This contract had been honoured for thirty-six years, but on this day in the second week of August the superintendent moved to prevent her and her two nurses from entering. 'I can't let you in, milady. The High Sheriff has issued instructions that no one gains admission.'

'I have the right, Joshua.'

'Not until after the trials, milady. Three dozen prisoners were removed last week by men claiming to be from the Taunton militia, and Mister Lewis is afraid it will happen again. They had papers purporting to come from the High Sheriff of Somerset, showing that each of the accused was from his county and should face trial there, but we learnt yesterday that none has arrived.'

'Meaning what? That they've absconded?'

'It looks that way, milady. They were amongst the first to be arrested and still bore the wounds of battle from Sedgemoor. You treated them when you were here last month.'

'Are you referring to the youths with sword slashes and musket balls lodged in their flesh who claimed they received their injuries scything hay?'

The superintendent nodded.

'Did their wounds heal?'

'So well, milady, that they were in good health when they were taken out of here by their friends. Mister Lewis says they'll be two hundred miles north by now.'

'Well, I trust he doesn't think I had anything to do with their escape, Joshua.' Jayne turned to her nurses. 'Did they ever tell us their names or where they came from?'

Without hesitation, Maggie shook her head. 'They were more intent on persuading us they were simple farmhands who'd been arrested in error, milady. I wouldn't describe any of them as men. I remember one telling me he'd just turned fourteen.'

'I think there was a James,' the second nurse said thoughtfully. 'He spent most of his time in tears because his mother would be angry with him for being in prison.'

Jayne nodded. 'I do recall them being young. Are these your escapees, Joshua?'

The superintendent bridled at what he took to be criticism. 'There were as many adults as there were youths, milady,' he said severely, 'and in answer to your previous query, the High Sheriff is suspicious of everyone, myself included. He questions how to explain such a brazen escape to the Lord Chief Justice.'

'If he has any sense, he won't try. I'm told you have more than three hundred awaiting him inside the gaol, so I doubt the Chief Justice will care about three dozen absconders unless someone's foolish enough to tell him.'

'Mister Lewis will feel obliged to do so, milady, if only because their names appear on the list Mister Milton is compiling of those who should be tried. He cited their wounds as evidence that they were at the battle of Sedgemoor.'

Jayne frowned. 'Who is Mister Milton?'

'A lawyer in London who's been tasked with deciding the merit of the cases against the accused prisoners, milady. To date, he has recommended the release of twenty-seven, though it made little difference to the numbers; another twenty replaced them within days of their discharge.'

'You have a lot on your plate, Joshua.'

'I do, milady.'

'Then I'll not add to it by demanding entrance.' She placed a sack of bread on the ground and gestured for her nurses to do the same with their sacks. 'You'll know best how to dispense this food, but my plea would be that you offer it first to those who receive nothing from their families. I imagine more fathers have disowned their sons than have chosen to support them.'

'They're afraid of being accused of treason themselves, milady.'

'Indeed.' She smiled. 'Good day to you, Joshua. I shall look forward to resuming our friendship once the Assizes are over.'

Jayne had little doubt that her son had been behind the 'brazen' escape. She had visited the gaol after Monmouth's execution and had described the rebels to Elias as gullible children. All had been arrested in the days following Monmouth's defeat, when farmers and householders told the pursuing bailiffs and militiamen that fugitives with bloodstained clothes and visible wounds were hiding in their barns or outhouses. The youngsters' claims to have cut themselves reaping hay were laughable, but they had no better idea how to explain their injuries. It had been clear to Jayne that not one had fully comprehended how dire his situation was, each clinging to the belief that only the rich and powerful paid the penalty for high treason.

She had recorded their names and treatments in her ledger, and Elias had studied the page with interest. He recognised several of the patronyms as common to south-west Dorset—Gale, Whetham, Symes, Hallett, Bondy—and wondered if the boys had tried to return to their families, only to find the doors closed against them. Rumour had it that even to give hospitality to rebels was treasonous.

Shortly afterwards, he had absented himself from Winterborne Houghton on the pretext of travelling to London to assess the mood in the capital. It was a journey he made several times a year, combining attendance at Parliament with affairs of business and visits to friends. He had been away for more than a fortnight, but Jayne had thought nothing of it until Joshua's mention of escape. Now, as the carriage left Dorchester, she leant towards her nurses, who sat on the seat opposite, and took their hands in hers.

'Thank you,' she said simply. 'You were under no obligation to support my blatant lie.'

Maggie chuckled. 'We were no keener than you to be accused of assisting rebels, Miss Jayne. In any case, who's to say the names they gave us were real?'

The second nurse, Emily, nodded. 'I'd have rescued them myself if I'd known how, Miss Jayne. They were that frightened, poor little mites. God bless their saviour is what I say.' Her raised eyebrows and twisted smile said she suspected Elias as much as Jayne did.

Elias listened to his mother's story. 'I've heard of similar escapes elsewhere,' he said. 'Word is spreading fast that the only sure way to avoid execution is not to appear before Lord Jeffreys. The King should be grateful they've gone. Even his most loyal supporters would struggle to watch children being drawn and quartered.'

'Where is "elsewhere"?'

'Exeter lost four, Taunton forty-three and Bristol ten.'

'All on the same day?'

'I believe so, Mama.'

'And all young?'

'Young, rebellious and extremely naive. I'm told they were looking for excitement and found more than they bargained for.' He changed the subject abruptly. 'Explain Mister Milton to me.

It's a rare lawyer who secures twenty-seven acquittals without the need of a judge.'

Jayne shook her head. 'I can't. I was more intent on distancing myself from the escape than quizzing Joshua about Mister Milton. All I know is that he has been tasked with assessing each man's case in advance of the Assizes. He appears to be making a list of those who should be tried and those who should not.'

'Who appointed him?'

'The High Sheriff.'

Elias considered for a moment. 'I hadn't realised Lewis was so inventive.'

The following morning, a maid entered the High Sheriff's parlour in Dorchester and told his wife that the Duke of Granville was in their hall. 'I said that the master was absent, ma'am, and His Grace wonders if he might speak with you instead.'

'Oh my word!' declared Mistress Lewis, thrusting her tapestry frame to one side and smoothing her bodice over her stomach. 'Sit up straight and pinch some colour into your cheeks,' she ordered her daughter. 'And for goodness' sake, don't smirk. You did that the last time he came to the house and he never gave you a second glance.'

'I wasn't smirking, I was smiling,' the girl answered peevishly.

'Well, don't do it again. Show His Grace in, Jenny, and then bring some cordial and a jug of ale.'

Elias, who had been watching the house since dawn for William Lewis to leave, was dressed in the manner that Mistress Lewis expected of a duke: embroidered knee-length coat, tight-fitting britches, polished leather boots and a long, loosely-curled wig. He bent a knee to both her and her daughter, and thanked them for receiving him. It was arguable which was the harder to read: the rigidly seated mother, who appeared to be holding her breath, or the wide-eyed daughter, who kept blinking at him.

'I hoped to find William at home,' he said, 'but I'm rewarded with the treat of conversing with two beautiful ladies instead.'

Unable to hold in her stomach for a second longer, Mistress Lewis expelled her breath. 'The pleasure is ours, my lord. Will you sit? The maid will be bringing cordial and ale shortly.' She gestured to her daughter. 'You remember Clarissa? She was honoured to meet you the last time you came.'

Elias stooped over the girl's hand. 'Your servant, Miss Clarissa.' He retreated to a chair as a pink flush rose in her cheeks and her lashes began to beat like butterfly wings. In a detached way, he wondered if she was about to faint and how that might affect his chances of acquiring the information he wanted. He addressed the mother. 'I trust I find you both well, ma'am.'

There followed fifteen minutes of inconsequential chatter about the minutiae of the women's lives. Mistress Lewis encouraged her daughter to turn her embroidery frame in order to display her flower tapestry, and Elias expressed deceitful enthusiasm for her unremarkable depiction of a rose. The girl contributed little, apparently set on keeping her mouth from moving, and Elias decided some of her teeth must be missing. He accepted a tankard of ale, congratulating Mistress Lewis on its excellence, before turning the conversation to her husband.

'How is William faring? He must feel he's carrying the weight of the world on his shoulders.'

'He's being driven to distraction by demands from all sides, my lord. When he's not receiving instructions from London, he's being waylaid by petitioners seeking the release of family members. We're all unsettled by it.'

Elias nodded sympathetically. 'I imagine you're counting the hours until this whole wretched business is over.'

'I am, my lord, though I fear it will get worse before it gets better.'

'How so?'

Mistress Lewis sighed. 'William's responsibility won't end when Lord Jeffreys leaves, sir. He'll have to enforce the executions, and that could take weeks. There aren't enough gallows or hangmen to cope with the number of men confined in Dorchester gaol.'

Elias adopted a thoughtful expression. 'And the cost of building extra gallows and hiring executioners from other regions will fall on Dorset's purse, presumably?' He took her silence for assent. 'Will the same not apply to Lord Jeffreys? He and his entourage will be living at our expense for months if he hears only one case at a time.'

'There'll be no need for trials if every man pleads guilty, my lord.'

Elias didn't have to feign his response. He was genuinely surprised by her statement. 'How will that be achieved?'

'Lord Jeffreys is considering lesser sentences for those who waive their right to trial.'

'Has he specified what the lesser sentence might be?'

Mistress Lewis shook her head.

Elias frowned. 'Then the pledge is meaningless and only the most gullible will believe it. If fifty men insist on their innocence and produce witnesses to prove it, the trials will last weeks. If one hundred insist, there'll be no end to them. Is William aware of that?'

'Rather more than you, my lord,' Mistress Lewis retorted sharply, stung into defence of her husband. 'He wrestles with the problem every day, and were it not for an attorney in London, he would be trying to solve it on his own. He's receiving precious little help from anyone else.'

Elias spread his hands in apology. 'I stand chastised,' he said, 'though, in fairness, I came to offer what assistance I could. Which attorney is it?'

'Mister Hugh Milton of Middle Temple. To date, he has identified more than two dozen cases that should not be brought to trial and expects to find more before the Assizes begin. The remainder—those he deems suitable for trial—will face Lord Jeffreys.'

Elias remarked that this seemed a sensible course of action, then turned the conversation back to the women. To probe any further into Mister Milton might alert Mistress Lewis to his reason for coming. He preferred her to believe that her daughter was the object of his interest. He had no guilt about the pretence. His only attraction for either woman was his title.

On the morrow, he rode to London and surprised the handful of servants who maintained his house in Bow Street. In normal circumstances, and because it was their custom to greet him on the forecourt with bows and curtseys, he gave them a week's notice of his arrival. Today, he was obliged to knock for five minutes to gain entry, and his elderly footman-cum-valet viewed him with alarm.

'We weren't expecting you, Master Elias,' he stammered, making vain attempts to smooth his sleep-dishevelled hair and crumpled tunic.

'Don't trouble yourself, Amos. I'm here for one night only and am happy to eat whatever your wife has in her larder.' He stepped through the doorway. 'I've ridden since dawn, with four changes of horse, and the last—the best of the hired bunch—is in the stable. I've unsaddled him and given him feed and water, but will you be kind enough to dry and blanket him? He needs rest and warmth before I leave again.'

'Is Simon not there, sir?'

'In a manner of speaking,' said Elias, moving into the hall, 'but he's made such a comfortable nest for himself in the straw that I didn't like to wake him. How old is he now?'

'The same as me, sir: a year past seventy. He wouldn't have lain down if he'd known you were coming.'

Elias shed his coat and tossed it across a chair. 'It's of no matter. Is Rose in the kitchen?'

'You'll shock her if you go in unannounced, sir.'

Elias laughed. 'Nothing shocks your wife, Amos.'

As he had predicted, Rose was untroubled by his sudden appearance. She was the same age as Amos and Simon and had known Elias since he was a boy. All three had worked at Winterborne Houghton until five years ago, when their advancing years had begun to take their toll, and Lady Harrier had suggested that Elias offer them the sinecure of maintaining the Granville property in Bow Street. Two or three local maids came in once a week to sweep and dust, but for the most part the elderly retainers were left to enjoy their retirement in peace. Rose liked to claim that she missed walking in the Dorsetshire countryside, but her knowledge of London theatres suggested she had found other ways to amuse herself.

She eyed Elias curiously as she placed a bowl of steaming broth on the table in front of him and cut some freshly made bread. 'It must be something urgent that's brought you here, Master Elias. From the dust in your hair, you look as if you've been riding hard for several hours.'

He grinned and took up a spoon. 'Surely you mean the smell of me?'

'I don't like to be rude, Master Elias, but you'll need to shed those garments before you conduct your business.' She filled a kettle from a bucket and hung it from a hook above the kitchen fire. 'If you're visiting friends, a shave and a good wash wouldn't go amiss either. I'll have warm water for you in a quarter-hour. Will that be soon enough?'

'It will, since I've yet to formulate a plan. I need to locate a lawyer who has chambers, or the use of chambers, in Middle Temple.' He dipped the bread into the soup. 'At the moment, I can't see how to do it.'

'There must be a list in the Temple that you can consult,' said Rose reasonably.

'Certainly, but it'll be held by the treasurer, and I'm not keen to draw attention to myself or the lawyer by asking for it.' He chewed the bread. 'I'd rather catch him unawares than give him advance notice that I'm looking for him.'

Rose took some cold mutton from her pantry and began to carve it into slices. 'The servants will know him.'

'They'll not speak to me without permission from their employers.'

'They might if you allow Amos to accompany you. He favours a tavern in Water Lane, and several of his drinking companions are employed at Middle Temple. He tells me they complain endlessly about their lot and envy him his position here.'

Elias took a slice from her platter and dropped it into his broth to warm. 'Why?'

'They're as old as we are and still expected to be on their feet all day. They call the lawyers cheating pettifoggers, having no more love of the breed than the rest of us. If you know the name of the man you seek, they'll be able to tell you where to find him.'

He bestowed a fond smile on her. 'Have I ever told you how much I love you, Rose?'

'More times than I can count, Master Elias,' she answered with a chuckle.

⁓

Amos removed a buff-coloured suit of thigh-length jacket, waistcoat and britches from a camphor wood chest and brushed each garment thoroughly while Elias applied a razor to his stubble and scrubbed himself clean with a cloth. The suit had been made for Master Elias's father, but it fitted his son perfectly. The likeness between the two men was extraordinary, and not just in looks, height and breadth. They had the same ability to assume any persona they chose, though the parts Master Elias played were more varied and accomplished than any Sir William had attempted.

As Sir William's valet for more than two decades, Amos had shared and guarded most of his secrets. After his death, he had doubted he would ever form such a close bond with a master again, yet Sir William's son had embraced him as closely.

Amos had no illusions about the nature of either man's work. The names to describe them were various—agent, infiltrator, emissary, envoy, spy—but Sir William's allegiances had always been easier to identify than his son's. Master Elias might have sworn loyalty to King James as the Duke of Granville, but Amos doubted the oath was sincere.

On Amos's advice, Elias was adopting the persona of an ageing merchant, that being more acceptable to servants than a person of rank. The pretence had the added advantage of distancing the Duke of Granville from the lawyer who had been charged with mediating cases against Dorsetshire rebels. Once dressed, he added twenty years to his appearance by donning a long grey wig with tight, unflattering curls and stooping over a stick to mask his height.

'What do you think?'

'I wouldn't know you if I came upon you unawares, Master Elias.'

'Sir William was a fine teacher, Amos.'

By then, it was late afternoon and the two men made their way along back streets to The Strand and thence to Fleet Street. The smaller roads were mercifully empty, but the thoroughfares were clogged with carriages, bringing wealthy ladies, footmen and maids to purchase novelties from the shops that lined the pavements. As ever, Elias contrasted the hedonism of London with the temperance of country areas. The capital squandered its money on transitory fashion; the shires guarded theirs carefully in the knowledge that a bad harvest or murrain in a flock would bring ruin. Such thoughts revealed that he was a Puritan at heart. In a choice between extravagance and restraint, he preferred restraint.

Amos indicated the tavern some fifty yards ahead when they turned off Fleet Street into Water Lane, then hung back to allow

Elias to enter the establishment alone. Both men felt that a chance meeting inside the drinking den would give rise to fewer questions than if they entered together, since the tavern maids, who knew Amos well, would be curious if he arrived with a stranger.

Amos's reputation for garrulity meant the chance meeting went unremarked, and no one queried his willingness to converse with a merchant over a tankard of ale. When the hour was past seven in the evening, he muttered to Elias that two Middle Temple servants were in the doorway. With feigned slurring, as betokened a man who had consumed several pints, he called them to his table and introduced his generous new friend, Mister Jonathan Bartram, who had a tale of woe about a cheating lawyer.

Mister Bartram ordered more tankards and a fresh pitcher of ale, encouraging the servants to wet their throats copiously. His own pretence at inebriation involved a rambling description of his wheelwright business in Dover and how Mister Hugh Milton had aided and abetted two of his creditors to swindle him out of payment for goods supplied.

'He uses Middle Temple as his address, though I'll wager that's as much a lie as his claim that my wheels shattered the first time they were used. I might believe it of one, but not two dozen, fashioned from the finest green oak and each as perfect as the next.' He fell into a morose silence.

Amos roused himself. 'I said you'd know this rogue if anyone did,' he told his friends. 'Mister Bartram's been near bankrupted by his double-dealing.'

'What will he do if he finds him?' asked one.

'Same as you or I would,' answered Amos. 'Drag him before a magistrate and make him admit what he's done.'

The other stirred. 'Except there's no Milton with registered chambers in Middle Temple,' he said staring pointedly from his empty tankard to the empty pitcher of ale. 'Which isn't to say I haven't heard the name.'

Elias ordered another pitcher. 'Continue,' he invited.

The man waited until his tankard was full again. 'Any member can use the Temple for the delivery of correspondence, and many do. In some cases, they authorise the receipt of letters under different names, and ask that they be repackaged and forwarded in their own names. They never give reasons for it, but we servants assume that such letters are from ladies other than their wives.' He took a long sup of ale.

'You think Mister Hugh Milton is an alias?'

The man chuckled. 'I know so, and from what you've told me, the member who's using it is trying to distance himself from his more questionable dealings. You're not the only one after him, Mister Bartram. At a rough guess, I'd estimate he's received in excess of fifty letters in the last four weeks. Our job is to send them on in batches of a dozen, and I've taken two of those batches to the post myself.'

'What's the name of the member?'

'That'll cost you, and the knowledge of where to find him will cost you more.'

'How much?'

The man studied him for several moments, clearly assessing how high he could go. 'Two guineas for both, but I'll need a pledge of silence from you. I'll lose my post if members learn of this transaction.'

Elias shook his head. 'You're an opportunist, my friend. You'll send me to the other side of London, looking for someone who doesn't exist, and you and your friend will be long gone by the time I get back.'

'My word is my bond, sir, and you'll need to travel a good deal farther west than London. The man you seek resides in Dorsetshire. I give you that detail for nothing, but his name and address will still cost you two guineas. I'll shake your hand to prove my honesty.'

Elias turned to Amos. 'Should I trust him?'

Amos shrugged. 'Dorsetshire's a mighty long way from Dover, sir. Are you aggrieved enough to travel that far in search of Mister Milton?'

'I am,' said Elias, taking two guinea coins from his waistcoat pocket and placing them on the table. 'First your hand, sir,' he instructed the servant, 'then the names. If they have the ring of truth, you may take the guineas and receive my pledge of silence.'

The man proffered his hand willingly. 'Mister Anthony Ettrick at number twelve, the Market Place, Blandford Forum in Dorsetshire. I can't tell you what he looks like, for I've never seen him, but I twice recited his name and address for the post-master.' He reached for the guineas. 'When you find him, you'll know I've not led you false.'

⌐⌐

Jayne looked at Elias's drawn face when he entered her office the following afternoon. 'You should have stayed longer,' she said. 'Only well-paid messengers ride to London and back in under thirty-six hours.'

Elias turned the chair and straddled it, resting his arms along the back. 'There was nothing to keep me. I concluded my business last night.'

'Successfully?'

'It depends on whether Mister Milton responds to my advice.'

'You've met him?'

Elias nodded. 'Twice, and my words fell on deaf ears both times.'

SEVEN

ELIAS HOBBLED HIS MARE IN woodland and walked across the fields to enter Mister Ettrick's house through the kitchen quarters. It was two hours before noon, and the cook, a day maid and Adam were busy preparing luncheon. The women clapped their hands to their hearts in shock at his sudden appearance, but Adam sketched a deep and respectful bow.

'We're at your service, my lord,' he said. 'Do you wish to see Elizabeth or Miss Althea?'

Elias's eyes creased with amusement. 'Why assume it's not Mister Ettrick I seek?'

'You'd have come to the front door, sir.'

'I can't argue with that,' Elias said, peeling off his gloves. 'Would you be kind enough to fetch Elizabeth? If she's busy, I'm happy to wait outside until she's free.'

The cook, realising belatedly who he was, bobbed a curtsey and pulled out a chair for him at the kitchen table. 'You're welcome to wait in here, my lord,' she said as Adam left the room. 'May I give you something to eat? I've made some sweet apple flapjacks which are still warm from the pan.'

'You're most kind, mistress.'

'Then sit, sir. I am Bridget and have been cook to Mister Ettrick since before Miss Althea was born. Your mother sat in here during the time she tended Miss Althea and was always most gracious about my food.'

Elias lowered himself obediently to the seat and took one of the honey-glazed apple tarts that she offered him on a wooden platter. 'With good reason,' he said, after swallowing a mouthful. 'It's a long time since I've tasted anything so delicious.'

Bridget was torn between delight and disbelief at the compliment. 'I doubt that's true, sir. Miss Jayne's cook will have far superior talents to mine.'

Elias finished the tart and licked his fingers. 'She likes to think she has,' he said, 'but her skill lies in making stews rather than pastries. Will you oblige me by transcribing the recipe so that I can take it home with me?'

Elizabeth heard the exchange as Adam escorted her into the room. Were Elias anyone else's son, she would question his motives in flattering Bridget, but he was too like his mother for Elizabeth to doubt his sincerity.

He rose to his feet as soon as he became aware of her presence. 'You must forgive my entering through the kitchen, Elizabeth, but I thought it wiser than approaching from the front. I'm unsure how I should announce myself to Mister Ettrick.'

'He still believes you to be Reverend Houghton, sir, but he's absent from home at the moment and we do not expect him back until sunset.'

'Then we have nothing to worry about. I have a question for Miss Althea, if she's willing to see me. It concerns a legal conundrum that her knowledge of the law may help me resolve.'

Elizabeth sent Adam to make the request, but the answer came back that it was declined.

'She's very busy, my lord,' said Elizabeth.

'Then will you ask the question for me, Elizabeth? It's a matter of urgency in view of the approaching Assizes. Is Miss Althea aware that the High Sheriff intends to coerce guilty pleas from those she assesses unfavourably?'

Elizabeth looked uncomfortable. 'It's a strange question,' she said carefully. 'Will she understand it?'

'I'd be surprised if she didn't, but if she requires clarification, you may add that the High Sheriff is under pressure from the Lord Chief Justice to keep trials to a minimum.'

Adam, who knew a good deal about what Miss Althea was doing, studied Elias covertly while Elizabeth delivered the message. Being young, he had an uncompromising view of life, and he was angered by Elias's hypocrisy. The last time the man had been here, he had shamed Miss Althea for not having a profession; now, he wanted to shame her for daring to take one.

Elias beckoned him forward. 'Your scowls suggest you think me unreasonable. May I ask why?'

Bridget tried to prevent Adam answering, but he ignored her. 'Miss Althea doesn't deserve your criticism, sir.'

'How have I criticised her?'

'By saying she's to blame for what the High Sheriff does.'

Elias gave the statement some consideration. 'My words could certainly be interpreted that way,' he conceded, 'but my intention is to warn her against placing too much trust in those tasked with delivering the King's justice.'

'She doesn't trust them at all, sir. Her aim is to prevent innocent men being sent to the gallows.'

'I presumed as much.'

'Then you have no argument with her.'

Elias heard the library door open and Elizabeth's footsteps hasten towards the kitchen. 'I wonder if she agrees with you,' he murmured.

⌁

Another table had been brought into the library to accommodate the quantity of correspondence that Mister Milton had received. Althea sat behind her desk, making notes in the margin of a letter, but she broke off to acknowledge Elias. He noticed that the hand holding the quill was trembling slightly, and he wondered if she was afraid of him.

If she were, she chose attack over defence. 'How did you know?' she demanded.

'You're not the only one who can solve equations, Miss Althea.'

'Have you told the High Sheriff?'

Elias shook his head. 'It would be against my interests, since you can reveal as much about Reverend Houghton as I can about Mister Milton.'

This thought had not occurred to her, and he saw some of the strain leave her shoulders. Her hair was as wild as the first time he had seen her, but the buttons on her jerkin were fastened, probably with the help of Elizabeth. 'Then why have you come?' she asked bluntly. 'To express disapproval?'

'Of what?'

She shrugged. 'Whatever offends you. My claim to be a man, perhaps?'

Elias smiled slightly. 'I find that more admirable than offensive. I was named after a close friend of my parents, Lady Alice

Stickland, who posed as a man for most of her life.' He paused. 'My objective in tracking down Mister Milton was to negotiate with him on behalf of the prisoners in Dorchester gaol.'

A frown creased Althea's brow. 'That is my objective also. I'm trying to effect the release of those who are innocent.'

'But you're condemning the rest. You may have succeeded in exonerating a few, but those you haven't excused will be pressed to admit their guilt and accept whatever sentence the Lord Chief Justice applies. It should have crossed your mind that William Lewis would employ any means he can to avoid prolonged and lengthy trials. There are too few hours in a day, and too few days in a month to hear hundreds of individual cases.'

Althea shrugged. 'That's why he's employing me—to weed out as many as I can.'

Elizabeth stirred. 'May we ask how you discovered the pretence, my lord? As far as we're aware, Mister Lewis accepted the references and recommendations that Mister Milton provided.'

'Only because it suited him to do so, and because he saw merit in Miss Althea's first assessments. Had he not, or if he had suspected the references were falsified, he would have made enquiries at Middle Temple as I did.' He shook his head at the sudden fear in both women's eyes. 'Your secret is safe. I purchased the information from a servant who believes me to be a wronged merchant seeking redress. He'll lose his position if he speaks of the transaction.'

'How can you be sure?' Althea asked.

'He was more intent on swearing me to silence than I him. Nevertheless, if I was able to link Mister Milton to Mister Ettrick so easily, then so will others. The first place they'll visit is your poste restante address in Blandford. Who lives at number twelve, the Market Place, and can they be trusted to keep your secret?'

Elizabeth answered. 'My cousin, Giles Haydock, and, yes, he can be trusted.'

Elias recognised the name. 'The tailor? I've used him for years but never knew the number of his shop.'

'But if you're acquainted with him, you know that he is not a gossip, sir.'

Elias nodded. 'Is your father aware of what you're doing?' he asked Althea.

She shook her head. 'Duty would oblige him to denounce me.'

Elias surveyed the piles of correspondence. 'Do these not make him suspicious?'

'He believes I'm writing a treatise on Euclid's *Elements*.'

Elizabeth added, 'The library is Miss Althea's domain, my lord. The master rarely enters it.'

Elias wondered whether it was naivety or misplaced trust that was leading them to answer so honestly. 'You're revealing too much,' he warned. 'My intention in coming here was to open your eyes to the damage you're doing, Miss Althea, but you've supplied me with a quicker way to achieve the result I want.'

'Which is?'

'An end to your mediation. It needs but a word to your father to cancel Mister Milton entirely.'

Althea asked Elizabeth to bring a chair from the salon for His Grace. 'You're too tall,' she said. 'I'll find it more comfortable speaking with you if you're seated.' She dipped her quill in the inkwell and finished the sentence she'd been writing.

'Where will Elizabeth sit?'

'Next to me. I keep a stool beneath the desk.'

When both were seated, Althea told Elias, 'I'm confused about what you want.'

'I came to warn you that your assessments are double-edged and to convince you to abandon them. Also, to use any means you can to dissuade accused men from pleading guilty. I'm told Lord Jeffreys will promise a lenient sentence to anyone who does, but the promise won't stand once the pleas are entered.'

Althea studied him thoughtfully. 'Who gave you this information?'

Elias shook his head. 'I'm not prepared to say.'

'Then I have no reason to accept it. You've cast two slurs against the Lord Chief Justice. First, that he would consider inducing guilty pleas from defendants; and second, that he would negate the terms of the inducement once a guilty plea was lodged.'

'He takes his instructions from the King, and the King won't permit clemency.'

'You must be well-acquainted with the King if you know his thoughts.'

Elias answered honestly. 'I was King Charles II's personal envoy and met his brother several times in that capacity. When James succeeded to the throne, he appointed envoys of his own choosing, but I still have friends at court. They speak of the King's fear of further anti-Catholic uprisings and his intention to make an example of Monmouth's followers. No mercy will be shown to anyone whom Jeffreys rules complicit in the rebellion.'

Althea nodded towards the shelves of books and pamphlets. 'I've read every case in which Lord Jeffreys has been involved, either as prosecutor or judge. His legal acumen is considerable, his oratory impressive and his judicial verdicts beyond reproach.

I find it hard to believe he'll act as the King's puppet during these Assizes.'

Elias leant forward. 'You would be wise to consider the possibility, however. The anger in Dorset will be considerable when three hundred Protestants are butchered alive on the orders of a vengeful Catholic monarch, and you can be sure that William Lewis will lay the blame at Mister Milton's door if the anger turns on him. You'll make the perfect scapegoat when he's accused of persuading poorly educated men to confess guilt on false promises of mercy.'

Only Elizabeth showed concern at the urgency of Elias's remarks; Althea remained unmoved. 'Why do you care so much?' she asked. 'Did you have sympathy with the rebellion?'

Elias answered the first question. 'Most of the rebels are simple folk, who took up pitchforks and clubs on Monmouth's pledge to defend Protestantism. They expected, as he did, that landowners would rally to his cause and bring their militias and weapons with them. When that didn't happen, defeat was inevitable.'

Althea shrugged. 'Landowners had more sense than to associate themselves with an ill-planned venture that couldn't possibly succeed.'

'You make my point very well, Miss Althea. The rich assess their chances of success while the poor fight for ideals, and dreams are rarely rooted in caution.'

'That doesn't absolve them of guilt. The law is clear. A person who levies war against the King or offers succour to his enemies in his own realm is guilty of high treason.'

'That's a fair description of Monmouth, but not of his followers. You asked if I had sympathy with his rebellion, Miss Althea. I did not, but I have unbounded sympathy for the men he misled.'

'In both senses of the word?'

Elias nodded. 'He persuaded an unarmed rabble to confront trained soldiers and then deserted them to save his own skin. Do you not have sympathy for them yourself, Miss Althea?'

Althea glanced towards the piles of correspondence on the other table. 'Perhaps you should read their letters, sir. They may not be as simple as you think. Some of their defences are quite imaginative.'

Elias accepted her invitation and examined every letter. There were closer to seventy than the fifty estimated by the servant from Middle Temple, and many were written in the same hand as a result of being dictated to a single scribe. He cross-checked the names against a list which Althea had compiled of those who had applied for mediation, giving brief explanations of why certain defences were accepted but others declined.

After half an hour of reading, he suggested there was room for mitigation in some of the rejected defences. He offered her one such letter as an example.

'This man admits he was at Sedgemoor but denies any part in the conspiracy against King James. He claims he was there to watch the battle, never saw or spoke to Monmouth, and the blood on his clothes came from his attempts to assist the wounded.'

'To succeed with that defence, he would have to prove that he tended only soldiers who wore the King's colours. If he assisted rebels, he offered succour to the enemy.'

Elias selected another letter. 'This man says he was fighting to safeguard the Protestant Church of England under King James. If Monmouth had different ambitions, he was unaware of them.'

'He became complicit in Monmouth's attempt to usurp the throne when he took up arms.'

'Even if he himself had no intention of deposing King James?'

Althea placed her elbows on the desk and cupped her chin in her hands. 'It's an interesting contention,' she agreed, 'but not one that Lord Jeffreys will accept. After the Rye House Plot, Lord Russell argued that a plan to levy an army did not indicate a design to kill the King, but his argument was rejected. The prosecutor in that case was George Jeffreys, so you can be sure he will dismiss any similarly pedantic interpretations of the law.'

Elias placed his hand on a third letter. 'What about a plea of duress? This man claims he was forced to fight by Dutch mercenaries who used the flats of their swords to prevent him running away.'

Althea shook her head. 'Duress can only be cited as an excuse in common law. A man is considered innocent if he can demonstrate that he committed a crime under threat of death to himself or those dear to him. It is no defence against high treason, for the law of high treason is predicated on a recognition that the sovereign's life has a higher value than the lives of his subjects.'

Elias eyed her thoughtfully. 'Is there any defence these men can offer?'

Althea lowered her hands. 'Proof of absence.'

'Go on.'

'If an accused person can provide witnesses to state that he was elsewhere during the rebellion, then he could not have taken part. A prolonged sojourn with family members in the north or east, covering the period from before Monmouth's arrival in Lyme Regis until his arrest on the Shaftesbury estate, should suffice.'

'Not every man can offer that defence.'

'There are different versions of it.'

'Such as?'

She took a moment to collect her thoughts. 'If five imprisoned men agree to swear on oath that a sixth was never party to their rebellion, there's a good chance the sixth will be released without trial. It depends how well the rebels understand the gravity of their situation, and whether they can be persuaded of the pointlessness of six dying when one can be saved.'

'If you were their lawyer, would you advise them to do that?'

'Not if all six were my clients, since my obligation to each would be the same. Lawyers deal with the facts of law, not the moral issues that surround it.'

Elias gave a low laugh. 'Indeed. It's a rare lawyer who puts morality before his fee.'

Althea didn't take umbrage because she agreed with him. There were as many charlatans claiming to practise law as practised medicine. 'The situation I'm proposing will force the men to question themselves. Such an act of selflessness will demand a level of commitment that they may not possess.'

'Could you persuade them to find it?'

She gave a small laugh. 'I doubt they'd believe an immoral lawyer in search of a fee . . . but they might listen to a charitable clergyman who donates his horse to the needy and whose honesty is beyond question. Do you know of such a person?'

Elias acknowledged the hit with a smile. 'Give me another version of proof of absence.'

'A debilitating illness, such as consumption, that would have left a man too weak to march and fight. Diagnosis by a trusted physician, who is willing to say he couldn't have left his bed to engage in rebellion, would be accepted.'

'Would the physician be required to say that under oath in front of Lord Jeffreys?'

She nodded. 'Unless the High Sheriff discharges the sufferer before the Assizes begin. You tell me he's looking for ways to avoid trials, so I imagine he'll seize on any reasonable excuse to let people go.'

'He's certainly amenable to releasing those you adjudge innocent,' Elias responded. 'Would you consider exploiting his trust to have guilty men released?'

Althea was unimpressed by the suggestion. 'There would be no trust to exploit if Mister Lewis doubted the honesty of my assessments. His suspicions would be aroused the first time I argued that a man's word alone was enough to exonerate him. You'll have gathered from the letters that duress, ignorance of Monmouth's intentions and helping the wounded are the most frequently cited justifications for participation, which tells me the prisoners are sharing ideas on how to mitigate their guilt. Do you think their gaolers are unaware of this and haven't reported it to Mister Lewis?'

Elias scratched his jaw. 'I could apply the same logic to those you've deemed innocent. They all claim false witness by neighbours as the reasons for their arrests. Why does that shared idea carry more credence than the others?'

'It doesn't unless I can substantiate what the appellant is alleging. I've refused at least ten men, using the same excuse, who were unable to supply me with proof of their claims.'

'What form does the proof take?'

'Witness testimony. Successful appellants supplied the names of people who would vouch for them. In every case, the witnesses responded immediately to my requests for information—often written by local parsons, who added personal statements of their own—and I submitted those documents along with my assessments to Mister Lewis. Long-held jealousies and grudges are the most commonly cited motives for false accusations.'

'It's a sorry world where a king's desire for vengeance inspires others to seek the same.'

'Indeed.'

Elias held her gaze briefly, then pushed back his chair. 'I'll leave you to your work, Miss Althea. Had I known your reasons for interceding, I would not have imposed on you.'

Her expression was unreadable, though Elias suspected she knew exactly what he was thinking. The suspicion was confirmed by her next statement.

'Witnesses must be open to verification by the High Sheriff and Lord Jeffreys. To that end, they must provide addresses and make themselves available should bailiffs call. They must also be willing to repeat their testimonies in court if Lord Jeffreys feels their written statements require further scrutiny. Do you understand?'

Elias rose to his feet. 'I do.'

'Then good day to you, sir,' she said, taking up her quill again. 'Elizabeth will show you out.'

She resumed her writing, demonstrating all too clearly that she had no further interest in him.

Elizabeth felt the need to apologise. 'She doesn't mean to be offensive, my lord,' she said as she escorted Elias to the kitchen. 'She values honesty and speaks in the same direct manner to everyone.'

'I am not offended, Elizabeth. I find her directness refreshing. Can you tell me why she decided to propose herself as a mediator?'

'Lord Shaftesbury's son, young Anthony, told her a farmer's wife had begged his father to intervene on behalf of her husband who had been wrongly arrested. The earl declined to help, but Anthony asked Miss Althea to read the letters and deeds that the woman provided.'

'Why was he interested?'

'He's enamoured of the couple's daughter.'

Elias smiled. 'That's as good a reason as any. What did the documents prove?'

'That the neighbour who made the false accusation was intent on acquiring the family's land. He offered the wife a pittance for it on a promise of retracting the accusation as soon as the deeds were transferred.'

'And Miss Althea invented Mister Milton to prevent that happening?'

Elizabeth nodded. 'But not as a mediator. She wrote a formal letter to the neighbour, using the Middle Temple address and citing his infringements of the law in his attempts to acquire the land. She allowed him one day to withdraw his accusation or face charges of demands with menaces, perjury, defamation and attempted theft.'

The servants in the kitchen were listening to this conversation through the open door, and Adam added a comment of his own as Elias and Elizabeth entered the room. 'The man's a weasel, my lord. Master Anthony said he has eyes for the daughter as well as the land.'

'And Miss Althea forced him to withdraw?'

The lad nodded. 'She would have used the same method to scare every malicious accuser if she'd known their names and the names of the men they'd accused. It was only by posing as Mister Milton that she could gain access to those who needed help.'

Elias buttoned his coat and pulled on his gloves. 'I trust the farmer and his wife have been warned to hold their tongues, and that you and Anthony haven't spoken about this to anyone else. I imagine the penalty for impersonating a lawyer is severe.' He smacked one palm across the back of his other hand to push the cuff of his leather gauntlet over his wrist.

Adam took a wary step backwards. 'Miss Althea has made us aware of that, sir, and we are all sworn to silence on the matter.'

'She has nothing to fear from us,' said Elizabeth firmly. 'Nor have you, my lord. We never gossip about anything that happens inside this house. You have my word on that.'

The cook handed him a scrap of paper. 'You asked for my recipe, sir. Take it with my blessing and know that Elizabeth speaks for all of us. We are too fond of Miss Althea to put her in peril.'

Elias thanked Bridget for her trouble and made his farewells. As he walked across the fields, he wrestled with his conscience. If William Lewis were to mention the lawyer's helpful assessments to the Lord Chief Justice, it would prompt a search of Middle Temple rolls that would lead inevitably to Mister Ettrick.

A selfless man would wait on the highway for the magistrate's return in order to warn him of his daughter's activities and give him the chance to rectify the matter before either was exposed. A ruthless man would exploit the daughter's trust and leave the father in ignorance.

EIGHT

THREE DAYS LATER LADY HARRIER received a summons from the High Sheriff, asking her to visit the Dorchester prison as a matter of urgency. His note, delivered by a messenger, spoke of several men showing clear signs of consumption and Lewis's fear that the disease would spread through the gaol's population. She showed the note to Elias.

'Why didn't Joshua mention this last week? The men must have had the disease for two or three months if the symptoms are noticeable enough for a layperson to recognise them.'

Elias shrugged. 'He was more concerned about them escaping than whether they were sick?' he suggested.

His mother dismissed that with a shake of her head. 'Disease of any kind alarms him. He lives in terror of catching something incurable from his prisoners.' She reflected. 'It's odd that several of them are displaying visible symptoms at the same time.'

'Why?'

'It implies they were all infected by a single source, but none has been incarcerated long enough for the source to be a fellow inmate.'

'It's not an uncommon disease, Mama. You'd expect to find a handful of cases in an overcrowded gaol.'

She studied him thoughtfully, in much the same way that Althea had done. 'Is that what you'd like me to tell the High Sheriff?'

Elias returned the note. It would be a red-letter day when he managed to get something past his mother. 'I'd rather you stressed the impossibility of men in the advanced stages of consumption being able to march long distances.'

'Assuming I agree with the diagnosis,' she said dryly. 'I'm not used to being told in advance what my patients are suffering from.'

Elias grinned. 'You'll not be disappointed, Mama. I'm reliably informed they've been coughing up blood and their thinness is so extreme their ribs are showing.'

'Informed by whom?'

'Your friend the superintendent. I chanced upon him yesterday and, as you say, he has a terror of incurable diseases. It was I who suggested he ask the High Sheriff to summon you.'

Jayne refolded the note. 'Why have you made these people your responsibility?'

'For the same reason you will, Mama,' he answered lightly. 'It's what your husband and my father would have done.'

<hr />

Jayne and her nurses were shown into a cell which housed nine men and one woman. On Joshua's instruction, the door was locked behind them, but the grille in the door remained open so that any conversation would be heard by the gaoler outside—not that it would be audible over the continuous dry coughing, Jayne thought, which came in bursts from one prisoner after the other.

There was no arguing with their thinness, but to Jayne's practised eye the pallor of their skins owed more to the application of chalk powder than sickness, while the nicks and scratches on their fingertips clearly accounted for the blood on the rags which they held to their mouths. She couldn't fault their commitment to playing their roles but questioned if she was prepared to jeopardise her hard-earned reputation by practising the level of deceit the charade would require. Even quacksalvers knew that consumption produced a fever which caused the cheeks to redden, and these white-faced people with their dry, phlegm-free coughs bore no resemblance to genuine sufferers, except in their thinness. She didn't doubt this was due to lack of food, though hunger would have been their constant companion long before they reached the gaol.

She beckoned the woman forward, guessing she was younger than her pinched, drawn face suggested.

'Tell me about yourself,' she said. 'How old are you and what is your name?'

'Grace, ma'am. I be seventeen and took work where I could until bailiffs snatched me off the street three weeks ago.'

'For what cause?'

She nodded to one of the men. 'They say my betrothed be a rebel, ma'am, and that I was with him at Sedgemoor.' She coughed into her rag. 'But we both be too sick to walk so far.'

'How old is your betrothed?'

'Seventeen, ma'am, same as me.'

Jayne glanced about the group. 'Who is the eldest amongst you?'

One stepped forward, and his frame was so skeletal that Jayne was amazed he was able to stand. 'I be, ma'am. My age is twenty-eight and I have a wife and three children at home.'

'What is your trade?'

'Farm labourer when there's work to be had, ma'am, but I'm willing to turn my hand to most anything for a penny.'

'What are you accused of?'

'Giving succour to the enemy.' He followed the girl's lead by coughing spittle into his rag. 'They say I raised my pitchfork against the King's army but I struggle to raise it even to lift hay.'

The others told similar stories, and Jayne came to the view that Monmouth had represented an escape from the hardship of their lives. Their emaciated frames spoke of prolonged and desperate poverty, and the chance to fight for something better would have been irresistible. The only mystery was who had selected them to masquerade as consumptives. Elias was accomplished at disguising himself, but he had escorted her too often on her visits to enter the gaol unrecognised.

With sudden decision, she exchanged a few murmured words with her nurses, then called to the gaoler to take her to the superintendent's office. Once there, she gave the impression of consumption without ever stating that that was her diagnosis.

'I applaud your sense in gathering them together in a single cell, Joshua, but you were irresponsible to refuse me entry last time. My best advice is that you release them to my care immediately, so that I can treat them in my hospital. And if you're worried that there are other sufferers, you must give me free access to all the cells. It takes a trained eye to spot phthisis in its early stages, and I doubt you or your gaolers have that ability.'

As she'd hoped, he fixed on her request to have them released. 'Mister Lewis won't permit it, milady. They've been charged with treason.'

She shook her head dismissively. 'You've seen them, Joshua. Their flesh has been wasting away for months. Do you honestly believe they were capable of marching with Monmouth, let alone strong enough to defend themselves against mounted troops?'

'It's not my decision to make, milady.'

'Then send a messenger to Mister Lewis and ask him to attend upon me here. He'll change his mind when he sees them for himself. I'm happy to wait, but you must permit me to examine the other prisoners in the meantime. You know as well as I the danger of allowing disease to spread unchecked.'

William Lewis arrived an hour after noon, and by then Jayne had added another three to the isolation cell. These were genuine consumptives, whose fevered sweats and laboured breathing showed the disease clearly. Her nurses had remained with the original ten while she went from cell to cell and, following her murmured instructions before she left to speak with the superintendent, these ten now displayed similar symptoms to the three who had joined them.

Maggie and Emily told her afterwards that two of the men had donated blood from their fingers to bring colour to cheeks, while bottled brine from the nurses' satchels had created the semblance of sweat on foreheads and tunics. Fortuitously, the resulting smearing of the chalk powder had given each so morbid an appearance that William Lewis, examining them through the grille in the cell door, hardly needed the additional evidence of panting breath to persuade him they were close to death.

He retreated hurriedly to Joshua's office and consulted the prison roll to discover who or what had caused the thirteen to be arrested. The reasons varied—*seen with a known rebel, absented themselves from home, spoke about Sedgemoor*—but in every case the words 'as told by an informer' appeared in brackets beside the explanation. Jayne, who was standing at Lewis's shoulder, saw the same phrase against most of the names on the roll, and remarked that it was gratifying to see how much support the King had in Dorset.

'His Majesty may hope so,' said Lewis, 'but I doubt it's admiration that induces people to inform. Ambition to advance or fear of being thought complicit are more likely incentives.'

'If you suspect that, why do you trust what they say?'

'I leave those judgements to the Lord Chief Justice, milady. My job is to arrest and charge, not adjudicate the merits of a case.'

'Of course,' Jayne answered apologetically. 'Forgive me. It was a foolish question. The judge will always take priority in such matters.'

Lewis straightened. 'Not always,' he said curtly. 'I have discretion when accusations are patently false.' He exchanged a glance with Joshua. 'The superintendent tells me you doubt these men would have had the strength to join the rebellion, Lady Harrier. Is that correct?'

'I certainly impressed upon him that a wasting disease, which causes difficulty in breathing, would make marching and fighting impossible. The question you must ask yourself is whether their extreme emaciation is of recent origin or predates Monmouth's arrival in June. I would suggest the latter. With or without phthisis, it requires more than a handful of weeks to reduce a flesh-covered body to a skeleton.'

'Would you be prepared to say that under oath to Lord Jeffreys?'

'By all means. Would you like me to write and sign a statement on phthisis to show him? If Joshua lends me his desk, a quill and paper, I can do it for you now.'

She took his nod for agreement and accepted Joshua's invitation to sit on his stool. He placed a quill and a piece of paper in front of her and she wrote a fluent paragraph on the symptoms and debilitating effects of phthisis, stressing the twin ills of progressive decline in respiratory function and chronic muscular atrophy which led ultimately to death. She added her signature and handed the page to Lewis.

'If you accept that this is a fair description of the thirteen people you observed, Mister Lewis, inscribe their names beneath what I've written and release them to my care. They will fare better in my hospital than here, and Joshua will have peace of mind, knowing they are not infecting him, his gaolers or the other prisoners.'

'Are you not afraid of infection yourself, milady?'

'If I were, I would not have made medicine my profession, sir. I've encountered worse diseases than phthisis these last fifty years.'

'How do you protect yourself?'

'Through two simple actions which can't be taken inside this prison, Mister Lewis: cleanliness and the isolating of infectious patients.'

Lewis took the quill and copied the thirteen names to the page. 'I presume I may visit Winterborne Houghton at any time to assure myself that these people are there, Lady Harrier.'

Jayne answered easily. 'Our door is always open to you, sir. And if you allow me the use of the prison wagon and a driver, you can be satisfied that my hospital is their destination.'

The wagon was the open cart that was used to transport convicted felons to the gallows, and the released prisoners eyed it warily as they emerged through the prison gates. Under the watchful gaze of Joshua, Jayne delivered a short speech in which she attempted with careful words to warn them that they might still face consequences.

'The High Sheriff has released you to my care because he is persuaded that you are gravely ill. In addition, he has granted me the use of the prison wagon and a prison driver to carry you to my hospital at Winterborne Houghton. I have impressed upon Mister Lewis that to walk any distance is beyond your ability, and he has requested the driver to report your safe arrival at Winterborne Houghton upon his return to Dorchester. Mister Lewis has further asked for my permission to visit the hospital at any time in advance of the Assizes to check on your progress, and I have given it readily. He hopes, as I do, that food and treatment in my hospital will allow you to improve over the coming weeks and months.' She looked from one to the other. 'Do you understand?'

They nodded, but it was impossible to tell from their expressions whether they recognised that she was cautioning them against leaving the wagon before they reached their destination. The temptation would be great, since the wagon's pace would be slow enough for them to drop off the back.

Whether by accident or design, Joshua muttered a comment that was loud enough to be heard by the group. 'You'll be held responsible if the driver reports any of them missing, milady.

Mister Lewis and his bailiffs won't take kindly to tracking them down after you took so much trouble to persuade him they can barely support their own weight.'

⌒

The long day had taken its toll on Lady Harrier by the time they reached Winterborne Houghton. She had a loathing of coach travel, and a round journey in excess of eight hours on hard seats had rattled every bone in her body, a discomfort made worse by her insistence on donating the cushions and blankets in her carriage to the shivering people in the cart. By stopping at a bakery on their way out of Dorchester and purchasing loaves, she had sated their hunger, but the unforgiving roads had drained their energy as much as hers.

Elias emerged through the front door as the two vehicles came to a halt on the forecourt and gave orders to his footmen and maids to assist the weary prisoners into the hospital. Having been assured by Maggie and Emily that they were capable of taking charge, he offered his hand and steadied each in turn as they stepped from the carriage. He told them beds and food had been prepared and that five maids were waiting inside to help.

'How did you know we'd be returning with patients, Master Elias?' Maggie asked in an undertone, so that the driver of the prison wagon wouldn't hear her.

'I watched you leave the gaol, then rode cross-country to warn Cook that she would have extra mouths to feed.' He sent her after Emily, then begged his mother's indulgence while he spoke with the prison driver.

The man was under instructions to return that evening with his report, but Elias persuaded him to accept some nourishment before he left. 'You still have four hours of light, and you'll make faster time with an empty wagon. I'll have grooms bring oats and water for your horses while you enjoy a tankard of ale and a bowl of stew in my kitchen. Does that appeal, my friend?'

Receiving an appreciative nod, he beckoned forward a groom to hold the lead animal's chinstrap and passed the driver to the care of a footman with instructions to ask Cook to feed him well. He then reached in to help his mother from the carriage and told his coachman to drive to the stable and send Timothy with oats and water for the prison horses.

'Can you walk?' he asked Jayne.

'As long as you lend me your arm. Were you really watching outside the gaol?'

'Listening also. I followed behind you for five miles in case your warnings went unheeded. Fortunately, the bread and blankets sent your guests to sleep. I'd have moved up on the wagon very fast if any had shown an inclination to leave.'

Jayne grasped his arm tightly as she mounted the doorstep. 'Who selected them?'

'A good friend. The gatekeeper accepted two gold sovereigns to let him inside at midnight to search the cells for his errant son, who went missing shortly after Monmouth landed.'

'Which good friend?'

Elias escorted her into the parlour and closed the door behind them. 'I suppose you'll keep pestering me until I tell you?'

'Of course.'

He lowered her onto a padded armchair and pulled forward a footstool. 'Isaac,' he said.

Jayne kicked off her shoes and placed her feet on the stool. She should have guessed, she thought. Only a competent doctor could have picked ten such plausible candidates. Isaac Morecott was her cousin Ruth's son from her first marriage. His stepfather was Jayne's brother Andrew, who had married Ruth after the death of Isaac's father, and through the tight bonds between the families Elias and Isaac had developed a close friendship despite choosing different paths in life.

Elias had followed his father into soldiering and diplomacy, while Isaac, who had spent his childhood years at Winterborne Houghton, had followed Jayne into medicine. His fascination with the hospital had been obvious from an early age and, with Ruth's permission, Jayne had encouraged him to learn from her. At fifteen, he had enrolled at Oxford to study medicine in earnest and, once given a licence to practise, had opened his own hospital in Weymouth, building a fine reputation for himself.

'How did you persuade him?'

'I didn't need to. We've been complicit in saving as many as we can since the rebellion ended. His task is to repair the wounded, mine is to spirit them away—usually by sailboat to France.' He gave a small laugh. 'He was doubly keen when I said you would confirm his choices.'

'He missed three genuine sufferers.'

Another laugh. 'Be fair, Mama. The gaol was in darkness, and the inside guards only allowed him a couple of minutes in each cell. With a single candle to show him what he was looking at, it's amazing he found as many potential consumptives as he did. Even more amazing that, half-asleep, they were alert enough to understand that he was trying to help them.'

'Did the gaolers allow him to speak with them?'

'He didn't try. He just looked them straight in the eye, asked if they could read, then pressed the folded instructions he'd written into their palms. He picked nine, but another four must have been added, because I counted thirteen outside the gaol.'

'Three were mine. Did Isaac pick a young woman?'

Elias shook his head. 'He was looking for a son. The women's cell was closed to him.'

The soft cushions of the chair were beginning to relieve some of Jayne's aches. 'Her name is Grace, and her young man must have found a way to pass the instructions to her. I find that touching. He must love her very much if he wasn't prepared to leave without her.' She flexed her toes. 'There's nothing to be done tonight except give them as much to eat as they can manage, but we'll need to make decisions about them tomorrow. I asked Maggie to put my three in the isolation room. Will you check that she's done that?'

Elias nodded.

'Tell her I'll be out presently to examine them more thoroughly.'

Her son answered with surprising firmness. 'You'll do no such thing, Mama. You're more fatigued than they are, and they'll still be alive tomorrow morning. I'll send Kitty to help you upstairs to bed and ask Cook to prepare a tray of food once you're settled.' He reached for her hand and folded it inside both of his. 'Thank you. You've done more than I expected this day. I hoped to free nine and you've given me an extra four.'

She eyed him curiously. 'Consumption was a clever choice. Was it you or Isaac who proposed it?'

Elias released her hand. 'Neither.'

'Who then?'

He made for the door with a grin. 'Your favourite solver of equations.'

Elias spoke with Cook and Kitty, his mother's personal maid, and then took the corridor to the hospital wing. Maggie waylaid him as he entered, muttering that the released prisoners were talking about leaving.

'They'll make a liar out of Miss Jayne if they do, Master Elias. She persuaded Mister Lewis they're too weak to put one foot in front of the other.'

'Where are they?'

Maggie nodded to a door on the right. 'In there, and looking closer to good health after two bowls of stew and a thorough cleaning by me and the other nurses. I've put the three Miss Jayne found in the isolation room at the far end of the wing, and they're showing no inclination to leave.'

Elias moved past her and opened the door. It was clear that the girl was the ringleader because she stood in front of the men, hands on hips and chin jutting aggressively. He caught the tail end of her argument, the thrust of which appeared to be that only fools would remain where the Sheriff and his bailiffs could find them. Better by far to take their chances outside than allow themselves to be trapped in a house, defended only by a frail old woman.

He moved into the room. 'Lady Harrier may seem old to one as young as you,' he said amiably, 'but to me and her household she's as strong as when she stood with my father and the besieged people of Lyme against seven thousand Royalists.' He ducked his head to the men. 'Good evening, sirs. I am Lady Harrier's son, the Duke of Granville, and I extend a warm welcome to you. If you have questions for me, I am ready and willing to answer them.'

He was greeted with a nervous silence.

'They're scared,' said Grace dismissively. 'I've had naught from them since we climbed into the cart.' She gestured to her young man. ''Cept from Billy, who wants me to hold my tongue.'

Elias cast a sympathetic glance in the lad's direction. 'You might be wise to oblige him, Grace. If these gentlemen thought your suggestions had merit, they would have answered you. Am I right, sirs?'

The eldest stepped forward. 'You are, my lord. We've had our fill of running, and would rather put our faith in Milady. She had no call to help us, but she did, and for that we thank her most heartily.'

Grace gave a snort of contempt. 'She encouraged the Sheriff to come visiting. What sort of help is that?'

Elias allowed the comment to pass. 'I gather you have Billy to thank for having you released from the women's cell. How did he pass the instructions to you?'

'They let me talk to him for a few minutes each day to stop me shouting from my cell. They said it disturbed the other prisoners.'

Elias turned to the men. 'By recollection, the last command on your written instruction was: "*We can only save a few. Do not share this message with anyone else.*" Did you abide by that request?'

The eldest nodded. 'All but Billy, sir. We know not if Grace abided by it.'

''Course I did,' she said contemptuously. 'You think I want timid women alongside me? It's bad enough that none of *you* dares say boo to a goose.'

Elias beckoned Maggie into the room. 'We have nine gentlemen who are ready to sleep,' he said, 'and one young lady who feels the need for action. Her favourite pastimes are lecturing and shouting. What do you suggest?'

Maggie, who had already received a strong dose of Grace's fiery rhetoric, folded her arms. 'Sarah needs help in the kitchen, Master Elias. There's meat to be diced and dough to be kneaded for tomorrow's meals, and I'll wager she and young Grace can teach each other a thing or two while they do it.'

Elias stroked his jaw thoughtfully. 'I doubt Grace has the stomach for a woman as fearsome as Cook.'

Grace's lip curled in disdain. 'No one frightens *me*.'

He gestured to the door. 'Then allow me to escort you to the kitchen.'

He led her down the corridor and instructed her to wait in the anteroom while he oversaw the driver's departure. Once the man had left, he took Sarah aside and begged her indulgence with a difficult patient, first asking if the driver had given the reason for why thirteen prisoners had been released to Milady's care. She said he had, but she hadn't believed him. People too sick to walk could never have consumed the amount of stew she was dispensing, and she had demanded the real explanation from Emily away from the driver's hearing.

'Which of them is causing a problem, Master Elias? I'll wager it's the girl. Emily says she's been nagging her poor young man since they arrived.'

Elias gave an involuntary laugh. 'Her name is Grace, Sarah, and I would estimate her age at sixteen or seventeen. She has confidence in her own abilities but none at all in those of Miss Jayne, whom she describes as a frail old woman. She wants to leave and take her young man with her, but I need them to stay. If I ask her to work with you, do you think you can talk some sense into her?'

Sarah jutted her own chin. 'Leave her to me, Master Elias. I don't tolerate insolence in my kitchen. Frail old woman indeed!'

⌒

Whatever passed between the two, Sarah was sympathetic enough to Grace's plight to ask Elias's permission to offer her and her young man employment in her kitchen. Both had been abandoned to parish poorhouses at birth, given little education, then turned adrift to live from hand to mouth. Sarah suggested their time at Winterborne Houghton would be better spent receiving elementary training in discipline, manners and kitchen skills than feigning consumption.

She made this request when Elias was taking leave of his mother in her office the next morning, so he deferred to Lady Harrier on the matter. Jayne gave her permission readily, telling Elias after Sarah had gone that, according to Maggie, Sarah had been deeply shocked by the girl's thinness.

'It touched her heart, apparently, even more so when Maggie took her to the room where the male prisoners are sleeping. They're all half-starved and in need of weeks and months of feeding. The eldest has a wife and children, whose situation will be worse than his, I imagine, since he was barely able to support them before he joined the rebellion.'

Elias lifted his saddle pack from the floor and slung it across his shoulder. 'We can accommodate a few more. Find out where his family lives and send Timothy to collect them. There's an empty cottage on the estate. They can stay there until we decide what to do with them.'

'How long will you be gone?'

'Three or four days.'

'Am I allowed to know where you're going?'

He shook his head. 'If Lewis comes calling, tell him I'm in London.'

'Doing what?'

'Looking for a wife,' said Elias with a laugh, as he headed for the door. 'It should end any ideas he may have that his daughter has captured my interest.'

Some half-dozen officers who had fought under Monmouth and Granville at Bothwell Bridge were scattered across the mid-English counties of Gloucestershire, Warwickshire and Worcestershire. Elias had kept close ties with them, largely through letter-writing, and each greeted him warmly despite the unexpectedness of his visit. He stayed no longer than two hours at any house, but in every case the request he made of his host was accepted and subsequently fulfilled.

Elias had expected no less. These officers had led men into battle, and not one could forgive Monmouth for abandoning his poorly equipped army to save himself.

RETRIBUTION:
THE BLOODY ASSIZES

September 1685

NINE

THE WESTERN ASSIZES BEGAN AT Winchester in Hampshire on 25 August. Reports of Judge Jeffreys' arrival in the town reached Dorchester within hours, and the description of the mighty procession of mounted lawyers, clerks and cavalrymen who rode behind and in front of the Lord Chief Justice's coach was alarming. King James was said to have dubbed the forthcoming trials a 'campaign' and had given Lord Jeffreys the rank of Lieutenant-General to denote his command of the operation.

Already known as a 'hanging judge' because of the harshness of his sentencing, Lord Jeffreys was rumoured to have named the campaign 'the Bloody Assizes' before he even left London. He was reported to revel in the fear he inspired, and he clearly intended that fear to be felt by every prisoner awaiting trial across the Western Circuit.

The only person to face charges of high treason in Winchester was a widow in her seventies, Dame Alice Lisle of Moyles Court near Ringwood. She was accused of allowing three fugitives from Sedgemoor to stay in her house overnight, but since her deceased husband, John Lisle, had been a presiding judge at the trial, conviction and execution of Charles I, few doubted that this was the real reason for her arrest. King James was known to have a long memory where his father's execution was concerned.

A letter addressed to His Grace the Duke of Granville arrived from Althea Ettrick on 29 August.

Honoured Sir,

In response to your request for information, we learnt this morning that Dame Alice Lisle has been convicted on all charges. She defended herself by saying she had known the fugitives for several years and offered them rooms out of friendship. She was unaware they were involved with Monmouth and claimed that infirmity and profound deafness precluded any meaningful conversation with them.

This defence was rejected by the jury after a severe hectoring from Lord Jeffreys when they said they were inclined to believe it. He has signalled his determination to punish every traitor, high and low, by making the harshest example of Dame Alice. She is condemned to burn at the stake, delayed until the second of September to give her family the chance to petition the King for a lesser sentence.

I regret the sad nature of this news.

Your obedient servant,
Althea Ettrick

Postscript: Although I'm reluctant to admit it, I fear your warnings about revenge taking precedence over justice may be accurate.

On 2 September, Elias rode to Winchester to witness Dame Alice's execution. The mood of the crowd grew ugly once they learnt that the only mercy the King was prepared to show the senile lady was to commute her sentence from burning to beheading. Elias wasn't alone in being repelled by the sight of one so confused being put to death by Jack Ketch, nor in questioning why London's executioner performed the task. From the muted mutters around him, the commonest view was that King James didn't trust local men to exact the brutal revenge he wanted.

Before returning to Winterborne Houghton, Elias paid an unannounced visit to the home of Hampshire's Lord Lieutenant, the Earl of Gainsborough. They were acquainted through their military service, and Elias hoped to tease the earl into revealing what he knew about Lord Jeffreys' campaign. He had no illusions that Gainsborough, a King's man through and through, would have any sympathy for rebels, but he thought he might have caveats about Jeffreys bringing an army into his county.

They greeted each other warmly and, once the pleasantries were concluded, Gainsborough took Elias to his private office. 'I don't say I'm displeased to see you, Granville,' he said, pulling out a chair for his guest, 'but what business brings you here?'

'Curiosity,' Elias said. 'I wanted to discover if the rumours we've heard in Dorset are true.'

'What rumours?'

'The King's so afeared the south-west will rise up against his Lord Chief Justice, he's provided six troops of cavalry to protect him.'

Gainsborough shook his head. 'Two at the most. I saw more clerks than soldiers in the convoy. They left for Salisbury, the next town on their circuit, three days ago, and the legal men were so dilatory it was a good half-hour before the tailenders cleared the town.'

Elias produced a wry smile. 'Such a long procession will convert easily to five hundred fighting men in the minds of Dorchester folk. They've convinced themselves that armed dragoons will be billeted in every house once the trials begin.'

'To what purpose?'

'The suppression of dissent when hundreds are dragged to the gallows on Jeffreys' instructions.' He shrugged. 'I've no idea how such stories start, Gainsborough, but there's a strong belief that the King expects a second rebellion when the ferocity of his revenge becomes known.'

'Who calls it revenge?'

'Your own people. I stood with the crowd to watch Dame Alice's execution, and most were angered to see her being mutilated by Jack Ketch. Not a person doubted it was an act of vengeance. May I ask why you absented yourself from the event?'

'My reasons are my own.'

Elias made no response, confident that he could endure a painful silence more easily than his host. It took a mere few seconds.

Gainsborough squeezed one fist inside the other, cracking his knuckles loudly. 'She didn't receive a fair trial,' he said abruptly. 'Jeffreys rode roughshod over the jury's concerns about her deafness.'

'So I've heard.'

'It was obvious to all that she couldn't follow anything that was said in the courtroom. A man was instructed to kneel at her side and shout the words into her ear, but it was more mockery than assistance.' Gainsborough shook his head in frustration. 'I tried to intervene after the jury was sent out to deliberate, but Jeffreys refused me entry to his chamber.'

'He takes instruction from the King. He can't afford to listen to reason.'

Gainsborough was set on his own thoughts. 'He assured me the night before that his reputation for harshness was exaggerated and he would conduct the trial with impartiality. It was a blatant falsehood. He refused to accept the evidence of his own eyes that Dame Alice was too confused even to understand why she was being tried.'

Elias gave a small shrug. 'The crowds this morning had no doubts. King James wanted his pound of flesh, and Lord Jeffreys delivered it for him. Perhaps he refused you entry to avoid having to admit it.'

Another frustrated shake of the head. 'He was drunk. I'm told he imbibed a flagon of wine at breakfast and then consumed a second flagon in the half-hour before the jury came back . . . and this on top of drinking himself to a stupor the night before.'

Elias eyed him with surprise. 'Was it obvious in court?'

'Not at all. He was ill-tempered and rude, but his speech was fluent and he was in control of himself. Take my advice and avoid Dorchester while he's there. His conceit is insufferable.'

At Winterborne Houghton the following morning, a footman announced that the High Sheriff was at the door. Elias sent the youth to alert Lady Harrier to an imminent inspection of her patients, then made his way to the front hall. To give his mother more time to prepare, he seized Lewis's arm with jovial good humour and drew him into the parlour, calling to a maid to bring some ale for his friend. The room formed the western corner of the house, with a large window overlooking the parkland and driveway, and a smaller one giving a view of the forecourt. Had Elias been there ten minutes previously, he would have seen Lewis's approach and could have prevented him entering.

'You look tired,' he said, pressing Lewis into a chair and drawing another close for himself. 'It's past noon. Will you take some luncheon with us?' He nodded to a table beneath the window. 'My mother and I eat in here, and it'll be no trouble to add an extra place.'

Lewis took a kerchief from his pocket and mopped sweat from his forehead. 'It would be much appreciated, Granville. I don't mind admitting I'm worn to the bone. My horse is blown from being ridden thirty miles at full gallop. I'll need the loan of one of yours if I'm to reach Dorchester by evening.'

'You may borrow one with my blessing. Where have you come from?'

'Salisbury. I spent the night there and have barely slept from worry. It's a bad, bad business.'

Elias used the hiatus of the maid's arrival with tankards of ale to consider his next question. He could think of only one reason why Lewis might go to Salisbury. 'Do I gather you've met Lord Jeffreys and the meeting didn't go well?'

Lewis took a long draught of ale. 'If you can call a conversation of half an hour with an inebriate a meeting. He alternated between bouts of maniacal laughter and unmitigated temper, then fell asleep and had to be taken to his room. The servants were all female, so the task of carrying and undressing him fell to me and my Wiltshire counterpart, John Davenant. It is not an experience I wish to repeat.'

'Where were Lord Jeffreys' own servants?'

'According to Davenant, his wife insists they remain at home. Travel disagrees with him and those who have accompanied him in the past have left his service within three days. Every High Sheriff has been ordered to provide him with suitable retainers for the duration of his stay.'

'He sounds most unpleasant.'

Lewis shuddered. 'He is. Davenant described him as a Welsh upstart, with little breeding and no manners. His first wife wasn't rich enough for him, so shortly after her death he married a second with money. It's doubtful either welcomed him as a husband if the speed with which he loses servants is any guide. Davenant wanted me to escort him to Dorchester today, but I refused and left early to be spared any more of his company than is necessary.'

Elias thought Davenant's patience must have been tested indeed to indulge in so much gossip. 'Has Jeffreys' business concluded in Salisbury?'

Lewis nodded. 'The calendar was light, with only six men arraigned for speaking seditious words. He ruled them guilty and ordered them whipped through the streets.'

Thoughtfully, Elias took a sup from his own tankard. 'Is he aware of the high numbers that await him in Dorchester?'

'He is, and threw wine in my face when I raised the matter.' Lewis crushed his kerchief in his fist. 'It's a mercy I've cut the Dorchester calendar by one quarter or he'd have broken the bottle over my head.'

'How many remain?'

'Five short of three hundred. I've released ninety-nine, who've been able to demonstrate malicious accusation, absence or ill health, though I'm inclined to recall them so as to oblige

Jeffreys to hear their cases. He'll have reason for ill temper if he's compelled to sit through weeks of evidence proving their innocence.'

Elias thought of the people involved in those releases, none of whom would welcome being interrogated by the Lord Chief Justice—least of all, Mister Hugh Milton. 'I wouldn't recommend it, my friend,' he said with a laugh. 'You'll suffer more than he does. My best advice is to forget the ninety-nine existed and keep the judge in ignorance of them.' He feigned a moment's reflection. 'I'm reminded of a woman I learnt about the other day. A cancer caused her such unremitting pain that she sought oblivion in brandy. Did Jeffreys look ill to you?'

'His complexion was unduly florid, but I put that down to inebriation. What are you suggesting?'

Elias shrugged. 'I'm wondering if there's a reason for his drunkenness. I was led to believe he's known for his sharpness of mind, legal acumen and impressive oratory, but your description of an ill-mannered oaf with little or no control over himself hardly fits that picture.'

'He can't hold his drink.'

Elias let the matter go and turned instead to the released prisoners. Where and how had Lewis acquired the evidence to prove their innocence? Lewis admitted that he had included thirty-six escapees in the figure, but of the rest, thirteen had been placed in the care of Elias's own mother, twenty-eight had produced witnesses willing to swear to the malicious nature of the accusations against them, seven had been exonerated by fellow prisoners, and the remaining fifteen had been able to supply invoices and receipts for work done and paid for by landowners in England's Middle Shires.

Elias pretended interest. 'What sort of work?'

'Stonemasonry. Landowners of good repute hired them before the rebellion began to transport Purbeck marble to estates across Gloucestershire, Worcestershire and Warwickshire. Their whereabouts from the beginning of June to the end of July were fully accounted for by their employers.'

'Why were they arrested at all?'

Lewis stared morosely into his tankard. 'Neighbours reported them for deserting their homes. It's the same with every prisoner. Friend informing on friend. I question whether there'll be any trust left in Dorset when the Assizes are over.'

'Precious little, I should think,' Elias said bluntly, 'and the fault lies with the King. It suits his purpose to set his subjects at each other's throats. There's less chance of another uprising if men disagree on where to direct their anger.'

'You're dicing with danger, Granville. Men were whipped through the streets of Salisbury for mouthing less.'

Elias gave a grunt of amusement. 'I doubt I've said anything you haven't thought yourself. His Majesty should have made do with Monmouth's head. He'll stoke a deal of hatred against himself if Jeffreys' judgements are seen to be unfair. I'm sure you're aware of the discontent in Hampshire over Dame Alice's execution. I was in the crowd and heard their mutterings.'

Lewis ran his kerchief across his brow again, and Elias wondered whether it was his wig or anxiety that was causing him to sweat. 'My hands are tied. Davenant tells me there's no reasoning with Jeffreys, nor with the four judges and prosecuting counsel who accompany him. All are set on delivering the harshest penalties possible.'

Footsteps sounded on the flagstones of the hall and Elias looked up to see his mother in the parlour doorway. He rose with a bow. 'We have a visitor for luncheon, Mama. William has ridden from Salisbury and is in urgent need of sustenance before he continues on to Dorchester.'

Lewis placed his tankard on the floor and pushed himself to his feet. 'Your servant, milady,' he said with a duck of his head. 'I trust I'm not imposing on you.'

Jayne entered the room with a welcoming smile. 'Not at all, sir,' she said, offering her hand. 'It's always a pleasure to see you.'

He stooped over her fingers. 'The pleasure is mine, milady.'

Above his bent head, Jayne lifted enquiring eyebrows at Elias.

'William has been telling me about an uncomfortable meeting he had with Lord Jeffreys, Mama. It seems our Chief Justice is an inebriate who drinks himself to a stupor. I found the idea surprising and mentioned that patient of yours who used brandy to deaden her pain. I believe her name was Gertrude.'

Jayne accepted the chair he drew forward for her and gestured to Lewis to retake his. The last set of patients that Elias had gifted her were the 'consumptives' and this sudden bestowal of Gertrude suggested that Jeffreys might be the next. 'Are you wondering if the Chief Justice has the same affliction as Gertrude?'

He held her gaze, and she knew his expressions well enough to recognise that he sought endorsement from her. 'That or something similar, Mama. It's odd for a man in his position to drink so heavily, don't you think?'

'Very odd,' she agreed, turning to Lewis. 'How old is he?'

'Not above forty, milady.'

'How strange. From his reputation for harshness, I'd assumed he was older. Describe him to me. Did he fidget? Have shivers? Look feverish?'

'All of those, milady. I put it down to his consumption of wine last evening. I doubt it's a regular occurrence.'

Elias shook his head. 'I fear it may be, Lewis. I spoke with the Earl of Gainsborough after Dame Alice's execution, and he informed me that Jeffreys was drunk when he delivered his verdict on her.'

Aghast, Lewis took to mopping his brow again. 'I was warned to expect irascibility but not drunkenness. The trials will be a mockery. What am I to do?'

'Eat,' said Elias, rising to his feet. 'You'll feel better with some food inside you. I'll tell Cook to prepare a third plate.' He gestured towards his mother. 'Meanwhile, allow Lady Harrier to advise you. She understands every disease, including the craving for alcohol.'

Jayne had a good understanding of how her son's mind worked. He wanted to meet Lord Jeffreys in a way that wouldn't raise Lewis's suspicions and had nominated her as the facilitator. She was curious enough to oblige him. 'You've been driving yourself too hard, Mister Lewis,' she said as Elias left the room. 'Were I your physician, I would insist you remain here for the night rather than return to Dorchester.'

'It's not possible, milady. I must be at my post when Lord Jeffreys arrives.'

'When will that happen?'

'He's due tomorrow, milady, but I fear he may have departed Salisbury already. He complained bitterly about the discomfort of the bed John Davenant found for him. He said it had left him in agony, and I can only pray the one we're providing is better.'

'Where will he be staying?'

'The lodgings in High West Street.'

Jayne pretended to ponder the matter. 'You would do well to make sure it's been thoroughly warmed and aired, Mister Lewis. By recollection, the mayor acquired that house two years ago for the use of visiting judges, and I doubt it's had much use in the intervening period. The last thing a sufferer of pain will want is dampness in the walls and in his mattress.'

'I've had maids working inside it for a week, milady.'

'Did you instruct them to open the windows and light fires in all the rooms?' She continued when he made no answer. 'If Lord Jeffreys has remained in Salisbury, you still have time, sir. I cannot stress enough that cold and damp are the enemy of pain.'

A tremor began in Lewis's upper lip. 'He will find fault with whatever I do, milady. He took against me most vilely last night. My nerves are shot to pieces because of it.'

Jayne was sympathetic. 'I can see that, sir. How sure are you that he has already left Salisbury?'

'Not at all, milady, but John Davenant was no keener to keep him than I to welcome him.'

'Would he accept a bed here for the night? We're close to the Salisbury–Dorchester highway and will welcome him gladly to give you further time to prepare. You have but to say the word and Granville will ride out to meet him.'

'I can't ask that of you, milady.'

Jayne smiled. 'Then you'll disappoint me, sir. Before the Civil War, I treated Sir John Bankes of Corfe Castle, who was Lord Chief Justice under Charles I. He, too, drank to excess, and I'm intrigued to discover whether the onerous nature of the position causes the drinking or whether Lord Jeffreys has a similar ailment to Sir John.'

'May I ask what that ailment was, milady?'

'Crippling gout, Mister Lewis. Sir John was quite the rudest and most ill-tempered man I'd met until I relieved his pain.'

'How, milady?'

'By removing his brandy and allowing him to drink only water.'

Lewis viewed her with alarm. 'That won't work with Lord Jeffreys, milady. His temper bordered on violence last night. He'll likely harm you if you deprive him of what he wants.'

'I wouldn't dream of trying, sir. It requires more than a single evening to persuade a patient to change his habits. I'm keener to discover why he behaves as he does, since it may be that he deserves your sympathy more than your dislike.'

Lewis's closed expression told her she was misguided, but he made no argument when Elias returned and agreed to convey his mother's invitation to Salisbury. Had Granville shown more enthusiasm for the task, Lewis might have questioned whether he was the instigator of the idea, but his reluctance to entertain an ill-mannered drunk was obvious.

Lady Harrier insisted they eat luncheon first, during which she described the condition of her consumptive patients and the remedies she was using to treat them. Lewis listened politely enough, but once the meal was over, he chose to accompany Granville to the stable rather than accept Lady Harrier's offer to have one of her nurses show him the hospital.

Maggie, who had hovered in the hall for just that purpose, gave way to giggles after the front door closed behind him. 'You might have spared him your descriptions of virulent green phlegm, Miss Jayne. He'll fancy himself infected all the way home.'

Jayne laughed. 'But think how relieved he'll be when he finds he's mistaken.'

Elias watched Lewis depart on a borrowed mount, then set about preparing his racing carriage. While the groom harnessed the horses, he retrieved blankets and soft cushions from his mother's coach and placed them beneath the seat before running the reins to the driver's position. Prior to mounting, he warned Timothy of the possible arrival of a cavalry regiment, since it was unlikely that Lord Jeffreys would travel without his army.

Leaving Winterborne Houghton, Elias steered towards Blandford and urged his horses to a fast trot. He was obliged to rein the animals to a walk through the busy town but, once clear, he increased his pace again. The highway, being a main thorough-fare, was well maintained. Ruts were common during the winter and spring, when the rain fell freely, but rare in summer when the ground was hardened by the sun. Several times he slowed to allow a vehicle to pass from the other direction, but none was grand enough to be carrying the Lord Chief Justice.

That encounter took place some five miles north of Blandford, though a bend in the highway meant Elias was unprepared for the advance guard of mounted troops that appeared in front of him. They rode four abreast and each column appeared to be five riders deep. He drew his carriage to an abrupt halt and, because he was positioned towards the centre of the road, the troop was obliged to halt likewise.

'Move aside!' an officer shouted. 'We travel on the King's business.'

'That may be so,' Elias called in return, 'but I need room to manoeuvre. Order your men to double file.'

'I do not take instruction from travellers. Your name, sir.'

'Colonel Lord Granville of our late King's Horse Guards. Who commands you?'

The officer—who was a captain, by the emblem on his collar—nudged his mount forward. 'The Lord Chief Justice, General Lord Jeffreys, sir. We escort him to Dorchester and request unhindered passage for his coach.'

Elias feigned a surprised laugh. 'He's the man I seek,' he said, drawing a letter from inside his coat. 'My mother asked me to give him this. Will you take it to him? I shall wait here until I receive his reply.'

He held out the letter but the captain remained where he was. 'He doesn't read petitions, my lord.'

'The Duchess of Granville doesn't write them,' Elias countered, knotting the reins to the rail above the carriage's front board and jumping to the ground. 'I'll take it myself. My horses are well trained and will stand steady until I return.'

The captain placed his hand on his sword hilt. 'I cannot allow you to pass, my lord.'

Elias crossed his arms. 'Then we'll be here a long time, my young friend. Mine is a racing carriage, and I'll wager there's not a man in your company who can drive it. My animals respond only to my instruction.'

With bad grace, the captain nudged his mount forward and held out his hand for the letter. His foot was so poorly inserted in his stirrup that Elias was tempted to knock it out and tip him from his saddle to teach him a lesson in soldiering, but he refrained. Instead, he passed him the letter, then recrossed his arms and prepared to wait. There was nothing he could add to his mother's invitation, which was penned in her usual forthright style.

Dear Lord Jeffreys,

I understand your stay in Salisbury has been far from comfortable, for which you have my sympathy. Should you wish to enjoy a restful night before you continue to Dorchester, my son, the Duke of Granville, and I would be glad to welcome you to Winterborne Houghton, which is situated five miles to the south-west of Blandford.

Our chambers are prized for the softness of their beds and our cellar for the excellence of its wine. In addition, Lord Granville served as a colonel for many years in the King's Horse Guards and is used to accommodating cavalrymen and their mounts.

My kind regards,
Lady Harrier, the Duchess of Granville

Elias remained straight-faced when the captain returned to inform him that General Lord Jeffreys requested his presence at the coach. The young officer's aggrieved expression suggested he had been on the sharp end of his commander's tongue, and Elias had no desire to rub salt in the wound. He ducked his head in acknowledgement and asked if the captain would be kind enough to escort him.

The young man dismounted and passed his reins to his neighbour before placing his right hand once again on the hilt of his sword and gesturing with his left for Elias to precede him. 'I am charged with Lord Jeffreys' safety, sir, and will defend him with my life if necessary.'

'As you should,' said Elias without rancour. 'However, if I had ill intentions towards him, my purpose in blocking the road would be to facilitate a flanking attack. I suggest you order your men to face the woodlands on either side to prevent such an assault occurring.'

He moved off as the captain gave the command, and his long stride took him to the coach well before the youngster caught up with him. With the window down, he had no difficulty seeing inside. He was surprised to find that Jeffreys was travelling alone, having expected his fellow judges to be with him; even more surprised by the pallor of the man's face, accentuated by his bizarre choice to travel in his formal red robes. To Elias's eyes, he looked very unwell, though whether from being inebriated the previous night or some other cause, he couldn't say.

He ducked his head. 'Your servant, sir,' he said, offering his hand in friendship. 'Elias Harrier, Duke of Granville. Allow me to welcome you to Dorsetshire.'

Jeffreys kept his own hands firmly in his lap. 'Your name means nothing to me,' he snapped, 'and the penalty for waylaying a traveller on the highway with the intent to rob him is hanging.'

Elias responded with a smile. 'I wouldn't be showing my face if my purpose was robbery, and nor would I have driven my racing carriage to meet you, since there is no more recognisable vehicle in this part of Dorset.'

Jeffreys tapped the letter on his lap. 'Who told Lady Harrier that my stay in Salisbury was uncomfortable?'

'William Lewis. He needed a change of horse if he was to reach Dorchester by this evening and asked to borrow one of mine. He values Lady Harrier's advice, so informed her of his concern that the judges' lodgings in High West Street might not meet with your approval. Her invitation was as much to assist him as you, since a delay in your arrival will allow him to ensure that acceptable servants are in place and the premises warmed and aired.'

'She presumes too much. I'm not in the habit of accepting unsolicited invitations.'

'The only presumption she may have made is that you'll decline, sir, for were your roles reversed she would do the same. Nonetheless, the invitation is sincerely meant.'

'You don't inspire me with confidence.'

Elias took a step backwards. 'Then I'll delay you no longer. I trust you find your lodgings in Dorchester agreeable.'

But Lord Jeffreys hadn't finished with him. 'What time will I arrive there?'

Elias glanced at the sun. 'Nine of the clock at the earliest,' he answered. 'You still have a good six hours of travelling ahead of you.'

'How many to Winterborne Houghton?'

'Three if you remain in this coach, less than one if you have the nerve to test my racing carriage.'

'Is it safe?'

'If you're willing to believe Lady Harrier. She's my most frequent passenger.'

The captain, who had been hovering at Elias's shoulder, intervened. 'I wouldn't recommend it, sir,' he told Jeffreys. 'It lacks a roof and sides and there's nothing to prevent you being thrown from the seat.'

'Except a strong leather belt about your waist and French-fashioned leaf springs to keep the seat level,' Elias answered mildly. 'I've not lost a passenger yet. Certainly not my mother, who has ridden in it more times than I can remember.'

Perhaps Jeffreys felt it ill-behoved a general to show less courage than a woman. Perhaps, too, he couldn't face another six hours in the coach with the likelihood of a damp bed at the end of it.

Whatever the reason, he dismissed the captain's concerns with a flick of his hand. 'Tell the driver to follow at his own pace and instruct your men to form their columns around Lord Granville's carriage. What stride should they adopt, sir?'

'A fast trot,' said Elias. 'Only my driveway is maintained to a high enough standard to achieve a canter.'

Jeffreys ordered the captain to open the door and pull down the steps. He spent a moment or two gathering himself, then gripped the doorframe and descended carefully to the ground. He was half a head shorter than Elias and his gait was unsteady, but his judge's robes and the undoubted dominance of his character gave him an imposing presence.

'For warmth and comfort, there are cushions and blankets beneath the seat,' Elias said as he led the Chief Justice to his carriage. 'Would you like me to arrange them for you?'

'Does Lady Harrier use them?'

Elias shook his head. 'She enjoys the wind. She says it gives her a greater sense of speed.'

Jeffreys used the step to hoist himself to the seat. 'She's an unusual woman.'

'Very unusual,' Elias agreed, reaching over him to pull the wide leather restraining strap across his lap in order to buckle it to the strap on his side. 'You'd be wise to grip the front board until you find your balance, my lord. This will be a very different ride from anything you've experienced before.'

TEN

JEFFREYS BARELY SPOKE DURING THE journey. Every so often, a groan whispered from his mouth, and twice he requested a pause to relieve himself at the side of the road. From the agony in his face, each urination was painful, but he performed the function without fuss and refused assistance in mounting to the carriage seat again.

The ride clearly exhilarated him, although his choice to remove his wig rather than lose it to the wind revealed a closely shaven head which made him appear considerably older than his forty years. His taciturnity towards his companion indicated that he viewed Elias only as a driver, despite being left in no doubt of Elias's rank during the convoy's slower progress through Blandford. Men hallooed him as the racing carriage hove into sight. 'You look well, my lord,' was the commonest cry, and his answer each time was, 'You also, my friend.'

Jeffreys broke his silence as they crossed the bridge over the River Stour and reached open highway again. 'Do you think it appropriate to court popularity amongst such people?'

'Appropriate to what?' Elias asked.

'Your standing. You lose authority by it.'

'If you say so,' Elias answered. 'For myself, I find a little civility goes a long way.'

Jeffreys snarled a reply, but his words were lost beneath Elias's call to the captain to increase his pace. There was no further conversation between them until Elias drew the carriage to a halt on the forecourt of Winterborne Houghton, having urged his horses to take the mile-long driveway that led to the house at a canter.

Jeffreys, clearly impressed by the magnificence of the building, pulled on his wig and looked beyond the groom and the approaching footmen. 'Where is Lady Harrier?'

Elias nodded towards the entranceway from where his mother was watching them, clad in a simple homespun kirtle and white apron. 'There, sir.' He beckoned a footman forward. 'Ask the captain of the guard to join us, Robert. You will find him at the head of the column.' He turned to Jeffreys as Robert set off at a run. 'I must see to your men's accommodation, but you and your captain will be in safe hands until I return.'

Jeffreys scowled. 'Only scullery maids wear homespun in my house.'

Elias laughed. 'You've risen in my estimation, Lord Jeffreys. I would have wagered good money that you'd never been near a scullery in your life.'

⸺

Jeffreys' greeting of Lady Harrier bordered on rudeness. His title of baron placed him several ranks lower than a duchess, but his only show of deference to his hostess was a brief nod of his head as he pushed past her into the hall. He refused to take her hand and told Robert to take him to his room.

'Instruct servants to bring my trunks and boxes to me as soon as my coach arrives. Meanwhile, you will serve as my valet. Is that clear?'

Robert turned to Lady Harrier. 'Do I have your permission, milady?'

'By all means, Robert. Lord Jeffreys is our guest and we should do whatever makes him comfortable.' She held out her hand to the captain, who had the grace to lift it briefly to his lips. 'Do you wish to accompany Lord Jeffreys upstairs, sir, or wait here for Lord Granville? I would entertain you myself, but I have patients awaiting me in my hospital.'

The captain cast an uncertain look at Jeffreys. 'My duty is to protect my general, ma'am.'

'Then Robert will have a bed set up for you in the anteroom to Lord Jeffreys' chamber for that purpose.' She smiled from him to Jeffreys. 'My household is at your disposal, gentlemen, but should you require my attention, Robert knows where to find me. Good day to you both.'

Jeffreys raised a hand to prevent her leaving, but she ignored him.

He glowered after her as she turned the corner into the corridor. 'What hospital?' he demanded of Robert.

'Her own, my lord. Milady is a physician.'

'Does she have a licence to practise medicine?'

'You must ask her, my lord.'

'I will. Escort me to the hospital.'

But Robert refused. 'Not without her permission, my lord. She endorsed your request that I show you to your chamber and act as your valet, but made no mention of anything else.' He gestured towards the stairs. 'Shall we proceed?'

'You have my instruction. Take me to the hospital.'

Robert lowered his head to hide the disdain in his eyes. Miss Jayne might forgive this man's rudeness to her, but Robert could not. 'If your preference is to wait here for Lord Granville's return, there are several seats that can accommodate you, sir.'

Spittle flew from Jeffreys' mouth as he retorted angrily, 'Do you know who I am?'

'Baron Jeffreys of Wem, sir. Lord Chief Justice and principal judge of the Western Assizes.'

'Then show the respect due to me, or find someone who can.'

Robert stepped back with a bow and went in search of Elias's valet, Zachariah.

Being an older man, Zachariah had more patience than Robert, but even he was tried by Lord Jeffreys' ill humour. Perhaps it was Jeffreys' need to use a piss-pot that persuaded him to follow the valet upstairs, but his temper was hardly improved by his efforts to use it. He found nothing to praise in Winterborne Houghton, belittling Lady Harrier's manner of dress, Lord Granville's fawning on the lower classes and the vulgarity of the French furniture in the chamber. He asked Zachariah if the dukedom was of recent origin, clearly believing that this was the explanation for his hosts' common tastes.

Zachariah had no difficulty understanding the thrust of the question. He also knew that it was a bare four months since Jeffreys had been created a baron. 'The Granville dukedom is six centuries old, my lord. My master and mistress have nothing to prove.'

A sour smile appeared on Jeffreys' lips. 'But others do?'

Zachariah ignored the question and motioned instead to the piss-pot. 'Allow me to empty that, sir. Would you care for some refreshment while you wait for your coach to arrive?'

'Send a maid with a jug of claret.' He turned his back on Zachariah and moved to look out of the window. 'And leave the vessel where it is. I'll be in want of it again shortly.'

'Would you like Lord Granville to wait upon you when he returns, my lord?'

'No. You may fetch me when I'm expected downstairs. Now, go. Your company irks me.'

Zachariah bowed and headed for the door.

Jayne learnt every detail of Robert's and Zachariah's conversations with Lord Jeffreys from her maid, Kitty, who had been her friend and companion for more than forty years. There wasn't a secret in the house that Kitty didn't know, including the secrets Elias kept from his mother, the most recent of which had involved a recipe for apple flapjacks.

According to Kitty, Elias had handed it to Cook on the evening he returned from speaking with Mister Milton. He had been irritatingly tight-lipped about who the lawyer was, but Jayne had had little trouble working it out for herself. He had told Cook the recipe came from the Shaftesbury estate and then cited his mother's favourite solver of equations in connection with the consumptives three days later.

Jayne had avoided showing too much curiosity, knowing from experience that it wouldn't be satisfied, and had remarked only that Elias should be careful about involving Althea too deeply in his schemes. Althea's inventive mind would not stop at consumption, and Jayne would hold her son responsible if he endangered her. Elias's answer had been teasingly opaque. A good fire usually nullified most problems, he had said.

That evening, the problem was Lord Jeffreys, and Kitty's task was to dispel any illusions he might have about Lady Harrier's lack of class. To that end, she chose a richly embroidered blue silk gown which hadn't been worn for more than year. 'I'll need to lace you into stays,' she told Jayne firmly, lifting a rigid undergarment from a chest. 'Your waist isn't as trim as it used to be.'

Jayne eyed her with disfavour. 'I'll not be able to breathe.'

'It's a small price to pay for looking elegant.' Kitty wrapped the stiffened fabric about Jayne's middle and began to thread the laces. 'Lord Jeffreys has trouble passing water. Master Elias told Zachariah he called a halt twice during the journey for the purpose of urinating, and he appeared to be in agony each time.'

'Has Zachariah observed the same here?'

'In a manner of speaking. Lord Jeffreys ordered him to wait in the anteroom when he had need of the piss-pot, but Zachariah heard a deal of groaning before being called to empty it. Each time he was ordered to return within a few minutes in case it was needed again.'

'What colour is the urine?'

'Brown, and Zachariah thinks there may be flecks of blood in it. He's keeping it in a covered bowl for you to examine. You should also know that Lord Jeffreys has consumed two flagons of wine in less than three hours and is halfway through another.'

'Is he drunk?'

'Not that you'd notice, though his temper has worsened.' Kitty gave the laces a sharp tug. 'Is that too tight?'

'Of course it's too tight,' Jayne retorted crossly. 'Why do you think I wear a kirtle most days?'

'Because you're lazy. It takes time and dedication to look pretty.'

'I don't plan to woo Lord Jeffreys, Kitty, merely ameliorate whatever ails him.'

'To what purpose? Every prisoner in the gaol would rather see him dead than cured.'

'He's still young, and is unlikely to die that conveniently. The best thing I can do for the prisoners would be to improve his temper.'

'I doubt that's possible. Zachariah says he's a miserable man.' Kitty tied off the laces, then lifted the silk gown over Jayne's head. 'There,' she said, pulling the skirt to the ground. 'You look as lovely as the day Sir William asked for your hand.'

Jayne laughed. 'You need eyeglasses, my dear. If William could see me now, he'd wonder what happened to the young woman he married.'

Kitty tugged the bodice edges together at the back and fed the buttons through their corresponding loops. 'He would say you're as beautiful today as you were then, Miss Jayne. He was a perfect gentleman. I wish I could say the same about your guest.'

Lord Jeffreys was surprised to find that Lady Harrier was alone when Zachariah escorted him into the salon. She stood by one of the large windows that overlooked the parkland and smiled as Zachariah announced their guest. 'How kind of you to join me, sir,' she said, offering her hand. 'I thought you might prefer to take your meal in your room.'

She looked very different from the dowdy woman he had met earlier, and he felt obliged to stoop over her fingers. 'I was led to believe your son would be here, milady.'

Jayne turned towards the window, drawing him with her. 'Your captain felt he should set a guard about the house, my lord. Granville has escorted him to the stables where his men are billeted. I'm waiting for his return. The evening's so pleasant, he'll walk back through the park.'

This was a blatant falsehood, since Elias was already standing at the corner of the house watching for Jeffreys' appearance at the window, which was the signal he and his mother had agreed upon. Jayne had asked for fifteen minutes alone with their guest, and the captain's request had given Elias a better excuse for tardiness than difficulty in dressing. The one smacked of consideration for soldiers, the other of foppish conceit, and Elias doubted that Jeffreys would care to engage with a fop. In truth, he doubted Jeffreys would engage at all, having heard from Zachariah how disagreeable three flagons of wine had made him.

Jayne's thoughts were similar as she led Jeffreys to a chair and invited him to accept a glass from a servant who stood nearby with a tray of filled crystal ware. 'The white is from the Loire Valley, and the red from Bordeaux, sir. My husband spent several years in France during the European wars, and became a connoisseur of the wines from the different regions. My son shares his enthusiasm, which is why we have such an excellent cellar.'

Jeffreys selected the claret, having already consumed a goodly amount of it; although, as Kitty had said, nothing in his demeanour suggested drunkenness. 'Do you also enjoy wine, Lady Harrier?' he asked as he waited for Jayne to sit.

'I do, sir,' Jayne answered, settling herself on a sofa and choosing a white, 'but not so much that I'll risk a sore head in the morning. Men are better able to withstand that horror than women, I find.'

Jeffreys lowered himself to the chair. 'We have stronger constitutions, milady. Myself, I never suffer from a sore head.'

'You're fortunate. My son has the constitution of an ox but it doesn't save him from the after-effects of over-imbibing. He has the grace to keep his complaints to himself, but his temper is unpredictable for several hours after waking.'

Jeffreys eyed her as he took a long swallow. 'Do you not have a cure for that, milady? I'm told you call yourself a physician.'

Jayne ignored the rudeness. 'Several,' she answered. 'The best remedy is to drink water, though ill-tempered men aren't easily persuaded of its benefits. They prefer to re-intoxicate themselves with alcohol.'

Jeffreys drained his glass and beckoned the footman forward to refill it. 'How do you measure intoxication, milady? By how much a man staggers or slurs his words?'

Jayne smiled. 'That's common in irregular drinkers, Lord Jeffreys, but not in those who live on wine and brandy.'

His lips thinned at what he perceived to be a criticism. 'Do you have a licence to practise as a doctor, Lady Harrier?'

She shook her head. 'I'm a woman, sir. Licences are granted only by universities, and universities are the preserve of men.'

'Are you aware that you can be prosecuted for claiming an entitlement you don't have?'

'To which entitlement are you referring?'

'The right to practise as a doctor.'

'I've never claimed that right. My standing is the same as any quacksalver or barber surgeon.'

Jeffreys seemed genuinely shocked. 'Yet you manage a hospital. No untrained quacksalver would dare embark on such an enterprise.'

'I didn't say I wasn't trained, sir.' Jayne motioned to Robert, who was standing by a table covered with papers. 'Bring Doctor Theale's certificate and King Charles's letter of endorsement, Robert. If those don't satisfy Lord Jeffreys, escort him to the table and allow him to read the letters of accreditation. I would hate him to think I have ever short-changed my patients through lack of a university education.'

Jeffreys took the documents and read them with the same diligence he applied to every piece of evidence that was placed before him. The certificate, prepared by Jayne's tutor, Doctor Richard Theale of Bridport, bore his Oxford seal and the words of the licence that had been granted to him upon his own graduation. He attested that Mistress Jayne Swift had studied under him for five years and had reached levels of distinction in both the theory and practice of medicine. A list of her attainments followed, together with the marks she had achieved in each discipline, concluding with the statement: *This candidate surpasses all others.*

King Charles II's letter bore the royal seal and stated simply: *His Majesty wishes it to be known that Lady Harrier's work in the field of medicine has his approval.*

Jeffreys tapped the page. 'What service did you perform to warrant this?' he asked.

'I don't make a habit of discussing my patients, sir.'

'Then I must assume this letter was purchased for you, either by coin or favour. Our late King was not known for his morality and, since I have no knowledge of Doctor Theale, the same may apply to him. Did you pay for the certificates?'

Jayne raised a calming hand to Robert. 'The judge seeks to establish the truth, as he would if we were in court, Robert.' She turned her attention back to Jeffreys. 'In order to remove any doubt, I shall answer your question. The men involved are dead, so I can't see that I'll be betraying their confidences by speaking of them. Nevertheless, I should like to record my objection to your maligning of Doctor Theale. Without wishing to seem discourteous, you have half his intellect and none of his principles.'

Surprisingly, Jeffreys smiled. 'Your objection is noted, Lady Harrier. Now, explain His Majesty's letter.'

'My son served in the Horse Guards with the Duke of Monmouth and, together, they made several visits to Winterborne Houghton. On one occasion, Monmouth arrived with the symptoms of typhus, commonly known as camp fever, and I placed him in quarantine in my hospital. He was fortunate to be young—barely twenty, as I recall—and responded so well to my treatments that he recovered quickly.'

'You should have let him die. From beginning to end, his life served no purpose.'

'On that we must differ, sir. I don't share your certainty about who is deserving of death and who is not.'

His eyes narrowed in irritation. 'My job is to deliver judgements, milady. If those judgements result in death, the responsibility lies with the culprits and not with me.' He tapped the letter again. 'Did Monmouth persuade his father to write this?'

'No, but he must have mentioned me to His Majesty, because I was summoned to attend upon the King some eight months later in London. His complaint was gout, for which his own physicians advocated purging and bleeding. He wanted to know if I had an alternative remedy.'

'Did you?'

Jayne nodded. 'The same that I used to cure one of your predecessors, Sir John Bankes of Corfe Castle. He was Lord Chief Justice to the first King Charles.'

'That would have recommended you to his son. Did His Majesty accept the remedy?'

Jayne shook her head. 'Not after I told him that he would have to abstain from liquor until the swelling in his toe joints reduced. He preferred bleeding and purging to drinking water.'

'Is water your cure for everything, milady?'

'There's no better way to cleanse a system, whether it be a sewer or a human body, sir. Had I been able to persuade King Charles and his physicians of that, he might be alive today. I was permitted only to examine his lower legs, and the gout was well advanced in his left foot. I was able to give him temporary relief from the pain, which is what prompted him to write the warrant, but his physicians refused to adopt the remedy.'

'Why?'

Jayne smiled slightly. 'They thought as you do, sir: that a woman has no place in medicine. Though in fairness to them, I advocated against the remedy's long-term use. To mask pain is no substitute for curing the cause of it. Patients die quicker if they're able to indulge their appetites without consequence.'

Jeffreys stared into his glass. 'What was the remedy?'

'Laudanum. It's a tincture of opium poppy seed, first discovered by Paracelsus in the last century. The elements required to make it are hard to come by—and few know how to make it—which is why I reserve it for the dying whose last hours would otherwise be spent in agony.'

'That would be a fair description of King Charles's death. Did you not think to offer the tincture then?'

'I would have done gladly had I known of his collapse, but the first we knew was that he had passed. I learnt the details from one of his physicians who was less critical of me than his colleagues and with whom I'd had some correspondence on the function of the kidneys. He sent me a copy of his notes the day after the King passed—which included symptoms and treatments—and asked if I could identify what had killed the King, since another physician suspected he'd been poisoned.'

'Could you?'

Jayne took a second or two to order her thoughts. 'If poison was involved, it was administered over a long period. His health had been declining for months. He struggled to breathe, his legs were ulcerated and the gout had spread to his knees and other joints. The immediate cause of death appears to have been a series of apoplectic strokes, but the ulcers and respiratory problems suggest they were brought on by failures in his internal organs, most likely his kidneys.'

'Caused by disease?'

Jayne nodded. 'At fifty-four, he was too young to be suffering the frailties of old age.'

'Which disease?'

'That I can't say. Our knowledge of why internal organs fail is very limited.' She paused. 'His physicians took two pints of blood and purged him mercilessly to reverse the symptoms of apoplexy, but the convulsions that followed demonstrated that neither treatment was effective.'

'What would you have done?'

'I'm sure you can guess, sir.'

Jeffreys eyed her in disbelief. 'You'd have administered *water*?'

Jayne smiled. 'I try not to harm my patients when I'm entirely ignorant of what ails them, Lord Jeffreys. As I understand it, the King was able to talk after his seizure and told his physicians they had no idea how much he was suffering. In those circumstances, my most pressing concerns would have been to relieve his pain and do all I could to prevent a second seizure, and in my experience the aggressive *removal* of fluid from a body does not achieve those purposes.'

'Have you ever treated a man with apoplexy, Lady Harrier?'

'Several, my lord. Women also. Some survive and some do not, though I have a better chance of success with those who retain the power of speech. They are able to tell me what they need—which, in the first instance, is usually water. Fear of what's happening to them makes their mouths intolerably dry.'

Jeffreys studied her for several long moments. 'What would you advocate for bladder stones?'

Jayne was surprised by the bluntness of the question, particularly in front of servants. She hadn't anticipated that he would be so open about what ailed him. From the information Kitty had given her, together with the dark cloudy urine that Zachariah had shown her, she had already suspected stones and gave him a straightforward answer.

'A high intake of liquid to assist them to pass, sir. A man who is prone to stones needs to expel them before they grow so large that they cause pain when he urinates.'

He closed his eyes briefly, but whether in shock at her use of the word 'urinates' or because pain was a constant companion, she couldn't tell. 'And you would recommend water as the liquid, presumably?'

'Pure well water is less likely to enlarge the stones than a sugary substance such as wine, sir. The purpose of taking copious quantities of liquid through the mouth is to flush the system, not assist in creating blockages inside it.'

This time, irritation caused him to inhale deeply through his nose. 'Most physicians believe that strong liquor dissolves the stones.'

Jayne nodded to his glass. 'Have you found that to be true?'

With great deliberation he raised the rim to his mouth and took a long swallow. 'I don't speak of myself, milady. I could as easily have asked what remedies you would recommend for the pox or the ague.'

'Tried and tested ones, Lord Jeffreys. I rarely resort to guess-work in the treatments I offer. I'm also reluctant to fail my patients so badly that they turn to a surgeon to help them. The risk of death is very high when incisions are made in the bladder and urinary tract.'

His discomfort was so obvious that she wondered if this was an option he was considering, but he was spared a response by the sound of the door to the terrace opening. Elias, clad in the same attire he'd worn to impress William Lewis's wife and daughter, strode across the floor, apologising for his tardiness.

'Your captain has asked me to tell you that he's placed guards about the building, Lord Jeffreys,' he said, before turning to his mother with a bow. 'You look radiant, Mama. You should wear that colour more often.' He lowered himself to a chair on the other side of Jeffreys. 'Please continue with your conversation. It was most discourteous of me to interrupt it.'

Jayne beckoned to the footman who was holding the tray of glasses. 'I'm sure Lord Jeffreys agrees that our conversation has run its course, Elias. Will you have some more of the claret, sir? My son rates it very highly and would welcome your opinion on it.'

Clearly relieved by the change of topic, Jeffreys was gracious, admitting freely that Granville's claret was superior to anything he had in his own cellar. From there, Elias steered him easily into talking about his life in London and naming acquaintances they might have in common. Jayne was content to listen and observe, and she came to admire their guest's fortitude. His constantly shifting position suggested back pain, but he gave no indication of it in his face.

His capacity for wine was extraordinary, but he excused himself only once, taking ten minutes in his chamber before being summoned to the dining room to eat. The room was smaller than the salon, with a long table running down its centre; for the sake of intimacy, Elias sat at one end with Jeffreys to his left and his mother to his right. Once settled, Jeffreys' consumption of alcohol continued unabated and the only ill effects he showed were increasingly sharp ripostes to Elias's conversation. Halfway through the meal, he fixed his attention on Jayne.

'Does your son forbid you to speak in his presence, Lady Harrier?'

'By no means, sir, but you and he have been directing your comments at each other. What can I talk about that will interest you more than mutual acquaintances in London?'

'Does it please you to travel, milady?'

'Not by coach. To sit for hours on a hard seat is tedious and uncomfortable.'

'On that we can agree. Their ponderous progress is beyond endurance.' He pushed his plate aside, his lips pressed together as if to prevent himself retching. 'I shall remember these Western Assizes for the dreadfulness of the travelling.'

Jayne smiled sympathetically. 'I feel for you, Lord Jeffreys. Was Granville's racing carriage an improvement?'

'Somewhat,' he agreed grudgingly. 'He tells me you're his most frequent passenger. Is that true?'

She nodded. 'He worries when I ride long distances on horseback, though I never understand why. I've been doing it for half a century without difficulty.'

Elias grinned. 'If you accepted the company of a groom, I'd have no reason to worry, Mama. You'll regret it when you're thrown and have to wait hours for a search party to find you.'

She smiled fondly at him. 'The same applies to you, my dear, but I would never insist that a caretaker follows you wherever you go. In any case, what use would a timid groom be in the event of an accident? He wouldn't know what to do if my shoulder were dislocated or my thigh broken. Wouldn't you agree, Lord Jeffreys?'

'I couldn't possibly say, Lady Harrier. I've never heard of a woman riding alone before.'

'Or astride either, I imagine.' She laughed at his look of disapproval. 'The frustration of travelling at the demure pace demanded by a side-saddle is as great as being confined to a coach. Progress is intolerably slow.'

'Then I'm not surprised Granville insists on driving you. Did your husband endorse such a flouting of convention?'

'Not only endorsed but encouraged, sir. Sir William considered the behaviour expected of women ridiculously limiting, as does my son. His concern is for his ageing mother's welfare, not whether she conforms to outmoded conventions. Do you not question such foolish concepts yourself?'

'I've never had reason to.'

'How fortunate for you,' she murmured. 'You must have a contented household. Even my mother, the gentlest of souls, railed against her position. She would have preferred to do something worthwhile with her life rather than give daily instructions to servants who knew their jobs as well as she did.'

There was a long pause, during which Jeffreys swirled the wine in his glass. One of the more interesting facts that Elias had learnt while he was in London was that George Jeffreys was afraid of his wife, who was said to have a ferocious temper. Amos had quoted a ballad about them, written before Jeffreys was elevated, which contained the refrain: '*Saint George killed a dragon and saved a maiden in distress; Sir George missed the maiden and married the dragon instead.*'

Jeffreys avoided any reference to his household. 'There are no women in my profession, milady. The law demands strong concentration, clarity of thought and the confidence to argue a case. The female mind, which is prone to excessive emotion, is unsuited to it.'

Jayne smiled. 'With respect, sir, I imagine there are as many men unsuited to the law as there are women. Have you considered arguing a case with a female before you condemn my entire sex for being overly emotional?'

'Are you proposing yourself, Lady Harrier?'

'If it pleases you. Of your more recent cases, I'm best acquainted with the trial of Dame Alice Lisle in Winchester. As I understand it, she was profoundly deaf and unable to follow what was said in court without a man shouting in her ear. I'm also informed that age had taken her wits. Would it interest you to revisit that case?'

Anger flared in his eyes. 'You take unwarranted liberties, Lady Harrier. My rulings are final.'

'Indeed,' she said calmly, 'but rearguing Lady Alice's case here in private is hardly a public challenge to your judicial competence, unless you choose to see it as such.'

Elias grasped Jeffreys' wrist before he could fling his wine in Jayne's face. 'I believe my mother has made her point, sir. Excessive emotion is not confined to one sex.'

Jeffreys made a visible effort to control himself. 'You found my weak spot, milady. I dislike having my verdicts pulled apart by people who were not present at the trial. A case must be heard in its entirety, not fed piecemeal to gossips.'

Jayne responded with a warm smile. 'I feel the same about my diagnoses and treatments, sir. It is tedious and irritating trying to explain diseases and cures to people who have no understanding of them. Shall we agree that we're both skilled at what we do, and cease annoying each other with silly suggestions?'

She was rewarded with an abrupt laugh. 'Touché, milady. I begin to understand why King Charles's physicians wanted him to take their counsel rather than yours.' He turned to Elias. 'You may unhand me now, sir. I never indulge in more than one bout of excessive emotion per evening.'

ELEVEN

COME EIGHT O'CLOCK, JAYNE ABSENTED herself to allow the men to talk freely. The chances of Elias learning anything meaningful about their guest's intentions at the Dorchester Assizes were small, however, since Jeffreys was close to unconsciousness. According to Elias later, the only intelligible remarks he made before slumping asleep at the table conveyed envy for his host's unmarried state. If Jeffreys had been born to a title, instead of having to acquire it himself, he would not have needed to tie himself to a virago whose only attraction was her father's wealth.

Elias hoisted the limp body over his shoulder and carried it upstairs. By then, the captain had returned and, with Zachariah's help, he stripped Jeffreys of his clothes and replaced them with a nightshirt. From the proficiency the young officer displayed, it was clear that putting his commander to bed was a regular occurrence, but Elias didn't embarrass him by asking. Even in battlefield conditions, it was beneath the rank of a captain to act as a servant. Elias's only request—one that his mother had asked him to make—was that Lady Harrier be allowed into the chamber to ascertain that the general was suffering nothing worse than intoxication.

'I would hate to have to explain to His Majesty that his Lord Chief Justice expired under my roof for lack of a little care.'

The captain shook his head. 'I've seen him worse, my lord. He'll not die.'

Elias stared down at Jeffreys' face. 'Nonetheless, I'd value my mother's opinion. It's not normal for a man to lose awareness so completely.'

The young officer shrugged. 'He never sleeps for more than two hours, but when he does it's the sleep of the dead. I can't see that it matters if she looks at him. He'll not know she's here.'

He came to regret that statement when Lady Harrier, dressed once again in a kirtle and apron, arrived with a nurse, a medicine satchel, a large pile of fabric, one empty bucket and another full of water. She shooed the three men from the chamber, closing the door behind them, and the captain wondered in alarm what she was proposing to do. He had had to walk softly around Lord Jeffreys for days, terrified of provoking the man's unpredictable temper, and he dreaded to think how he would react to being woken by a woman.

Elias put a comforting arm around his shoulder and urged him through the anteroom into the corridor. 'Your imagination is running away with you, my friend,' he said, steering him towards the stairs. 'Lord Jeffreys will bless you for Lady Harrier's intervention. I warrant her skills are ten times that of his own physician.'

The captain tried to resist the pressure of Elias's arm. 'I should be at his side. She may be harming him.'

Zachariah chuckled. 'With what, sir? Kindness? Milady seeks to assuage a person's troubles, not make them worse.' He addressed Elias as they reached the bottom of the stairs. 'Do I have your permission to take the captain to the kitchen, sir? Sarah has fresh ale on tap and stew bubbling over the fire, and it will ease the captain's mind to hear what the servants say about their mistress.'

'By all means,' said Elias, releasing the young man to Zachariah's care. 'But spare a thought for your guards, captain. They, too, might like a bowl of stew and a sup of ale, if only to alleviate their boredom. The threat of an attack against Lord Jeffreys is non-existent, since no one outside this house or the stables knows he's here.'

He watched them turn towards the kitchen then made his way to the salon, where he lounged in a chair, drinking brandy and clouding the air with pipe smoke. All the while, he kept an eye on the dragoon pacing about the terrace, and when the man was finally called away, he abandoned his unfinished glass and pipe and left the house unobserved.

Jayne's single intervention while Jeffreys slept was to place a large pad of absorbent fabric beneath his hips and another between his legs. She needed Maggie's assistance to roll him onto his side in order to position the bottom pad, but once done, she sent Maggie back to the hospital and placed the second pad over and around his genitals herself. Thereafter, she lit an hour candle, which she placed on the stand beside his bed, drew up a chair and, by the candle's light, made notes in a ledger.

Jeffreys awoke with a cry of pain when the candle had burnt for two hours, almost to the minute. Unable to contain his need to urinate, he tried to raise himself from the pillows, but Jayne stood, pressed her right forearm across his lower abdomen and used the fingers of her other hand to drum the skin above his pubis. The method, designed to stimulate a more extreme urge to urinate, resulted in a scream of pain and a sudden rush of liquid into the pads.

Without fuss, Jayne scooped them into the empty bucket before they could saturate the mattress and then assisted Lord Jeffreys to a sitting position. She placed the pillows behind his back, pulled the coverlet to his waist and washed her hands in the basin on the stand. She dried them on a clean napkin as she resumed her seat.

'You were lucky, sir. The stone was not so big that you couldn't pass it with a little assistance. The method has a higher chance of success when the patient is lying down.'

He stared at her in horror, struck dumb by the humiliation she had just inflicted upon him.

Jayne continued matter-of-factly. 'I would have suspected bladder stones even without your mention of them, Lord Jeffreys. You show all the symptoms. Difficulty passing water . . . pain when doing so . . . reluctance to strain too hard . . . inability to remain asleep . . . ill temper . . . nausea . . . constant backache.'

He found his voice. 'I don't make a play of backache.'

'Not knowingly, perhaps, but it was obvious to me.' She lifted the flap of her medicine satchel and removed a vial of willow bark tincture and a silver spoon. 'This will ease the pain of the stone's passing as well as the ache in your back.' She filled the spoon and offered it to him. 'You will sleep better for it, Lord Jeffreys.'

'Will I wake again?'

Jayne smiled. 'I'm not in the habit of poisoning my patients, sir. I've built my reputation on keeping people alive.' She noted his surprise at the pleasant taste of the medicine. 'I infuse the willow bark with honey to allay the bitterness. If you find it beneficial, you may take a vial away with you tomorrow.'

He returned the spoon. 'You're not my physician, Lady Harrier.'

'Indeed, but I hate to see any of my guests suffer. Stones have been known for centuries and, judging by the number of patients I treat each year, their incidence is increasing. Either that, or word of my prowess in dealing with them is spreading so fast that more and more patients are seeking my services.'

He showed renewed horror. 'You handle other men the way you handled me?'

'When necessary, but most dislike the experience and prefer to accept my advice rather than repeat it. I can't prove that wine enlarges the stones, Lord Jeffreys, but I *can* prove that water keeps them small enough to pass with ease.'

'How?'

She nodded to the saturated fabric. 'By examining them. The stone you've just expelled will be twice the size of those expelled by water drinkers. Water produces a larger quantity of urine than wines or spirits—and is of a clearer consistency—which tells me water keeps flushing the stones rather than allowing them to settle and grow.' She took a silver tankard from her satchel and dipped it into the bucket of well water. 'Will you oblige me by trying?'

'I wouldn't dare. If your tincture helps me sleep, I'll soil your bed.'

'I'll wager one shilling that you won't,' she said, pressing the tankard into his hands. 'And I'll wager a second shilling that the next time you wake, you'll be clear-headed and free of pain. Do we have a bet, sir?'

He watched her over the rim of the vessel as he drank the contents. 'I have never known a woman to behave and speak as you do, Lady Harrier.'

'You don't watch or listen hard enough.'

He handed her the empty tankard. 'It would be a waste of my time, since all I hear is criticism. And no, I will not accept your bet. Only a fool wagers money that he fears he will lose.'

Jayne placed the vessel on his night stand. 'You have more wisdom than most of my male patients,' she told him, standing and looping the strap of the satchel over her shoulder before moving the chair away from the bed. 'Few can resist a bet.' She left the bucket of water but stooped to grasp the handle of the one containing the saturated fabric.

His horror returned. 'You shame me anew. Can you not instruct a maid to do that?'

She straightened with the bucket in her hand. 'How does it shame you if I do it, sir? My intention is to keep these night's events between ourselves, not allow them to become a subject of gossip in my kitchen.'

'Your rank is higher than mine, Lady Harrier. Everything you've done for me is beneath your position.'

'Only in your eyes, Lord Jeffreys. My hope in coming to your chamber was to ease your pain. Have I achieved that?'

'You have.'

Jayne ducked her head in acknowledgement. 'Then we can both sleep well tonight. I value my reputation as a physician far above my rank. Farewell to you, sir, and may your dreams be pleasant ones.'

She carried the bucket to the hospital laundry where she emptied the contents into a large stone bath, which contained other soiled items soaking in water. The unenviable task of scrubbing and boiling these assorted fabrics fell to her nurses, although they had found willing helpers in the oldest released prisoner and his wife. Overwhelmed with gratitude to be living with their three young children in a cottage on the estate, the pair accepted every unpleasant job they were asked to do, and according to Kitty they were greatly liked by the rest of the household because of it.

Elias was considering offering all the 'consumptives' permanent positions once the Assizes were over, but for the time being they were required to hold themselves ready for inspection, most especially while Lord Jeffreys was in the house. Grace, who remained suspicious of Lady Harrier's ability to protect them, had taken a bowl of blood from the kitchen to transform every face from growing health to high fever and the results were pleasingly grisly.

Jayne closed the laundry door behind her and went in search of Elias. The footman at the front door thought he was in the salon, but the only evidence that he had been there was a half-smoked pipe and a barely touched glass of brandy. The hour was close to midnight, the candles were beginning to splutter in their sconces, and Jayne would have taken herself to bed had she been less curious about where Elias had gone.

She took the chair he had occupied and watched the guard pace back and forth across the terrace. He was close enough to the house for the interior light to reflect off his silver buttons and sword blade, and she guessed that Elias had turned the seat towards the window in order to do what she was doing. If so, there could have been only one reason—to wait for an opportunity to leave the house without being seen—and from there, it was a logical assumption that the guard was now a barrier to his returning.

In the hope that Elias was standing at the corner where he had waited for Jeffreys to appear at the window, she opened the door and walked to the opposite side of the terrace. The guard, startled by her sudden appearance, hurried to admonish her. 'You shouldn't be here, woman,' he said, clearly taking her kirtle and apron for the garb of a maid. 'My orders are to keep everyone inside.'

'Forgive me,' Jayne responded, 'but I've been working so hard and the night is so clear that I couldn't resist a few minutes outside.' She pointed to the south-west. 'My husband tried to teach me the names of the stars, but I was a disappointing pupil and could never retain them in my head. Do you see the one just above the trees? Do you know what it's called?'

The dragoon followed the direction of her finger. 'They all look the same to me.'

'Surely not. There's a cluster of two or three dull stars and a brighter one to the right, where the line of trees dips slightly.' She placed her free hand on his arm to prevent him turning away. 'Indulge me a little longer. It's a rare treat to be able to look at the heavens with a companion. My husband has been dead seven years, and I miss him most dreadfully.'

The dragoon shuffled his feet, torn between sympathy and duty. 'I'm sorry for that, miss, but I'm ignorant about the sky and you need to go back inside.'

'Do you not follow the stars when you ride at night?'

'Not me. I stick to the tail of the horse in front of me.'

'Who leads the column?'

'Our captain, and he follows the highway.'

Behind them, the overly vigorous jiggling of the latch on the door sounded loud in the still night air. 'I've been looking for you, Mama,' called Elias. 'What are you doing outside?'

She turned with a smile. 'Enjoying the sky,' she answered. 'You should copy my example, Elias. Fresh air is infinitely preferable to the filthy smoke you belch in the salon.'

He crossed the terrace and tucked her hand inside his elbow. 'I'm a soldier, Mama, and soldiers do not keep guards from their duties.' He nodded to the dragoon. 'Thank you, my friend. You must blame me for this disturbance. I omitted to inform Lady Harrier of General Lord Jeffreys' order that the household remain confined until his departure.'

The dragoon seemed more anxious that he'd been talking to a duchess than that she had disobeyed an instruction. 'I hope you didn't think me rude, milady. If I knew anything about the stars, I would have been honoured to name them for you.'

'It's of no matter,' she assured him. 'Your kindness in listening to me was enough, and for that I thank you most heartily. I trust the rest of your night will be without incident. Farewell to you.'

She said nothing more until Elias had closed and bolted the door behind them.

'What on earth induced you to agree to this house becoming a prison?' she demanded.

'I need the guards to swear that I never left the house, otherwise I might be suspected of causing the rear axle on Jeffreys' coach to shatter.' He smiled at her expression. 'I don't intend to keep him here, Mama, merely offer myself as his driver for as long as it takes our people to fashion and fit a new axle.'

'How did you leave without being seen?'

'I slipped out when the previous guard was called away. Cook is pledged to feed them stew and ale through the night and, mercifully, they're so young and poorly trained they're willing to accept a summons from a footman rather than wait for their replacements.' He escorted her to the sofa and sat beside her. 'Thank you. Your distraction was greatly appreciated.'

Jayne looked at him. 'What do you plan to do with Jeffreys?'

'The same as you. Persuade him to consider alternative remedies.'

'I would need several weeks to achieve that. He's too arrogant to relinquish his strongly held opinions and too eager to throw the contents of his glass at anyone who provokes him.'

'He holds the King's mandate as Lord Chief Justice,' Elias responded. 'He has reason to feel superior. No one dares take him to task over anything.'

Jayne studied him. 'You're not responsible for Monmouth's followers, Elias. They knew what they were doing when they joined his rebellion.'

'I should have done more to stop him.'

'It wasn't possible. You said yourself he was in too deep.'

'Then I need to stop Jeffreys,' he said lightly.

He was so like his father, Jayne thought. She could never tell when he was joking and when he was serious. 'Don't do anything rash,' she warned. 'I won't forgive you if my house and hospital become forfeit because you want to teach Lord Jeffreys some manners.'

Elias's face split in its familiar grin. 'I already have, and he reacted better than I expected. I envisioned being drenched in my own extremely expensive claret after I told him you'd won the argument.'

'He's not a toy, Elias.'

'I'm aware of that, Mama, and I don't intend to provoke him further. My aim is to urge him to stand by his promise of leniency for those who plead guilty, and I'll have a better chance of success if I appeal to his intellect rather than his manners.'

Jayne rested her head against the back of the sofa, wishing she shared his confidence. Lord Jeffreys hid the severity of his illness well, but she suspected that his prodigious consumption of wine went far beyond the need to dissolve and expel stones. 'Your success will be governed by how sober he is when you speak with him,' she advised. 'Alcohol bolsters his sense of status and authority, and he'll reject every reasoned argument you make while under its influence.'

Elias thought of his mother's words when Zachariah told him the following morning that his guest had yet to leave his bed and had been drinking claret for two hours. This information came in response to him asking if Lord Jeffreys was ready to leave for Dorchester. By then, the household had been awake and at work for five hours, the captain had had his troops mustered since dawn in preparation for an early departure, and the coachman had let out a shriek after setting the vehicle in motion, only for the rear axle to collapse.

Elias had restored both the captain's and coachman's composure by offering to drive Lord Jeffreys in his racing carriage. He further offered the services of his joiners, smith and wheelwrights for the repair of the offending axle and undertook to make the explanations to Jeffreys himself. However, it appeared his efforts would come to naught when Zachariah told him his guest was still in bed.

'Is he drunk?' Elias asked, in an echo of his mother the previous day.

The valet shook his head. 'Not that I can see, Master Elias. If anything, his temper has improved. He tells me he slept well and has asked me to congratulate you and Miss Jayne on the softness of your pillows and mattress.'

'I need him dressed and out of the house, Zachariah.'

'Indeed, sir, but he takes no notice of anything I say. I'm afraid you'll have to tell him yourself, though I can't guarantee he'll respond as you wish. He's talking of postponing the trials to next week and wonders if you can send word of that to his fellow judges.'

'Absolutely not,' Elias said firmly, heading for the stairs. 'I'm not his damned clerk.'

He strode through the anteroom and entered Jeffreys' chamber without waiting for a reply to his light knock.

'It's time to rise, General,' he said cheerily, pulling the coverlet from Jeffreys' legs and removing the glass from his hands. 'Your troops are mustered and my racing carriage awaits you. We'll take food for the journey, and you'll be pleased to hear the ride will be mercifully short, as I expect to have you in Dorchester in under three hours.' He placed a hand beneath Jeffreys' armpit and hauled him unceremoniously from the bed. 'Can you dress yourself or would you like my assistance?'

In the confined space of the room, the contrast between the two men could not have been greater. Elias, booted and clad in his long black coat, with the fresh scent of the outdoors in his hair and on his clothes, towered over the stale-smelling, barefooted Chief Justice in his rumpled nightshirt. Aware of it, Jeffreys shook himself free and ordered Elias from his chamber.

'Send the valet,' he snapped.

But Elias shook his head. 'Consider me your aide-de-camp for the next thirty minutes. Your men have been waiting on you for five hours and I've taken responsibility for delivering you to them. There's more to being a general than assuming a rank, Lord Jeffreys. You have a duty to lead your campaign in the field as well as in court.'

'Are you lecturing me?'

Elias moved to the chest at the foot of the bed and lifted the lid. 'Only as your aide-de-camp,' he said affably. 'I chose mine for their willingness to remind me of my obligations, and I'm returning the favour.' He took out the clothes that Jeffreys had been wearing the previous day and laid them on the bed. 'Will these do or would you prefer something else?'

'Why your racing carriage and not my coach?'

'An axle on your vehicle has shattered. My wheelwrights can repair it, but the work will take time. William Lewis expects you in Dorchester this afternoon, so I've offered to drive you.'

Jeffreys made a dismissive gesture with his hand. 'It's not necessary. I'll remain here until the carriage is ready. Instruct my captain to send a dragoon to Dorchester to inform Mister Lewis of the delay.'

'We're not a common tavern, Jeffreys, and if we were, I doubt your purse runs deep enough to compensate me for the cost of feeding and accommodating you and your troops for a week.' Elias nodded to the jug of claret on the nightstand. 'A single cask of that fine Bordeaux wine costs one hundred shillings, and my bottler tells me you're well on the way to emptying it. I'm happy to give you one night of drinking it for free, but no more.'

Jeffreys' mouth dropped open. '*One hundred shillings?*'

'You wouldn't enjoy it so much if it were cheaper.' Elias nodded to the clothes on the bed. 'Do you don your hose before or after you pull on your britches?'

'Before.'

Elias handed him a pair of stockings. 'Shall we proceed? Your lodgings in Dorchester will cost you nothing and I'm told the cellar has several palatable wines. To make the transition less arduous for you, I will ask my bottler to decant a couple of flagons to accompany us on our journey.'

'What of my trunks and boxes?'

'They'll follow behind us in a cart. You can oversee their loading yourself, though I'd prefer you to place anything of value in my carriage. I'd hate you to think my carter was a thief because you misremember what you brought with you from London.'

Jeffreys subjected him to a long stare before sitting on the chair and drawing a stocking over his right foot. 'The coach was thoroughly checked before we left London. What caused the axle to shatter?'

'The poor state of our roads,' Elias answered easily. 'Collapsed wheels are common in Dorset.'

Jeffreys unrolled the second stocking. 'You and your mother unsettle me, Lord Granville. I pride myself on being able to tell a liar from the way he answers my questions, but you and Lady Harrier are unreadable.'

'My mother never lies, Lord Jeffreys. I'll swear to that before God.'

'And you?'

Elias grinned. 'I was King Charles's personal envoy, sir. It was my duty to lie whenever the situation demanded it.' He handed Jeffreys his britches. 'In the matter of the axle, however, you can trust my honesty. I have no interest whatsoever in keeping you from the task that awaits you in Dorchester.'

Jeffreys drew an immediate and, from his expression, *satisfying* link between 'envoy' and Jayne's testimonial from King Charles. 'Half-truths are akin to lies,' he said, pushing his feet into the britches and standing up. 'Lady Harrier omitted to mention that you were instrumental in winning praise from the late King. She wanted me to think it was her suggested treatments that secured his approval.'

Elias lifted the shirt off the bed and shook out the creases. 'And so they did,' he said, 'since I wasn't appointed an envoy until several years later.' He waited while Jeffreys drew up his britches. 'You'd be nearer the truth if you said my mother was instrumental in helping me, since King Charles was well disposed towards anyone bearing the patronym Harrier.'

Jeffreys fastened the ties at his waist. 'I find that hard to believe. A man of his prodigious appetites wouldn't remember a woman he met only once.'

Elias gave a good-natured shrug as he passed over the shirt. 'I warrant you'll remember her yourself when your doctor drains you of blood and money to no effect, sir. You may even come to agree with King Charles that licences are not worth the paper they're written on unless the men who flaunt them can provide a cure.'

TWELVE

LORD JEFFREYS ACCEPTED LADY HARRIER'S invitation to view her hospital before he left, but he refused to enter any of the rooms, preferring to see her patients from the safety of the corridor. This was particularly true of her consumptive patients, whose feverish faces and racking coughs alarmed him. He was more at ease in her office, where she decanted willow bark tincture from a large glass jar into a vial.

He surveyed her shelves, comparing them with the shelves in his own physician's office. There were no purges, no leeches, no woodlice, no bitter vinegar, no spirit of human skull and no poultices to blister the skin. Instead, the labels beneath the flagons described remedies derived from plants, such as lavender, calendula and thyme.

'Do you not see merit in waging war on sickness, Lady Harrier?'

She eyed him with amusement. 'Should I take that to mean you think sickness can only be defeated by aggressive remedies, my lord?'

'It's not my field, milady, but my own physician has rather more'—he sought for a word—'*exotic* medicines.'

'Such as?'

'Woodlice for respiratory conditions . . . spirit of human skull for seizures.'

'I've never found infusions of pulverised bones and insects in sour wine or vinegar to be effective, Lord Jeffreys, and certainly not when treating the conditions you mentioned. In my experience, patients with epilepsy or breathing constriction respond better to the calm-inducing benefits of St John's wort or valerian.'

'Taken with water presumably?'

Jayne laughed. 'Of course, though I doubt you need another lecture on why.' She handed him the vial. 'I have nothing to add to the advice I gave you last night, sir, except to remind you that to mask pain is no substitute for curing the cause of it.'

He tucked the vial into his coat pocket, grateful for her discretion. Such innocuous comments would signify nothing to the captain who was waiting in the corridor. 'You were right to predict a peaceful night, milady. I would have lost the wager had I been foolish enough to accept it.' He stooped over her hand. 'Allow me to thank you.'

'I'm glad to have been of service, sir,' she said, escorting him to the door and passing him to the care of his captain. 'May the remainder of your stay in Dorset be as tranquil.'

⸻

In view of Jeffreys' earlier scepticism about his mother's memorability, Elias found his fascination with her amusing. He appeared unable to discuss anything else during the journey to Dorchester, though his views were somewhat confused. In one breath, Lady Harrier was a woman of rare intelligence; in another, she was stubbornly wedded to the benefits of natural substances. He thought her parting remark surprisingly uninformed.

'She wished me tranquillity during my time in Dorset,' he told Elias. 'But why? Was she mocking me?'

'I imagine she was suggesting that the gift of calmness is in your hands. As long as the trials are seen to be fair, there should be no trouble.'

This didn't satisfy Jeffreys. 'She should have considered the discomfort of sitting on a hard bench for hours on end. What would she recommend for that?'

'A soft cushion,' Elias answered, steering to the left to avoid a depression in the road. 'Have you considered ways to reduce the size of the list?'

Jeffreys didn't answer, signalling clearly that the conduct of the trials was none of Granville's business. They drove in silence for several minutes before he returned once again to the subject of Lady Harrier.

'Would she knowingly have treated a rebel if he'd asked for her services?'

'Certainly,' said Elias honestly. 'She never turns anyone away. Which isn't to say she had sympathy with Monmouth or his foolish rebellion, merely that she continues to honour the pledge she made before the Civil War—to treat anyone in need, regardless of belief or allegiance.'

'Had she done so, I would have sentenced her to burn.'

'Then we're fortunate that no one presented himself with a battle wound. Lady Harrier became skilled at extracting musket balls and suturing sword slashes during the Civil War and would have recognised such an injury immediately.' Elias nudged the lead horse back towards the centre of the highway.

'The majority of the prisoners you'll be trying are from south Dorset. Here in the north-west we never saw Monmouth in person so remained unmoved by his rhetoric.'

'Your mother told me you were friends as young men.'

'We served in the Horse Guards together.'

'And afterwards? Did you continue the friendship?'

Elias shook his head. 'My straight speaking conflicted with his ambitions. He preferred men who flattered him.'

Jeffreys considered this for several moments. 'It's a trait you've inherited from your mother. I found her directness alarming. She refers to body parts and their functions by name rather than euphemism.'

'Does your own physician use euphemisms?'

'Of course not.'

'Then why expect them from my mother?'

'She's a woman.'

Elias smiled slightly. 'But a physician first, who has spent a lifetime proving herself better than most men. Does the same apply to you, or can you rest on your laurels certain that no one dares question your ability?'

'There's nothing to question. My ability is known. Why else would His Majesty have confidence in me?'

'It depends who you listen to,' Elias answered. 'Opinion is divided on whether you're his puppet, willing to deliver the judgements he wants, or a man of strength and independent thinking, ready to offer honest justice.'

Jeffreys leant over the side of the carriage to spit onto the dirt of the road. 'That's all I care for Dorset opinions,' he said coldly, straightening again.

Elias gave a lazy shrug. 'You have my sympathy,' he said. 'I feel the same about London opinions. There's no honour or honesty in a city that's dedicated to the pursuit of wealth.'

He flicked his reins, calling to the troops in front to increase their speed, and any answer Jeffreys gave was lost beneath the drumming of hooves. Thereafter, conversation between them lapsed until they entered the outskirts of Dorchester and the column came to a halt shortly after crossing the River Frome.

'I trust you don't question *my* honesty,' Jeffreys remarked, pulling on his wig and straightening his robes.

Elias ignored the question, nodding instead to the captain who was riding towards them. 'He needs directions to his men's barracks. William Lewis has instructed that no mounted dragoons be seen on Dorchester's streets for fear of inciting anger against the King.'

Jeffreys dismissed the remark with a petulant wave of his hand. 'My orders override the High Sheriff's. We will continue as we are. There is more I wish to say to you.'

'I'm Dorset born and bred, Lord Jeffreys; you won't like my responses. Also, I suggest you bow to the High Sheriff's superior knowledge regarding the likelihood of rioting before, during and after the Assizes.' Elias tied off the reins and jumped to the ground to address the young officer. 'Your accommodation is some four hundred yards down a side street, captain. If you think you can drive this carriage at walking pace, lend me your horse and I'll take your place at the head of the column.'

The captain dismounted. 'I believe I can, my lord. I've watched how you handle the unusual harnessing.'

'Good man. The general chose his officers well.' Elias swung into the saddle, leant down to lengthen the stirrups, then rode past the troops and led the procession to the sprawling tithe barn that had been prepared for them.

~

A second platoon of troops, which had accompanied the bulk of Jeffreys' cavalcade, was already billeted in the barn. The captain spoke with his deputy, a lieutenant, and learnt that they had arrived some hour previously, having left Salisbury at dawn. The High Sheriff had been waiting for them on the forecourt, along with two unremarkable coaches which would transport the judges and the prosecutor to their lodgings.

'He said he wasn't expecting trouble but preferred not to provoke it by making the judges' arrival conspicuous enough to attract crowds,' the lieutenant finished.

'What of the clerks and lawyers?' the captain asked.

'The Sheriff's people walked them to their accommodation.' He glanced at the racing carriage where Jeffreys sat hunched in irritation. 'The general is required to wait here until the Sheriff returns with a coach.'

The captain groaned. 'He'll not stand for it. He wanted me to drive him to his private quarters rather than follow the column and he'd have made it an order if I'd known where they were.'

'Be grateful you didn't. There's no hiding who or what he is in those robes.' His friend nodded to Granville, who was speaking with the owner of the barn. 'Who's that?'

'The Duke of Granville. We spent last night on his estate.'

'He's not dressed like a duke.'

'He doesn't behave like one either. He treats people with respect, unlike the general. Look at him—face like a shrivelled prune and wrinkled mouth ready to spit at the poor idiot who instructs him to wait for the High Sheriff.'

His friend jabbed his arm with a sharp finger. 'Your responsibility. Your task. Consider it punishment for going on bended knee to win your captaincy by taking this command. You can't say you weren't warned.'

'I can and will,' the captain muttered. 'No one told me I'd be nursing a drunk around the West Country.' He stepped forward as Granville approached. 'My lord?'

'The farmer tells me the High Sheriff has left instructions for Lord Jeffreys to remain here until his fellow judges are settled in their accommodation. Is that correct?'

The captain nodded. 'Yes, sir, though I doubt the general will want to hear it. He regards waiting as a waste of time.'

'Then I have a proposition for you, captain. If you're willing to hand charge of his safety to me, I'll convey him to his lodgings myself. If his current expression is anything to go by, he'll have worked himself into a fine fury by the time the High Sheriff is ready for him.'

'As long as he has no objection then neither do I, my lord. Should I raise the issue with him or will you?'

'I'll speak with him,' Elias answered easily. 'If he agrees to my conditions, we'll depart immediately, and I'll ensure he's comfortably settled before you report for duty yourself.'

'Where should I come, sir?'

'Number six, High West Street. Accompany the High Sheriff. His name is William Lewis, and he'll be keen to satisfy himself that Lord Jeffreys is content. Meanwhile, you can organise your troops and horses. The farmer is contracted to supply all reasonable needs for the duration of your stay.'

The lieutenant stirred. 'With respect, my lord, what's to stop you taking Lord Jeffreys hostage?'

Elias eyed him thoughtfully. 'Nothing at all, except a strong disinclination to forfeit my life and property on a fruitless exercise. What can I hope to achieve by it?'

The lieutenant shrugged. 'The rebels' freedom in exchange for his.'

'You have an inventive mind,' Elias murmured, 'but in future, keep such ideas to yourself. An enemy would report you as a rebel sympathiser, ready to incite others to threaten the life of your commander.'

The young man blanched. 'That wasn't my intention, my lord.'

'Then watch your words,' Elias advised, removing his coat and striding towards his carriage.

The officers watched as he leant in to converse with Jeffreys. They expected impatience and anger, but instead the Chief Justice descended from his seat and, divesting himself of his robes and wig, traded them for Lord Granville's coat. Granville folded the wig inside the robes, tucked them beneath the seat, laced his hands to hoist Lord Jeffreys back into the carriage, then rounded the vehicle to climb into the driving position. In short order, the horses circled the forecourt and disappeared down the road at a smart trot.

'Will he report me?' the lieutenant asked.

The captain shook his head. 'He's not the sort to inform on people.'

～

Jeffreys was silent until Elias slowed his horses to a walk and steered them onto High East Street. Being the main thoroughfare through Dorchester, there were wagons and coaches clogging the road, and people by the dozen making their way along the pavements. 'You never answered my question.'

Elias halted the carriage to allow a woman and two small children to cross in front of him. 'Which one?'

'Do you doubt my honesty?'

Elias set the horses moving once more. 'I don't know you well enough to say. Ask me again when the Assizes are over and I've had a chance to see how faithfully you deliver justice.'

Jeffreys gave a snort of derision. 'It's not in your interests to rule in my favour. You'll cast doubt on my judgements in the same way your mother did last night in regard to Dame Alice.'

'To what purpose?'

'The number arraigned to appear before me in Dorchester is surpassed only by Taunton. If all are found guilty, Dorset will be dubbed a county of traitors. I imagine her landowners will do anything to mitigate so unwelcome a reputation.'

'A few dozen rebels hardly represent the whole county, Lord Jeffreys.'

'There shouldn't be *any*,' came the tart response. 'There'd be no need for trials if your people had the same respect for the King as is shown in London.'

Elias pulled out to pass a stationary wagon. 'I imagine the poor of London would have been as easily swayed by Monmouth as the poor of the south-west had he entered England through Tilbury docks rather than Lyme Regis. Did you ever meet him?'

'No. The Act of Attainder was passed by Parliament, negating the need for a trial, so I wasn't obliged to sit in judgement on him.'

'He looked like his father and had his father's appeal. To simple farm workers and artisans, the illegality of his claim to the throne wasn't as apparent as it was to Parliament.'

'That's no excuse,' Jeffreys snapped in reply.

'I didn't say it was,' Elias answered. 'I was merely explaining why humble folk rallied to his standard. King James is unknown to them, while Monmouth was the embodiment of King Charles.'

Jeffreys shrugged. 'It makes no difference. My orders are clear. Anyone convicted of involvement in the rebellion must face a traitor's death.'

'Then I feel for you,' Elias said. 'The King has placed you in an unenviable position.'

'How so?'

'The rebels' executions will weigh on your conscience and not on his.'

Jeffreys gave a dismissive flick of his fingers. 'Your mother was similarly exercised by the subject last night, and I gave her a similar answer: the person to blame for a traitor's death is the traitor himself.'

Elias ignored the comment. 'We're about to enter High West Street. Your lodgings are some fifty yards on the left.'

'Will you accompany me inside?'

'If you wish.'

'I do.'

Elias gave a nod of agreement, and shortly afterwards drew to a halt in front of number six, a small, tired-looking Elizabethan house with latticed windows. The door was opened by a smartly dressed footman of wide girth and middle years who had been watching for Lord Jeffreys' arrival, but he seemed to doubt that either of the men in the unorthodox carriage was the person he had been told to expect. Curious bystanders were gathered in a throng on the pavement, drawn to the lodgings in the knowledge that the Lord Chief Justice would arrive before long, and they, too, appeared disappointed in what they saw until a woman called to Elias.

'I am Greta, Lord Granville. Your mother cured my little Lucy of measles. You drove her to us and waited four hours outside until Lucy's fever calmed. We thanked you and Lady Harrier most deeply for your trouble.'

'I remember,' said Elias, dredging his memory for that one event amongst many. 'Is little Lucy well?'

'She is, my lord. Do you bring us Judge Jeffreys?'

'That depends on whether anyone is willing to guard my horses, Greta. Are the strapping lads beside you your sons? If so, I'll give them a penny each to hold the chinstraps until I return.'

The boys needed no further inducement, stepping forward briskly to grasp the leather straps. Elias tied off his reins, then jumped to the ground and walked around the rear of the carriage to assist Jeffreys to dismount. He kept himself between Jeffreys and the crowd, told the boys that he wouldn't be above a quarter-hour, then addressed the rapidly growing press of people.

'We need a path to the door,' he said pleasantly, spreading his arms to encourage them to separate. 'I'll force a way through if necessary, but there'll be bloody noses if I do.'

A man of some sixty years, dressed in the manner of a merchant, took it upon himself to act as marshal. 'I served under this gentleman's father during the Civil War,' he said as he shooed the bystanders aside. 'Sir William Harrier was the bravest man I've ever known, and if his son fights as well as he did, you'll have bloody noses indeed.'

Elias leant past Jeffreys to pull from beneath the seat a leather satchel containing valuables, the folded robes and a basket with two flagons of claret, then shepherded the Chief Justice towards the door. He paused only to speak with the merchant. 'Thank you, my friend. Will you accompany me to the White Horse Inn when I'm finished here and recount your memories of my father over a tankard of ale? I never tire of sharing stories with those who knew him.'

The man bowed. 'It would be my honour, sir.'

'Mine also,' Elias answered, following Jeffreys across the threshold. He waited while the footman closed the door behind them, then gave him their names, along with the satchel, robes and basket. 'Lord Jeffreys' boxes and trunks will arrive within the next three hours. In the meantime, is his chamber ready for him?'

'It is, my lord.'

Elias turned to Jeffreys. 'Then I'll take my leave of you, sir. Your captain and the High Sheriff will be here shortly.' He offered his hand.

Jeffreys took it more willingly than Elias had expected. 'Will you sit with me a while? Those boys will wait as long as necessary if I add another penny to their wages.'

Elias shook his head. 'My horses suffer when they stand in harness too long.' He tried to withdraw his hand but Jeffreys' grip tightened.

'You'd rather drink ale with a stranger?'

Elias smiled. 'No one who served under my father is a stranger, sir, and I spoke truthfully when I said I enjoy reminiscing about Sir William.'

Jeffreys released his hand. 'Why Sir William and not Lord Granville?'

'That's how his soldiers knew him. He inherited the dukedom after the Civil War ended.'

'Which side did he support?'

Elias turned away with a laugh. 'Not the one you would have supported,' he said, lifting the latch on the door. 'Sir William stood with the people.'

Jeffreys, still wearing Elias's coat, moved into a small salon to watch his departure through the window. The crowd in front of the house had thinned, and he had a brief conversation with the merchant before paying the two lads a penny each. After that, he hoisted himself into the carriage and set off up the road.

Jeffreys snapped his fingers to summon the footman. 'Did you hear what Lord Granville said to the man on the pavement?'

'He asked him to wait for him at the White Horse Inn, my lord.'

'Where is that?'

'High East Street, my lord. You will have passed it if you came from the barracks.'

'Which side?'

'The opposite side to this, my lord.'

Jeffreys turned back to the window. 'Take the satchel, garments and basket to my chamber. I'll sit in here. Do not disturb me again until the High Sheriff arrives.'

The footman, who was usually employed in William Lewis's house, did as he was bid, then returned downstairs and instructed the kitchen servants to be as quiet as possible. Thereafter, he stationed himself in the dining room, which was situated across the hallway from the salon, to watch for Mister Lewis's coach. When it drew up an hour later, he went to open the front door.

'Is he here?' Lewis asked, crossing the pavement.

'Yes, sir. He awaits you in the salon.'

Lewis clapped him on the shoulder. 'Thank you, Edward. Be good enough to announce me.'

The captain, following a few steps behind Lewis, drew his sword when they found the room empty. 'What have you done with him?' he demanded of the footman.

Edward, a timid fellow at the best of times, lost every vestige of colour at the sight of the blade. He tried to speak, but words wouldn't come.

Lewis ordered the captain to sheathe his sword. 'There's nothing to be gained by intimidation,' he said. 'Breathe deeply, Edward, and tell us where you think Lord Jeffreys might be.'

Edward stammered out an explanation. 'He ordered me to take some items to his chamber. I believe he must have left the house then.'

'What would cause him to leave?'

'I don't know, sir, but he seemed very curious about where Lord Granville was going.' Edward repeated what he had told Jeffreys about the merchant and the White Horse Inn.

Lewis turned to the captain. 'Is he likely to have followed Granville to a tavern?'

'I don't know, sir.'

Lewis recalled his own interaction with Jeffreys in Salisbury. 'The only reason would be to confront Granville. Was there enmity between them last night or this morning?'

The captain shook his head. 'Not that I noticed, sir. If anything, I'd say the general rather took to Lord Granville and his mother.

I watched him take his leave of Lady Harrier, and he was unusually civil to her.'

Edward stirred. 'He may have been upset by Lord Granville's parting remark, Mister Lewis. Lord Jeffreys asked him which side his father had supported in the Civil War, and Lord Granville implied that his father supported Parliament. Could it be that Lord Jeffreys, being a King's man, harbours grudges about the Royalists' defeat?'

'If he does, he's picked the wrong opponent in Granville; he won't hear a bad word said against his father. How was Lord Jeffreys dressed? Was he recognisable as the Lord Chief Justice?'

'Not at all, sir. I wouldn't have known who either of them was had Lord Granville not told me. Lord Jeffreys was bare-headed and wore a black coat.'

The captain intervened. 'The coat belongs to Lord Granville, Mister Lewis. He lent it to Lord Jeffreys after insisting the Chief Justice remove his robes for the journey here.'

Lewis considered for a moment. 'Then he's clearly chosen to return the coat himself rather than send a servant with it. I'm not inclined to pursue him over a courteous gesture, but the White Horse Inn is within walking distance if you feel it's your duty to do so, captain.'

'What will you do, sir?'

Lewis nodded towards the dining room. 'Sample some of my cook's food,' he said. 'My wife has donated her to Lord Jeffreys for the duration of the Assizes, but our kitchen is missing her badly . . . and so am I.'

The captain followed his gaze. 'May I join you, sir? If this man is correct to say that the general is unrecognisable as the Chief

Justice, I'd prefer not to draw unwelcome attention to him by appearing in uniform.'

Lewis agreed readily, though he suspected the captain's reluctance to seek out Jeffreys had more to do with the mouthful of abuse he was likely to receive than reluctance to expose the judge's identity. The chances of the man remaining sober and civil in a tavern were small, and Lewis didn't envy Granville having to deal with him.

Elias had planned to reclaim his coat later that evening after William Lewis had taken Jeffreys through the onerous list of cases that faced him on the morrow. Jeffreys had blocked Elias's previous attempt to raise the issue of leniency, but Elias hoped he would be more amenable after seeing the list.

He was irritated, therefore, to find Jeffreys deep in conversation with the merchant when he entered the White Horse Inn. They made a strange tableau, sitting side by side at a table, with their heads inclined towards each other in what appeared to be intimate friendship. It was hard to tell which of the two found the other more engaging, though Elias doubted it was Jeffreys. The only reason a man of his intellect would be encouraging a lesser man to speak freely would be to discover truths that were best kept hidden.

He lifted the chair opposite Jeffreys and turned it, so that its back was resting against the tabletop. 'I wasn't expecting you, my lord,' he said, straddling the seat and folding his arms across the top rail. 'Are your lodgings not to your taste?'

Jeffreys hadn't met Granville's gaze so directly before, and he was disconcerted by the contempt in the other man's eyes. The impression was fleeting—derision transforming almost immediately to mild curiosity—but Jeffreys was left with a sense that he had misjudged the man. He had assumed that Granville's willingness to accommodate and accompany him stemmed from boredom with the unfulfilling life of a country squire, but he wondered now if he'd been wrong.

He brushed the sleeve of the coat. 'I felt obliged to return this. You departed in such a hurry you left it behind.'

Elias answered honestly. 'On purpose. I wanted an excuse to return this evening.'

'To what end?'

Elias nodded towards the merchant. 'The same that brought you here. A desire for information. I trust you've slaked your curiosity about Lady Harrier's husband and my father.'

Jeffreys wasn't easily intimidated. 'Not entirely. Mister Hendry has yet to tell me whether Sir William supported General Cromwell in the matter of King Charles I's trial and execution.'

The merchant stirred. 'That question hasn't been put to me, my lord, and I wouldn't have answered if it had. It's not my place to speak for Sir William in such matters.'

Elias gave a nod of acknowledgement. 'Thank you, Mister Hendry. My father would have applauded your discretion.' He turned again to Jeffreys. 'Why do Sir William's views on the trial and execution interest you?'

'The second King Charles had a great hatred of Cromwell because of the part he played in his father's death. Was he aware of Sir William's friendship with Cromwell—which Mister Hendry has described most eloquently—when he wrote your mother's testimonial and appointed you as his envoy?'

'Sir William was his envoy before I was, Lord Jeffreys.'

Jeffreys' mouth thinned in irritation. 'You didn't mention that.'

'You didn't ask.'

'You're an annoying man, sir. Should I assume your father hid his friendship with Cromwell in order to win the position of envoy?'

'You can assume what you like, Lord Jeffreys, but every assumption you make will be wrong. You're too wedded to the idea that talented men can only be found London.'

'What talents did Sir William have?'

'Many. Those that appealed to King Charles were his fluency in foreign languages, his commitment to seeing a task through to its end, his judgement, his foresight and, above all, his restraint. He had no desire to flaunt the role he played for the King.'

Jeffreys was sceptical. 'He must have been ambitious or the King wouldn't have known of him.'

Elias shook his head. 'He was known to Parliament for the clandestine work he performed during the war. The members needed someone to travel freely between England and France without drawing attention to himself and they chose Sir William.'

'For what purpose?'

'To negotiate the terms under which King Charles could be restored to his father's throne.'

Jeffreys' mouth opened and closed like a trout's, and it was several seconds before words came out. 'King Charles would never have accepted a friend of Cromwell as a mediator.'

'My father was opposed to the military dictatorship that England became under General Cromwell and put friendship aside to argue against him. King Charles knew that.'

His words angered Jeffreys. 'You're lying.'

Elias rose to his feet. 'Then we have nothing more to say to each other. Be kind enough to leave my coat at your lodgings when you depart.' He ducked his head to the merchant. 'I look forward to speaking with you another time, Mister Hendry.'

The merchant watched him make his way towards the exit. 'He's every inch his father,' he murmured.

'You think he was telling the truth about Sir William?'

Mister Hendry drained his tankard before placing it back on the table. 'I know he was.' He reached into his jacket pocket. 'This should cover the cost of the ale, my lord,' he said, placing three-pence on the table, 'but you'll forgive me if I, too, take my leave.'

Jeffreys clamped his hand over Hendry's wrist to prevent him standing. 'What did Granville mean by "clandestine work"?'

'The same that it usually means, my lord. It was no accident that Royalist movements and plans were known to Parliament.'

'Sir William was a *spy*?' Disapproving spit sprayed from Jeffreys' mouth.

'The best and bravest Parliament had. He faced treason charges every time he crossed enemy lines.' Hendry pulled himself free. 'You're ignorant of the choices men were forced to make when they were ordered to take up arms against each other, sir. You owe your appointment to King James and see the conflict through his eyes—as a son whose father was executed by his subjects.'

'At the behest of a warmonger—Oliver Cromwell—whose ambition was to steal the throne for himself.'

Hendry gave a low laugh as he rose from his chair. 'Sir William's favourite saying was that the first casualty in war is truth, but I didn't expect a judge to prove it to me. General Cromwell championed the rights of the people, sir, just as Sir William did.' He took his leave with a small, ironic bow.

On his way through the tables, he paused to speak with other customers, but Jeffreys' fear that he would name his drinking companion was ill-founded. Not a single glance was directed towards the Lord Chief Justice, and Jeffreys was left with the thought that, if Granville had told the truth, Sir William had trained his men to be as reticent as he was.

THIRTEEN

Dusk was falling when Jeffreys emerged through the tavern doors. Nothing about his appearance suggested he had consumed eight pints of strong Dorset ale, but his decision to turn left rather than right indicated confusion about where he was. He walked some fifty yards in the wrong direction before Elias, following on the other side of the road, took pity on him. He lengthened his stride and crossed to intercept Jeffreys before he reached the less savoury part of town.

'I doubt your reputation will withstand being apprehended by watchmen, Lord Jeffreys. Only footpads and men in search of whores frequent this area at night.' He took the man's arm and turned him around. 'Your lodgings are this way. Do you require my assistance to find them?'

'Were you following me?'

'Only to ensure that you didn't come to harm. I made you my responsibility when I drove you to High West Street and felt duty-bound to return you there intact.'

Jeffreys reversed the position of their arms, so that he was leaning on Elias for support, their earlier dispute apparently forgotten. 'Your assistance would be appreciated. Dorset ale is stronger than I'm used to.'

Elias set him moving. 'You hold it well. Not many men would be standing after eight pints.'

'How do you know my consumption?'

'The innkeeper kept me informed. He allowed me to sit in his kitchen until you left.'

'You're acquainted with such people?'

Elias steered him across the road. 'Well-acquainted. Lady Harrier has tended him and his family since she first became a physician. Her favourite patient is his mother May, who is past eighty and suffering from arthritis. Lady Harrier visits her once a month to alleviate her pain and knead her fingers to keep them supple.'

'Why? What does so much effort achieve in one so old?'

'You've been imbibing her product all evening; May is the best brewer in Dorchester.' Elias assisted Jeffreys over the kerb on the other side. 'Do you not weary of searching out the worst in people?'

'What else would you expect from a judge?'

'Impartiality,' Elias suggested.

Jeffreys gave a sour laugh. 'You're a dreamer. It makes no difference if I have sympathy with a person's motives—the law is inflexible. Guilt attracts punishment.'

'Do you never question the level of guilt? Is a woman who steals bread to feed her starving family as deserving of the gallows as a man who clubs a shopkeeper to death in order to rob him of his savings?'

'The law makes no allowance for circumstance. In both your examples, the defendants knew they were committing a crime, as did Dame Alice Lisle when she invited rebels into her house. Your mother challenged me on that case, but the lady's defence of ignorance, deafness and feebleness of mind did not excuse her actions. By giving succour to the King's enemies, she committed high treason and her punishment reflected that.'

Elias was impressed by Jeffreys' ability to speak and argue fluently when the cool dusk air was having the opposite effect on his gait. Without support, his staggering would cause him to lose his footing, and Elias didn't doubt that unconsciousness would follow shortly afterwards. In a strange way, the contrast between strength of mind and weakness of body evoked Elias's admiration. From the length of time his mother had spent in Jeffreys' chamber the previous night, he guessed the judge was sick as well as inebriated.

'I bow to your superior knowledge,' he said. 'but would you have been so strict with Dame Alice if you'd tried fifty hardened rebels alongside her, all of whom bore the scars of battle? Her contribution to the rebellion would have seemed small compared with theirs and deserving of a lesser sentence.'

'There *is* no lesser sentence for high treason.'

'Not in your gift, perhaps, but the King can show mercy. Across the Western Circuit, well in excess of two thousand are awaiting trial for treason. Can His Majesty afford the levels of hatred that the drawing and quartering of so many will cause him? For every butchered man there will be twenty friends and relatives mourning his loss, turning two thousand disaffected persons into forty thousand. Is he prepared for such an outcome?'

'He takes a more expedient view. As long as the living are frightened into obedience, he will count the campaign a success. Fear deters rebellion. Mercy encourages it.'

'His brother Charles showed more intelligence. His willingness to forgive all those who took up arms against his father earned him the love of his subjects. Isn't that the example King James should be following?'

Jeffreys slowed to a halt, obliging Elias to do the same. 'Why are you so concerned about the fate of rebels?'

'I'm not,' Elias answered. 'My concern is for King James. He's been on the throne too short a time to pursue vengeance so ruthlessly. He needs to win the hearts and minds of his subjects, not turn them against him.'

Jeffreys began to sway. 'Justice is not vengeance.'

'It will be seen that way when two thousand Protestants are hanged, drawn and quartered on the orders of a Catholic king. The streets of the south-west will be awash with blood and hate.'

Jeffreys eyes rolled. 'Ride to London and argue your case with His Majesty.'

Elias caught him before he collapsed. 'That's your job,' he muttered, stooping to hoist the insensible body over his shoulder for the second time in twenty-four hours. 'The pity is you lack the courage to do it.'

—

He apologised to Lewis and the captain as he carried Jeffreys into the dining room. 'It wasn't my doing,' he said. 'I merely rescued him after he consumed a gallon of ale. Where do you want me to put him?'

Lewis groaned. 'The trials begin tomorrow. I have lists to show him.'

The captain stood. 'There are padded chairs in the salon, my lord. He'll come round if he's seated in one of them.' He lifted a jug of wine and a glass from the table. 'His first request will be for wine, but he'll be himself again once he has it. I've watched it happen before.'

All might have proceeded as the captain predicted had Elias not wanted his coat. Once inside the salon, he set Jeffreys on the floor in front of a high-backed armchair, inserted his hands beneath his armpits to hold him upright and asked Lewis to strip him of the garment. Lewis had barely begun when Jeffreys' eyes snapped open and he flailed his fists at the man in front of him. Elias took a punch to his eye and several to his chest before he transferred his right hand to Jeffreys' throat and lifted him six inches off the ground.

'Pull harder and quicker,' he said unemotionally.

'You'll strangle him,' Lewis muttered, turning the coat inside out by peeling it from Jeffreys' shoulders.

'I never kill men who can't fight.'

Lewis's actions had the benefit of forcing Jeffreys' arms to his sides, though the irate judge began swinging his fists again as soon as they were free.

Elias dropped him unceremoniously onto the chair and stepped away. 'I have more need of this than you do,' he told Jeffreys, taking his coat from Lewis and pulling the cuffs back through the sleeves. 'The journey to Winterborne Houghton takes longer in the dark and the night air is cold.'

Jeffreys looked from him to Lewis, intelligence returning. 'Forgive me. I was confused about where I was.'

Elias shrugged on the coat and pulled a chaperon hood and gloves from the pockets. 'It seems to be a common occurrence with you, Lord Jeffreys,' he said, tugging the hood over his head and sliding his hands into the leather gauntlets. He turned to Lewis and the captain. 'My respects, sirs. I trust the rest of your evening is free of incident.'

Jeffreys spoke to prevent him leaving. 'Will you accept my apology, Lord Granville?'

Elias studied him coolly. 'Does it mean anything?'

'It's as sincerely offered as your mother's invitation yesterday.'

A small smile twisted Elias's mouth. 'Then allow me to accept it in the same spirit. We can part in the happy knowledge that we match each other in candour and honesty.' He gave a brief duck of his head before walking into the hall and unlatching the front door.

After it closed behind him, Jeffreys instructed his captain to hand him a filled glass. He addressed Lewis. 'Granville's honesty is questionable. He expects me to believe that his father negotiated the terms for our late King's restoration to the throne.'

The remark was more question than statement, and Lewis was clearly expected to answer. But he was conscious that Jeffreys had the means to saturate him in wine if the answer displeased him. 'He spoke the truth, my lord,' he said, taking several steps backwards. 'Sir William was Parliament's courier in the matter, and such was the trust King Charles placed in him, he appointed him an envoy after his succession.'

'Lady Harrier made no mention of it last night. She tried to persuade me she earned her royal warrant through her own efforts. Now I discover that both her husband and son had influence with King Charles.'

Lewis stared at a point above Jeffreys' head. 'I doubt Lady Harrier has ever used either of them to gain advantage, sir. She has no need. Her prowess as a physician means she is better known than they are.'

'In Dorset, perhaps, but not in London.'

'Her saving of lives during the Civil War brought her to the attention of King Charles I's nephew, Prince Maurice of the Palatinate. I imagine he may have mentioned her name outside Dorset—even to his cousin, King Charles II, perhaps.'

Jeffreys studied him curiously. 'She said it was the Duke of Monmouth who mentioned her.'

'That is equally probable, sir, since he and her son served together as young men.'

Jeffreys drained his glass. 'Then I'm perplexed. Why does a woman who is so well connected and so renowned for her skills content herself with this backwater county when she could be feted in London?' He held out his glass for the captain to fill and saw the same contempt in Lewis's eyes as he'd seen in Granville's earlier. 'You don't like my referring to your county as a backwater?'

'I would have no objection if it were true, Lord Jeffreys, but your presence here—and the three hundred alleged rebels in my prison—suggests it isn't. As for Lady Harrier, I don't believe mindless flattery appeals to her.'

Jeffreys gave an abrupt laugh. 'You're as disdainful of London as Lord Granville is.'

'Most Dorset folk are, my lord. The capital takes our taxes but gives us little in return.' Lewis drew his lists from inside his coat. 'May I show you these?'

'What are they?'

'The cases that will come before you tomorrow.'

Jeffreys motioned to him to sit. 'How many are likely to plead guilty?'

Lewis lowered himself to the neighbouring chair. 'I can't say, my lord. It will depend on whether you offer leniency to those who do. The idea is being much discussed inside the prison.'

Jeffreys frowned. 'I wrote to you in confidence about that possibility. Have you revealed it to others?'

Lewis kept a wary eye on the wineglass and refrained from saying that he had told his wife. 'I have not, but even the least intelligent person can see the impossibility of trying three hundred in the handful of days you've allotted for the Dorchester Assizes. The prisoners are debating ways to persuade you to curtail the list.'

'Such as?'

'Dragging out the proceedings by submitting not-guilty pleas. They're gambling you'll lose patience and free them.'

'Unlikely. What else?'

'The arduous nature of the penalty for high treason. To hang, draw and quarter three hundred condemned men will require considerably more executioners than Dorset possesses, and those we hire will need knowledge of how to eviscerate a half-strangled but still living man. The prisoners are wagering that you'll order them whipped through the streets rather than burden the county with so difficult a task.'

Jeffreys considered him thoughtfully. 'Are you and Granville in collusion to win mercy for rebels?'

Lewis's surprise was so obvious that Jeffreys couldn't doubt his denial. 'I've had no conversations with him on the matter, my lord. The only view I've heard him express is that the King will stoke hatred against himself if you're seen to deliver vengeance rather than justice.'

'Do you agree with him?'

Lewis hesitated. 'Resentment is rife, but it has more to do with birthright than distinctions between vengeance and justice. There are no men of rank on my list, so the perception is that only the lower classes are being singled out for punishment.'

'Are there none from the professional classes?'

'A handful. Two trained soldiers, an attorney from Dorchester and a constable from Chard. The rest are artisans or farm labourers, few of whom have any great fluency in reading or writing. Their pleas of innocence will almost certainly be based on their ignorance of Monmouth's intentions.'

Jeffreys took a swallow of wine. 'Who did they think they were fighting when the King's army confronted them at Sedgemoor? Germans? Frenchmen?'

Lewis smiled in spite of himself. 'They'll have an answer, sir. They have answers for everything.'

'I don't doubt it. No mind is as cunning as the criminal mind, Lewis. Monmouth fomented rebellion in the full knowledge of what he was doing, then used his last days to persuade his uncle that others were to blame for his actions. His followers will do the same. I had no sympathy for him and I have no sympathy for them.'

Lewis proffered the list. 'Do you wish to read this, sir?'

Jeffreys shook his head. 'It's not necessary. We'll offer them leniency in return for guilty pleas. I imagine most will accept.' His eyes closed briefly. 'I'm in need of rest. Instruct the footman to take me to my chamber.'

⁓

Lewis gave a start of shock when Elias emerged from an alleyway. There were so few lights in windows that the street was wrapped in darkness, and he knew Elias only by his height. With neither holding a lantern, both faces were pale glimmers in the night.

'I thought you long gone,' Lewis said.

Elias fell into step beside him. 'I was concerned for you, my friend. After the mauling Jeffreys gave me, I wasn't sure what state you'd be in when you left. I thought I'd accompany you to wherever your horse is stabled, and lend you an arm if you needed it.'

It was a poor excuse but Lewis accepted it. 'That's most considerate, but he behaved better after you left. I can't make him out at all, Granville. He had shopkeepers whipped through the streets of Salisbury for mouthing minor seditions but is willing to offer leniency to men caught fleeing Sedgemoor as long as they plead guilty. Explain that to me.'

'It's a trap,' Elias answered bluntly. 'The promise of leniency will be rescinded as soon as they admit their guilt. Jeffreys made it clear to me that there is only one penalty for high treason and the King expects it to be imposed.'

Lewis halted. 'It won't work. If the promise to the first man is broken, those who follow will plead innocence.'

'I imagine the offer will be made to them inside the prison. They'll be asked to submit their pleas before they attend the court, and Jeffreys won't sit until every prisoner has done so. The proceedings will be swift if fifty guilty persons at a time are brought before him. His only duty will be to pass sentence.'

Lewis squeezed one fist inside the other. 'There'll be rioting in the cells if you're right. Men yet to appear will have nothing to lose by trying to break out.'

Elias nodded. 'You should make that clear to Lord Jeffreys and his fellow judges.'

'They'll tell me the prison is my responsibility.'

'It's a difficult problem,' Elias agreed. 'Another solution would be to get word to the prisoners that promises of leniency may not be honoured. They'll have no reason to riot if they're warned in advance that a guilty plea carries risk.'

Lewis looked towards the White Horse Inn, where his horse was stabled. 'I'll pretend you didn't say that, Granville. Jeffreys suspects you of trying to win mercy for the rebels and he'll believe it for a fact if I repeat those remarks.'

Elias sounded amused. 'I imagine he thinks the same of anyone who quotes the numbers he faces—as you did also, perhaps?'

'He accused me of colluding with you when I said that Dorset had too few executioners to draw and quarter three hundred.'

'Then I'm not surprised he thought we were conspiring. I spoke in similar terms, but the figure I quoted was two thousand. Did you know so many are awaiting trial across the south-west?'

'I've been too pressed with Dorset's business to concern myself with other counties.' Lewis took a moment to reflect. 'It'll be a bloodbath.'

'Indeed, and the King will be hated for it.'

'Did you warn Jeffreys of that?'

'I did. His response was that I should make the case to His Majesty.'

'Will you?'

Elias shook his head. 'Two of his closest advisers have already tried and their warnings went unheeded. The King is set on deterring future uprisings by making an example of Monmouth's followers.'

'He may be correct.'

'I don't think so, Lewis. People are angry that Monmouth's followers must endure torture before they die, while their

leader—the man who abandoned them—was permitted a dignified death. High Sheriffs across the West Country fear rioting in
the streets once the butchery begins.'

A candle appeared in the window of a house close to where
they were standing, spilling light across their faces.

'We may be overheard,' Lewis said nervously. 'You endanger
us both by what you say.'

Out of the corner of his eye, Elias watched a young girl place
the candle on a mantelpiece before stooping to sweep ash from
a dead fire. 'Calm yourself,' he murmured. 'It's just a maid going
about her business.'

'I have more to lose than you.'

Elias made no answer.

Lewis continued irritably, 'I've no reason to disbelieve the Lord
Chief Justice. If he promises leniency, I'm willing to accept that
he'll keep his word. Anything else would be improper.'

'I doubt Jeffreys will put propriety before the King's orders, Lewis.'

'There's nothing I can do. I, too, am bound by oath to deliver
what His Majesty wants.'

'Then I'll trouble you no further.' Elias pulled up his coat collar,
obscuring the lower half of his face, and gave a brief nod before
crossing the road to disappear down a side street.

FOURTEEN

DAWN WAS BREAKING OVER WINTERBORNE Houghton when Kitty woke her mistress and told her a patient had need of her services. It was such a common occurrence that Jayne roused herself immediately and prepared to dress. 'Who is it?' she asked.

'Lord Jeffreys, Miss Jayne. His captain has ridden from Dorchester, requesting your help. He says the general has been crying out in pain since midnight but refuses to see a Dorchester physician.' She helped Jayne into her woollen kirtle. 'I told him you'd give him some medicine to take back with him.'

'I doubt medicine will suffice. Leave me to finish dressing and send Zachariah to wake Master Elias. Order his carriage to await us on the forecourt.'

Kitty buttoned the kirtle and took a clean white apron from a chest. 'He's already tried. Master Elias didn't come home last night.'

'Then I'll need my britches and a cloak.'

Kitty shook her head. 'It's too dangerous for you to ride at this time of the morning. Master Elias will tear me to shreds if I allow it. The sun's not properly up.'

Jayne moved the maid aside and pulled her britches from the chest. 'Master Elias needs to be here if he wants to dictate my travelling arrangements. I'll be safe enough if I follow the captain, which I'm told is what his men do.' She sat on a stool and fed her feet into the britches. 'Tell him I'll be with him shortly and send Zachariah to the stable with a message for Timothy to saddle my chestnut mare. As quickly as possible, please.'

Kitty abandoned the apron and headed for the door. 'I'm doing it under protest, Miss Jayne.'

'Of course you are, my dear. You do everything under protest.'

Kitty paused in the doorway. 'I wouldn't mind so much if you were endangering yourself for someone pleasant, but it's madness to do it for an ill-tempered brute like Lord Jeffreys.' She clicked her tongue in disapproval. 'He won't be content until every gallows in Dorset is full.'

Jayne stood to tie the tapes of her britches before dropping her kirtle skirt over them. 'You're as judgemental as he is.'

Kitty chided her. 'Don't pretend you think differently. We wouldn't have thirteen consumptives in our hospital if you condoned the hanging of rebels.'

'True,' Jayne agreed, 'but the person to blame is King James, not the sick man who has been tasked with his dirty work. Now go, and inform the captain we'll be leaving within a quarter-hour.'

The young officer who was waiting in the hall looked nonplussed when Lady Harrier descended the stairs alone and asked Robert if her mare was ready. On being told that it was, she then enquired of the captain if his own mount was rested enough to make the journey back to Dorchester.

'Yes, milady. I couldn't ride her hard in darkness so she's far from spent.'

Jayne opened the flap of her medicine satchel, which Robert was holding for her. 'All's well then,' she said, checking the contents. 'We'll set off at a trot and only move to a canter when the light is stronger.' Satisfied, she re-buckled the flap and requested Robert to attach the bag to her pommel.

The captain ran his tongue across his lips, his anxiety obvious. 'I'd be happier if your son drove you, milady.'

'He would be, too, captain, but he appears to have remained in Dorchester for the night. Have no fear: we'll make faster speed on horseback.'

The young man shook his head. 'He's not in Dorchester, milady. He removed his carriage from the barracks an hour before midnight and headed towards the Blandford Road. Had he not, I would have asked him to bring Lord Jeffreys to you rather than waste time fetching you to him.'

'That would certainly have made more sense,' Jayne agreed, buttoning her cloak at the neck and walking to the door. Ribbons of orange streaked the sky above the horizon to the east, and the silvery grey of dawn was rapidly dispelling the black of night. 'I think it would be wiser if you followed me,' she said over her shoulder. 'I know the road well and can avoid the worst of the ruts.'

The captain's shock at a woman wearing britches beneath her kirtle quickly gave way to feelings of inadequacy at her ease with riding astride. He judged her to be the same age as his grandmother, but not only did she lead him the twenty miles to Dorchester in dim light without incident, she also took her horse from a canter to a gallop for the last three miles of the journey and left him struggling to keep up. By the position of the sun as they entered the outskirts of the town, they had covered the distance in a little over two hours, and she slowed to a walk only when they crossed the River Frome.

She halted opposite the first street to the left. 'I must go on foot from here, captain. Dorchester loves to think it embraces modernity, but her people are still not ready for a woman who refuses to ride side-saddle. Normally, I would lead my mare to the White Horse Inn and stable her there, but I'll reach Lord Jeffreys quicker if you're willing to take charge of her.'

'I'll stable her at our barracks, milady. Will you be safe walking the streets on your own?'

'Yes,' she said, handing him her reins before dismounting and smoothing her kirtle over her britches and leather boots. 'Dressing like a servant has its advantages.' She released her satchel from the pommel and placed the strap over her head and across her shoulder. 'Have you told anyone that Lord Jeffreys was asking for me?'

'Only my lieutenant, milady. I had to explain why I was absenting myself.'

'Then keep it between the two of you, captain. Lord Jeffreys' business is his own, and you'll earn his distrust if he becomes the subject of gossip.'

'You have my word, milady.'

'Thank you.'

With a nod of farewell, she crossed the road to enter the side street, and the captain was disappointed that, despite their journey together, he had had so little conversation with her. At the very least, he would have liked to express his gratitude that she had agreed to help Lord Jeffreys.

Jeffreys was anything but grateful. His back was crippling him, the pain in his abdomen was so severe that he'd vomited twice, and his aching head had prevented him sleeping. He'd sent the captain to summon her hours ago. Why was it only now that she was here? His own physician would have come immediately.

Jayne placed her palm on his forehead to feel for fever. 'It takes longer to travel a dark highway than the lit streets of London, Lord Jeffreys.' She transferred her hand to his wrist to measure his pulse between her thumb and forefinger. 'What did you drink last night?'

'None of your business.'

'Then I'll accept the footman's account. According to him, you consumed a gallon of ale at the White Horse Inn before being carried here in a stupor by my son, drank half a flagon of claret downstairs, another full flagon in this chamber and then ordered brandy.' She lifted an empty glass from the cabinet beside the bed and sniffed the dregs at the bottom. 'Which you appear to have finished.'

Jeffreys glowered at her. 'You're worse than my wife.'

Jayne ignored him to inspect the chamber-pot. 'Your bladder seems to be draining freely. The footman tells me he's emptied this three times during the night and you've obviously used it this morning. Would you care to explain why you put such fear into your captain that he felt obliged to ride through the night to summon me from my bed?'

'I've never experienced such pain,' he told her petulantly. 'I feared a stone of enormous size had dislodged.'

'You would be running a fever and your heart would be racing if that were true. There may have been a stone, but it was small enough for you to expel yourself.'

'Then why did the cramps in my belly cause me to vomit, and why are my head and back troubling me so badly?'

'You're unused to Dorset ale and were unwise to add wine and brandy to it. As to your back, I doubt your spine has benefited from being levered over Lord Granville's shoulder.'

Jeffreys dismissed her diagnosis with a disdainful wave of his hand. 'I need stronger medicine than your willow bark tincture. I have trials to conduct and I can barely stand for pain. Did you bring me laudanum?'

Jayne walked to the door and called down the stairs to the footman. 'I need a bucket of fresh water now and some food as soon as your cook can prepare it,' she told him. 'A dish of bread, bacon and eggs for preference, please.'

'You're wasting your breath,' Jeffreys snapped. 'Instruct him to fetch a flagon of claret.'

Jayne allowed her disdain to show. 'I feel for your poor wife, sir. She must be deeply disheartened to find herself tied to an ill-mannered fool when she thought she was marrying a man of stature and intellect.'

His eyes flared angrily. 'You're being offensive, madam.'

'It's a fault of mine, sir. I have little tolerance for dedicated inebriates who draw their courage and self-worth from a bottle.' She stooped to lift her satchel from the floor where she had placed it. 'If you want my help, you'll do as I say. If you don't, I shall leave. The choice is yours.'

FIFTEEN

MISTER ETTRICK'S COACHMAN HASTENED TO the door of the stables when he heard the sound of wheels on the gravel driveway. The sun had yet to rise, and he couldn't conceive of anyone calling on the master so early in the morning. The groom, whose job was to meet incoming carriages, was barely awake, and though Henry had donned his britches and tunic, he had yet to pull on his boots.

With some relief, he watched the slow-moving vehicle turn onto the fork that led to the stables rather than continue towards the forecourt, and dim though the light was, he guessed by the harnessing of the horses that the driver was Lord Granville. He thrust his feet into his boots, calling to the groom to get dressed, then stepped outside to greet their visitor as Elias pulled up his horses and tied off the reins.

'Forgive me for coming at such an ungodly hour, Henry,' he said, vaulting to the ground, 'but I must see your mistress immediately. How can that best be achieved?'

Henry was rendered temporarily speechless. 'I don't know, my lord,' he managed finally. 'Neither Mister Ettrick nor Miss Althea rise before day is fully broken. Where have you come from?'

'Dorchester.'

'In the dark, my lord?'

Elias took the coachman's arm and escorted him back inside the stable, where a lantern was burning. 'Indeed, but at a slow walk. I've been stationed at the top of the driveway for two hours, waiting for lights to show in the downstairs windows, and I'm guessing that most of the maids are now up. Will Elizabeth be one of them?'

'Most certainly, my lord, but she makes sure the servants know their tasks for the day before she clothes herself. You'll embarrass her greatly if you see her in her night attire.'

Elias scratched his stubbly jaw. 'That wouldn't do at all. Will it embarrass her if you see her?'

'No, sir.'

'Then take her this message.' He paused to marshal his thoughts. 'Lord Granville is in urgent need of Mister Milton's help and begs a meeting with Miss Althea in order to explain why. He hopes to leave again before Mister Ettrick becomes aware of his presence.'

'I can't promise how she or Miss Althea will respond, sir.'

Elias gave his shoulder a friendly pat. 'You can only do your best, Henry. While I wait for an answer, do you have a razor I can use? I wouldn't want to scare Miss Althea if she does agree to see me.'

Henry nodded to a table at the back of the stable which held a bowl of cold water and a tin mirror. 'It's not what you're used to, my lord.'

Elias thanked him. 'It's luxury compared with a battlefield, my friend. Try hard for me. Without Miss Althea's help, I am all that stands between three hundred prisoners and a judge intent on having every last one of them slaughtered.'

Elizabeth's immediate response was refusal. Nothing was so important that it justified Lord Granville disrupting the household in this way. Did he expect her to dress herself and Miss Althea in the blink of an eye? And what made him think Mister Ettrick wouldn't be woken by the commotion of doors opening and closing and Miss Althea bumping herself downstairs on her bottom? Elizabeth might be able to contrive a meeting in two hours, but not now.

They were speaking in the kitchen and Henry placed himself in front of the door to the hall to prevent her leaving. 'At least wake Miss Althea and give her Lord Granville's message. He impressed upon me the urgency of the matter.'

'He was exaggerating. The man charms servants into doing whatever he wants. Look at Bridget. She's already thinking about making flapjacks for him.'

Bridget chuckled. 'And why not? It's rare to cook for someone so appreciative.'

Adam intervened on Henry's side. 'Miss Althea ought to hear the message, Miss Elizabeth. She'll wonder why Lord Granville is asking for Mister Milton's help rather than her own.'

Elizabeth wagged a finger at him. 'She gives you a little teaching, and you think you know everything.'

'I know she'll be curious,' Adam answered. 'I mean, why would Lord Granville drive in darkness when he could have stayed in

Dorchester and ridden at speed in daylight? I'm guessing he needs something from Mister Milton to take back with him before the trials start.'

'It's most irregular. Gentlemen don't come calling on young women at this time of the morning. We'll all be dismissed if Mister Ettrick discovers him.'

'He'll not discover anything if she speaks to the gentleman in here,' Bridget said. 'In all the time I've worked for him, Mister Ettrick has never once set foot in my kitchen. I'll act as chaperone to Miss Althea while you keep the master occupied in the breakfast parlour. I'm sure you can find something to lecture him about.'

Elizabeth cast her a sour glance. 'There'll be an enormous fuss when I tell Miss Althea she has to dress in something suitable and come downstairs without waking her father.'

'I'll carry her,' said Henry. 'I've done it many times before.'

'Why does she have to wear something suitable?' Adam asked. 'It's not as if Lord Granville has ever seen her in fancy clothes. It's not as if *I've* ever seen her in fancy clothes.'

Henry chuckled. 'He's no oil painting himself at the moment. He has a black eye, his hair and coat are covered in dust from the road, and I left him using cold water and my razor to scrape the growth from his jaw. Miss Althea's more likely to find fault with his appearance than he with hers.'

⸻

Althea was more intrigued than critical. 'Who struck you?' she asked when Henry ushered Elias through the back door.

The kitchen was lit by several candle trees, and the light was bright enough to show the developing bruise around Elias's left eye. The same was true of his badly scraped stubble and dust-powdered hair, which gave him the appearance of a rake. Althea found this reassuring, since his unkempt state supported Henry's view that his business with her was both urgent and genuine.

'Lord Jeffreys. He took exception to my wanting my coat back.' Elias shook his head before she could ask for further explanation. 'The story's a long one and I need to return to Dorchester before the prisoners make their pleas.'

Althea, who was sitting at the kitchen table with her nightshift covered by a shawl about her shoulders and a blanket over her knees, nodded to the chair opposite her. 'Be seated, sir, and tell me what you need from Mister Milton.'

As was his custom, Elias turned the chair around and straddled it, resting his arms across the back so that he could look at her directly. 'I need him to write as many letters as he can in one hour,' he said. 'Each should be addressed to an imprisoned man whose defence he dismissed for lacking merit, in the hope that that man will repeat what is written to other prisoners. You have more than fifty names recorded on written submissions in the library, and Mister Milton's advice can be given in one sentence. "While your innocence may be hard to prove, I urge you to try, since a promise of leniency in return for a guilty plea will not be honoured." If you're willing to write this, I will ensure the letters are delivered.'

Althea folded her hands beneath her chin. 'You know this for a fact?'

Elias nodded. 'The High Sheriff confirmed to me last night that Lord Jeffreys intends to offer the inducement.'

'Did he also confirm that it won't be honoured?'

'No, but Jeffreys stayed a night under my roof and I drove him to Dorchester yesterday. I've been conversing with him for a day and a half, and I wouldn't risk my life on his honesty.'

Another woman would have plagued him with questions about why Jeffreys had been at Winterborne Houghton, but Althea addressed the inducement. 'It depends on how he defines leniency. If he interprets it to mean that a simple hanging is more merciful than drawing and quartering, he can honour his pledge by passing that sentence.'

'He won't. He told me in no uncertain terms that there is only one sentence for high treason, and the King expects it to be implemented.'

'Then the legality of the proceedings will be challenged. A judge who coerces a defendant into offering a plea that is contrary to his interest will be in contempt of the law and not in accordance with it.'

Elias was conscious of the minutes slipping by. 'But not until the condemned men have been butchered. William Lewis fears rioting when the prisoners discover they've been tricked. I urged him to warn them of the possibility of deceit, but he refused.'

'He can do no else. A High Sheriff is bound to support the King's judges. Can't you spread the word yourself?'

'Not in the short time I have. Visitors are banned and the gaolers require considerable persuasion and bribery to leave an outside door unlocked.'

Althea wondered how often he'd used bribery in the past. 'What makes you think letters from Mister Milton will be allowed? If the superintendent is aware of Lord Jeffreys' plan, he'll question any attempt to communicate with prisoners on the first day of the trials.'

Elias acknowledged the point with a nod. 'In that case, your efforts will have been wasted.' He studied her closely. 'You're under no obligation, Miss Althea. I'll write the letters myself if you're willing to supply me with a list of prisoners still inside the gaol.'

'Signing yourself as Mister Milton?'

He gave another nod. 'The superintendent's more likely to admit them if they're endorsed by a name he recognises. But the handwriting will be so different from yours that Mister Milton can deny involvement.'

Althea gave an involuntary laugh. 'Mister Milton is in no position to deny anything.' She broke off for several moments' thought. 'A single letter will invite less suspicion, particularly if it's unsealed and the superintendent can read it. Father told me a couple of weeks ago that a Dorchester lawyer has been charged with treason. His name is Matthew Bragg and he's accused of guiding known rebels to a place of safety in order to avoid capture. He adamantly denies the charge, saying he was stopped in the street by three strangers who asked him for directions to a particular address, and he intends to defend himself strongly.'

Elias couldn't recall a Matthew Bragg amongst the names in the library. 'Did you adjudicate his case?'

'No. He never applied. Being a lawyer, I imagine he's confident of winning an acquittal through his own efforts. Father assumes he will, because there's no evidence that he had a previous acquaintanceship with the strangers or knew of their connection with Monmouth. He was merely being courteous in helping them on their way.'

'Dame Alice Lisle used the same excuse.'

'Indeed, which is why I wish Mister Bragg had applied to me. I would have advised his release, since the informant who witnessed the encounter appears to have spoken out of malice.'

She smiled at Elias's obvious irritation at what he believed to be a fruitless discussion. 'Mister Bragg will be better educated than most. I can construct a letter to him that will contain the warning but will not raise the superintendent's suspicions.'

Elias was sceptical. 'It will mean putting all our eggs in one basket. What if he keeps the information to himself?'

Althea tugged at her shawl to stop it slipping down her arms. 'Not our eggs—yours,' she reminded him. 'I need better evidence that Lord Jeffreys intends to offer a fraudulent inducement. I'll write the letter because I don't trust you not to bring bailiffs to our door by using Mister Milton's name on letters of your own.' She turned to Adam, who was standing by the door. 'Will you fetch paper, pen and ink from the library, please? This table will serve well enough as a desk.'

With more time wasted while Adam crept quietly to the library to avoid alerting Mister Ettrick to anything untoward happening, Elias regretted coming. He would have done better to haunt the prison in the hopes of bribing a gaoler than squander the entire night on the risky gamble that a recluse would be amenable to persuasion. When Adam returned, he asked Althea if she would prefer him to wait outside. She shook her head.

'You won't disturb me unless your own disturbance causes you to fidget. I presume you blame yourself for not doing more to stop your foolish friend's rebellion.'

'You read thoughts?'

'Very easily when they're as transparent as yours.' She squared the paper in front of her. 'The time to be angry with me is after you've read what I've written. If you still think ten communications will serve better than one, you may take me to task. If not, you may borrow Griselda to carry Mister Bragg's letter to Dorchester at a gallop.'

&

Dear Mister Bragg,

As a practised adjudicator, I was interested to read the details of your case. A mutual friend at Middle Temple presented them to me because he wanted reassurance that I would have mediated in your favour. Having considered your situation, I told him I would have done.

I presume you intend to cite actus reus non facit reum nisi mens sit rea[*] *and have the necessary evidence to prove that you had no* ex ante[†] *knowledge of the strangers who asked for directions nor,* <u>more importantly</u>, *could have guessed by their words or demeanour that they were rebels?*

You will know that mens rea[‡] *is notoriously difficult to refute, but your case has more merit than Dame Alice Lisle's, whose use of the same defence—that she had no reason to believe her visitors were rebels—was rejected on the grounds that her previous acquaintanceship with them should have told her they were followers of Monmouth.*

As an attorney of good standing, acting in propria persona[§], *you will be able to argue your case more strongly than she did, and the following words spoken by the*

---

[*]   The act is not culpable unless the mind is guilty
[†]   Prior
[‡]   A guilty mind
[§]   In one's own person

great Roman lawyer and statesman, Cicero, may serve
as inspiration:

'Cave promissiones misericordiae. Non honorabuntur.
Hoc dicia aliis.'*

Your servant and fellow attorney at law,
Hugh Milton
Middle Temple

Althea handed the page to Adam and asked him if he could work out the Latin phrases that she'd ascribed to Cicero. He traced the first sentence with his finger.

'I know that *cave canem* means "beware of the dog" and *mater misericordiae* means "mother of mercy", Miss Althea, so since *promissiones* is close to "promises", I'm guessing the first sentence says, "Beware promises of mercy."'

'Good. The next one?'

'*Non* means "not" and *honorabuntur* is part of a verb. Is it the verb "to honour"?'

Althea nodded.

'Then does it say, "Not to be honoured"?'

'Close. The verb ending is third person plural and gives a future passive meaning. It translates as *they will* not be honoured. Now the last phrase.'

Adam placed his finger under each word in turn. 'This . . . say . . . all?'

---

* Beware promises of mercy. They will not be honoured. Tell this to others.

'Almost. *Dicia* is an instruction to "tell" and *aliis* is the dative plural of "others". You need to put "to" in front of it.'

Adam read the line aloud. '"Beware promises of mercy. They will not be honoured. Tell this to others."'

Althea smiled her approval, then retrieved the letter and passed it to Elias. 'If Adam can decipher the warning after a mere handful of lessons, then Mister Bragg will have no trouble with it. Latin is the language of the law and he should have a good foundation in it.'

Reading the page, Elias recognised immediately that he could never have composed anything as fluent and clever as Althea had conceived. Not only had she included a general warning to the prisoners, but she had also alerted Bragg to the flaw in his defence: namely, his need to prove that he could not have guessed the strangers were rebels.

He returned the letter for Althea to fold and address. 'Are you concerned that Mister Bragg isn't properly prepared?'

She brought the four corners of the letter to the middle to form a diamond shape, then turned it over to flatten the folds. 'I am,' she said, inscribing Mister Bragg's name on the front. 'I fear he's relying on his good name as an attorney to exonerate him.'

'What else can he do?'

'Produce witnesses to testify that there was nothing about the strangers to raise suspicion. Others must have passed them; he needs to persuade one or two of those people to come forward.'

'He may have tried and failed,' said Elias, taking the letter and tucking it into his inside pocket. 'Most would rather distance themselves from accused men than be seen to assist them.'

'But not you?'

He rose with a smile. 'The operative word in the sentence was *seen*, Miss Althea. Invisibility allows for greater freedom, I find.' He turned the chair the right way around and tucked it beneath the table. 'Whatever ensues, you have my word that Mister Milton will remain a secret between us.'

'Will you take Griselda?'

He shook his head. 'I've imposed enough already, and Henry will have no credible explanation if your father finds his horse gone and an unknown carriage in his stable. I'll return to Winterborne Houghton and ride cross-country from there.' He held her gaze. 'Being untraceable is as desirable as being unseen at times like this, Miss Althea. A blaze in the library hearth and a strong caution to the occupant of your poste restante address to stay silent should serve the purpose.'

Her piercing blue eyes lit with amusement. 'There's no compulsion on you to deliver the letter, Lord Granville.'

'There was no compulsion on you to write it, Miss Althea.'

'Indeed. We're as complicit as each other. Good day to you, sir.'

'And to you.' He sketched a bow and left through the back door with Henry.

Adam gathered up the paper, ink and pen. 'What did he mean, Miss Althea?'

'I'll explain later,' she told him, pushing her chair away from the table and moving it towards the door with her good foot. 'First, you need to fetch kindling and logs for the library fire.'

⌒

Elias reached Winterborne Houghton an hour and a half after his mother had left. He learnt of her departure from Timothy, who instructed an undergroom to release the horses from the racing carriage while he saddled and bridled a black stallion. As he fed the bit into the animal's mouth, he nodded to the neighbouring box, which normally housed Lady Harrier's mare. 'Miss Jayne left for Dorchester at sun-up, Master Elias. She was accompanied by Lord Jeffreys' captain, and the young man was clearly terrified at the thought of being responsible for her.'

Elias groaned. 'Couldn't you have stopped her?'

'Not without tying her to a post, Master Elias. If it's any consolation, she had more charge of the captain than he of her. Miss Jayne set the pace and he followed.'

'That's no consolation at all. The poor wretch will be a quivering wreck by the time they reach Dorchester. What did he want with her?'

Timothy buckled the chinstraps. 'Attendance upon Lord Jeffreys. He's in extreme pain and has been crying out for Lady Harrier.'

'Good,' Elias commented cheerfully. 'Let's hope his agony is bad enough to delay the start of today's proceedings.' He took the reins and swung himself into the saddle. 'If I ride like the wind, I won't be far behind Lady Harrier. All being well, she and I will be home by mid-afternoon.'

⌐

By riding cross-country at a fast gallop in daylight, he reached Dorchester an hour after Jayne and the captain. His first port of call was the official 'post' in High West Street where letters were sorted and distributed. For a small fee, he persuaded the postmaster to include Mister Bragg's letter with others for the prison, requesting that they be delivered immediately. To ensure this happened, he watched from across the street and followed the first youngster to emerge. The lad made his way directly to the gaol and handed a bundle of letters to the doorkeeper.

Satisfied that he could do no more, Elias retrieved his mount from where it was tethered and rode the short distance to the White Horse Inn. He expected to find his mother's horse in the stables and cursed roundly when he didn't. His first impulse was to retrace the route she would have taken. His second was to check the barracks to see if the captain had returned.

⁓

'Is Lord Granville your only child?' Jeffreys asked, laying his fork on his finished plate.

The question held an implied criticism. Wives were valued for their fecundity and not their independence of spirit. 'He is,' Jayne answered, moving the plate to a table beneath the window.

'That must have disappointed your husband.'

She ladled water from a bucket into a tankard. The Chief Justice's rudeness had been unrelenting from the moment he'd agreed to accept her treatment. In the absence of alcohol, it appeared to be his only method of maintaining his sense of self-importance. 'Not that I noticed,' she said, carrying the tankard to the bed. 'Drink this, please.'

He did so with bad grace. 'You're fortunate he was too courteous to make his disappointment obvious.'

'You're even more churlish sober than when you're drunk, sir,' Jayne countered, removing the tankard and placing it on the nightstand. 'Is your own marriage so wretched that you must disparage mine?'

'I've been wed twice, milady, and my wives have produced twelve children between them.'

'How gratifying for you. You've proved your potency with two different women.'

'Most died in babyhood.'

It was hard to tell if their deaths were a cause for regret, but Jayne expressed sympathy as she took his wrist between her thumb and forefinger. 'I'm sorry to hear that.'

'Would they have lived if you had been my family's physician?'

'You know full well I can't answer that question, Lord Jeffreys. A charlatan might claim he could, but not me. Your pulse is strong and your colour has improved. Does your back still ache?'

'Yes.'

'If that persists, I'll give you something to ease the pain once you're dressed. I'll ask Edward to help you.'

He raised an imperious hand. 'I have more questions for you. Start by explaining your husband.'

The request was so absurd that Jayne laughed. 'I can't. Justification for a person's existence is God's preserve.'

Jeffreys was unmoved. 'Your son told me he was a Parliamentary spy and close friend to General Cromwell during the Civil War. He then betrayed the cause in order to negotiate the return of King Charles II, for which he was rewarded by being appointed His Majesty's personal envoy. Explain that.'

'Lord Granville never describes his father in such terms.'

'The interpretation is mine.'

'I assumed so.'

'Then give me the correct interpretation.'

Jayne would have refused had his version of the story not been so prejudicial to William. She had little doubt that the belittlement of her husband was just another prop to his self-esteem, but she found she wasn't willing to let it pass. Jeffreys wasn't so sick or unhappy that she was prepared to forgive his rudeness indefinitely.

'Your statements were poorly configured and inaccurate,' she said. 'A correct rendering would be as follows: After the death of the Lord Protector and the failure of the republic, Parliament tasked its most trusted courier, Sir William Harrier, with travelling secretly to France to present the terms for the restoration of the monarchy—'

Jeffreys broke in with a scornful laugh. 'Sir William was a *messenger*?'

'It was certainly his intention to pass for one. He was fluent in French, having fought for ten years in the European wars, and he had more freedom to come and go as a humble courier. Had he flaunted himself, King Charles would not have placed so much confidence in him.'

'Your logic escapes me. Where was the virtue in secrecy?'

'In what it demonstrated. Sir William was an honest broker who acted through principle and not for personal aggrandisement. King Charles preferred his advice to that of the sycophants in Parliament who told him what he wanted to hear.'

'A man in the pay of the enemy can never be an honest broker.'

'Sir William was a free agent. He refused rewards of any kind, either from Parliament or the King.'

Jeffreys' lips twisted cynically. 'I don't believe you. His Majesty would never have trusted a man who took up arms against his father.'

'Half the country took up arms against his father, Lord Jeffreys,' Jayne responded in a tone as dry as dust. 'Had it been it otherwise, there would have been no Civil War. Fortunately for his people, King Charles was wise enough not to hold grudges.'

Jeffreys took the remark personally. 'You think I do?'

'It certainly sounds like it. You're too young to remember the conflict, so I assume you've adopted King James's view. He was never as willing as his brother to admit that there were rights and wrongs on both sides.'

'With reason. The monarchy would not have been restored if right had been on Parliament's side.'

'I suggest you live through two decades of chaos before you make that statement again, Lord Jeffreys. It took men of vision to recognise that tolerance was preferable to perpetual enmity.'

'Your husband being one such man?' Jeffreys gave the now familiar dismissive flick of his hand. 'You're like your son. You want me to think well of Sir William.'

'I doubt Lord Granville cares any more for your opinion than I do, Lord Jeffreys. Had you met Sir William, it might be different, but since you did not, you have nothing on which to base an opinion.'

'Should I regret that?'

'No,' Jayne answered honestly. 'Your ill-mannered arrogance would have bored him. He had no ambitions to be lauded and admired wherever he went.'

Jeffreys' lips thinned in annoyance. 'Is that how you see me?'

'Yes.'

'Were you as direct with him?'

'Always.'

'Then I'm not surprised you have only one child,' he said waspishly. 'I imagine he stayed as far away from you as possible.'

Jayne found the taunt more amusing than vexing. 'You're half right,' she conceded. 'Soldiering and diplomacy took him from home a good deal in the early years of our marriage, which made conception difficult. I was past thirty when Elias was born, and women are like mares, Lord Jeffreys: their fertility wanes with age.'

Annoyance turned to disapproval. 'I don't wish to hear that. Some things shouldn't be said.'

'Indeed, so let's stop teasing each other.' Jayne paused at the sound of the front door opening and the murmur of voices as Edward greeted a visitor. 'That will be your captain. Would you prefer his assistance in dressing?'

'I'm not well enough to leave my bed.'

She pulled back his blanket. 'I expect every man you sentence to a traitor's death will say the same,' she responded. 'And with rather more justification.'

'You have sympathy for them?'

'I'd be an unfeeling physician if I didn't,' she said, interlocking her arm with his and pulling him to a sitting position. 'They face the unbearable pain of having their bellies sliced and their entrails torn from their bodies while still alive. I question how anyone can remain steadfast in anticipation of such agony.'

'They shouldn't have joined the rebellion.'

Jayne grasped his ankles and forced him to turn towards her. 'Who shall I call? Edward or your captain?'

Jeffreys lowered his feet to the ground. 'Why are you so eager for the Assizes to proceed?' he asked. 'It must have occurred to you that I can't pass sentence if I'm confined to my bed.'

'I see no advantage in it. You'll be as bound by the King's orders tomorrow as you are today, and delay will merely increase the anxiety of everyone involved. Hopelessness is widespread inside the prison, with half the inmates weakening in body and mind from going unfed. For you to feign illness while others are suffering intolerable despair would be neither right nor just.'

'You've been listening to gossip,' he said dismissively. 'The High Sheriff made no mention of the conditions you're describing.'

'Mister Lewis shares his superintendent's dread of catching diseases. He rarely accompanies me to the cells.'

Jeffreys stared at her. 'You've *visited* the place?'

'Once a month for nearly four decades. I never rely on gossip for my information.' Jayne turned towards the door. 'I'll ask Edward to help you. Your captain will be weary from riding through the night to fetch me.'

Edward shook with fear at the prospect of dressing Lord Jeffreys, saying the judge would abuse him vilely if he made a mistake. Lady Harrier asked if the captain had arrived and Edward gestured to the dining room. 'He and Lord Granville are eating breakfast, milady. Do you wish me to announce you?'

'Lord Granville?' she echoed in surprise.

'He accompanied the captain, milady. I believe he intends to escort you home.'

'Then announce me by all means, Edward. It will be a relief to see friendly faces.'

She smiled as both men leapt to their feet at her entrance. The captain sketched a deep bow while Elias reached for her hand and raised it to his lips. 'You look as enchanting as always, Mama.'

She gave his fingers a sharp pinch. 'Between the two us, I'm hard-pressed to say whose appearance is worse.' She turned to the captain. 'Lord Jeffreys needs assistance with dressing, sir. Are you able to provide it?'

He gave a reluctant nod and removed the napkin from around his neck in preparation for leaving. Elias forestalled him. 'Allow me,' he said. 'I performed the task yesterday, so have some idea of what he likes.'

The captain hesitated. 'He might want to fight you again, my lord. You didn't part on the best of terms last night.'

'All the more reason to make amends,' Elias said, heading for the door.

The young officer turned anxiously to Jayne. 'I should go with him, milady. There's no saying how Lord Jeffreys will react. He punched Lord Granville most aggressively yesterday.'

Jayne gathered from this that Elias owed his black eye to Jeffreys. 'Have no fear,' she said calmly. 'My son is too courteous to respond in kind.' She gestured towards the table. 'Will you draw out a chair for me and ask Edward to bring me eggs and bacon? I confess to being inordinately hungry after watching Lord Jeffreys gobble his.'

SIXTEEN

ELIAS STOOD IN THE OPEN doorway of the chamber and surveyed the hunched figure on the side of the bed. Two white legs dangled pathetically from beneath a nightshirt while the torso was folded in on itself as if in agony. Had anyone but his mother been ministering to this man, he would have believed the play-acting. As it was, he guessed Jeffreys had been expecting the footman or the captain, either of whom would have scurried back downstairs to fetch Lady Harrier.

He was curious about Jeffreys' motives. What did he want from her that she hadn't given him already? An excuse to delay the trials? He announced himself by rapping his knuckles against the door panels.

Jeffreys raised his head, his feigned expression of pain turning quickly to irritation. 'What are *you* doing here?' he demanded.

'I came to escort my mother back to Winterborne Houghton. I worry when she rides alone.' He nodded to Jeffreys' wooden chest. 'Shall I select your clothes or would you rather do it yourself?'

'Why didn't you drive her in your racing carriage?'

'Your captain was so alarmed by your condition that she chose the fastest mode of travel. She left on horseback before the sun was fully up and I was only alerted to her absence an hour and a half later. I trust you were suitably grateful for the effort she made on your behalf.'

A sly look entered Jeffreys' eyes. 'I was unforgivably rude. Will you fetch her back? I wish to apologise to her.'

Elias lifted the lid of the chest. 'You can make your apologies downstairs, though I doubt you'll need to.' He removed hose and britches and laid them on the bed. 'Lady Harrier is used to ill-tempered patients who imagine themselves to be sicker than they are.'

'I'm in terrible pain. My own physician would have given me something more than water to ease it.'

Elias removed a shirt and laid it beside the britches. 'Naturally, and the more evil-tasting the concoction the higher the price. Every quacksalver prays for men such as you to fill their purses.'

'You're as offensive as your mother.'

'Lady Harrier is never offensive to patients. You must have provoked her beyond endurance. What were you talking about?'

'None of your business.'

'Then I'll hazard a guess that the topic was Sir William. Did my mother tell you what you wanted to know?'

'She said I would have bored him. Is she right?'

'In person, perhaps, but as a topic of conversation he would have found you fascinating. Ambitious men always interested him, particularly those who had a need to parade their status.'

'He was born to his dukedom. If he'd had to earn it, he'd have felt differently.'

Elias shook his head. 'Sir William made his own way in life, just as you have done. He never expected or wanted to inherit the dukedom, which is why he used the simpler form of address—Sir William Harrier.'

A flicker of triumph showed in Jeffreys' eyes. 'You must have disagreed with him or you wouldn't have assumed the title on his death.'

'I never disagreed with my father. I admired him prodigiously.'

This clearly displeased Jeffreys. 'Then why take the title?'

'I made a promise to my great-grandfather that I would keep the Granville name alive. Our family patronym is Harrier, the dukedom is Granville, and a good deal of our wealth derives from careful hoarding by previous owners of the title.' He lifted the hose. 'Shall we begin?'

Jeffreys ignored him. 'The only way for a name to continue is to marry and have children. Why haven't you done that?'

'I've yet to find a wife with wider interests than stitching tapestries and preening herself in front of a mirror.'

Jeffreys took him seriously. 'It's your mother's fault. She's spoilt you for other women.'

To Elias's ears, the words sounded perilously like a compliment. 'Lady Harrier may be unusual, but she's not unique, Jeffreys. Your landlady of last night easily matched her in intelligence and competence when she was younger.'

'She's not from your class.'

'More's the pity. I've met a hundred young women who aspire to be duchesses, and not one can string a sentence together without simpering. I'd sooner marry a quick-witted servant girl than tie myself to a nincompoop.'

'Your Granville blood will be tainted if you do.'

'With what? We all bleed red, including you.'

Jeffreys' mouth screwed in disapproval. 'Have you no care for propriety?'

'None at all.' Elias held out the hose. 'Will you don these yourself or must I do it for you? You can't hide in here forever.'

Jeffreys took the stockings reluctantly. 'Will you stay for the trials?'

'No.'

'How will you judge my fairness in delivering justice?'

'By the length of time you remain in Dorchester.'

Jeffreys unrolled the hose. 'Then your judgement will be harsh. The Exeter Assizes begin in less than a week, and I'm told it takes a day to journey there.'

'You're the Lord Chief Justice. The Western Circuit is yours to order as you choose.'

'You may think so,' was Jeffreys' only response before he applied himself to dressing.

William Lewis arrived after Lord Granville and Lady Harrier had left and was told by Edward that he'd missed them by a quarter-hour. He questioned why they had been there, and Edward—fearful of being overheard by Lord Jeffreys, who was sitting in the salon—answered in a whisper. As a result, Lewis received a somewhat garbled explanation, involving screams of pain, Lady Harrier riding at a gallop, Lord Granville refusing to allow Lord Jeffreys to remain in his bedchamber and the demand for a flagon of wine in the salon. He braced himself for ill temper and was relieved to be greeted with something resembling pleasantness.

'Seat yourself, Lewis. Would you care to join me in a glass of Lord Granville's excellent claret?'

Lewis perched on the edge of a chair. 'No, thank you, sir. I'd rather keep a clear head in view of what awaits us this morning.'

Jeffreys flicked the concern aside. 'You worry unnecessarily. The proceedings will go smoothly once the defendants see the sense of pleading guilty.' He turned the glass and watched the light from the window play across the red liquid. 'My captain appears to be in thrall to Lady Harrier and Lord Granville. He has deserted me in order to escort them to the barracks.'

Lewis produced a suitably vague response. 'They have many admirers in Dorset, my lord.'

'Do you know them well?'

'Well enough to be on visiting terms.'

'I find their conceit infuriating.'

Lewis lowered his gaze. Conceit was a term he might apply to Jeffreys, but not to a duchess who never used her title and a duke who greeted everyone as his friend, irrespective of class. 'They're certainly out of the ordinary,' he agreed.

Jeffreys jabbed a finger at him. 'My point precisely. They make a virtue of their refusal to conform.'

Lewis wondered how much claret the man had imbibed. The heightened colour in his cheeks suggested more than a single glass, and he thought it likely he'd downed them in the fifteen minutes since Lady Harrier's departure. 'We should be leaving, sir. Your fellow judges await you in the courtroom.'

'Who will protect me from the crowds?' He subjected Lewis to a withering stare. '*You?* I'd rather have the duke at my side.'

Lewis ignored the insult while questioning whether Jeffreys wasn't in greater thrall to Granville than his captain was. 'We will not encounter crowds, sir. The Oak Room, where the trials will be held, is in Antelope Walk and can be accessed by a tunnel. There are several beneath this town, one of which links this house directly with the Oak Room.'

'How long is it?'

'No more than a quarter-mile . . . possibly less.'

Jeffreys looked at him in disbelief. 'A quarter-mile! I've never heard of such a thing. Is it passable?'

'Easily so. The entrance is through the cellar, and the passageway is wide enough to take two people side by side. I had it swept of dust and cobwebs three days ago.'

'When and why was it constructed?'

'No one knows, my lord. So few people are aware of the tunnels' existence that their history has been forgotten. My predecessor theorised that their purpose was to assist priests to escape persecution during Queen Elizabeth's reign.'

'Those were evil days for Catholics.'

Lewis avoided an answer by rising to his feet. 'It is time, sir. The other judges are eager to speak with you before I order the first batch of prisoners to be brought to Antelope Walk.'

'I'm told there are catacombs in Rome where the curious get lost and die.'

'There's no chance of getting lost, my lord. Edward has prepared candles and the tunnel has only one exit.'

Jeffreys sighed. 'More's the pity,' he murmured in a conscious echo of Elias. 'Have you ever wished to pass your burdens to someone else, Mister Lewis?'

'Frequently, my lord. I would do so now if I could.'

'I also,' said the Lord Chief Justice, draining his glass and placing it on the table beside him. He rose to his feet and adjusted his heavy robes across his shoulders.

Jeffreys belaboured Lewis with complaints as they made their way along the tunnel. The smell was unpleasant. The candles gave off too much smoke. It was an undignified way for the Lord Chief Justice to access a courtroom. He should have processed through the streets with his fellow judges so that the people of Dorchester and Dorset understood the gravity of these Assizes.

Lewis gave tactful responses, while wondering what Jeffreys would make of the Oak Room. Would he consider it a proper courtroom when it was merely a large salon in a hostel? Lewis's nerves were shredded enough without further anxiety being piled on his shoulders. Granville's warnings about dishonoured pledges of leniency had been playing on his mind all night, as had his prediction of rioting in the streets.

He gestured towards a flight of steps. 'We've reached our destination, Lord Jeffreys.'

The judge halted, making sure that his chain of office sat squarely atop his robes and his wig was as it should be. 'The lions' den awaits us,' he murmured, holding out his hand for the ledgers and papers that he'd entrusted to Lewis. 'Proceed with courage, sir. You're trembling so much you have more the air of a sacrificial lamb than a Daniel.'

The exhortation was unnecessary. Lewis went unnoticed the moment Jeffreys entered the Oak Room. The steps led into an antechamber and his only role was to usher the Lord Chief Justice through the interconnecting door to the oak-panelled salon and allow him to dominate. He did so easily, receiving bows from the assembled judges, lawyers and clerks before taking his place at the centre of the justices' table.

Thereafter, the topic for discussion was how to manage the day's proceedings. Sir Henry Pollexfen, the prosecutor, asked Lord Jeffreys if he had considered his proposal: that the defendants record their pleas before being brought to the court. Jeffreys said he had but that he wasn't prepared to adopt it until he had assessed the honesty of the first thirty men. According to the documentation provided to him, most of them had been caught with weapons in their hands or with the scars of battle on their persons, and only a plea of guilty would suffice. If they attempted to prolong the Assizes with fraudulent declarations, Sir Henry's proposal would be enacted.

He turned to Lewis and asked him if he could acquire a scythe and a sickle before the trials began. 'I note that over a dozen of these men claim to have been injured during haymaking.'

'There's a blacksmith close by, my lord. He has a good supply of such tools and will be willing to loan them.'

'Send a servant with the instruction. We'll begin as soon as he returns.'

Lewis nodded to a bailiff who was standing guard by the entrance door, and the man, who had heard the exchange, gave an answering nod before departing. Lewis then told Jeffreys that it would take a good half-hour to assemble the first batch of prisoners. Meanwhile, the minister of Dorchester's parish church, which was almost adjacent, had offered to say prayers for him, his fellow judges and the Assizes. Would they be gracious enough to attend his service?

Jeffreys scowled. 'Why did you not tell me of this earlier?'

'You didn't give me the opportunity, my lord.'

The remark brought surreptitious smiles to several faces in the room, as if an inability to communicate information to the Lord Chief Justice was a common problem.

Jeffreys pushed himself to his feet. 'Our time will be as well spent in prayer as wasting it here,' he said ungraciously, beckoning to Pollexfen and the other four judges to join him. 'Give the order to summon the prisoners, Mister Lewis, and then lead us to the church. I trust the minister is not a sermoniser.'

He trusted wrong. The reverend, a thoroughly Christian man, delivered a short sermon on the Beatitudes, repeating one line several times. 'Blessed are the merciful for they shall obtain mercy.' Jeffreys tolerated the first two citations, but grinned so savagely at the third and fourth that the minister wisely brought his sermon to a close. The service ended with a blessing for the Lord Chief Justice, the judges and all those who were about to appear before them.

'Damned impudence,' Jeffreys muttered loudly enough for everyone to hear.

It was hard to say if the Chief Justice's short temper during the first set of trials was caused by the reverend's strictures, lack of wine or the defendants' pleas of innocence. He fidgeted constantly, broke the points of two quills by jabbing fiercely at his ledger, and delivered his questions with scathing contempt. Lewis watched defendant after defendant trip over himself in his attempt to outsmart him, but none succeeded.

Those who claimed that the wounds on their arms or chests had occurred during haymaking were handed a sickle or scythe and ordered to demonstrate how they or another had caused the injury. Each failed because the curved blades of the implements and the angled settings of the handles could not replicate the thrust or slash of a straight-bladed sword. Those caught fleeing Sedgemoor with weapons or claiming to be mere observers of the battle were similarly dismissed as liars.

The last man to appear was the lawyer, Matthew Bragg. He endeavoured to present a confident air, but his terror of Lord Jeffreys was obvious. He stuttered through his defence, declaring himself to be a lawyer of good standing and quoting Latin phrases to exculpate himself, none of which impressed the Lord Chief Justice.

Jeffreys viewed him with mounting disdain, and Lewis wondered if he saw in the lawyer a chance to demonstrate that he was as willing to condemn the professional classes as those from humbler stock.

'Let me understand you, sir. You saw no harm in assisting three strangers in the street because nothing about them suggested they were rebels?'

'Yes, my lord.'

'You say your own home is situated in that street, and you walk it regularly. How often do you encounter people unknown to you?'

Bragg tugged nervously at his waistcoat. 'Not frequently, my lord, but newcomers to the town have been known to lose their way. I assumed that was the predicament of these three men.'

'They were hardly lost, sir. They were so close to the house they were looking for that you were able to escort them to the front door.'

'Courtesy demanded it, my lord.'

'Did you ask them where they came from or why they were on foot and not on horseback?'

'No, my lord. I didn't feel it was my business.'

'High treason against a lawful king is everyone's business, Mister Bragg. You encountered these strangers two days after the traitor Monmouth was defeated by His Majesty's army, yet it never occurred to you that they might be fleeing capture?'

Bragg ran a nervous tongue across dry lips. 'There was no reason why it should, my lord. They were seeking a specific address. I assumed they were artisans who had been summoned to work in the property.'

'Were you the only person in the street?'

'No, my lord. There were other passers-by and servants in doorways.'

'Why are they not here to testify on your behalf? Your argument that these men could not be taken for rebels might carry weight if others agreed with you.'

Bragg wrung his hands. 'I couldn't persuade them, my lord. They fear being taken for Monmouth sympathisers themselves. I beg you to understand what a weight of oppression has descended on our county since neighbour was invited to inform on neighbour. I am a victim of this myself, being entirely ignorant of who named me to the bailiffs.'

Jeffreys consulted Lewis's list. 'These notes say the homeowner reported you. He knew these men for rebels as soon as he saw them and refused them admittance. He watched you lead them away.'

Bragg's mouth dropped open in shock. 'That's not true, my lord. They entered his house and I never saw them again.'

'Why would he lie?'

It was a moment before Bragg could produce an answer. 'Perhaps he was worried that I would report him for harbouring rebels and decided to report me first. When did he make the accusation?'

Jeffreys looked at the notes again. 'Within a day. His house was searched and no rebels were found.'

Once again, Bragg was obliged to hunt for an explanation. 'They must have left or been hidden. Did the bailiffs search his cellar? There's no better way to deflect suspicion from one's own premises than to accuse someone else.'

'You seem confused, Mister Bragg,' Jeffreys said caustically. 'A moment ago, these strangers were artisans, now they've become rebels in need of a hiding place.'

'You invited me to speculate about the homeowner's motives in accusing me, my lord. Why is he not here to answer your questions? No one else took the strangers for rebels. Certainly not I.'

'Then produce witnesses to that effect. You cannot cite *actus reus non facit reum nisi mens sit rea** without offering proof of an innocent mind.'

'I would have called my accuser as a witness if I'd known his name, my lord. It is he who should be accounting for the strangers. What became of them? Have they been arrested? Do they admit to being rebels?'

Jeffreys glanced at Lewis. 'Do you have an answer, Mister Lewis?'

Lewis stepped forward. 'Three men according closely to the description Mister Bragg gave were taken in charge some two miles

---

* The act is not culpable unless the mind is guilty

north of Dorchester. They spoke in Somerset brogue, bore the scars of battle and claimed to come from Taunton. They were returned to that town under guard and will face the Assizes there in three weeks' time.'

Bragg reacted angrily. 'I saw no battle scars, and my description covered half the artisans in Dorset. Dark of hair, dressed in tunics and britches, and of average height. Where's the proof that yours are the same three men as mine?'

'My bailiffs made a thorough search of the house, Mister Bragg, and nothing untoward was found.'

'But it makes no sense,' Bragg protested. 'Why would they ask me to lead them to a man who was likely to inform on them? You must see the absurdity of what you're suggesting.'

Lewis addressed Jeffreys. 'The previous renter of the property is said to have been a Monmouth sympathiser, my lord. He abandoned the house shortly after the rebellion began, and the present occupier moved into the residence one week before the strangers came to his door. Since Mister Bragg was given an address and not a name, the bailiffs believe he expected to find that the previous tenant had returned. He was closely acquainted with the man, having represented him over a disputed debt.'

'How do you respond to that, Mister Bragg?'

Bragg levelled a trembling finger at Lewis. 'The High Sheriff twists facts to suit his purpose, my lord. I had a single meeting with the previous tenant and then avoided him, for he was in such dire financial straits that he was unable to pay for my services. Further, my knowledge of him was so small that I cannot recall his name, and I was entirely ignorant that he had left the property or might have had sympathy with the rebellion.'

Jeffreys leant forward to stare at him. 'Let me understand you anew. You now want me to believe that an upright lawyer took three honest artisans to the house of a debtor without warning them that they would not be paid for work done?'

Bragg wilted under his glare. 'Yes, my lord, for it is the truth.'

'I don't believe you, sir.'

Bragg sank to his knees and held out his hands in supplication. 'I swear by all that is holy that I am the victim of unfortunate circumstance and entirely innocent of the allegations being made against me, my lord.'

Jeffreys dismissed him with a scornful flick of his fingers. 'You knowingly gave succour to the King's enemies and are guilty of high treason.' He read from a document in front of him. 'You will be taken to a place of execution two days hence. There, you will be hanged then cut down alive. Your bowels will be drawn and burnt in front of you, your head smitten off and your body quartered and divided at the King's will. God have mercy on your soul.'

SEVENTEEN

THE STAMP OF HOOVES AND the crunch of coach wheels on the forecourt were audible in the parlour. Elias stood to look through the small, west-facing window. The vehicle was nondescript, but he recognised the driver immediately. The only question was who was inside.

'Is it a patient?' Jayne asked.

'I won't know until the carriage door opens.'

He watched one of his grooms hasten forward to take charge of the horses while Henry lowered himself gingerly to the ground by placing his toe on the front wheel. Advancing age required him to take a moment to straighten his back before he moved to the carriage window and asked for orders from the occupant. There was no mistaking the face of the person who leant forward to speak with him, but Henry made no attempt to open the door.

'You'll have to excuse me, Mama. I doubt our visitor will find the courage to enter the house unless I insist upon it.'

'Will we require extra places at the table?'

Elias smiled as he straightened his jacket. 'It depends on how persuasive I am,' he said.

Jayne waited until he had left the parlour, then rose to peer through the latticed panes. By then, the carriage's occupant was no longer visible at the window and the coachman was walking towards the front door. His face meant nothing to Jayne, for she'd never seen him, but Elias's words and his emergence onto the forecourt with a wheeled chair gave her a good idea of who their visitor might be. He greeted the coachman as an old friend, spoke to him briefly and then pushed the chair towards the carriage.

Jayne stayed at the window long enough to see Althea lean forward to watch Elias's approach and then resumed her seat. Her only remaining query was how well her son and Althea Ettrick knew each other.

With the carriage door open, Elias could see Elizabeth sitting beside Althea. He bowed to them both and said he hoped their journey hadn't been too arduous. Elizabeth assured him it had not, but Althea's expression suggested the opposite.

'You don't agree, Miss Althea?'

'I hadn't expected it to take so long. I understand now why you built your racing carriage.' She lowered her gaze to the wheeled chair. 'Is this another of your inventions?'

'Hardly, since the idea was yours. Lady Harrier was so impressed by your chair that she asked me to make one for her patients. Will you try it? I'm interested to know if the larger wheels will allow you to propel it by hand.'

Althea's immediate reaction was to refuse but, in truth, she was intrigued by the design. At the front of the chair was a single wheel, some twelve inches in diameter, set centrally on an axle with thin metal footplates on either side. At the rear were much larger wheels, some three feet in diameter, each of which had knobs placed at intervals around its rim.

She subjected Elias to her penetrating blue gaze. 'Are the footplates for steering?'

He nodded.

'Did you manufacture it yourself?'

'With help from my workers.'

Althea looked at his hands, which were clasping the finials on either side of the top rail. She had been so drawn to his bruised eye and scruffily shaven face that morning that she hadn't noticed the cuts and calluses on his fingers. All in all, he bore more resemblance to a labourer than a duke, and she thought how different he was from the aloof picture young Anthony painted of his lower-ranked father, the Earl of Shaftesbury.

'I came to tell you about Matthew Bragg. Also to admit to being wrong about Lord Jeffreys. Both can be done as easily from this coach as from a chair.'

Elias nodded towards the rapidly dipping sun. 'Even if you leave now, your journey home will be in darkness. Henry will endanger himself and you if he tries to pick his way by the light of a lantern.'

'He's done it for my father, and you yourself drove through the night to speak with me this morning.'

'Under a bright moon and a cloudless sky. You will not be so fortunate, Miss Althea; the weather has been building from the west since noon.' He moved the chair closer. 'Oblige Lady Harrier by staying the night. We can accommodate you all with ease, and she will sleep better knowing you are safe.'

This time, Althea made her refusal plain. 'That's not possible, sir. We were able to come because my father is absent from the house, but we expect him back tomorrow morning and must be there to greet him.'

Elias saw from Elizabeth's expression that this was an untruth, though he guessed the falsehood related to the time of Mister Ettrick's return rather than his absence. 'Then you must permit me to accompany you. It would be a shocking dereliction of duty if I allowed two ladies to travel alone at night with only their coachman to protect them.'

The idea of being in a confined space with him alarmed Althea. 'I wouldn't advise it,' she said stiffly. 'You will find this coach a deal less comfortable than yours.'

'I'm not planning to ride with you, Miss Althea. My intention is to return to my bed afterwards and I will need my own mount for that.' He nodded towards the house. 'You should eat before we depart. Elizabeth and Henry also. If you thought the journey long and slow in daylight, you will find it intolerable once night falls.'

Elizabeth stirred. 'Lord Granville speaks the truth, Miss Althea. You've forgotten how draining coach travel is. You're worn out from having to stop yourself falling sideways each time the wheels encountered a rut.'

'There was nothing to stop you bracing me, since you have the benefit of two workable feet,' Althea countered sourly.

Elizabeth responded with acid of her own. 'On the one occasion I tried, you told me you weren't a child and I wasn't your mother.'

'Well, you're *not*,' said Althea crossly, 'but you always *behave* as if you are.'

Henry stepped forward. 'Remember your manners,' he chided them both. 'We are not at home.'

There was a short silence.

'I've yet to meet anyone who tolerates coach travel with good humour,' Elias said amiably. 'My mother has a particular loathing for it, being unable to endure the slowness or the hardness of the seats. Allow me to tempt you inside for some food, Miss Althea. To escape your prison for half an hour will make the return journey more bearable.'

'It was not my intention to impose on you, Lord Granville.'

'It is no imposition, Miss Althea.'

'Your servants will think me poorly dressed.'

Elias avoided the obvious answer: that it didn't matter what his servants thought; instead, he canted his head to one side to examine her. Under pressure from Elizabeth, her hair had been neatly braided and, instead of a jerkin and skirt, she wore a simple primrose gown with a dark blue woollen cloak about her shoulders. She even appeared to have shoes—or perhaps boots—on her feet to judge by the leather toes that peeped out from beneath her hem.

'I can't see why,' he told her truthfully. 'You look very elegant to me.'

A flush rose in her cheeks. 'It's one of Gertrude's gowns,' she confessed. 'She didn't always wear wide skirts.'

He smiled at her honesty. 'Well, it suits you to perfection, Miss Althea. Your stepmother chose well, even if she meant the gown for herself. Will you come inside? It will please Lady Harrier to see you.'

Althea saw little sense in refusing again. Apart from the fact that he was the most persistent person she had ever met, Elizabeth was nudging her arm to persuade her to say 'yes' and Henry patted his stomach as if all he could think of was food. She ducked her head in a nod. 'Thank you. You're very kind. I will enjoy meeting Miss Jayne again.'

'May I lift you into the chair?'

Her eyes widened in horror, and Henry stepped forward immediately. 'With respect, sir, the responsibility for carrying Miss Althea has always been mine. We've developed a fine trust in each other over the years.'

'Of course,' said Elias, pulling back a couple of paces. 'I'll hold the chair steady for you.'

He was touched by the care Henry took to make sure that Althea's gown and cloak remained tucked about her body and that her skirts covered her feet. He looked to be the same age as her father, but she was so slight of build that he was never in danger of dropping her. At no point during the transfer from carriage to chair did he allow her hem to ride up, and once she was safely seated he knelt to ensure the fabric hung neatly and evenly from her knees.

He rose. 'Is there anything more I can do for you, Miss Althea?'

She clasped his hand briefly. 'No, thank you, Henry, though I'm sure Elizabeth would appreciate some assistance in descending. I'll move back to create more space.'

He took a firm grasp of the chair arms to prevent her extending her foot. 'I doubt Lord Granville expects you to move the machine yourself, Miss Althea.'

'Indeed not,' said Elias, drawing her backwards. 'Allow me to be your driver for the length of your stay.'

He assumed her twisted foot was encased in an unattractive boot and was tempted to tell her she was worrying unnecessarily, as he and his mother had seen worse in the hospital, but Althea had gone to so much trouble to present herself well that he didn't want to discomfit her. When Elizabeth had descended from the coach, he asked the groom to escort Henry and the carriage to the stable, then took the two women into the house himself.

Robert bowed to them both when they entered through the doorway, and his efforts brought an amused retort from Elizabeth. 'I'm no better than you,' she told him. 'My rightful place is in the kitchen.'

'Elizabeth teases you,' Elias said mildly. 'She will be joining Miss Althea, Lady Harrier and myself in the parlour for supper, as will their coachman, Henry. Please escort him here as soon as his horses are fed and watered. We expect to depart again in one hour.'

Robert ducked his head in acknowledgement. He was well-used to his master's unorthodox behaviour, but he couldn't recall a coachman being invited to eat with Lady Harrier in the parlour before. It made him intensely curious about the young woman in the wheeled chair. Who was she? Robert assumed her inability to walk meant she was a patient, but that hardly accounted for Master Elias's insistence on treating her servants as equals.

⌒

Timothy had better success in the stable after Steven, his youngest groom, recognised Henry as the man who had returned Master Elias's mare. Timothy greeted him warmly, thanking him for the care he had taken with the animal. 'I trust your mistress is well,' he said. 'His Grace was most impressed by her ability to solve equations.'

Henry gave a surprised smile. 'Do you know what the equation was?'

'Judging by the fact that His Grace was dressed as a parson when he left on the mare and you asked my groom if he recognised the animal when you brought her back, I'm assuming your mistress guessed that the parson wasn't who he said he was . . . though how she worked out that he was the Duke of Granville is beyond me.'

'She's clever.'

'My master would agree with you. His precise words were: "No equation is too difficult for her."'

Henry needed no further persuasion to talk about his mistress. As he and Timothy ministered to the needs of the horses, he expatiated on Miss Althea's qualities. She had the brains and courage of a man, treated her household as friends and was a good deal prettier than she believed herself to be.

'She sounds like the master's mother,' Timothy murmured, bringing forward a bucket of water. 'How far have you travelled?'

'From Wimborne St Giles.'

'Miss Althea's business must be urgent if she was willing to journey so late in the day.'

Henry nodded. 'There's fear of rioting in Dorchester. Outlying magistrates have been summoned to the town as a matter of urgency. Mister Ettrick left on horseback at three o'clock and we departed a half-hour later to alert Lord Granville. Miss Althea felt he should know after his visit to her this morning.'

This intriguing exchange was ended by Robert's arrival with instructions to escort Henry to the house. Timothy sent him on his way, placing blankets over the horses' backs to keep them warm, then turned his mind to Elias's precipitate arrival that morning with a black eye and half-shaven face. Was that before or after he'd visited Miss Althea? After, he decided, since the master's clear intention as he spurred his mount to a gallop was to make up time on Miss Jayne.

A slow smile spread across Timothy's face. He knew of only one woman who might be willing to receive a male visitor at dawn, and that was Lady Harrier. Could it be that Master Elias had finally found his mother's equal?

Althea would have kept her head down had the ceiling of the entrance hall not been so extraordinary. Carved oak beams rose in arched tiers to support the vaulted roof, reminding her of an engraving she had seen of Henry VIII's palace at Hampton Court. The hall was a good deal smaller than the one depicted in the pamphlet, but she thought how disappointing the black-and-white etching was when compared with reality.

It forced her to recognise that confining herself to her father's house had been more limiting than liberating. By looking up, she couldn't avoid the gazes of servants, and the mockery she had anticipated didn't happen. Maids and footmen looked her in the eye with a welcoming smile and she felt increasingly emboldened to smile back. She wasn't so naive that she thought all households would be as accepting—people in worse condition than herself must present themselves at the hospital every day—but for one evening at least, she allowed herself to feel at ease in the company of strangers.

The table in the parlour was circular and large enough to sit five people in comfort. Lord Granville placed Althea between Elizabeth and his mother, himself next to Elizabeth, and Henry between himself and Lady Harrier. This meant that he was sitting opposite Althea, and he stared at her as directly as he had that morning.

'You came to tell me about Mister Bragg,' he prompted her, once the maids had served each of them a bowl of scented chicken broth.

'Can I speak freely?' she asked. 'I took your advice and set a fire in the library hearth.'

'My mother is the soul of discretion and our servants are as loyal as yours,' he told her. 'Speak as freely as you wish.'

'Very well, but the news isn't good. We were visited by a bailiff early this afternoon. He notified my father that a lawyer who was in the first group to appear before the judges persuaded the twenty-nine men alongside him to plead not guilty even though their culpability was obvious. Lord Jeffreys sentenced them all, including the lawyer, to be hanged, drawn and quartered in two days' time.'

Elias took a spoonful of broth. 'Are you blaming yourself?'

'No. The sentence would have been the same if they'd pleaded guilty.' Althea took a sup from her own bowl. 'I regret to say you were right in your assessment of Lord Jeffreys. He was so irritated to have the first session of the morning wasted on meritless cases that he sent the prosecutor, Sir Henry Pollexfen, to the prison with the offer you predicted. Men who pleaded innocent but were later found guilty would suffer the same fate as the first thirty. Men who saved the court's time by pleading guilty might escape execution at the King's mercy.'

'Might?' echoed Elias. 'Does that make the inducement legal?'

'Lord Jeffreys will argue that it does, though his subsequent rulings suggested the opposite.'

'Go on.'

'The second morning session lasted under an hour. Sixty-eight men pleaded guilty and all were condemned to be hanged, drawn and quartered as speedily as the first thirty. Rumours of potential rioting are rife, and the High Sheriff has summoned Justices of the Peace from across the county to assist the town magistrates in maintaining order.'

'Your father being one?'

Althea nodded. 'According to the bailiff, Lord Jeffreys has instructed that nothing must impede the Assizes. He's demanding that magistrates sit through the night in order to make examples of troublemakers.' She gave an unexpected laugh. 'Papa's response was colourful.'

Elias smiled. 'What did he say?'

'That Lord Jeffreys is an idiot. There are no punishments available. The prison is full, there is only one pillory, and men capable of administering a whipping have been ordered to set up gallows for the ninety-eight executions in two days' time.'

'Did the bailiff agree with him?'

'So much so that he added "dangerous" before "idiot". Lord Jeffreys is threatening to impose soldiers on the town if Mister Lewis fails to keep control.'

'When was this threat made?'

'In the wake of the second session. The convicted men were marched back to the prison, and they called to the watching crowds that they had been deceived. The answering shouts of sympathy could be heard in the courtroom. Lord Jeffreys reacted angrily to having his decisions questioned so publicly and warned the High Sheriff he would use his army to quell the unrest if Mister Lewis couldn't do it himself.'

Lady Harrier stirred. 'Was he drunk?'

Althea turned to her with a look of curiosity. 'Why do you ask?'

'He has an appetite for alcohol. It makes him ill-tempered.'

Althea seemed unsurprised. 'Lord Jeffreys' predecessor as Chief Justice, Sir Francis Pemberton, has accused him several times of being an inebriate, but I've never known if the allegation was true. Sir Francis bears such a strong grudge that I've always suspected most of what he says to be malicious.'

'Why?'

'He blames Lord Jeffreys for his dismissal. Sir Francis was the presiding judge at Lord Russell's trial for treason after the Rye House Plot, and George Jeffreys, as prosecuting barrister, made it clear that he thought Sir Francis was favouring Russell by allowing him too much leeway in presenting his defence. George Jeffreys won the case and gained in reputation and influence because of it, while Sir Francis was damaged and ultimately discharged.'

'To be replaced by Jeffreys?'

'Yes. The Crown rewarded him well for delivering a traitor's head.'

There was a brief silence before Elias spoke. 'He can't have foreseen having to deliver thousands more when he accepted his reward. I don't envy him his choices.'

'Which are?' his mother asked.

'To play the puppet or bite the hand that feeds him.'

Althea pushed her unfinished bowl away and placed her arms on the table in order to lean towards him. 'There is a third choice, but it depends on whether Lord Jeffreys has kinder feelings towards you than your bruised eye suggests.'

Elizabeth prepared to raise an admonishing hand to remind Althea of her manners, but Lady Harrier gave a tiny shake of her head followed by a barely perceptible wink. She was enjoying Althea's blunt speaking with her son.

'He has a liking for my claret and my racing carriage,' Elias answered, 'but his feelings towards me appear to be mixed. What is it you wish me to do?'

'Talk with him again. Persuade him to pass sentence without specifying when the executions should take place.'

'How will that help?'

'Delays will give him time to negotiate a concession from the King.'

'I'm listening.'

'His Majesty has the power to mitigate all sentences. Should he choose, he can commute hanging, drawing and quartering to penal transportation to the Americas. The system has been in place since before 1620 and is applied to those who have committed a hanging offence but are deemed worthy of being given a second chance at life, albeit in slavery.'

Elias pushed his own bowl aside. Althea was correct in what she said, but attitudes had changed since the Civil War, when Parliament had drawn its support from the very classes—the lowest—which were most likely to be transported. King Charles II, valuing his subjects' devotion, had rarely resorted to it, but his brother might think differently.

'King James is a vengeful man,' he said. 'Why would he want to give rebels a second chance?'

'For money,' Althea answered matter-of-factly. 'Plantation owners in the West Indies pay ten to fifteen pounds for a slave. His Majesty can take the profit himself or follow the custom of his father and grandfather who granted the sale rights to courtiers in order to keep them loyal.'

'It's a vile trade.'

'Indeed, but faced with the cruellest and most barbaric of deaths, do you not think Monmouth's followers would agree with Cicero's contention, *dum anima est, spes esse*—while there is life, there is hope? At the King's mercy, the period of slavery can be limited to ten years. Thereafter, a man is permitted to live free in the country to which he's been taken, or pay his passage home if he and his family can find the money.'

Elias's gaze held hers. 'You seem to have discovered some sympathy for rebels, Miss Althea.'

'They are not being treated fairly, sir. Elizabeth heard the bailiff tell Papa that Mister Bragg was quite unprepared for Lord Jeffreys' interrogation. I should have written to him sooner. His defence might have succeeded if he had allowed me to assist him.'

Elias shook his head. 'From your description of the day's events, Lord Jeffreys was set on finding every man guilty.'

'I could have tried.'

'You did so in your letter this morning,' Elias said. He then spent several seconds in thought. 'There are well in excess of two thousand men awaiting trial across the south-west. The King might content himself with a few hundred being butchered if he can take profit from the rest. What makes you think Lord Jeffreys is the man to persuade him?'

'It's in his interest to establish the legitimacy of his inducement. He had a taste today of the feelings that deceitful justice inspires and will not want that stain against his name. His manner may be offensive, and often is, but his knowledge of the law is impeccable and he's a persuasive orator. The use of fraudulent inducements does not accord with that reputation.'

'How do you know he didn't speak with the King on these matters before he left London?'

'He would have shown leniency today if he had the authority to do so.'

Elias couldn't disagree with her, since Jeffreys had said as much himself. 'I don't wish to dash your hopes, but he's too afraid of losing his position to challenge the King. I urged him to do it last night and he gave me a poke in the eye for my efforts.'

'You told me it was because you wanted your coat back.'

'That, too. I was tempted to tell him that the last person I lent it to was Monmouth, but I didn't think he'd find the idea as amusing as I did.'

Althea smiled. 'He'd have given you two black eyes.'

Elias returned the smile. 'No man is that lucky twice.'

There was a momentary pause, during which she searched his face thoroughly. 'Even so, will you make the attempt again? If your desire to mend the damage your friend did is sincere, the King may agree to mitigate the punishments of his followers.'

'Why are you so confident that I can inspire Jeffreys with the necessary level of courage?'

'I'm not,' she answered candidly, 'but I can hardly do it myself.'

Jayne waited in the hall for Elias to return the wheeled chair. Beyond him, Henry was tucking a thick woollen blanket across Althea's and Elizabeth's knees before closing the carriage door and climbing into the driver's seat. She watched Zachariah place a heavy fur cloak about Elias's shoulders and fasten it at the neck before handing him his thick leather gauntlets.

'Will you ride to Dorchester from Wimborne St Giles?' she asked.

'It would make sense. I'll sleep longer if I rent a bed at the White Horse Inn rather than come back here and leave again at dawn.'

Jayne nodded. 'Then take this with you now.' She handed him a vial. 'Lord Jeffreys will be in pain—it's a constant problem for him—so tell him I've sent him laudanum and advise him to take it in a spoonful of sweetened water. There's enough for two doses, but warn him that the effects wear off in four hours.'

'And if he's not in pain?'

'He will be.'

Elias, who had seen the effects of laudanum on his mother's patients, tucked the vial into his pocket. 'Are you hoping to suppress his ill temper towards the prisoners?'

'Towards you also. May I give you some advice?'

Elias smiled. 'As long as I'm not obliged to accept it.'

'Never,' she said. 'I'm a very undemanding mother.'

He bent to drop a kiss on her cheek. 'What's the advice?'

'Don't propose the idea yourself. Allow Lord Jeffreys to think of it. He'll reject any suggestion that comes from you.'

'Why?'

'He's jealous of you. He envies your confidence and the easy relationship you had with your father.'

'My mother also?'

'Perhaps.'

Elias eyed her closely as he pulled on his gauntlets. 'Do you want me to succeed? To replace an hour of agony with a lifetime of misery is a desperate bargain, and not one that I would choose for myself.'

'Maybe not, but I agree with Althea. Hope is worth nurturing. Were your father alive, he would tell you that not every man listed for transportation will reach the Americas.'

A thoughtful expression settled on her son's face. 'Thank you, Mama. I believe that's exactly what Papa would have said.' He walked outside with his hand raised in farewell.

EIGHTEEN

EDWARD SHOOK HIS HEAD WHEN Elias presented himself at the door of the lodgings in High West Street the following morning and asked if Lord Jeffreys was dressed and able to receive him. 'He's refusing to see anyone, my lord. He won't even speak to his captain.'

Elias stepped into the hall. 'What's troubling him?'

The captain emerged from the dining room. 'We don't know, my lord. I've tried his door several times but he's placed something behind it. I've heard him groaning, but he won't respond to questions.'

'Has he been drinking?'

'He hasn't asked for anything from the cellar but he may have supplies in his room. I believe you gave him some of your claret.'

'Not enough to impair him two days in a row,' Elias said, shrugging off his cloak and handing it to Edward. 'We need to enter his room.'

He and the captain went upstairs and took it in turns to put their shoulders to the door. After several strong heaves, enough of a gap was created for Elias to slide past the large oak chest that was blocking the entrance. Jeffreys was lying on his back on the floor near the bed, the coverlet tumbled haphazardly over him, and Elias's first thought was that he was dead. His second, as Jeffreys peered at him through half-opened lids, was that this was a performance, designed to win sympathy.

'Are you in pain?' he asked unemotionally.

Jeffreys' response came in a whisper. 'Every movement is agony.'

'Did you fall from the bed?'

A small shake of the head. 'I pushed the chest.'

'And you've been lying here ever since?'

A nod.

'Do you want me to help you stand?'

This time the shake of the head was vehement.

He reminded Elias of men wounded in battle. Those with the severest injuries always begged to be left where they fell rather than endure the torment of being carried from the field. He took the vial from his pocket. 'This is laudanum. Lady Harrier said you know what it is and that I should give it to you if you complained of pain. Since I'm not a physician, I have no idea if now is the right time. The choice must be yours.'

'Now,' Jeffreys managed.

Elias called to the captain to bring a spoon and a cup of sweetened water from the kitchen. While he waited, he lifted the lid of the chest and found stacks of leather-bound ledgers. He opened one and read the title page: *Dorchester Assizes, 1662*. He raised the covers of those in neighbouring stacks and all bore the same title with different dates.

'You're stronger than you look,' he murmured. 'There's half a ton of criminal history in here. You must have had an urgent need for privacy to move it.'

No answer.

Elias nodded towards an abandoned ledger on the floor beside Jeffreys. 'What did you hope to find? Reassurance that you're not the only Chief Justice to offer fraudulent inducements?'

No answer.

'You'd have been disappointed. I can't speak for London, but I don't believe they've been used in Dorset before.'

Jeffreys stared at him with dislike.

Elias tilted his head. 'I hear the captain coming. Do you wish him to enter?'

Another vehement shake of the head.

Elias moved to the gap in the doorway and took the cup and spoon. 'Thank you, captain. Your general will summon you when he's ready.'

He waited until the young man had returned downstairs, then mixed the laudanum with sweetened water in the spoon and knelt to raise Jeffreys' head to help him take the liquid. He knew from watching his mother administer the remedy that it took minutes to work, so he lifted the ledger from the floor and perched on the edge of the chest, flicking through the pages. Dated 1651, most of the recorded cases related to matters arising from the Civil War, such as forfeiture of land and compensation for theft of stock.

After ten minutes, Jeffreys spoke. 'I expected to find your father's name.'

'I guessed as much.'

'His service to Parliament would have given him the right to demand the forfeiture of Royalist estates. Did he?'

Elias shook his head. 'He preferred to live in peace with his neighbours.' He closed the ledger. 'Has your pain diminished?'

'Yes. Will you help me to sit?'

Elias stepped around him to pull pillows from the bed. 'I suspect my mother would advise against doing anything in a hurry,' he said. 'Let's start by propping you against the nightstand.' He stacked the pillows behind Jeffreys and then eased him to a sitting position. 'Have you the strength to shuffle backwards?'

He made the suggestion deliberately for he wanted reassurance that the Chief Justice hadn't lost the power of his limbs; a paralysed judge would be of no use to him at all. His relief when Jeffreys employed his arms and legs to push himself against the pillows must have been obvious because he was rewarded with a surprisingly good-humoured smile.

'My back has troubled me for a long time. At its worst, I can barely breathe or speak for pain. I moved the cabinet when my captain informed me that the High Sheriff was downstairs, insisting on questioning my decisions.'

Elias resumed his seat on the chest. 'With reason. You require him to apply the law while ignoring it yourself.'

'Is that what he told you?'

Elias shook his head. 'It's the opinion of angry bailiffs on the streets of Dorchester.'

'Anger is not an opinion. It's an emotion born of ignorance. We were warned of rioting, and Lewis acknowledged his responsibility to deal with it.'

Elias stretched his long legs in front of him, crossing them at the ankles. 'The warnings were unfounded. I saw only two examples of unrest on my way here: the words "Bloody Assizes" daubed in red paint on the door of the Oak Room and a straw effigy wrapped in crimson fabric with a rope about its neck dangling from a nail hammered into the doorframe. The message across its chest read "The Hanging Judge". I assume it represents you.'

Jeffreys seemed to find this amusing. 'You think I care?'

'Not now, perhaps, but you will when the laudanum wears off. The physical and mental anguish you faced during the night will surface again by noon, made worse by the complaints of magistrates who were drawn from their bailiwicks to deal with non-existent rioters in Dorchester—on your instruction, I'm told.'

'By whom?'

'The bailiffs who were taking down the effigy and removing the daub. They were out of temper with you after being required to patrol the streets all night.'

'On Mister Lewis's orders, not mine.'

Elias's only response was a nod of acknowledgement.

'I trust you made that clear to them.'

'It wasn't necessary. They knew he had no choice once you threatened to impose military rule on his town.'

'That's an absurd exaggeration.'

'Is it? Your clear motive in tempting men to plead guilty is to limit the amount of time you spend on a hard bench. To that end, you declared yourself ready to quell any disagreement at the point of a sword. What is that if not military rule?'

Jeffreys offered a lecture. 'It depends on your interpretation of the term. Ordinarily, it applies to the governance of a country where power resides in the army, as during the republic under Oliver Cromwell. In its secondary meaning of "martial law", it refers to situations where, for reasons of discontent and rebellion, legal administration cannot operate without military protection.'

An ironic twist lifted the corner of Elias's mouth. 'I stand corrected. I should have said you threatened to impose martial *law*.'

'Those words never crossed my lips. If Mister Lewis took that to be my meaning, he was mistaken.'

'I believe you. The mind of a reasonable man is no match for a skilled lawyer who uses niceties of language to obscure deceit . . . as I'm sure the prisoners who were tricked into pleading guilty yesterday will agree.'

'No trickery was involved. The offer was read to them, and they accepted the terms. As they should, since their culpability was obvious.'

'Maybe so, but I'm surprised you didn't see the sense of exercising some discretion. The wording of the offer gives you that leeway, and to have applied more lenient sentences to a few would have encouraged those on today's list to take the gamble.'

Jeffreys' eyes narrowed. 'How do you know what was in the offer? It was made inside the prison.'

'All Dorchester knows. Before the end of the day, the knowledge will have spread across the county and thence into Devon and Somerset. By the time it reaches Taunton, it will have become a dire warning: under no circumstances plead guilty.'

'Mercy is the prerogative of the King—a truth that is stated clearly in the offer.'

Elias rose. 'Then I'm in error. I assumed you represented the Crown in your delivery of justice.' He moved to the window, where he watched servants with wicker baskets form a queue outside the bakery on the other side of the road. 'What is the purpose of a Lord Chief Justice who has no authority?'

'Cease plaguing me!'

'Someone needs to. You can't hide in here all day. I'm your aide-de-camp and duty-bound to remind you of your obligations. Another two hundred men await trial before you leave for Exeter, and they'll need a more attractive enticement than the promise of hideous torture within forty-eight hours to plead guilty.'

'What would you suggest?' Jeffreys asked sarcastically. 'You have no training in the law, and the penalty for high treason is immutable.'

Elias pretended to think about it. 'Are you obliged to set a date for the executions?'

'It's customary, but not compulsory.'

'Then leave the date of the executions open and explain why you're doing it—to give His Majesty time to consider whether any of the convicted men are deserving of a more lenient sentence.'

Jeffreys gave a grunt of amusement. 'How well do you know King James?'

'Hardly at all.'

'I guessed as much. He won't be satisfied until every last rebel is dead.'

Elias watched the queue outside the bakery lengthen. 'Is he aware of how long that will take? Even butchering a pig takes two hours, and you've allocated a mere day for the disembowelment and quartering of ninety-eight men.' He turned. 'There's no better argument for leaving the executions open than the impossibility of fulfilment.'

Jeffreys yawned. 'It won't persuade His Majesty towards leniency. I suggested transportation but he wouldn't countenance it.'

Elias frowned to keep himself from smiling. Nothing should ever be this easy. 'I'm glad to hear it. I share my father's view that profiting from slavery is a loathsome practice.'

Predictably, mention of Sir William brought an immediate contradiction. 'Charitable would be a better description. The life of a condemned man is already forfeit. To allow him to keep it, even in servitude, is an act of kindness.'

Elias added fuel to the fire. 'Sir William wouldn't have agreed with you. In a choice between a quick death and the lingering torment of bondage in the Americas, he would have chosen death. As would the soldiers who served under him. They fought to defend their freedoms, not surrender them to an oppressor.'

There was no response and a silence developed between them. In other circumstances, Elias would have given his father's true motive for denouncing the practice of transportation—the impossibility of a fair trial when the King had a financial interest in the verdict—but to hint at complicity between a corrupt monarch and a corrupt judiciary would achieve the opposite of what he wanted.

Several minutes passed before Jeffreys spoke again.

'Jack Ketch is a ruffian, but he knows his business and warned me in Winchester of the difficulty of disembowelling the hundreds awaiting trial across the south-west. I wrote to His Majesty from Salisbury on the matter and received his reply yesterday afternoon. His mind is unchanged. He expects the full penalty to be applied to every convicted rebel.'

'Did Ketch say how many he could dispatch in a single day?'

'Ten to twelve on the first, seven to nine on the second, and no more than five on the third. With an accomplished assistant, they might achieve more, but thereafter they would be too weary to continue without a period of rest. Inexperienced executioners wouldn't manage half those numbers.'

'First, find someone willing to try,' Elias said. 'The last person in Dorset to suffer the punishment was a priest on the eve of the Civil War. I'm told the barber paid to perform the task was so inept that his victim took upwards of an hour to die despite having his liver removed along with his entrails. As to removing the head and limbs, that was completely beyond the barber. He was so disturbed by what he'd done that he woke screaming every night for the rest of his life.'

'I don't wish to hear that.'

Elias shrugged. 'The story is well known in Dorchester. I doubt there'll be many wanting to follow in the barber's footsteps.'

Jeffreys pushed himself off the pillows and rolled onto his knees. 'You're an irritating man,' he snapped. 'These should be Lewis's concerns, not mine.'

'I'm sure they are,' said Elias, moving to assist him to his feet. 'I imagine he's half-mad with worry over the ninety-eight executions you've ordered for two days' time. If Ketch can only manage a dozen, Lewis will need another two score men to deal with the rest. Where do you suggest he finds them? Will you offer your youthful captain and his troops for the purpose?'

Jeffreys shook him off to sit on the side of the bed. 'Enough! I'm willing to accept that to specify a date is unreasonable. Does that content you?'

'As long as you adjust yesterday's sentences.'

'Only for those who pled guilty. The first thirty, who wasted the court's time, must face their punishment. His Majesty won't tolerate anything less.'

Elias gave a nod of acknowledgement. 'May I offer another suggestion?'

'If you must.'

'Write to His Majesty again, repeating Jack Ketch's words verbatim. The incapability of meeting his demands will not go away simply by leaving the date of the executions open. Even if Lewis succeeds in dispatching twenty-five a week, which is questionable, the bloodletting will continue until Christmas.'

'Why should that concern His Majesty?'

'When resistance to the executions grows—which it will—a single gaoler open to bribery can release a hundred men in a single night. He'll disappear with them, probably towards the north, and there'll be little chance of tracking them once they're outside William Lewis's jurisdiction.'

Jeffreys narrowed his eyes. 'Do you *enjoy* plaguing me?'

Elias smiled. 'Not at all, my friend. I'm your loyal aide-de-camp. Allow me to help you dress.'

Lewis was in no mood to be courteous when he arrived to escort Lord Jeffreys along the tunnel to the courtroom, having spent a sleepless night placating angry magistrates who had been kept from their beds for no good reason.

His irritation lost some of its sting when Edward showed him into the salon and Lord Jeffreys offered a prompt apology for refusing to receive him the previous evening. He blamed his churlishness on the need for quiet reflection. 'I'm fully conscious of the difficulties you face, Lewis, and have been considering different ways to ameliorate them. Please sit and allow me to explain my thinking.'

Lewis gave him grudging thanks, while questioning whether anything he said would be worth hearing.

Jeffreys leant towards him. 'We have a shared responsibility to comply with His Majesty's orders, but our tasks are hardly comparable. To pass sentence takes minutes, to put three hundred to death will take weeks.' He paused to deliver a prodigious yawn. 'I've decided not to specify dates for the executions. This will allow you to determine the frequency of their occurrence and give His Majesty time to consider whether a lesser penalty is acceptable. I have suggested transportation to him once before, but I am minded to suggest it again. Does that meet with your approval?'

Lewis made a conscious effort to keep his mouth from gaping. 'It does, my lord,' he managed. 'The prospect of dispatching so many as speedily as the King would like has caused me a deal of anxiety.'

Jeffreys yawned again. 'I make no guarantees, but if His Majesty agrees that removing rebels from the country and depriving them of their freedom suits the same purpose as death, I presume that marching columns of prisoners to a port will be a simple exercise.'

'Rather simpler than executing them, my lord. We use local militias to assist us when we have numbers to move.' Lewis closed his mind to the three dozen who had been liberated from Dorchester gaol by men claiming to be from the Taunton militia. 'We've had no problems to date, and I do not foresee any in the future.'

'I'll include that in my report to His Majesty. Is it time for us to leave?'

Lewis rose. 'I'm afraid so, my lord.'

Jeffreys extended his hand. 'Then I'll need your assistance to stand. A night of searching for solutions has drained me of energy.'

After returning Jeffreys to his lodgings at the end of the morning sessions, Lewis instructed Edward to take food to the judge's room when he refused to sit in the dining room or salon. 'I imagine he'll demand wine, but he'll be in no state to conduct further trials unless he eats.'

Edward bowed. 'I'm sure Lord Granville will persuade him, sir. We expect him again shortly.'

'Again?' Lewis echoed. 'When was he here last?'

'Eight o'clock, sir. Lady Harrier sent him with a remedy to relieve Lord Jeffreys' pain.'

'Which direction did he take when he left?'

'I believe his intention was to return to the White Horse Inn, sir. He said he needed more sleep.'

As do I, Lewis thought sourly, nodding to Edward to open the front door. He stepped onto the pavement and searched both ways for Granville's tall figure. Not seeing it, he stationed himself in the alleyway from which Granville had emerged two nights previously. His patience was rewarded after five minutes when he saw Granville crossing from High East Street into High West Street.

He accosted him before he could pass the alleyway. 'Explain,' he said.

Elias arched an enquiring eyebrow. 'What?'

'Lord Jeffreys' change of heart. He's now stressing the possibility of mercy and leaving the dates of the executions to me. He also hopes to persuade the King to commute death to transportation. How did you convince him?'

'I helped him dress.'

Lewis dismissed this with a shake of his head. 'What was this remedy you gave him?'

'A reliever of pain.'

'How did your mother know he needed it?'

'He allowed her to treat him during his stay with us.'

'Is the remedy the reason for his good temper? Even the prisoners found him pleasant. He exonerated two on no better evidence than the attorney offered yesterday and gave hope of mercy to those who pled guilty. Meanwhile, he was in constant danger of falling asleep. His yawns were so huge they were copied throughout the courtroom, even by his fellow judges. I've never seen the like.'

Elias feigned a moment's reflection. 'My mother would argue that pain is the cause of irritability, and contentment comes when a person is freed from it.'

'Then he needs further relief. He snapped my head off when I suggested I join him for luncheon. Are you expecting a better reception?'

'I don't know, my friend. He asked me to return at noon, so here I am. Is there something you wish me to say to him?'

Lewis searched his face. 'The only words I have are for you. Do nothing to provoke him. He leaves for Exeter the day after tomorrow, and every warrant he's signed will stand once he's beyond Dorset's borders. For the sake of peace in our county, I would prefer to keep it that way.'

Elias's expression was unreadable. 'In that case, demonstrate your intent to dispatch the thirty from yesterday morning's session as swiftly as possible. Jeffreys has his own burdens to carry, the weightiest of which is his need to please the King.'

Lewis gripped his arm. 'By the time he departs, he will have condemned another two hundred and sixty-five. Do you advise the same for them?'

Elias wrestled himself free. 'My advice is to pray that the King is satisfied with thirty,' he murmured, heading on to the judge's lodgings.

Edward informed Elias that Lord Jeffreys was in his chamber and asked if he wished to join him. Elias declined. Instead, he entered the salon where he'd seen a desk with paper, quill and ink. He took a few minutes to scrawl a note, then took the vial of laudanum from his pocket and instructed Edward to give it to Lord Jeffreys.

'You'll administer it better than I, my lord.'

'He'll do it himself,' said Elias, handing him the folded note. 'Just make sure he reads this first.'

Dear Jeffreys,

The pain-numbing properties of laudanum are miraculous, but the accompanying euphoria quickly becomes a craving. Be wise and hold this second dose in reserve until your desperation for it is as great as it was this morning.

I must return to Winterborne Houghton to ensure that your carriage is ready for your journey to Exeter. All being well, your coachman will deliver the vehicle to your regiment's barracks tomorrow afternoon.

Your friend,
Granville

In his private journal, Lewis recorded that Lord Jeffreys was *sour-faced* and *impatient* during the day's remaining sessions.

I expected him to recant his earlier promises but, mercifully, he did not and proceedings went as smoothly as this morning. In excess of two hundred men have now been condemned, but only the first thirty require speedy management. In order to show good faith, and while I can utilise the services of Ketch and his assistant, I have nominated thirteen to be executed on Gallows Hill tomorrow. Lord Jeffreys intends to send a report of our Assizes to His Majesty at the conclusion of business, and I trust his mention of these first executions will be received well. My wife reminded me that 13 is an unlucky number, but she is confident that any misfortune will be visited on the rebels and not on me. I pray she is right. God have mercy on their souls.

NINETEEN

ELIAS'S FIRST INDICATION THAT THE executions had begun was when Lord Jeffreys' coach came to a standstill a mile outside the town. The driver called down to him that there was stationary traffic ahead as far as he could see, and Elias, who had been dozing on the seat inside, roused himself to lower the window and call back.

'What's causing it?'

'I don't know, my lord.'

'Is there much coming the other way?'

'Only a man on horseback, sir.'

Elias flipped the latch on the door and jumped to the ground. He had ordered the crests on both doors to be obscured by canvas flaps to deter the curious and readjusted the one on his side to make sure it hung straight. The rider, a farmer by his dress, was still some fifty yards distant and his willingness to answer questions from every vehicle in the queue was reflected in the slow pace of his mount. When he drew close, he gave an explanation without being asked.

'There's nowhere for vehicles to go,' he told Elias. 'Every road and street in Dorchester is clogged.'

'Why?'

'The executions. They're set to continue till nightfall and folks are flooding in to watch.'

'How many are planned?'

The farmer shook his head to say he didn't know. 'I witnessed one poor wretch being mutilated and that was enough. There's more blood on Gallows Hill than in my slaughterhouse.'

'When were they announced?'

'I'm told the names were posted yesterday evening and word has been spreading ever since.' The farmer nudged his mount forward. 'You'd be wise to turn back if you haven't come to gawp. Those ahead of you say they've been stopped here an hour already.'

Elias raised a hand in thanks and walked forward to address the driver. 'There's little sense in us both being forced to wait. I promised to deliver you to the regimental barracks but I can achieve that by riding ahead and sending a dragoon to lead you in.'

The driver nodded. 'Thank you, my lord. Even London's roads are never this bad. Dorset must be starved of entertainment if executions draw these sorts of numbers.'

Elias pondered these words as he made his way to the back of the coach and unhitched his mare. His intention had been to ride home as soon as he had fulfilled his pledge to the driver, but he wanted to learn what had brought so many to watch rebels being punished. If agreement with their sovereign's desire for vengeance or, worse, a yearning for amusement were their motives for coming, then his efforts to persuade Jeffreys to petition King James to adopt a more lenient penalty would prove fruitless. Both men sought endorsement for what they were doing and reports of enthusiastic crowds on Gallows Hill would spur them to even greater excess.

The captain came out to greet him when he reached the barracks. Elias explained the need to send a dragoon to the coach, then asked permission to stable his horse in the barn. 'There's no need to unsaddle her,' he said, dropping to the ground. 'I don't expect to be away above an hour.'

The captain glanced towards the sun, which was now three hours past its zenith. 'If it's Lord Jeffreys you seek, he'll not receive you, sir. He planned to write a report for His Majesty at the end of this afternoon's session and left instructions that no one was to disturb him until it was finished.'

Elias shook his head. 'It's reassurance I seek, and your general can't give me that.'

'Is it something I can help you with, my lord?'

'Only if you're willing to accompany me to Gallows Hill to watch rebels being killed.'

The young officer ran a nervous tongue across his lips. 'Is that an order, sir?'

Elias turned away. 'No. Your reluctance is reassurance enough.'

He was reminded of his parents' account of their first meeting as he forged a path through the press of people that thronged Dorchester's streets. It had occurred on the day the priest had been eviscerated by an incompetent barber. His mother had been summoned by her cousin Ruth to tend to her dying son Isaac, and the impossibility of making her way through the crowds had put her in the way of Sir William. Without his help she would not have reached Isaac in time to save him. Both had spoken of the people's excitement to watch an elderly man being tortured for his Catholicism, and Elias searched faces to see if that same glee was replicated today. The easiest to read were those coming away from Gallows Hill—presumably having stayed for a single execution, as the farmer had—and their eyes were more haunted than exultant. Some even called to the oncoming streams to think twice about continuing, the thrust of their cries being that a brutish, bloody sight awaited them.

Predictably, the description whetted appetites rather than suppressed them and the push to keep moving forward grew stronger. Nevertheless, as Gallows Hill drew close, Elias was struck by the increasingly large numbers coming away from it. For ease of passage, the streams divided, with leavers passing to the right of those approaching. Many of the former held kerchiefs to their mouths and noses, and Elias understood why when the street opened out to reveal the expanse of land on which the scaffold stood.

A sickening smell of raw flesh, spilt blood and boiling entrails pervaded the air, along with the vile odours of faeces and urine. From the overpowering stench, the condemned men weren't the only ones emptying their bladders and bowels, and Elias remained at the edge of the killing ground to avoid treading in piss or excrement.

He had thought he could withstand the savage cruelty of evisceration, but found that he could not. A barely clad figure was being lowered from the scaffold as he arrived, and the wretch's gasps for air as Jack Ketch and his assistant tossed him onto a table demonstrated that he was still alive. He looked to be about eighteen, the same age as Robert, and his anguished cries for his mother as Ketch inserted a knife into his abdomen were piteous. The cries turned to screams when the knife sliced him open and

Ketch inserted an iron hook into his gaping belly to haul glistening entrails from the cavity.

Unable to watch, Elias turned his head to study the crowd to his left. Like him, many were averting their gazes from the hideous spectacle, while those who continued to watch did so with sombre expressions on their faces.

The youngster's screams faded to a rattling sigh as his life left him, and a groan of sympathy ran through the assembled watchers. Elias saw a woman shake her fist in the air before shouting something at Jack Ketch. Her words were inaudible but others were emboldened to copy her. Men's rougher chords cast slurs against the King, the Bloody Assizes and the Hanging Judge, only to be countered by cries from the other side of the open ground in support of His Majesty.

Elias looked to where William Lewis, dressed in the full regalia of High Sheriff and surrounded by stony-faced bailiffs, was standing on a raised dais. Appearing unmoved by the competing voices, they gazed unwaveringly at Jack Ketch and the business of the execution. Elias felt an intense sympathy for them. They had no choice but to appear committed to the task in hand, and he wondered if their nights would be as troubled as those of the incompetent barber more than forty years ago.

He left as the thwack of an axe, slicing through a neck and into wood, sounded in his ears. He wasn't alone. People were departing from all around the crowd, and he took heart from their comments. Most expressed revulsion.

A voice spoke at his shoulder. 'They came out of curiosity, my lord, but they'll not return. If the executions continue, there'll be no witnesses to them.'

Elias turned to see the merchant who had served under his father. 'What makes you think I care, Mister Hendry?'

'You showed your distaste for the procedure too clearly, my lord. I was twenty yards to your right and saw you turn away at the same moment that I did.'

Elias glanced towards the man on Hendry's other side, who was leaning in to listen. 'If you have an hour to spare, Mister Hendry, now might be a good time to share memories of Sir William over a jug of May's ale,' he said, nodding towards an alleyway ahead. 'That lane will take us to the White Horse Inn.'

Mister Hendry accepted the invitation gladly and Elias steered him through the oncoming crowds. He kept the conversation light, questioning Mister Hendry about the nature of his business. Discovering he was a wool merchant, he regaled him with stories of his flocks as they made their way to the tavern. It was arguable who was the more bored by the time they entered through the door and seated themselves at an empty table.

Elias called for a jug of May's brew and leant forward to apologise. 'Forgive me, sir,' he murmured, 'but I was wary of expressing sympathy for the poor lad in public. The Assizes may be over, but the informants who supplied the names of the condemned men to the bailiffs are still amongst us.'

Hendry studied him curiously. 'Has that risk not passed, my lord? Lord Jeffreys departs for Exeter tomorrow.'

'Leaving upwards of three hundred men awaiting death in Dorchester prison with no idea if or when their executions will take place. I prefer to be thought indifferent to their fate, Mister Hendry.'

Reserve crept into the other's expression. 'May I ask why, my lord?'

'The appearance of impartiality opens doors. It was a trick my father taught me.'

A sigh of relief escaped the merchant's mouth. 'I thought I'd misjudged you, sir.'

Elias shook his head. 'I'm a true product of both my parents, Mister Hendry.'

They refrained from speaking while a maid placed a flagon and two tankards on the table. The merchant filled one and pushed it across the table to Elias. 'Is there hope of leniency for the condemned men?'

'It depends on whether Lord Jeffreys petitions His Majesty. If he does, he'll recommend transportation.'

'Slavery is hardly leniency.'

'Indeed, but transportation might be easier to escape. I'm told passage to the West Indies is notoriously unpredictable. Ships are sunk or driven off course by storms.'

Mister Hendry mulled over this as he took a sup of ale. 'Are you aware that your father posed as an importer of cloth during the two years before the Civil War began, my lord?'

Elias accepted the change of topic easily. 'I am, sir. The imposture allowed him to travel freely around the harbours of the south-west without drawing Royalist attention to the purpose of his visits.'

'Quite so. Both sides understood how crucial control of the seas would be in the forthcoming conflict. Sir William's task was to identify the ports that would align with Parliament. Do you know how many shipping invoices he forged to maintain the deception?'

Elias shook his head.

'In excess of one hundred. To my knowledge, the only genuine invoice he ever wrote was for the Earl of Carnarvon, who commissioned fabric from him for Royalist uniforms. Sir William fulfilled the order by using a firm of weavers in France with whom he'd done business during the European wars. His favourite jest was that he could spot Carnarvon's troops anywhere on a battlefield, simply by the quality of the material they were wearing.'

Elias had heard this story, too, but pretended he hadn't. 'I knew I'd enjoy speaking with you, Mister Hendry. You've told me something I didn't know.'

'Your father was a fine man, my lord. I learnt a great deal from him.' Hendry took another swallow of ale, watching Elias over the rim of his tankard. 'Half my trade involves the exportation of wool to the continent and I have extensive knowledge of the documents required for the carriage of cargo abroad. I am also familiar with the time and effort required to trace consignments that get lost in transit or are delivered to the wrong port. For the most part, it's not worth the bother of looking. Products that disappear into back alleyways are impossible to find.'

Humour creased Elias's eyes. 'First, the cargo must reach the wrong port, Mister Hendry. How is that achieved when the captain of the commissioned ship has orders to travel in the opposite direction?'

'I can think of two ways. Pay the commissioned captain to alter course—with little likelihood of the transaction remaining secret—or find a trusted alternative to replace him. I know of one who might be sympathetic to the enterprise.'

'Does he command his own ship?'

A nod.

'The cargo will be highly lucrative. Why would the first captain give way to him?'

'We must change his orders.'

A small laugh issued from Elias's mouth at the merchant's matter-of-fact tone. 'When? And why would he accept the change?'

Mister Hendry answered the last question first. 'It's not unusual for a ship to be diverted to a different port when problems arise in the delivery of freight. As to *when* . . . A captain rides at anchor outside a port for several days until he's notified of his cargo's arrival. Such notifications—be they amended orders or an invitation to moor alongside a quay—are carried by harbour officers in hired skiffs whose owners earn a fee for the service.'

'On the instructions of the harbourmaster?'

'Indeed.'

'And how do we convince the harbourmaster that the amended orders are genuine?'

Hendry chuckled. 'We don't try. Skiffs come two a penny, and any confident man can pose as a harbour officer. I imagine the chosen port will be Bristol. It's the largest in the south-west and does a goodly amount of trade with the Americas. Traffic in and out is continuous, and the departure of a ship anchored well away from the harbour will go unremarked if another of similar size takes its place shortly afterwards.'

'Bearing the same name?'

Hendry shook his head. 'Crudely painted letters will attract attention.'

'Why would a ship with a different name be given the cargo? Theft would abound in ports if any vessel can present herself for loading.'

'The deliverer of the cargo will have a manifest, bearing the name of the substitute ship, stating what the cargo is and how many pieces must be loaded. As long as that manifest conforms to the one held by our trusted captain, the transaction will go smoothly.'

Elias closed his eyes briefly. 'You mount challenge on challenge, Mister Hendry. The deliverer is likely to be a subaltern in a county militia. In my experience, such men accept sealed documents from their commanders, tuck them inside their jackets and extract them only when they're satisfied that they're in the presence of the recipient. How can his manifest possibly accord with a fraudulent one on a fraudulent ship?'

'Your father made sure the orders were correct *before* they were placed inside a jacket, my lord.'

Elias took a long drink. 'That's a skill I'd like to learn. Did he tell you how he did it?'

'Commanders write and seal their orders in advance, then leave them lying on a desk until they're needed. Sir William made the switch then. He said he never knew a commander to break his own seal in order to confirm what was on the page.'

'That would be what he called the art of confusion.'

'It would, my lord, and it was an art he practised better than anyone. I have it on good authority that he could replicate the seal of four of the King's generals. He used Lord Goring's seal to convince the Royalists besieging Taunton that two thousand mounted dragoons approaching at a gallop had come to reinforce them and not the beleaguered Parliamentary garrison. They were so taken by surprise when the dragoons drew their swords that they fled the field and the victory went to Parliament.'

Elias nodded. He knew this story also. 'He couldn't have done it if Goring hadn't believed him to be a friend.'

'Don't waste your sympathy on Lord Goring, sir. He was a drunkard and a thief who cared nothing for the Royalist cause and fought only for enrichment.'

'I wouldn't dream of defending Lord Goring, Mister Hendry. I was reflecting on my friendship with various lord lieutenants and High Sheriffs.' Elias tapped the lip of his tankard against the one the merchant was clasping. 'To your health, sir. Assuming I can rise to your challenges, I look forward to doing business with you.'

TWENTY

ELIAS RODE CROSS-COUNTRY TO AVOID the traffic on the highway, but five miles short of Winterborne Houghton he made a sudden decision to veer east towards Wimborne St Giles. By then, the hour was past seven and the sun was setting. Thirty minutes of hard riding in gathering night brought him to Magistrate Ettrick's house but, as he slowed to a walk at the top of the driveway, he questioned why he had come. His chances of speaking to Althea away from her father were so slim that a letter would have been a more sensible way to recount his meeting with Jeffreys.

He halted well short of the fork to the stables, and looked towards its interior. Oil lamps hanging from rafters showed the groom releasing horses from the shafts of a carriage while a liveried coachman slapped dust from the skirts of his coat. Realising Mister Ettrick had visitors, he twitched his reins and prepared to depart as quietly as he had come.

'Did you wish to speak with Miss Althea, my lord?' asked Henry's voice from the darkness of the verge.

Elias gave a start. 'I didn't see you, my friend.'

Henry stepped from behind a tree, his unsteady gait suggestive of drink. 'I was composing myself, sir. I lose patience on these evenings.'

'Which evenings?'

'When the master is forced to entertain Reverend and Mistress Hughes. They take a free meal off him twice a year in return for blessing his house.' He gave a loud belch. 'Apologies, my lord. It's not my place to criticise the master's guests.'

'You'll find no disagreement from me, Henry. Joshua Hughes is a pompous ass and his wife a duplicitous shrew. Does that match your description of them?'

'It does, my lord. Why does Lord Shaftesbury tolerate them?'

'He lacks the will to wield the axe. Hughes was appointed by his father and has been the minister here for as long as anyone can remember.' Elias paused. 'Is Mister Ettrick likely to mention meeting Reverend Houghton? Emily Hughes is as able as Miss Althea to put the patronym together with my description.'

'You're safe on that count, my lord. Miss Althea had the same worry and told her father the truth this morning. He's pledged to keep the story of the parson to himself.'

'Was he angry?'

Henry shook his head. 'Not at all. He's grateful to your mother for saving Miss Althea's life, and wishes he could have told you of the debt he owes her. If you were to present yourself at his door now, it would please him.'

Elias gathered his reins together. 'But not Reverend and Mistress Hughes,' he said with a laugh. 'Our dislike is mutual. Farewell, my friend.'

Emboldened by drink, Henry moved to block his path. 'It's past time they knew the truth about Miss Althea, my lord. We'll be living with Elizabeth's anger for days because of their ignorance.'

'Are you referring to a specific ignorance or paucity of knowledge in general?'

'The late Mistress Ettrick persuaded them that Miss Althea is an imbecile, sir, and since Miss Althea refuses to prove them wrong, the master conducts these evenings alone. The minister and his wife never ask after her and, if Mister Ettrick mentions her name, Reverend Hughes commends him for his tolerance towards unfortunates.'

Elias made no answer.

'He says Lady Harrier thwarted God's will, my lord. He calls her a meddlesome woman for keeping an imbecile alive.'

Elias groaned on behalf of his mother, then tossed his reins to Henry and slid to the ground. 'Your master and I will need Miss Althea to present herself in person if our arguments are to succeed.'

'She won't do it, my lord.'

Elias clapped him on the shoulder. 'Then sober up and persuade her, my friend. I can't prick the conceit of a bloated hog like Joshua Hughes without evidence to prove my case.'

Adam's surprise to find Lord Granville at the front door turned to impish excitement when Elias spoke. 'I thought Mister Ettrick might appreciate some assistance in entertaining his guests,' he said, stepping inside and peeling off his gauntlets. 'You'll need to warn Elizabeth and Bridget that there'll be another mouth to feed.'

Adam helped him out of his coat. 'I will, sir.'

Elias smoothed his waistcoat, then gestured towards the salon, where Joshua Hughes's abrasive tones were reverberating about the room. 'The reverend knows only how to preach, so you'll have to shout over him. Can you manage "His Grace, the Duke of Granville" at full voice? Our aim is to shock your master's tormentor to silence, Adam.'

The young footman tackled the task with enthusiasm, roaring the announcement at such a pitch that it was heard all over the house. He achieved the required silence in the salon, but it was clear that Mister Ettrick was far more startled than his guests by Lord Granville's appearance.

Elias approached him with an outstretched hand. 'Forgive my intrusion, sir, but knowing how urgently you and Miss Althea await news from Dorchester, I thought I'd pay you a visit before returning to Winterborne Houghton.' He ducked his head to the Hugheses. 'Sir, ma'am.'

They eyed him sourly. They were accustomed to having Mister Ettrick to themselves on their biannual visits, and to compete for his attention with a person as flippant as the Duke of Granville was displeasing. Both were strangers to humour. Joshua Hughes was unable to forego moralising even for a minute, while self-righteous Emily pressed her lips together at any attempt to lighten the mood.

She offered Elias a limp hand, which he raised obligingly to his lips. 'You look well, Mistress Hughes. Few ladies wear grey as confidently as you.'

Her mouth turned down immediately. 'I don't dress to be flattered, Lord Granville.'

'I can see that,' he agreed solemnly before releasing her fingers and turning to her corpulent husband. 'Are you well, sir?'

'As well as can be expected, my lord.'

Elias adopted a look of sympathy. 'Does something ail you? Should I ask my mother to call upon you?'

Hughes shuddered. 'I was referring to the dire times in which we find ourselves, sir. Rebellion in our land, the leader of the rebels discovered on this estate, and his followers being rightly punished for their treason. Evil is everywhere, as I have impressed upon Lord Shaftesbury.'

Elias gave a small laugh. 'Does that explain the increase in your stipend? Shaftesbury tells me you've spent it on a new mount. Do you find horses a successful antidote to evil?'

As Hughes spluttered an indignant response, Adam retreated to the kitchen. 'Lord Granville is here. He's poking fun at the reverend and his wife.'

'We know,' said Elizabeth, adding plates to the piles on the table. 'If your screeching hadn't told us, Henry's headlong arrival would have done. He's with Miss Althea in the library. Make haste to join him and lend support to what he's saying. I'll bring the primrose gown to the library and dress Miss Althea there if she agrees to Lord Granville's suggestion. Tell her we all want to watch the fat man and his skinny wife eat humble pie.'

⌐

Adam struggled to hide his smiles as he filled glasses and listened to Elias's relentless teasing of the reverend and his wife. He tried to remember every remark so that he could impart them all to Miss Althea on the morrow, but Lord Granville's ripostes were so quick that most of the exchanges finished as soon as they began. Only the last remained with him.

'We heard that you entertained Lord Jeffreys at Winterborne Houghton some days ago,' Mistress Hughes remarked. 'My husband and I wonder why Wimborne St Giles wasn't given the distinction, since Lord Shaftesbury's support for His Majesty is well known.'

'I wasn't aware that Shaftesbury had offered an invitation, ma'am. Jeffreys made no mention of it.'

'We assumed the High Sheriff had granted you the privilege.'

'By no means. I took matters into my own hands and waylaid Jeffreys on the highway. Had the same idea occurred to Shaftesbury, you and Reverend Hughes could have satisfied your curiosity as successfully as Lady Harrier and I did.'

'We're above vulgar curiosity, sir.'

'I'm relieved to hear that, ma'am. I'm quite talked out on the subject of Lord Jeffreys. Name me another subject that interests you.'

The ensuing silence was broken by the arrival of Elizabeth, who ordered Adam back to the kitchen before busying herself with rearranging the settings on the table that Mister Ettrick had used for Monmouth's hearing. Mistress Hughes muttered to her husband that Elizabeth had miscounted, there being four chairs and five place settings, but his answer was pre-empted by Elizabeth announcing that supper was ready to be served.

She pulled out chairs for Reverend and Mistress Hughes on the side closest to the salon door, gestured for Mister Ettrick to place himself at the head and asked Elias to seat himself next to Mister Ettrick, facing the door. 'Please take your seats, lady and gentlemen. Your first course will be a dish of pickled salmon.'

Mistress Hughes leant towards her host as Elizabeth's footsteps faded into the hall. 'You should consider replacing her, Anthony. Her mind is going. Our meal has been shockingly delayed, she has set one too many places and has forgotten that I told her the last time we were here that my husband and I do not do fish.'

Mister Ettrick cast a thoughtful eye towards the extra setting, then tucked his napkin into his collar. 'The word "do" may have confused her, Emily; "like" might have been a better choice. As for replacing her, my daughter wouldn't allow it. Without Elizabeth our house would descend into chaos.'

Reverend Hughes tut-tutted. 'Each man is master of his own home, sir. It is written in Proverbs that he shall not surrender his strength to wives or daughters.'

He started in shock as a female voice spoke directly behind him.

'Forgive me for contradicting you, sir, but if you're referring to Proverbs Thirty-one, you've misquoted the verse and taken it out of context.'

The reverend clapped his hand to his heart as Adam pushed Althea's chair into view. Her progress across the floor had been so quiet that only Elias had been aware of it, and he gave nothing away after she placed a finger to her lips to prevent him acknowledging her. With the wheels of her chair moving soundlessly and Adam walking in stockinged feet, even her father had failed to notice her.

She smiled at Mister Ettrick now. 'The Bible doesn't oblige you to close your ears to me, Papa. The man in question was a future king who was unmarried and childless. His name was Lemuel and he was recalling his mother's advice on how to reign wisely. Verse three says: "Give not thy strength unto women nor thy ways to that which destroys kings." She was urging her young son to avoid the temptation of harlots.'

Mister Ettrick reached for her hand. 'You look quite lovely, my dear. If I didn't know better, I'd say I was looking at your mother.' He gestured to his guests. 'You've met Lord Granville, but allow me to introduce you to Reverend and Mistress Hughes. Joshua, Emily, this is my daughter Althea.'

The pair were so dumbstruck that Elias rose to his feet with a bow. 'You do us a great honour, Miss Althea. Is your treatise on Euclid's *Elements* finished? I would hate to think we've interrupted an important train of mathematical thought for something as frivolous as pickled salmon.'

The remark made her laugh. 'Bridget would be mortified to have "frivolous" attached to the dish, my lord. She prides herself on the artistry she brings to its preparation. And, no, I have yet to finish my treatise. The *Elements* consist of thirteen books, and the propositions and their proofs take time to translate and abridge.'

Elias moved his chair to the empty place setting, then walked around Mister Ettrick to stand in front of her. 'May I have the privilege?' he asked. 'I like to think I'm becoming as practised as Adam at steering your vehicle.'

'You may,' she said, 'though it doesn't turn as easily as yours.'

'You have need of a chair, too, my lord?' Mister Ettrick asked in surprise.

'Not personally, sir, but my mother was so taken with Miss Althea's invention that she asked me to construct one for her patients.' He stationed Althea next to her father and seated himself on her other side. 'She was kind enough to try it when she came to Winterborne Houghton two days ago.'

Althea, who hadn't confessed everything, pinched her father's knee beneath the table to persuade him to close his mouth. 'Lord Granville's design is superior to mine, Papa. By dint of using larger wheels at the rear, he has created a vehicle that can be operated by the sitter's hands.' She turned her gaze on the reverend. 'Do you find human inventiveness as intriguing as I do, sir?'

Her assessing stare clearly unnerved him and he took a mouthful of wine before answering. 'God guides every hand,' he managed. 'The inventiveness is His not man's.'

She laughed. 'Do you apply the same logic to Archimedes' inventions? He was Greek, worshipped Zeus, and was born nearly three hundred years before Christ.'

'Heathen inventions are of no account.'

'Archimedes was a hardly a heathen, sir, except in the narrowest sense of not being a Christian.' Althea waited while Adam and Elizabeth served the pickled salmon. 'Without his understanding of mathematics and physics, we wouldn't have levers and pulleys to move heavy objects.'

Mistress Hughes's lips thinned to threads, but whether at Althea's criticism of her husband or the food on her plate, it was hard to say. '*All* men were heathens before Our Lord was born,' she said sternly.

'Even the prophets and scribes of the Old Testament, whose writings inspired His life and teaching, Mistress Hughes?'

'Of course not,' came the sharp response. 'They foretold His coming.'

'But not by name, ma'am. The term used in Greek and Roman translations of the Bible is *messias*, which is derived from the Hebrew *mashiah*. The Jewish scribes were foretelling the coming of the Messiah.'

A scornful smile twisted the woman's mouth. 'Jesus and the Messiah are one and the same.'

'Only to Christians, ma'am. Jews still await the coming of their saviour.'

Mistress Hughes pushed her plate away. 'You shouldn't allow such heresy in your house, Anthony.'

Mister Ettrick took a large forkful of food to excuse himself from answering.

More obligingly, Elias swallowed the last of his salmon and wiped his lips on his napkin. 'Quite delicious,' he said. 'Allow me to respond on your behalf while you enjoy Bridget's artistry, Miss Althea. Mistress Hughes has raised an interesting topic for debate. While the truth may be offensive to Christians, is it heretical to state the known fact that Jews don't accept Jesus as their Messiah? Perhaps her husband can enlighten us?'

Outside in the hall, Elizabeth and Adam clapped their hands to their mouths to stifle their laughter. Revenge, even when slow in coming, was delightfully sweet.

⁓

Mistress Hughes couldn't contain her irritation at having her and her husband's ideas challenged and asked for their carriage to be brought to the front door once her barely touched plate of beef and mushroom pie had been removed. With indecent alacrity, Mister Ettrick dispatched Adam to the stable and invited the Hugheses to join him in the hall for a private prayer. As they left the salon, he nodded to Elizabeth to remain.

Elias rose to his feet. 'As chaperone, your place is beside your mistress, Elizabeth,' he said, pulling out his chair and beckoning her forward. 'You've earned your rest after being on your feet all evening.'

'It wouldn't be appropriate, sir.'

'Then the chair will remain unoccupied,' he said. 'I need to pace before I resume my saddle.'

'Bridget has made a cider syllabub, my lord. She'll be disappointed if you don't eat it.'

Elias walked around the table. 'Then I'll eat it with pleasure. Her syllabub will be twice as pleasant without a sermon to accompany it.' He turned to Althea with a smile. 'You made your case to perfection, Miss Althea. Did you enjoy yourself as much your father and I did listening to you?'

Elizabeth spoke when her mistress didn't answer. 'You did us proud, my dear. I've never seen that pair so disconcerted before.'

Althea instructed her to take Elias's seat. 'Lord Granville's right,' she said. 'You must be worn out. I hadn't appreciated how much work these evenings involved. Does Mistress Hughes always inspect her food as if it's covered in maggots?'

'Always,' Elizabeth assured her, taking the chair. 'She eats nothing and her husband consumes her plate as well as his. Why do you think she's so thin and he's so fat?'

Althea had clearly considered that point already. 'He's a bully and has trained her to behave in a way that suits him.' She looked at Elias. 'I enjoyed surprising them,' she conceded. 'I also understand why Anthony finds his tutorials with Reverend Hughes so unrewarding. For a teacher, his mind is shockingly narrow.'

'He has no incentive to broaden it. Preaching political and religious orthodoxy pays the best stipend in this part of Dorset.'

'And how will my proving I'm not an imbecile change that?'

'It won't, though I doubt the reverend and his wife will be so keen to impose themselves on your father in the way they've done in the past.'

She shook her head. 'They'll be even keener,' she said. 'And next time they'll be better prepared. Reverend Hughes will come armed with obscure biblical texts, and his wife will have a list of criticisms from this evening. She's bound to have noticed that I'm wearing one of Gertrude's gowns.'

'And you'll silence her as easily as you did tonight.'

'But it's all so pointless,' she protested. 'What does it matter if they think me an imbecile? I care nothing for their opinion.'

'There'll be many who do,' Elias countered. 'Not least young Anthony. He wouldn't have to keep his visits here a secret if Lord Shaftesbury knew the calibre of your learning and teaching.'

'He wouldn't enjoy his lessons so much if his father knew about them.'

Elias smiled, knowing she was right. 'But where's the sense in hiding your light under a bushel when your intelligence is superior to that of everyone around you? Aren't you pleased that you argued a case in person as successfully as Mister Milton argued upwards of fifty in writing?'

'Several of which emanated from you,' she said matter-of-factly. 'You're fortunate it was I who assessed them, since it was obvious that your friends in the Middle Shires were all working to the same instruction.' She paused. 'Why did you come here this evening? I can't believe that persuading me to confront Reverend and Mistress Hughes was the cause.'

'To share a burden,' he answered honestly. 'William Lewis ordered thirteen men to be butchered today on my advice.'

Althea's surprise was obvious. 'For what reason? Papa attended yesterday morning's trials and he said Lord Jeffreys left the dates of the executions open to give His Majesty time to consider alternative sentences. Did Jeffreys renege on the policy afterwards?'

Elias shook his head. 'He introduced a delay to all except the first thirty. He said His Majesty would not consider leniency in their cases.'

'And you advised Mister Lewis to expedite those executions?'

'I suggested he'd be wise to give Jeffreys something positive to report to His Majesty before he leaves Dorset.'

'I would have made the same recommendation. Why are you questioning yourself?'

'I attended one of the executions—a lad barely older than Adam—and there were as many applauding the spectacle as turning away from it. If both Lewis and Jeffreys report only the applause, His Majesty will stand firm.'

Althea searched his face. 'Such reports are always biased towards what the King wants to hear. You know this. It must be the young man's death that's troubling you. Have you persuaded yourself you're responsible for it?'

'Lewis wouldn't have acted so quickly if I hadn't prompted him.'

She shook her head. 'You give yourself too much credit. He'll have made the decision himself. Who was the executioner?'

'Jack Ketch, the same man who dispatched Lady Alice. Lord Jeffreys brought him and his assistant with him from London.'

'Then they are the more likely explanation for Mister Lewis's haste. He used practised executioners while they were available to him.' Her gaze held his and he saw a softness that he hadn't seen before. 'You've always known that some would have to die.'

Elias nodded.

'And I've always known that sooner or later I would have to emerge from my hiding place,' she said. 'It seems we must both learn to live with the choices we've made.'

Outside, hooves and coach wheels crunched on the forecourt, followed by the sounds of muttered voices, the opening and closing of a carriage door and the click of the coachman's tongue as he set his horses moving again. A few seconds later, Mister Ettrick re-entered the salon, advancing towards them with his arms outspread and a beam of happiness on his face.

A mischievous gleam sparked in Althea's eyes. 'Brace yourself, sir,' she murmured. 'I believe my father intends to hug you.'

TWENTY-ONE

THE LANTERN CLOCK IN THE entrance hall of Winterborne Houghton House showed half after eleven when Elias let himself in. Robert, who had been dozing on a chair, leapt to his feet and took his coat. 'Your mother's waiting for you in the parlour, Master Elias. She's fallen asleep on the sofa, but Kitty said not to disturb her unless you failed to return by midnight.'

Elias frowned. 'Has something happened?'

'I would say so, Master Elias. Lord Jeffreys and his captain rode here on horseback to see Miss Jayne. They stayed an hour and left again while it was still light. The captain asked to be remembered to you.'

'But not Lord Jeffreys?'

Robert shook his head. 'He was pleased to find you absent, Master Elias. His only interest was in talking to Miss Jayne.'

'She must have had something he wanted, Robert.'

'That was my thought, Master Elias.'

'Did she give it to him?'

Robert nodded. 'I believe so. He looked a good deal happier when he left than when he arrived.'

Elias clapped him on the shoulder. 'Tell Kitty to expect her mistress in a quarter-hour, then take yourself to bed. I'll ensure that Miss Jayne reaches her chamber safely.'

He made his way to the parlour and sat on a chair beside the sofa. His mother was a light sleeper from years of being woken by summonses from patients and, though he moved quietly, the soft scuff of his shoe on the rug caused her eyes to open. She took a moment to acquaint herself with where she was, then pushed herself to a sitting position. 'How late is it?'

'Close to midnight.'

'Have you eaten?'

Elias smiled. 'Very well, thank you, Mama. I've had pickled salmon, beef and mushroom pie, cider syllabub and a goodly amount of brandy.'

'Where?'

'I'll tell you when you've told me what you gave Lord Jeffreys. Robert says he left in a better mood than when he arrived.'

Jayne debated with herself whether discretion towards a patient should always outweigh curiosity. 'Would you be content if I said I gave him advice?'

Elias shook his head. 'Laudanum might have persuaded him to mount a horse and come here in person, but not advice.'

'Perhaps I gave him both,' she said. 'Why are you so interested?'

'I'm wondering what you're hoping to achieve. You're not usually so generous with it. Did you warn him of the cravings it induces?'

'I didn't need to. He said you already had.' She paused. 'He persuaded me he couldn't survive the long journeys and the hard benches of the Western Circuit without an effective palliative and, knowing his condition, I agreed with him. Does that satisfy you?'

'By no means. My best guess is that you want to prolong his good humour until the Assizes conclude and he returns to London.'

'Is that a bad ambition?'

'Not if you're willing to keep supplying him with laudanum. I'd prefer him to be in a high state of euphoria when he argues the case for leniency before His Majesty. He'll not find the confidence to face him otherwise.'

Jayne rested her head against the back of the sofa. 'Did I ever tell you of Richard Theale's experiments with tinted water and bitter almond oil?'

'No.'

'Isaac and I have repeated and proved the experiment many times. If a patient is given a medicine that looks and tastes the same as a treatment he has had before, he experiences the same benefits as were granted by the original remedy.'

'Why?'

'We're not sure. It seems to be a trick of the mind. As long as the patient is convinced the cure will work, the body profits. I gave Lord Jeffreys six vials. Three contain laudanum and three contain coloured water, but he won't know the difference from the appearance or the effect.'

'Why include laudanum at all?'

'To remind his body that the remedy works. Deceptions are more successful when they're mixed with truth. Your father taught us that.'

Elias grinned. 'He was never as devious as you, Mama.'

'Possibly not, but if Lord Jeffreys finds relief from tinted water, I'm happy to supply him with it. He's a good deal sicker than he pretends, my dear. Now, tell me where you enjoyed this meal of salmon, beef and syllabub.'

'Mister Ettrick's house.'

'On your own?'

He shook his head. 'The other guests were Joshua and Emily Hughes. I was persuaded by Miss Althea's household to prove to them that she's not an imbecile.' He took pity on his mother's frown of incomprehension and told her the story. 'Ettrick was so delighted by how the evening went that he plied me with brandy and tobacco in his parlour, which is why I was late coming home.'

'What of Althea?'

'She retired when the Hugheses left.' He smiled at his mother's expression. 'You have nothing to concern yourself about, Mama. Mister Ettrick is as forthright and honest as his daughter, and his view appears to concur with hers: that, apart from her brothers who procure books for her, he will be the only man in her life.'

'Are you looking to change their minds?'

He ignored the question. 'I sent word to Kitty that I would have you in your chamber within a quarter-hour.' He pushed himself to his feet and offered his hand.

'I'll not forgive you if you raise Althea's hopes only to dash them when you grow bored,' Jayne warned, allowing him to pull her upright.

He folded her arm inside his and escorted her to the stairs. 'It won't happen,' he said. 'I've never met a young woman so resistant to my title and charms. Can you manage the steps yourself or do your advancing years require me to assist you up them?'

Jayne withdrew her arm with a laugh. 'You're as infuriating as your father,' she said. 'He always resorted to teasing when

I broached subjects he didn't want to address.' She mounted the stairs alone, pausing at the top to look down at him. 'Will I see you tomorrow?'

Elias shook his head. 'I'll be leaving for Bristol at dawn. Wish me well, Mama.'

'I always do, my dear.'

Bristol was sixty miles north-north-west of Blandford and, rather than resort to a relay of horses in order to do the journey in one day, Elias stopped overnight at a tavern in Warminster, a market town in Wiltshire known for its wool and malt trades. Posing as a soldier on a week's furlough, he engaged the landlord in conversation. He said he had a fancy to explore the town before retiring for the night. Which inn did militiamen favour? The Rose and Crown, he was told. And which inn should he avoid? The Fighting Cock, home to subverters and troublemakers.

Following the landlord's directions, he made his way to the Rose and Crown, where he joined three reserve soldiers in drinking good health to His Majesty and perdition to rebels. He learnt that Warminster men were attached to the Somerset militia, there being no Wiltshire militia. Demands on their time were few. They had been ordered to stand ready to fight at Sedgemoor, and it was a cause for deep regret that their presence hadn't been needed. Taunton men had covered themselves in glory by pursuing Monmouth from the field and capturing him in Dorset.

After an hour, Elias excused himself, pleading an early start the following morning. In an alleyway off a neighbouring street, he reversed his jacket, rubbed dirt on his face and hands, tied his hair into a knot on the nape of his neck and made his way to the lower end of the town.

The Fighting Cock was located close to one of the malt houses, and the air inside was thick with pipe smoke. He took a seat at a table of grim-faced men who viewed him with suspicion until his Dorset brogue, heavily patched jacket and claim to be a farm worker in search of employment began to elicit responses from them. He bemoaned the difficulty of securing a lasting tenure; they bemoaned the poor pay and arduous nature of their work—steeping and raking barley by the ton in order to produce malt. And when all were agreed that they worked for ungrateful masters, Elias steered the conversation towards Monmouth's rebellion.

Had they heard the news from Dorchester that thirteen Dorset men had been executed for high treason and another two hundred and eighty had been condemned to the same fate? He received several nods, and the man next to him muttered that there was one law for the poor and another for the rich. His friends hushed him immediately, casting wary glances at Elias, but Elias shook his head, saying they had nothing to fear from him.

'Your friend speaks the truth. Only the poor face execution.'

Another man spoke. 'We heard the judge offered mercy.'

'You heard wrong. He told the condemned men that the King might consider it, but few believe he will.'

The first man spat on the floor. 'He's a Catholic. He wants all Protestants dead.'

There were more attempts to silence him, but he was too aggrieved to heed them.

'There's no mercy in him. He might spare rebels the knife, but he'll string them up and leave them to hang from their gibbets for months as a lesson to the rest of us.' He turned to Elias. 'Am I right?'

Elias shrugged. 'There's a rumour in Dorchester that he may commute the sentences to transportation as a means to fill his coffers.'

'Slavery's worse than death.'

'But easier to escape. It's a long march from Dorchester to Bristol, and a lot can happen on the way. Me, I'd choose life every time and pray that God smiles more kindly on Protestants than Catholics.'

This was greeted with laughter, and the conversation turned to methods of escape. Each man thought in terms of a single prisoner slipping his shackles, but Elias prompted them to consider an entire column disappearing off the highway. When they said it wasn't possible, he proposed the idea of Dorset militiamen being gulled into handing their charges to Wiltshire men, dressed in the uniform of the Somerset militia.

'The best place to do it would be Yeovil. It stands close to the border between Dorset and Somerset, and columns from Dorchester are bound to pass through it on their way to Bristol.'

'Are Dorset men easily gulled?' the first man asked.

'All men are when they're presented with the right papers. Soldiers claiming to be from the Taunton militia freed three dozen rebels from Dorchester gaol simply by showing an order signed and sealed by the High Sheriff of Somerset.'

'Where did they get it?'

'A good forger can replicate anything for a price.'

'What if the Dorset men have orders to escort the prisoners all the way to Bristol? They'll not hand them over in those circumstances.'

'They will if their High Sheriff sends a messenger after them with an amended order. A document bearing a correct and unbroken seal will always be accepted.'

There was a short silence.

The man opposite Elias stirred. 'What happened to the prisoners who were released from Dorchester gaol?'

'They were marched to a barn where a blacksmith removed their shackles, and were then guided north in groups of three. By the time the deception was discovered, they were spread across several counties, and no one thought it worth the trouble of tracking them.'

Elias's neighbour subjected him to several seconds of close scrutiny. 'Were I a wagering man, I'd say you were behind that escape. You may have the Dorset brogue and calluses on your fingers, friend, but you speak too prettily for a farm labourer. What's your interest in helping rebels?'

'The same as yours,' Elias answered easily. 'I object to a Catholic king taking vengeance on the Protestant poor of the south-west. Monmouth's head should have been enough for him.'

'Your name, friend.'

Elias shook his head. 'Keep calling me "friend". Whatever name I give you will not be mine.'

The man opposite smiled cynically. 'You've got him all worked up to help you. Me and some others, too, maybe. How can we do that if we don't know who you are?'

Elias took note of their empty tankards and called for another jug of ale. 'I'll return in seven days,' he said. 'If you're still of the same mind, we'll talk again. If not, we'll take our leave of each other with no hard feelings.'

'You're very trusting. What's to stop us bringing bailiffs here to arrest you?'

'Nothing,' Elias said good-humouredly. 'But they won't thank you when I fail to appear. A wise man does not enter an establishment like this without knowing who's inside.' He rose to his feet as a servant girl approached with a jug. 'This should cover your evening's ale, gentlemen,' he said, placing a florin on the table. 'Enjoy it with my good wishes.'

⁓

He reached Bristol at noon the next day and made his way to St Augustine's Reach, a large excavated harbour where the River Frome met the River Avon. Ships of all sizes were moored along the quayside, disgorging or taking on cargo, and carters waited in line to deliver goods or carry them away. The scene was one of intense activity, as befitted England's second largest port, but with so many people milling haphazardly across the cobbles, Elias questioned how the harbourmaster could control what was being loaded and unloaded.

A multitude of shops, taverns and warehouses lined the road that ran around the harbour, and all were as busy as the quay. Sailors finding their land legs crowded the pavements in front of the taverns; porters with wheelbarrows were conveying rope, candles, soap, tar and pitch from the chandlers to the ships; and warehouses were taking incoming goods through one door and sending outgoing goods through another. To Elias, the colour, noise and constant movement represented confusion, but he wasn't so naive that he believed confusion to be the reality.

He turned back the way he had come and headed for a stable that he had passed some three streets from the quay. He paid the ostler to keep his horse for twenty-four hours and asked him for directions to the harbourmaster's office. Turn right onto the quay, he was told, walk two hundred yards and look for the red-brick house next to the Anchor Inn. He asked next if the ostler could recommend somewhere clean to lay his head that night. But of course, the ostler told him. His mother's hostelry was the best in Bristol and stood adjacent to the stable.

He unbuckled Elias's saddle pack and handed it to him. 'My family is as honest as the day is long, sir. While you go about your business, you may leave this with my mother without fear of anything going missing.'

Elias hid his scepticism as he hoisted the pack over his shoulder. 'Then I will happily reserve a bed in her hostelry. I'll check on my mare when I return this evening, so don't stint on her oats and blankets.'

The man protested that such a thought would never occur to him, and Elias departed with a feigned nod of appreciation. As he walked to the neighbouring house, he lifted the flap of his pack to retrieve the leather pouch that contained his purse and letters of accreditation and transferred it to a pocket inside his jacket. The letters lent credence to whomever he claimed to be and would make interesting reading for the ostler and his mother if he were foolish enough to give them the chance.

Mistress Dorey—the title displayed above the hostelry's door—was stooped and old, but her eyes were bright. She echoed her son's assurances about honesty as she wrote Elias's name—Jonathan Speedwell—in her book and relieved him of his pack. He told her he would be back by sunset, and asked if he could eat supper in her establishment. But of course, she said in the same glib manner as her son. Her food was the best in Bristol. She would, however, require money in advance. Two shillings and sixpence should suffice for supper, bed and breakfast.

Her beady gaze followed Elias's movements as he withdrew some coins from his waistcoat pocket and selected a half-crown. As he passed it to her, he was amused to see that she was counting the remaining coins in his palm. In places such as this, he secreted his leather pouch beneath his mattress before he went to sleep, but he made a special note to keep a tight guard on all his pockets when he returned that evening. Mistress Dorey might be old and bent but the fingers that took the coin looked remarkably nimble.

He made his way to the Anchor Inn and took a seat at a table near a wide doorway, which gave him a view of the people entering and leaving the harbourmaster's office. After an hour of watching, he was satisfied that he could identify the men in the master's employ. Their uniform was consistent—dark blue britches and jackets—and when not entering the premises alone, they were escorting merchants or seamen with documents.

He abandoned the inn to walk from one end of the quay to the other, pausing every so often to watch cargo being loaded onto a ship. His purpose was twofold: to acquaint himself with the harbourmaster's methods of controlling the importation and exportation of goods, and to memorise faces. The uniformed men numbered in excess of a dozen, but he was as interested in the thirty or so urchins who hung around them in twos and threes, ready to do their bidding. The boys' commonest task was to run to the harbourmaster's office, most often with papers, but at other times with queries because they appeared to have answers when they returned.

With the setting of the sun, the crowds on the quay thinned and the day's work concluded. The carters departed, the warehouses closed their doors and only the taverns remained open. Elias made his way back to the Anchor Inn and mingled at the entrance with sailors whose clear intention was to souse themselves before stumbling back to their ships. He bantered in French with a group from Bordeaux while watching the urchins form a queue outside the harbourmaster's office. After ten minutes, a fat man in a gold-braided naval uniform emerged through the front door and gave each child a half-penny on the promise of more work tomorrow.

Elias excused himself from the Bordeaux sailors and followed fifty yards behind the tallest boy as he headed away from the quay. He had so outgrown himself that the sleeves of his tunic barely reached his elbows or his britches his knees, but his frame was too slender to fill their width. He had been noticeable as the lad most often singled out to run errands, yet his pay had been the same as every other urchin.

Their route ran parallel to the street that Elias had ridden earlier, and he wondered if he was being led back to the stables when the lad turned right into a side street. It seemed not. Within seconds, the boy returned to the main thoroughfare, clutching a small loaf to his chest. Elias glanced into the street as he passed and guessed that the half-penny had been used at a bakery which was still open. Shortly afterwards, the lad disappeared into a narrow alleyway behind a large warehouse. Reluctant to follow too closely, Elias stopped at the corner and listened for footsteps. Not hearing them, he inched sideways and saw a door closing halfway down a row of dilapidated houses.

He waited a few minutes, then trod on soft feet along the passage. Smoke from chimneys and the acrid stench of urine on cobbles assailed his nostrils, and he paused only briefly beside the house where the door had closed. The shutters were so warped that a six-inch gap gave him a glimpse of the interior, and the tableau that presented itself was easy to read. A single guttering candle, an emaciated mother sitting on a stool with a newborn clamped to her breast, three skeletal children lying pale-faced and wide-eyed on straw at her feet, and the slender youngster carefully tearing the inadequate loaf into equal pieces.

Elias had no qualms about using him for his own purposes. A prosperous port like Bristol should be ashamed to have such poverty in its midst.

Following supper that evening, Mistress Dorey showed him to his room. The bed, a large one, was already occupied by a fellow traveller, whose sleep was so deep that the opening of the door and the introduction of candlelight to the chamber didn't wake him. Suspecting collusion between the landlady and her alleged guest, Elias asked what it would cost to have a room to himself. Another half-crown, he was told.

He insisted on seeing the room before he agreed, and Mistress Dorey led him up another flight of stairs to an attic room. She raised her candle high to illuminate the narrow bed, saying it wasn't as comfortable as the other, but Mister Speedwell could be assured of privacy. Elias placed his pack on a chair and released the lower button on his jacket. This allowed him to retrieve the required coin from his waistcoat pocket, but he made a point of reattaching the button immediately.

Mistress Dorey chuckled. 'You're not very trusting of us, are you, sir?'

'I don't trust anyone in large cities, Mistress Dorey. A lad ran into me on the quay earlier and I queried his motives until one of the harbourmaster's men spoke up for him. He called him Alan and said he worked harder than any of the other urchins. It seems he was running an errand, though I question where he found the energy for such a task. He had outgrown his clothes and was little more than skin and bone.'

'That would be Alan Dugdale. He's yet to reach twelve but his mother relies on him.'

'Where's his father?'

'In Taunton prison. He joined the rebellion and was captured at Sedgemoor.' Her mouth turned down in disapproval. 'You were right to be wary of the lad. He has no more regard for the law than his father had.'

'In what way?'

'I caught him stealing bread from my waste bucket only last week.' She placed the candle on a nightstand. 'Snuff this out before you go to sleep and place the chair in front of the door if you fear intruders. Good night to you, Mister Speedwell.'

'And to you, Mistress Dorey.'

⌒

Elias was waiting on the other side of the road when Alan Dugdale turned out of the alleyway shortly after dawn and headed past the warehouse towards the harbour. With the main thoroughfare beginning to fill with people, he was quickly lost to sight, and Elias crossed to walk down the alley. He was alone in doing so and no one appeared to be stirring in the other houses. His light tap on Mistress Dugdale's door was answered by a weak, 'Come in', and he raised the latch.

The scene that greeted him was the same as the previous night—the mother on her stool, her children at her feet—but he was struck by how cold the room was. With no glass in the window, no fire in the hearth and the high wall of the warehouse excluding the sun, there was nothing to warm it.

He remained in the doorway. 'Don't be afraid, Mistress Dugdale,' he said quietly, reluctant to disturb her neighbours and conscious that a man's presence would alarm her. 'I come as a friend to your husband and beg just a few minutes of your time.'

'You know Peter?'

'Not in person, ma'am, but I'm acquainted with many from Dorset who fought alongside him. May I enter and shut the door behind me? My words should be heard only by you.'

She sighed. 'There's nothing I can do to stop you, sir.'

With sunken cheeks and dark rings beneath her eyes, she looked older than she was. In order not to frighten her further, Elias took a single step away from the closed door, then dropped to a squat to address her at her own level.

'I could give you a name to call me by, but it would be false,' he said. 'Will you take on trust that I am here to help as many of Monmouth's followers as I can, including your husband Peter?'

'Do I have a choice in the matter?'

'Yes. Ask me to leave, and I will.'

She assessed him for several seconds. 'What do you wish to say?'

'The Taunton Assizes are due to begin in three weeks' time. Is Peter aware of the punishment he will face if he's found guilty?'

She nodded. 'He's resigned to it.'

'He might do better to make plans for escape.'

'There is no escape.'

'Not yet, perhaps, but things may change when the King understands the impossibility of executing the high numbers who still await sentence. Rumour has it that His Majesty is considering commuting death to transportation.'

'Rumours are rarely true.'

Elias shook his head. 'Unless the facts suggest they might be. In Dorchester, the Chief Justice declined to set dates for the executions. If he continues with that policy, a substitute punishment will have to be found.'

'And you expect transportation to be the preferred substitute?'

'I do. Selling men into slavery is highly profitable.'

Her body might be frail, but her intelligence was strong. 'Which is why you're here . . . because Bristol trades in slaves?'

Elias nodded. 'This is where I believe your husband and his fellow rebels will embark.'

'And you hope to help them escape?'

'Yes.'

A small laugh fluttered from her mouth. 'But why tell me, sir? I can barely stand. What in the name of heaven do you think I can possibly do?'

'Permit me to ask your son for assistance, ma'am.'

Her eyes flared in alarm. 'No! His father is lost to us. We cannot lose Alan as well. He is all that stands between us and starvation.'

Elias took a cloth bag from his jacket pocket and laid it on the floor in front of him. 'This contains five shillings in the form of sixty pennies. I give it to you without condition, although I urge you to be wise in how and where you spend it. A sudden increase in wealth will attract attention from your neighbours and thieves.' He touched the bag with his forefinger. 'To avoid raising suspicion, Alan should continue to use his half-penny to buy bread from the baker in the next street. Everything else should be purchased from retailers as far away from the docks as he can manage.'

Tears of despair welled in her eyes. 'You'll take Alan from me if I accept.'

Elias shook his head again. 'I would have left you the money even if you had refused to speak with me. This also.' He removed a large muslin-wrapped package from his other pocket and laid it on the cloth purse, loosening the ties to display a round cheese which he had purchased from Mistress Dorey. 'You and your children need to eat if you're to regain your strength.'

She dashed the tears away with the back of her hand. 'If you're counting on Alan asking where it came from, sir, I'll lie and say a kind lady brought it.'

Elias smiled. 'You may say whatever you like, ma'am,' he answered, pushing himself to his feet and reaching for the latch. 'I'll take my leave before your neighbours become aware of my presence. A gentleman of my height isn't often mistaken for a lady . . . kind or otherwise.'

He was rewarded with a glimmer of amusement in the sad eyes. 'And if I decide to tell the truth?'

'I'll be on the quay tomorrow. Alan will recognise me from your description of my appearance. Farewell, Mistress Dugdale.'

A letter from Lady Harrier to Miss Althea Ettrick at
Holt Lodge:

Dear Althea,

*I am in need of your help. I have been sent a treatise on
phthisis by a Swiss doctor who is exploring new treatments
for the disease. However, since it is written in German, I am
unable to decipher it. Might you be able to visit me one day
this week in order to translate it? You will do my consumptive
patients a great kindness if you consent.*

*Please tell your father that you will not require a
chaperone if Elizabeth is too busy to accompany you.
Granville is away from home and I will be your only
company.*

With kind regards,
Jayne

TWENTY-TWO

November 1685 (eight weeks later)

ANDREW HENDRY LOOKED UP AS a shadow fell across his table. He was sitting in the window of a tavern on the Bath Road and, as ever, would not have recognised Lord Granville if he hadn't been expecting him. This was their seventh meeting in as many weeks, always in different establishments where neither was known. Today, Lord Granville had the look of a carter with greying hair and grizzled beard. He ducked his head in deference to the merchant's superior class.

'I be told you have need of a carrier, zurr.'

Hendry motioned to the seat opposite him and beckoned to a maid to bring ale. 'I do,' he agreed, as the girl brought a jug and a second tankard. 'What is your name and hourly rate?'

Elias seated himself. 'Jeremiah Hobbs, zurr. It be two shillings for deliveries in Bristol and four for journeys outside.'

Hendry waited for the maid to leave. 'You're overcharging,' he muttered. 'I can get a carter for half that price in Lyme.'

'Lyme doesn't deal in slaves,' Elias responded, also in a low voice. 'Here they trade in flesh from Africa and everyone benefits, including carters. It's a wretched business. The city's awash with money earned from human misery.'

'Have you seen these Africans?'

Elias shook his head. 'They're kept chained in holds until they reach the Americas. My youngster was paid to empty buckets of water through a hatch on one of the ships, and his shock was so great he couldn't speak for three hours.'

'What did he see?'

'People chained together like animals. His job was to cool them but they caught the water in cupped palms, drank it and then held out their hands for more. Did you know such a trade existed?'

'Only through rumour.' Hendry shook his head at Elias's expression. 'We can't save the world. Content yourself with Englishmen and harden your heart to the plight of foreigners. I've received word that the *Santa Maria* was sighted off the fishing port of Padstow yesterday, so she should be entering the Bristol Channel late this night or tomorrow morning. Are you ready for her?'

Elias nodded. 'What of the *Hopewell*?'

'She's been at anchor in Swansea Bay since Saturday. John Prowse estimates twelve hours sailing time to Bristol and suggests I alert him when the *Santa Maria* departs. It will take a day for the message to reach him, by which time the *Santa Maria* should have cleared the Channel. He's anxious not to be seen by Captain Jackson. He has some acquaintance with the man and says he'll be suspicious about his diversion to Plymouth if he passes a vessel large enough to carry two hundred slaves.'

Out of the corner of his eye, Elias kept a continuous watch on their neighbours at the next table, but the three men appeared as keen as he to keep their conversation unheard, bending their heads close and speaking in undertones.

'We'll have ten days from the time of the *Santa Maria*'s departure to conduct our business,' he muttered. 'Three for Jackson to sail to Plymouth and seven while he waits at anchor for his cargo. My Devon counterpart is confident he can contain him for a week—I've supplied him with the necessary letters, explaining the delay—but no longer.'

'Prowse must depart well before that if he's to escape detection.'

'Agreed, and the timing will be tight. Dorset dispatched her prisoners from Dorchester two days ago, and Somerset's prisoners left Taunton yesterday. At their present rate, both columns have another four days of marching ahead of them. I'll hand Jackson his amended orders at dawn on the day after tomorrow. That should allow Prowse to arrive at his anchorage at least twenty-four hours before the cargo arrives.'

'You're cutting it too fine,' Hendry warned. 'Jackson could reach Plymouth before Prowse even begins loading.'

'I have faith in my Devon counterpart.'

'Who is he?'

'The son of Colonel John Metcalfe, my father's second-in-command. Do you remember him?'

'Very well. He was a fine man. I fought beside him at Lyme when he was still a major. I heard he died some five years since.'

Elias nodded. 'Sadly so, but his son is cut from the same cloth. My parents stood sponsor for him at his christening, and the bond between him and my family is strong. He'll not let us down.'

'What's his connection with Plymouth?'

The same as yours and mine with Bristol, my friend. *None.* When our tasks are done, it will be as if we never existed.'

For all their sakes, Hendry hoped he was right. It needed but one element of this fragile enterprise to fail, and their heads would roll. Lord Granville had told him at their last meeting that King James had granted this batch of prisoners to his wife, and the name of the ship that her private secretary had commissioned to carry them was the *Santa Maria*. Granville wouldn't say how he came by the information—he played his cards close to his chest and guarded other people's secrets as diligently as his father had done—but Hendry had been more shaken than he cared to admit by the revelation. It was one thing to defraud a courtier, quite another to defraud the Queen.

'Are your plans for protecting Prowse in hand?' he muttered. 'We'll all be unmasked if he's put to the question. Torturers will use the rack and hot irons to break him.'

His fear was so palpable that Elias answered with more confidence than he felt. He, too, worried about the fragility of their enterprise. 'My lad will replace Prowse's signed manifest with one supplied by me, which he'll take to the harbourmaster. Assuming it's accepted, the harbourmaster's ledger will state that the cargo was received by the *Santa Maria*, and the manifest will bear my representation of Captain Jackson's signature.'

'What about the deliverers' manifests? Will they accord?'

Elias nodded again. 'I've ridden hard between Bristol, Dorchester and Taunton these last three days.'

'Do you have the originals with you?'

'They're in my cart. We'll have fewer witnesses if I hand them to you there. Both bear Captain Jackson's signature in the same hand as the ship's manifesto. Providing Prowse can switch them successfully, the militia commanders will have receipted orders conforming to the manifest in the harbourmaster's possession.'

'My messenger will take them with him to Swansea.'

Elias refrained from urging him to impress upon Prowse the importance of the task. Both men knew as well as he that if the switch wasn't made, two High Sheriffs would be presented with fraudulent orders, naming the *Hopewell* as the receiving ship. 'Excellent,' he said. 'I wouldn't want William Lewis reading my forgery.'

Hendry took a nervous gulp of ale. 'There's a lot can go wrong.'

'Indeed, so I suggest you leave for Dorchester immediately after dispatching your messenger. My lad and I will handle the rest.'

'Can he be trusted?'

'I believe so.'

'What if the harbourmaster decides to oversee the docking?'

A faint smile played across Elias's lips. 'It will be a first. He's too lazy to leave his office.'

'What if your imposture as one of his officers is challenged?'

'I'll be boarding the skiff away from the harbour. Who's to see me?'

'Captain Jackson.'

Another faint smile. 'I'll try not to raise his suspicions.'

'You mustn't underestimate him, my lord,' Hendry cautioned, his nervousness betraying itself in his accidental use of Elias's title. 'Prowse tells me he's as cunning as a fox.'

Elias glanced towards the men at the next table, but they were still deep in conversation. 'I don't doubt it, my friend,' he murmured. 'He's made a small fortune through trade with the

Americas. His preferred cargo is African slaves. He rations their water and feeds them pig swill to increase his profits and will do the same with Englishmen unless we prevent him.'

From a distance, Captain Jackson lived up to expectation. Tall in stature, he stood at the bow of his ship, eyes narrowed against the rising sun, watching the approaching skiff. He was bearded and ruddy of face, and held a cat-o'-nine-tails in his hand, which he tapped rhythmically against his other palm. Two of his crew hovered at his side, their fear of him obvious, since his only discernible expression was hostility.

The *Santa Maria* had been riding at anchor in the estuary since the previous morning and, despite having observed her for several hours from the southern bank, this was the first time Elias had seen the captain. He seemed intent on intimidating his visitor, and Elias wondered if this was his usual welcome for skiffs flying the flag of the harbourmaster.

Terror was certainly being felt by the owner of the skiff. A fisherman by trade, he delivered a stream of curses under his breath as he luffed his sail to slow his vessel. He was father to a rebel in the column coming from Taunton, and his willingness to help his son was evaporating rapidly in the face of an angry giant with a whip.

Elias rose to his feet as the skiff turned broadside to the *Santa Maria* and nudged against her side. With a reassuring nod to the fisherman, he seized a hanging line and hauled himself up and over the gunnel, grasping hold of the mast's shrouds to pull himself upright as he stepped onto the deck. Having loosened his harbour officer's uniform to make the climb, he rebuttoned it neatly before ducking his head to the captain.

'Your servant, sir,' he said in a soft Bristol accent. 'Do I have your permission to come aboard?'

Unexpectedly, Jackson laughed. 'Where did you learn to scale a rope so easily?'

'In His Majesty's navy, sir. I served on the *Westergate* until she foundered in 1668. Thereafter, I served ten years on the *Nightingale* before being released to work under the harbourmaster here.'

'Would you consider employment with me? You'd be worth three of the useless crew I have now.'

Elias examined the two sailors at his side. 'Not if you're as free with your cat-o'-nine-tails as your men's knocking knees suggest, sir.'

Another bark of laughter. 'I pay them well. Can you say the same of Bristol's port authorities?'

A hint of a smile lifted Elias's mouth. 'No, but a comfortable berth is better than a wretched one. Your ship stinks, sir. We smelt the reek of human excrement from two hundred yards away.'

Jackson grinned, as if straight speaking appealed to him. 'You get used to it. My crew finds the stench preferable to cleaning the holds by hand.'

'You'd not find me any more willing, sir. Have you considered offering buckets to your human cargoes?'

Jackson launched a globule of spittle onto the deck at his feet. 'They're savages. If you show them kindness, they claw at your eyes.' He thwacked the whip against his palm. 'Are the prisoners close? I expected two or three days of rest before being summoned to load them.'

Elias drew a sealed letter from his jacket and walked forward. 'I don't know, sir. My only instruction was to give you this. I shall take your reply back with me.'

Close to, they were of a height, although Jackson's bulk gave him dominance over Elias's slenderer build. The captain slung the whip across his shoulder, took the letter and snapped the seal without looking at it. 'Goddamn it!' he snarled as he read the contents. 'I'm minded to tell His Majesty to go hang himself.' He screwed the paper into a ball. 'How's that for a reply?'

'I've heard worse,' said Elias.

Jackson raked the fingers of his free hand through his beard. 'This letter tells me that two hundred men have been abducted off the highways leading to Bristol in the last week. Is that true?'

Elias shrugged. 'We've heard rumours, sir, but I can't vouch for two hundred. We know that a hundred went missing outside Yeovil. The ship commissioned to transport them travelled light as a result, and her captain wasn't happy. He hoped to make more profit from the journey.'

'Which captain?'

'Harold Greenwood of the *Penny Rose*, sir. He departed five days ago with only half his expected cargo, and his invectives were fruitier than yours.'

A full-throated guffaw issued from Jackson's mouth. 'I know him. His language is rancid.' He tossed the ball of paper to Elias. 'Read it. His Majesty deems it safer to send columns south. Am I any more likely to receive a full cargo if I follow this lickspittle's order to move the *Santa Maria* to Plymouth?'

Elias made a play of smoothing out the page and deciphering the crumpled words. 'The gentleman is writing on behalf of

Her Majesty, the Queen, sir. The slaves, and the money earned from their sale, have been granted to her.'

'*His* Majesty, *Her* Majesty. Where's the difference? Wives obey their husbands.'

'Not always, sir. My mother would advise you to trust the Queen's honesty over the King's.'

'Why?'

'Men squander money. Women safeguard it. Were my mother promised enrichment through the sale of goods, she would be as diligent as Her Majesty in ensuring the pledge was honoured.'

'What's her name?'

'Sarah Goodheart. Her earnings as a laundress kept my sisters and me from starvation.'

'What of your father?'

Elias answered unemotionally. 'Dead of drink twenty years since. He's not missed.' He returned the letter to the captain. 'A written reply would be more acceptable than a spoken one, sir. Without evidence that I delivered Her Majesty's letter, my own truthfulness may be questioned.'

Jackson gave a grunt of amusement. 'I doubt that, my friend. You have an honest face.' He nodded towards the cockpit. 'I keep my quill and ink in there. If you lend me your back, I'll oblige Her Majesty with a response.'

━

When the *Santa Maria* was lost to sight by a bend in the river, the fisherman lowered the harbourmaster's flag while Elias stripped off his uniform jacket and bundled it with the flag into a knapsack. He pulled the tails of his shirt free of his britches, tied his hair in a knot and began running a fishing net between his hands.

Like many before him, the fisherman wondered who this man was. The only name he knew him by was 'friend', yet he had seen him in three different guises—a merchant in a tavern, a harbour officer and, now, a humble worker on a skiff. 'Did you convince the captain?' he asked.

'We won't know until he weighs anchor, but he scrawled a message beneath the Queen's seal to say he expected to be in Plymouth before the week is out.'

'I thought he'd take his whip to you.'

'The opposite. He was irritatingly pleasant.'

'Why irritatingly?'

Elias stooped to loosen a tangle in the net. 'My conscience troubles me less when I create problems for men I dislike.'

The fisherman gave a snort of contempt. 'What's to like? You said yourself he'd treat the prisoners badly if the stink from his ship was any guide.'

'Indeed. People can be very contradictory.'

There was a short silence while the fisherman considered the contradictory nature of his passenger. 'You needn't concern yourself over Captain Jackson. He'll tell his story and his crew will back him up. His only problem will be loss of revenue from his promised cargo.'

'Not entirely,' Elias countered mildly. 'If all goes as planned, the harbourmaster's records will show that the prisoners were loaded onto the *Santa Maria*, and my jovial dupe will curse the day he told me I had an honest face.' He nodded ahead towards a wide dip on the southern side of the river where cattle had trampled a stretch of the bank in search of water. 'That would be a good place to drop me off. I can cut across the fields to watch Captain Jackson's departure.'

'Will we meet in the tavern tonight?'

Elias shook his head. 'Two nights' time,' he said, reaching for the knapsack as the skiff altered course. 'By then, the *Hopewell* should have arrived and your son will be a day away from freedom.' He touched his forehead in salute. 'He and his comrades have a lot to thank you for, my friend. As do I.'

The fisherman luffed again and watched Elias leap for the dip in the bank. He was undecided whether to admire the stranger or distrust him. Honest of face he might be, but his talent for deception was remarkable. Only a man with ice in his veins could have scaled the *Santa Maria*'s rope with as little fear as this one had shown.

Alan Dugdale felt a similar confusion every time he spoke with Elias. To date, he had performed every task set him, but the two this morning were the most perilous. He had accomplished the first: running to the harbourmaster with news that the prisoners to be loaded onto the *Santa Maria* had arrived, relaying the master's order to summon the *Santa Maria* to berth number fifteen to Elias, then waiting until Elias returned and handed him a counterfeit order instructing a harbour officer of his choosing to oversee the loading of the prisoners onto the *Hopewell*.

Alan had chosen the officer who used him the most often, but his heart had been in his mouth from beginning to end of the task. Now, he was waiting to perform the second: to be first in line to receive the manifest signed by the captain of the *Hopewell*, and replace it with the one that Elias had given him. Fear of discovery was his constant companion, and his mother's warnings kept ringing in his ears. Do not be lured by false promises into doing something foolish, she had told him.

'Keep heart,' Elias murmured in his ear as the *Hopewell* dropped her anchor some fifty yards from the quay. 'You have my word that your father is amongst the prisoners. You will see him pass when the columns are loaded but he has been told to ignore you. You must do the same. To show recognition will endanger you both.'

'You promised he wouldn't be taken by the boat.'

'Nor will he. You must trust me on this, Alan.'

The boy stared at him in anguish. He longed to trust him—he was the kindest and most generous person Alan had ever met—but he was a stranger without a name. Yesterday, he had been a merchant, three hours ago a harbour officer, and now he had charge of a donkey cart laden with sacks of flour. His excuse for every request he made of Alan was that it would help his father, but he never explained why, saying the less Alan knew the safer he and his father would be.

They stood in a queue of carters, some waiting to accept goods, others with goods to deliver, and the harbour urchins milled around them. Each lad was looking to be tipped a farthing for matching a wagon to a berth number or a ship's name, though carters, being notoriously mean, rarely rewarded them.

'My mother says I shouldn't trust you, sir. She's frightened of losing me.'

Elias watched a tender row out to the now-stationary *Hopewell* to receive her mooring ropes. 'She'll not lose any of her family as long as you keep faith with me, Alan.'

'But I don't know who you are.'

Elias stooped to look into the boy's eyes. 'You will soon,' he said. 'For now, you must allow me to help all the prisoners. Do you have the document?'

Alan nodded. 'Inside my tunic.'

'Then be first in line and look for your father in the column. You can decide whether to switch the pages when you see him. Is that acceptable to you?'

'Yes.'

Elias nodded to the tender which was on its return journey, hauling the mooring ropes behind it. 'You need to move now. There will be no saving anyone if you miss your place at the front.'

He watched the lad run towards the quay, then mounted his cart and waited patiently for the *Hopewell* to be winched against the quay and planks run out from her side. After thirty minutes of intense activity, Captain John Prowse left his ship and presented his manifest to the harbour officer who had overseen the docking. The officer beckoned the subalterns in charge of the prison columns to approach. Each presented his orders and saluted smartly when the manifests agreed and the officer instructed them to begin loading their human cargo.

Alan could barely contain his shock when he saw his father in the line of prisoners. Shackled to the men in front and behind him, his thinness was in stark contrast to their broader frames and, but for the close support of their bodies against his to keep him upright, he would have fallen. If he recognised his son, he gave no sign of it and was quickly lost to Alan's sight when he reached the deck.

People crowding the quay hurled insults at the prisoners, calling them traitorous scum, and Alan felt rage at their cruelty grow inside him. Even so, he raised his voice along with the other urchins and shouted slurs himself, recognising that to do otherwise would single him out. He needed no better lesson that lies and pretence could be used in a good cause.

The strongest memory he had of that morning was the kindness of the two prisoners who had supported his father. He did not know their names, any more than he knew Elias's, but all three were at the forefront of his thoughts as he ran to the harbourmaster's office with the false manifest. Not one of his father's former friends or neighbours had come to his aid . . . but strangers had.

John Prowse had stocked his ship with what he needed in London to avoid urchins running along the line of carters and shouting 'Hopewell' and her berth number for everyone to hear. The docking officer might recall the name from the manifests, but without anyone else to vouch for it, the harbourmaster's record citing the receiving vessel as the *Santa Maria* would stand. With twenty or more vessels a day being loaded with cargo, and no questions about a particular cargo likely to be raised in under a week, one out of one hundred and forty ships could easily be misremembered.

As the only carter bearing goods for the *Hopewell*, Elias steered his wagon out of the queue when the last of the prisoners had disappeared into the hold. By then, John Prowse and the subalterns were satisfied that the full cargo had been loaded and, by dint of summoning a crew member to bring him his quill and ink and then using the harbour officer's back to sign the three manifests, Prowse substituted the subalterns' pages with those handed to him by Hendry's messenger. The exchange was so neatly done that only Elias noticed.

Prowse beckoned the subalterns forward. 'Who's from Taunton?' he asked.

'I am, sir.'

'This is yours,' he said, folding the paper so that the broken edges of Somerset's seal came together before handing it to him. 'And this yours,' he told the second subaltern as he did the same with William Lewis's seal. 'You've performed your duties well. My compliments to you both.'

'Thank you, sir,' they answered in unison, tucking the documents inside their jackets.

'Which tavern would you recommend for these worthy fellows and their men, sir?' Prowse asked the harbour officer as he handed him his signed manifest.

The harbour officer snapped his fingers at the front lad in the line of urchins and passed the manifest to Alan without reading it. 'The Rising Sun, sir. They serve good English ale and attract fewer foreign sailors. You'll find it down there, gentlemen.' He nodded towards a side street, then turned to Elias, who had dismounted from his cart. 'Yes?'

'I were told to bring flour to this ship, zurr.'

'Do you have your order?'

Elias jerked his chin towards a man hurrying down the gang-plank. 'He came hisself to make the request. There's nowt in writing.'

Captain Prowse followed his gaze. 'That's my cook,' he said. 'We were cheated out of some dried goods in London, and he's been complaining to me ever since. I told him to see what he could get here.'

'Make haste then,' said the harbour officer. 'You need to vacate this berth within the hour.'

Prowse called to his boatswain. 'Send men to unload this cart. And *you*, check each sack as it comes aboard,' he told his cook. 'I don't want you grumbling afterwards that there are more weevils than grain in them.' He turned to Elias. 'You'll be paid when he tells me your produce is pure. Good day to you.'

He was shorter than Captain Jackson, but no less impressive, and Elias was confident that Hendry had chosen well as he pulled twelve sacks from the cart and handed them to the sailors who came to collect them. Elias was obliged to kick his heels for a quarter-hour before two were returned to him as being unfit. With a muttered growl, he pushed his hand into the slits the cook had made in the hessian and withdrew a fistful of flour from each. The harbour officer laughed when he saw more desiccated black beetles than flour on Elias's palm.

'That'll learn you,' he said.

'It weren't me that filled 'em,' Elias snarled, letting the sacks collapse back onto the cart bed and staring angrily at the two sailors who had placed them there. 'You owe me for ten good 'uns.'

One of the men counted five florins into his palm. 'That's all the captain says they're worth.'

'He's a damned thief.'

'Do you want to repeat that to his face?'

Elias spat on the ground and heaved himself up to the driving seat. 'Just tell him I said it,' he grunted, slapping the reins against his donkeys' rumps. 'We'll not do business with him again.'

'Nor he with you,' the sailor shouted as the cart headed away from the ship.

Elias drove down a narrow lane to a small stone barn some two miles outside Bristol on the Bath Road. It had been his and the donkeys' home for several weeks, and they snorted when they recognised it. He jumped to the ground to raise the bar on the double doors, then stood aside as the donkeys moved forward and allowed him to close the doors behind them.

Leaving them to stand in harness, he lowered the backboard on the cart and pulled the left-hand sack towards him, untying the cord at the mouth and peeling the hessian off the skeletal figure inside. He felt for a pulse in one of the emaciated wrists, then lifted Peter Dugdale in his arms and carried him to a makeshift bed in a corner of the barn. Peter's face was smeared with traces of flour that had caught in the hessian when the *Hopewell*'s cook had emptied the sack, and Elias squeezed out a cloth in a bowl of water and wiped it clean. The cool touch of the fabric caused the man's eyes to open, and he stared at Elias in bewilderment.

'Who are you?' he whispered.

'A friend of your son's,' said Elias, filling a beaker from a flagon of water and holding it to Dugdale's lips. 'You should be proud of him, Peter. He's worked hard these last few months to keep his mother and sisters alive.'

'Where are they?'

'Close. First, you must eat.' Elias reached for a knapsack at the side of the bed. 'It's a miracle you managed the march from Taunton.'

Tears coursed down Peter's sunken cheeks 'Two men I barely knew supported me. What has become of them? They were more deserving of your help than I am.'

'I doubt your son would agree with you,' Elias said with a smile as he removed a loaf and some soft cheese from the pack. 'He's a brave lad, Peter. You and your fellow prisoners owe him your lives and your freedom.'

A letter dispatched from Plymouth on 22 November to Mister
Jonathan Speedwell at a poste restante address in Bristol:

Dear friend,

*My work is done. I depart Plymouth within the hour and
will drop this letter at a post on the outskirts of town. Should
you wish to contact me, you will find me at my usual address.*

*My dealings with your customer ended this morning when
he became enraged at my inability to provide him with the
goods he wants. We negotiated on amicable terms for seven
days, but he now suspects me of acting in bad faith. I have
therefore decided to cut my losses and leave.*

*You would be wise to do the same. His anger was
impressive. Cover your tracks well. He accused me of
conspiring with a Bristol harbour officer to defraud him.
Hoping your own business has been successful.*

Your brother in God

A reply sent by Elias to Matthew Metcalfe on 25 November
to an address in Lyme Regis from a post on the
Bristol–Yeovil highway:

Dear friend,

*Your assistance has been invaluable. Despite his jovi-
ality, I never doubted my customer's capacity for anger.
Fortunately, my other business proceeded without mishap,
although the ill health of one of the participants kept me
longer than I wished.*

Your letter was a reminder of the passage of time. I am now on the road and, while my travel is necessarily slow, I am confident that the journey can be accomplished safely.

Give my regards to your family, and visit us soon. My earnest wish is to thank you in person.

Your brother in God

TWENTY-THREE

30 November 1685

LADY HARRIER RAISED HER HEAD as wheels crunched on the forecourt. She was reading a brief history of Geronimo Fabrici, a sixteenth-century professor of anatomy in Italy, which Althea had translated for her and delivered by hand. They sat on either side of the fireplace in the parlour, and Althea's discomfort at the thought of being forced to meet strangers was obvious. She had conquered her fear of leaving her father's house when she knew what awaited her, but her dread of the unforeseen remained strong.

Certain that the visitor was a patient, Jayne rose to her feet and walked to the west-facing window. She couldn't contain her surprise. 'Good lord! Well, now I've seen everything.'

'Who is it?'

'Elias, dressed like a vagabond and driving a cart pulled by donkeys. It appears to be full of hay. What on earth would possess him to present himself in such a state?'

The question would have been appropriate to a daughter or a close friend, but Althea, being neither, was unsure how to respond. A daughter would say her brother had got himself into hot water and had needed an escape; a close friend would advise Lady Harrier to wait for her son's explanation. But what would a patient say?

'I'm sure he has a good reason,' she murmured.

'Without doubt, but he doesn't usually bring his masquerades to the front door.' Jayne beckoned Althea to join her. 'See for yourself. He'll be the subject of gossip in the hospital.'

Althea suspected another ploy to encourage her to stand, but she was too curious to refuse. At Lady Harrier's invitation, she had been visiting Winterborne Houghton once a week for the purpose of finding the courage to walk, and Milady's ruses to draw her from her chair—usually posed in the form of a challenge—were numerous and effective. After nigh on three months of relentless exercise, particularly being made to stand on her good leg against a wall for an hour at a time, bending her knee and straightening it again, she could rise from her chair unaided and maintain her balance for as long as was needed.

She was also adept at using her hands to propel Lord Granville's chair, and had drawn the design on paper in the hope of finding a joiner in Blandford to replicate it. As yet, this had proved unsuccessful, but part of her enjoyment in coming to Winterborne Houghton was to spin at speed down the length of the uncluttered salon. Now, she drew alongside Jayne, pushing herself upright to survey the sight of Lord Granville, tousle-haired, bearded and in ragged clothes, handing his reins to a groom and sliding wearily to the ground.

'He makes a convincing carter,' she said. 'How far do you think he's travelled?'

'Lord only knows. I haven't seen him since he told me in September that he was going to Bristol.'

This was the explanation for why Althea hadn't encountered him on her visits, which had arisen from Lady Harrier's constant requests for help in translating documents. Occasionally, Althea had wondered if these, too, were a ruse, but if they were it was a ruse she enjoyed. She was never sure whether to be relieved or disappointed by Elias's absence, and had resisted asking after him for fear Lady Harrier would misconstrue her reasons. She watched him walk to the rear of the cart and unhook the backboard.

'He seems to have passengers,' she said. 'The hay is heaving.'

Together, they watched him lift three little girls to the ground, clap a lad on the shoulder as he slid off the cart and then offer his hand to a woman who was clasping a baby to her chest. She took it gratefully, lowering herself with as much dignity as she could muster. Lastly, he scooped an emaciated man into his arms and led the family towards the entrance, calling to the grooms to treat his donkeys as considerately as they treated his horses.

'He's brought me a patient,' Jayne said briskly. 'You'll have to come with me, my dear. Shall I push you or will you propel yourself?'

Althea lowered herself to the chair and moved it backwards, her face expressing alarm. 'What are you expecting me to do?'

'Look after the mother and children while Elias and I take the father to the hospital. They'll be cold from the journey, so escort them in here and allow them to sit beside the fire. Tell Robert to bring cordial and sweetmeats.'

Althea wanted to protest that she wasn't qualified for such a task. She knew nothing about children or nursing mothers, and her palsied leg and wheeled chair were bound to frighten them. But Lady Harrier was already heading for the door, and Althea, cursing the sense of obligation she felt towards her, followed. In truth, she was just as nervous about meeting Elias, since he was even more likely than his mother to assume that he was her reason for being there.

She reached the hall as he and the family were entering. Lady Harrier greeted them with her usual kindness, then beckoned Althea forward to take charge of the woman and the children. Elias, seemingly unsurprised by her presence, smiled at Althea as he accompanied his mother down the hospital corridor, cradling his frail burden in his arms.

At a loss for what to do, Althea turned pleading eyes on Robert, who was standing to one side. He stepped forward immediately.

'Did Milady express a preference for where you should take your guests, Miss Althea?'

'The parlour,' she managed. 'She said they'd be cold from the journey and would need cordial and sweetmeats.'

Robert turned to the woman with a respectful bow. 'May I have your name, ma'am, so that I can acquaint you properly with Miss Althea?'

The woman looked helplessly at her son.

'We are the Smiths,' Alan said carefully. 'My parents are John and Mary Smith, I am James Smith, and my sisters are'—he thought hard—'Rose, Violet and Daisy.'

'And the baby?' Robert asked.

Further thought. 'Lily.'

'Then allow me to introduce you to Miss Althea, who is a close friend to both Lady Harrier and the Duke of Granville. Miss Althea, may I present Mistress Mary Smith and her children, James, Rose, Violet, Daisy and Lily. While you escort them to the parlour, I shall go in search of refreshments.'

His mischievous wink as he recited the clearly invented names suggested the same friendly support for Althea that Adam always gave her. She was also absurdly moved to have him describe her as a close friend to his master and mistress.

She managed a smile for the visitors. 'Will you follow me, Mistress Smith? The parlour is comfortable and pleasantly warm.'

The woman stared at her anxiously then whispered something to her son. 'Mama wants to know who the Duke of Granville and Lady Harrier are,' the boy said.

Althea was taken aback. 'The gentleman who brought you here is Lord Granville, and the matriarch who greeted you is his mother, Lady Harrier.'

'Do they live here?'

'Yes. Lord Granville's estate is Winterborne Houghton and this is his home.'

The boy stared in awe at the vaulted ceiling. 'We call him Mister Friend, and he never said nothing about bringing us to a place like this . . . just somewhere safe.'

Another urgent whisper from the woman.

'Mama says this is too fine for us,' the boy told Althea. 'We're dirty from hiding in the barn and cart for ten days and will likely shed hay on the floor.'

Althea couldn't disagree—they truly were filthy—but what to do? She was as much a stranger to this house as they were, being acquainted only with the salon and parlour, and she had no idea where else to take them. 'We'll rid you of the hay outside,' she said with sudden decision, giving her wheels a strong push and spinning the chair towards the entrance. 'The rest we can deal with once you're warm and fed.'

The boy danced beside her. 'Can't you walk?'

Althea had never been asked that question so directly before and answered honestly. 'I was born with a palsied foot. It makes walking difficult.'

He gestured towards the baby. 'Hannah has palsy. Mama says it's because she had too little to eat when she was nursing her. Was it the same for you?'

Althea's willingness to satisfy another's curiosity was very limited. 'You said the baby's name was Lily.'

'It is. I get mixed up sometimes.'

She drew to a halt on the wide front step and turned to his mother. 'I can't go further without someone to lower my chair to the forecourt, Mistress Smith. Are you able to brush the hay from your children's clothes yourself?'

The woman took a trembling breath. 'Not with the babe in my arms, ma'am. I'll need both hands to clean them properly.'

'Can your son hold the baby?'

'Not easily, ma'am. If you permit it, she'll be safer in your lap. Her shawl is clean. Mister Friend'—she corrected herself—'Lord Granville purchased a new one for her a week ago and insisted on wrapping her in it himself.'

Althea couldn't recall ever seeing a baby before, and knew for a certainty that she'd never touched one. 'Did he hold her?'

'Yes, ma'am, and has done so many times. He's a most considerate person and relieved me whenever I became weary.' A shy smile lifted the woman's mouth. 'I believe you're the reason he took to the little one, ma'am. He said he had a friend with palsy.'

In any other circumstance, Althea would have dismissed the remark as duplicitous flattery, designed to win compliance, but she doubted Mistress Smith was so calculating. With an inward sigh, she tapped her lap. 'You'll have to show me what to do. I'm not as accomplished as Lord Granville in the matter of babies.'

The woman settled the swaddled infant inside the crook of Althea's left elbow, easing her forearm across the child's chest. 'Her back is weak, but she'll not trouble you if she's in a tight embrace with her head supported against your shoulder.'

Althea brought her other arm around to make the embrace firmer. 'What age is she?'

'One year and three months, ma'am, but always taken for a newborn. I thought it was my lack of milk that was stunting her growth until I noticed that she can only clasp my finger in her right fist. She has no strength on her left side. A midwife told me in June that she has palsy and that I should let her die.'

'But you couldn't?'

'No.'

With that, Mistress Smith took her other children down the steps to the forecourt and removed their top garments in order to shake off the hay and dust. Each was as thin as the next, and Althea didn't doubt that their mother would be the same had modesty not demanded that she slap and brush her kirtle rather than remove it. It was a humbling glimpse of genuine suffering, and Althea made a silent pledge never to complain about her own situation again.

When Elias came to the parlour some two hours later, Althea turned the chair one-handed to face him, the swaddled infant asleep inside her arm. The boy, wearing a tunic and britches which had once belonged to Robert, hovered at her side. Behind them, the mother, draped in a woollen shawl supplied by Kitty, sat on a cushion by the hearth with her other three daughters, wrapped in blankets, sleeping beside her.

They were all rosy-cheeked from the heat of the fire, including Althea, and she felt she should explain why. 'Your mother told me to keep them warm,' she said, 'so I asked Robert for more logs.'

'Splendid,' said Elias, moving into the room, bringing with him the odour of sweat and donkey. He held out his hands to the flames. 'Your husband has revived and is taking broth and water, ma'am,' he told Mistress Smith. 'Lady Harrier says you'll be able to speak with him soon.'

A smile lit her tired eyes. 'Thank you, sir.'

The boy plucked timidly at Althea's sleeve, and she gave him a small nod. 'James wonders if Lady Harrier knows what caused his father to lose consciousness, sir. He tells me it happened very suddenly.'

Elias lowered himself wearily to a chair and leant towards the lad, his hands clasped in front of him. 'I fear it was my warning that we were approaching a tavern with bailiffs outside. Your father has endured more than most men can withstand over the last few months, and the thought that he might be taken from you again was too much for him.'

'He was scared?'

Althea spoke before Elias could. 'By no means,' she said firmly. 'A man as brave as your father is never scared, and he wouldn't be eating and drinking now if the sickness had been real.'

'He was pretending?'

'Certainly.'

'Why?'

'To keep you, your mother and sisters safe. Let us suppose the bailiffs had stopped the cart and found you hiding under the hay. Which would frighten them more? A man ready to fight while knowing he couldn't win against so many, or one so diseased that he was close to death?'

'Disease?'

'Always. People fear sickness more than anything. Am I not right, Lord Granville?'

Elias blanked the image of Peter Dugdale, broken in body and spirit, being brought to reluctant wakefulness by the acrid smell of burning feathers beneath his nose. 'You are, Miss Althea. My young friend's father puts his family before everything.'

Althea longed to ask questions. What had happened? Why had Elias brought them here? Who were they? Why was he responsible for them? But now was not the time to satisfy her curiosity, and she doubted Elias would be forthcoming if she tried. He guarded secrets better than any person she had ever met—bar, perhaps, his mother.

The boy had let slip enough to give her some understanding. He never used the term 'rebel' to describe his father, but Althea didn't doubt that that was what the man was. She learnt that Elias had taken him off a ship and kept him and his family in a barn for five days because the father was too weak to stand. When they left, they left suddenly. Travelling in the cart had been cold and slow, but Mister Friend had built fires each night to warm them and allow them to eat. He was a kind person.

'I must leave,' she said. 'I promised Papa I would be home before nightfall and Henry has been waiting on me for more than an hour.' She lifted the infant from her lap and offered her to Elias. 'I'm told you're experienced in the handling of babies, sir.'

A teasing gleam lit his tired eyes as he took the bundle. 'I have a particular fondness for this one, Miss Althea. She reminds me of you.'

Grateful that her cheeks were already flushed from the heat of the fire, Althea used her good foot to push the chair backwards. 'She'll do well under your and Lady Harrier's care,' she said, before turning to Mistress Smith. 'God be with you and your family, ma'am. I shall be thinking of you in the days to come.'

The boy began dancing again. 'Can I push you?' he asked eagerly. 'I should learn how to do it for when Hannah has a chair.'

Althea nodded. 'You may, though you need to decide on which name you want to call her. For myself, I prefer Hannah because it means loveliness.'

He took a firm grip of the finials and steered her towards the doorway. 'Which would you choose between James and Alan?'

'Alan. It means handsome and clever.'

'John and Peter?'

'Peter. It means strong and wise.'

As their voices faded down the hall, tears spilt onto Mistress Dugdale's cheeks. 'She has given me so much hope, sir. I had despaired of Hannah's future until I met Miss Althea. Were it not for her honest replies to Alan's questions, I would never have guessed she had palsy.'

Elias, malodorous, dirty and deeply fatigued, smiled as he touched a finger to the infant's nose.

A letter from Mister Hendry to the Duke of Granville,
dated 3 December 1685:

Your Grace,

I am pleased to inform you that your recent consignment was shipped safely to its port of destination in France. I received word this morning that two hundred items of freight were disembarked without trouble and cleared the dock shortly afterwards.

I trust this meets with your approval and that you will consider me again, should you have further business to conduct.

Your servant,
Andrew Hendry
Merchant

TWENTY-FOUR

ON THE FIFTH DAY OF December, Lady Harrier was summoned from the hospital by Robert, who told her the High Sheriff was in the front hall, asking for His Grace. 'He became heated when I said I didn't know where Master Elias was, so I offered to fetch you instead, Miss Jayne.' He glanced towards the room which housed the Smiths and lowered his voice so that it wouldn't be heard in the hall. 'Mister Lewis is so agitated I was afraid he might come looking for His Grace himself.'

'That wouldn't do at all,' Jayne agreed quietly. 'Bring ale to the parlour and then wait with us until I give you an excuse to fetch Lord Granville. Ask that he wears his coat and comes in from outside, otherwise the High Sheriff will question why neither of us knew where he was.'

She greeted Lewis warmly, apologised for her son's absence and invited him into the parlour. 'You look perturbed, sir,' she said with concern, taking the seat beside the hearth that faced the doorway and motioning him to take the chair opposite. 'Is there something I can do for you?'

Lewis squeezed his hands between his knees. 'Only if you know why some of my prisoners have disappeared, milady.'

She feigned surprise. '*Disappeared*? From the *prison*?'

'Hardly,' he snapped. 'We guard that well. They vanished outside Yeovil on their way to Bristol. Orders were counterfeited, and an entire column—one hundred men—melted away.'

'Good heavens! I've never heard of such a thing. When you say melted away, do you mean they became vapour? Was this witnessed?'

Lewis glared at her. 'I was speaking figuratively, milady. A more appropriate choice of words would be "escaped from lawful custody".'

Robert's appearance with a tankard of ale and a glass of lemon cordial gave Jayne a minute or two to consider her response. She took a sip of her cordial while Lewis consumed a third of his tankard in a single swallow. 'Why were they being taken to Bristol?' she asked. 'Are the rumours of transportation true?'

'You must know the answer to that, Lady Harrier. It was your son who suggested transportation to Lord Jeffreys.'

Jayne gave a small laugh. 'You're mistaken in your first assumption, sir. My son is annoyingly abstemious in what he chooses to disclose. As to the second, I find it hard to believe that Lord Jeffreys would accept another's suggestion. I've never met a man so unwilling to listen to advice.'

'Be that as it may,' Lewis responded irritably, 'the sentences have been commuted, and I'm faced with explaining why one hundred Dorset men failed to reach Bristol three weeks ago.'

'You think Lord Granville can tell you?'

'He makes no secret of his view that King James's pursuit of vengeance is misguided.'

'I share the same view, Mister Lewis. It's a foolish monarch who courts the hatred of his subjects. Do you conclude from this that I, too, have knowledge of your prisoners' escapes?'

Lewis's glare grew more ferocious. 'A messenger, wearing the livery of one of my officers, intercepted the column four miles south of Yeovil and gave the commander of the militia amended orders which bore my seal and signature. Lord Granville is the only regular visitor to my office who has expressed sympathy for rebels, and, since the counterfeit orders allowed impostors to take charge of the column when they crossed the border into Somerset, I suspect him of purloining my seal and substituting his orders for mine. I'm told your husband acted similarly during the Civil War.'

Jayne allowed a second or two to pass. 'Sir William was also reputed to have fought the seven-thousand-strong Western Army single-handedly in order to secure victory at Lyme, Mister Lewis,' she responded mildly. 'Very few of the stories about him are true. Does the description of the messenger accord with Lord Granville? His height is distinctive.'

'Of course not,' Lewis snapped. 'He wouldn't be so foolish as to make his involvement obvious.'

'I would agree with that,' Jane said lightly. 'What date was your seal stolen? Perhaps I can reassure you that Lord Granville was nowhere near Dorchester that day.'

Ferocity turned to sourness. 'By "purloined" I meant "used", milady. The seal has never left my office. Nevertheless, a set of counterfeit orders carried its impression and my signature, and a column of prisoners was abducted off the highway.'

'By whom?'

'Soldiers dressed in the uniforms of the Somerset militia, who bore similarly fabricated orders bearing the seal of Somerset's High Sheriff.' He drained his tankard. 'They marched the column away and none of the prisoners has been seen since.'

'Mister Lewis needs more ale,' said Jayne, turning to Robert with a nod of instruction to fetch Elias. 'I'm saddened to see you in such low spirits, sir,' she finished, once Robert had left.

'With reason, milady. The King expects to be recompensed for the loss of a hundred slaves. I received a letter to that effect three days ago, and the figure quoted was two thousand pounds.'

This time Jayne's surprise was genuine. 'That's an extortionate amount. I remember Sir William telling me that previous monarchs considered themselves fortunate to receive ten pounds per head for slaves. You must argue strongly against it, Mister Lewis.'

'How can I? The responsibility for the prisoners was mine.'

Jayne studied him for several moments, her mind running through what he'd said. 'It seems to me that Somerset must have played a part,' she said thoughtfully. 'Wasn't it Taunton militiamen who relieved you of three dozen prisoners in August? Whose seal was on their orders?'

'The superintendent claimed it was the High Sheriff's, but when I sought clarification both the Sheriff and the Taunton militia denied any knowledge of the affair. They'll deny this also.'

'As should you,' Jayne said reasonably. 'It would be the honest response, would it not? I presume you dispatched the prisoners in the full expectation of them reaching Bristol.'

'Of course.'

'Then you have no reason to berate yourself. I can conceive of several interpretations of the limited facts you've given me, and none involves you or Lord Granville.'

He eyed her suspiciously. 'Name one.'

'The story you've been told is untrue.'

His face reddened with annoyance. 'I'm not a fool, Lady Harrier. My first act was to seek verification of the report I received. The militia commander showed me the counterfeit order and it was very convincing. A ship's captain in Plymouth is claiming similar deceit for the loss of two hundred prisoners, half of whom were from Dorset, though mercifully his amended orders bore the Queen's seal, making the loss her responsibility and not mine.'

To Jayne's relief, since the Queen, a ship's captain and Plymouth were well beyond her extemporising abilities, they were interrupted by the return of Robert with a jug. 'Cook wonders if Mister Lewis would care to stay for luncheon, milady,' he said, pouring a froth of sweet-smelling ale into the man's tankard. 'She has a sirloin turning on the spit, and dumplings, carrots and turnips simmering in a rich beef broth.'

'I fear he's too angry with me to accept,' Jayne remarked wryly, 'but ask him, nonetheless. His company will be most welcome.'

'Sir?'

Lewis groaned, clearly finding the choice between succulent beef and maintaining his sense of grievance a painful one. 'My anger is for the King, milady, not for you. His Majesty seems to think Dorset is made of money. He offers us nothing towards the cost of the executions, which has been prodigious, and then demands redress because his own purse will lose revenue. Is that fair?'

'Not at all, sir. How many executions have there been?'

'Seventy, milady, and all performed under duress from the King, who demanded that Dorset set an example for the rest of the south-west to follow. He instructed that I conduct them throughout the county—from Lyme Regis in the south to Sherborne in the north—so that no one was left in ignorance of the consequence of rebellion, and it has not been a happy experience for anyone—least of all me.'

'I can see that,' Jayne said sympathetically. 'Your situation is most disagreeable. You are held responsible whichever way you turn.' She paused at the sound of steps on the flags of the hall. 'I believe that's Lord Granville. He'll be better able to settle your mind on these matters than I can.'

Elias entered the room and bowed to his mother as he peeled off his gauntlets. 'Forgive my tardiness, Mama. The road from Salisbury has developed so many ruts, I was obliged to rein the horses to a walk for long stretches.' He turned to allow Robert to remove his coat and raised surprised eyebrows to see Lewis. 'I wasn't expecting you, my friend. What brings you here?'

With renewed ire, Lewis voiced his suspicions, but Elias had the advantage of having learnt of them from Robert outside the Smiths' room. Rather than revert to indignation at being accused of theft, he allowed Lewis to vent his spleen before pointing out how easy it was to make a mould from a wax seal.

'Authority is a tradeable commodity, Lewis. You know this. You also know that postmasters are open to bribery. Some make the impressions themselves from unbroken seals, others allow forgers to do it. Either way the impression is sold to the highest bidder.'

'I use trusted messengers for precisely that reason.'

Elias was standing in front of the fire, warming his back. 'They're as easily corrupted. At the right price, anything can be bought.'

Lewis bridled. 'You doubt my ability to select honest men?'

'Not in the least, my friend, but I wouldn't care to vouch for your predecessors. I imagine Dorset's seal has been in the hands of forgers for decades, along with those of every other High Sheriff in the south-west.' He paused. 'If it's any consolation, your counterparts in other counties are in the same position. John Davenant told me yesterday that he heard Somerset has lost well in excess of two hundred prisoners, and Devon upwards of seventy.'

Lewis stared into his tankard before taking another long draught. 'Do they know who's responsible?'

Elias shook his head.

'Who would you name if I asked you to guess?'

'The list would be a long one. Our Catholic King has made a host of enemies through his brutal treatment of Protestants, and I imagine the same is true of you. There'll be a goodly number in Dorset wishing you ill for delivering His Majesty's vengeance.'

Lewis refused to be diverted. 'I would guess at rebel sympathisers rather than enemies of the King.'

'They're one and the same,' said Elias, walking to a desk in the corner and removing a folded letter. 'I received this last week from the Constable of the Tower.' He passed the page to Lewis. 'It came in reply to a request from me, which is explained in the first line.'

Lewis read the two paragraphs.

Dear Granville,

Yes, the streets of London are ringing with talk of the Bloody Assizes. Shock is general, as is agreement that more have been butchered for high treason in the south-west these last two months than in the capital for three centuries.

You are right to assume that His Majesty's willingness to commute the sentences to transportation is an attempt

to quell criticism, but it may not achieve the end he desires.
Accusations of profiteering are rife.

Yours ever,

George Legge

Lewis returned the page. 'How does this help me? I can't cite profiteering as a reason to refuse the King's demands for compensation.'

Elias resumed his place in front of the fire. 'Explain.'

Lewis did so, and Elias's reaction was similar to his mother's.

'Twenty pounds per head? That's usury. I trust you didn't read the letter in the presence of the messenger.'

Lewis shook his head. 'One of my officers took receipt of it.'

'Then you have time to consider what to do.'

Lewis viewed him with disfavour. 'That's easily said, but what choice do I have other than to agree? It will mean raising taxes on every parish in the county, and this time the rioting will be in earnest.'

Elias took a second or two to ponder the matter. 'You can burn the letter,' he suggested, then smiled at Lewis's appalled reaction. 'There's only your officer's word that you received it, and he'll be cheaper to bribe than the King.'

'His Majesty will write again, with double the demand for putting him to the trouble.'

'Not for several days, and his first request will be that you answer his previous letter. However, since you're claiming ignorance of it, you can only send copies of responses to earlier correspondence. That should create enough confusion to carry you through Christmas.'

'What will that accomplish except to further annoy His Majesty?'

Elias shrugged. 'A month is a long time, Lewis. The cries of profiteering will only get louder.'

AN ANONYMOUS PAMPHLET, DISTRIBUTED WIDELY IN LONDON ON 14 DECEMBER 1685, AND SENT TO THE DUKE OF GRANVILLE BY GEORGE LEGGE, CONSTABLE OF THE TOWER.

The message accompanying it read: *Is there truth in this?*

The Lord of Misrule

History tells us that Queen Elizabeth (much loved and of revered memory) allowed her jester to sit on her throne during Christmastide each year. He was titled the Lord of Misrule, and his task was to bring joy and laughter to the festivities, dispensing goodwill and charity to Her Majesty's subjects.

The tradition, along with Christmas itself, was abolished after the Civil War, when humour and jollity were outlawed by the serious men who governed us during the sober years of the Protectorate. Mercifully, our late lamented King Charles II restored the twelve days of Christmas and played the role of generous jester himself.

A monarch with the common touch knows the value of winning his subjects' affection. One who surrounds himself with servile flatterers does not. The clamour of discontent over the number of Catholics being appointed to positions of power by King James is growing louder, as are the voices demanding to know why revenue from selling English Protestants into slavery has been promised to courtiers and not to the public purse.

Rumours of double-dealing are rife. Weaker convicts who are unlikely to attract a good price have failed to reach their port of embarkation, but compensation at twice their value is being demanded from the counties of the south-west. Suspicion is strong that frail men are being marched to their deaths to satisfy the greed of Catholic sycophants.

Misrule will be the least of the accusations whispered against King James if these stories are true.

The Duke of Granville replied with a single sentence on 16 December: *Your guess is as good as mine, my friend.*

TWENTY-FIVE

WILLIAM LEWIS'S UNEXPECTED ARRIVAL A mere half-hour before the Christmas Eve festivities were due to begin caused a ripple of fear to run through the Granville household. The hour was four of the clock and dusk was giving way to night. With only farmhands and their families expected, Robert had stationed Grace's young man, Billy, at the front door to complete his training as a footman, while Grace, who had been elevated to the status of housemaid under instruction from Kitty, stood at Robert's side, waiting to show guests to their places.

Lord Granville and Lady Harrier followed tradition by inviting everyone who lived on the estate, old and young, to a banquet on the night before Christmas. The salon, brilliantly lit by a multitude of oil lamps and candles, was bedecked with holly and ivy interlaced with ribbons; and rows of tables were laid for in excess of one hundred and twenty people. Billy and Grace had nothing to fear from making mistakes. No guest was of higher status than they or likely to find fault with them.

Hearing horses' hooves on the forecourt, Billy pulled the door ajar to see who it was. He slammed it shut again and turned, white-faced, to Robert. 'It's the High Sheriff with bailiffs,' he stuttered.

The 'consumptives' hadn't lost their fear of William Lewis, despite his indifference to what had happened to them. On the few occasions he had visited, they had hidden themselves away—although, as Lady Harrier pointed out, the chances of him recognising them were negligible. A diet of healthy food had filled them out, and they bore no resemblance to the starving wretches he had released to her care.

Grace gave a shriek and ran for the kitchen, while Billy, consumed by panic, stood his ground for a bare few seconds before following her. Cursing under his breath, Robert stepped forward and opened the door himself. He half-believed that Billy had imagined bailiffs, but the sight of mounted men carrying lanterns told him otherwise.

He watched as Mister Lewis dismounted, passed his reins to the rider next to him and approached the steps. His actions suggested that only he intended to enter, and Robert swept an extravagant bow. 'Welcome, sir. Is it His Grace or Lady Harrier you wish to see?'

'His Grace,' said Lewis. 'I assume he's at home, since we saw lights in the salon from the end of the driveway. Is he expecting guests?'

'Yes, sir, the servants and farm labourers.'

Lewis pushed past him into the hall. 'Is he in the salon now?'

Robert moved ahead of the Sheriff to block his path. 'No, sir. He's dressing. May I give him a message from you?'

'Ask him to spare me a few minutes in the parlour. I'll not keep him long.'

'The parlour is occupied, sir. Can I ask you to wait for him here?'

Perhaps Billy's hasty slamming of the front door had roused the High Sheriff's suspicions because he frowned. 'By whom? Servants? Does a man of my standing not take precedence?'

'Always, sir. If you'll allow me a moment, I'll clear the room for you.'

Robert backed away from him to ensure that he stayed where he was, then opened the parlour door and slipped inside. 'The High Sheriff is in the hall, Miss Althea, asking to speak with Lord Granville, but I'm reluctant to leave him alone in order to fetch the master in case he comes in here. He's accompanied by six bailiffs who are waiting with their horses on the forecourt. Will you engage him while I fetch the master?'

Althea watched the colour drain from Mary Smith's face as she stared anxiously towards her husband. Unlike Grace and Billy, they were still painfully thin, and John Smith's prison pallor had not improved by being closeted in the hospital since his arrival. She felt a sudden dread for herself—*Had someone betrayed her? Had Mister Milton been exposed?*—but young James's immediate move to stand between his frail father and the door shamed her into action. She lifted Lily from her lap and handed her to her mother.

'I will, but you'll have to make haste, Robert. I'll not be able to keep his attention above a few minutes.'

She refused to let him push her chair, saying she would be more interesting to Mister Lewis if she propelled herself. For once, she restrained her speed so that Robert was able to keep pace. He, as ever, wondered why she was so fond of decrying herself when everyone who saw her found her memorable. This evening, she was dressed in a blue silk gown that matched her eyes, and Robert thought her mighty pretty.

In the hall, he bowed to Lewis. 'May I present Miss Althea Ettrick, who is a guest of Lord Granville and Lady Harrier, sir? Her father is Magistrate Ettrick of Holt Lodge, Wimborne St Giles.' He bowed to Althea. 'Miss Althea, allow me to introduce you to our esteemed High Sheriff, Mister William Lewis.'

Lewis was so taken aback by a female in a wheeled chair that he responded discourteously. 'I asked for Lord Granville.'

Robert made another bow. 'I will fetch him for you now, sir.'

Althea offered her hand as Robert scurried for the stairs. 'I've long wanted to meet you, sir,' she said. 'My father speaks highly of you. He tells me you've coped with our county's recent difficulties in exemplary fashion.'

Lewis bent over her fingers, trying to recall if he had ever heard mention of a daughter in the Ettrick household, particularly one as remarkable as this. He did his best not to stare, but it wasn't easy. Not only was a chair on wheels outside his experience, but so was the young woman's willingness to move it herself, since such an overt display of strength wasn't usual in females. (His wife asked him later if Miss Althea was a beauty, and he said he wasn't much of a judge in such matters, but her jet-black hair and astonishingly blue eyes compelled attention. The description displeased Mistress Lewis, suggesting, as it did, that her husband had dwelt on the girl's face longer than he should have done.)

'Your father is most kind, Miss Althea. It was he who issued Monmouth's arrest warrant, was it not?'

'It was, Mister Lewis. Viscount Lumley and Sir William Portman brought the pretender to our house.'

'Did you meet him?'

Althea shook her head. 'The circumstances didn't allow it, sir. We had an army camped on our forecourt and two dozen men in our salon, arguing over who should be awarded the bounty. Mister Ettrick doubts he would have survived if he had ruled that their prisoner was *not* Monmouth.'

'Was it in question?'

'Not after his clothes were returned to him and he was loaned a wig. I understand that his likeness to his father was extraordinary. The pity is he lacked King Charles's intelligence. His rebellion was always doomed to fail.'

Lewis responded soberly. 'My life would have been a good deal easier these last few months if Dorset men had realised that, Miss Althea.'

'I'm sure of it, sir.'

He made no response and Althea wished she were better at small talk. A long uneasy silence might encourage him to suggest they go to the parlour. She reversed her chair away from him and asked if he would care to see the salon.

'It more closely resembles a woodland than a gracious hall,' she said, turning in a tight circle, 'but you'll need to give me a wide berth. My steering isn't always as accurate as it should be.'

Lewis looked around for a maid or a footman, querying the propriety of accompanying her. Where was her chaperone?

She seemed to read minds as well as drive vehicles. 'We'll not be alone, sir,' she said, setting herself in motion. 'My father's housekeeper is arranging my contribution to the evening. You will be intrigued by it, I think.'

Lewis doubted he could be any more intrigued than he already was. 'Is Mister Ettrick here also?' he asked, falling into step beside her.

Althea shook her head. 'He is spending Christmas in London with my brothers and their families. He sees them so rarely that it will be a pleasure for him.'

'You didn't choose to join him?'

Her answer was matter-of-fact. 'It wouldn't have been possible, sir. There's no space in our coach for my chair, and Lady Harrier had already invited me here.'

She gave a thrust of her wheels to move ahead of him into the salon. Beyond her, a grey-haired matron stood behind the high table, head canted to one side, surveying what looked like a representation of this very house. She raised her head with a smile as her young mistress approached.

'Bridget and Henry have done us proud,' she said. 'The pieces fit together perfectly.' Her smile turned to a frown of suspicion when she saw a man she didn't recognise accompanying her charge. 'Sir?'

Althea spoke lightly. 'This is Mister William Lewis, the High Sheriff of Dorset, Elizabeth. You will have heard of him from my father in reference to the trials and executions of rebels. Sir, this is my chaperone and companion, Mistress Elizabeth Harvey.'

Lewis thought he saw momentary shock in the woman's eyes before she lowered her head to perform a curtsey, but there was no sign of it when she straightened again. 'It's a privilege to meet you, sir. Mister Ettrick has mentioned your name several times.'

'Warmly, I trust?'

'Very warmly. Will you be staying this evening?'

'No. I am due in Blandford within the hour.' He moved to inspect the edifice on the table. 'Is it a cake?'

'Yes, sir, flavoured with almond and honey. The windows are crystallised sugar infused with lemon, and the doors and tiles are made of biscuit. It was Miss Althea's idea.'

'My cook makes round cakes.'

'The wooden hoops in which they are usually baked are circular, sir, but Miss Althea asked our coachman to make rectangular moulds. The result is as you see. The house is built in layers, with softly creamed cheese between them. Our cook would have assembled it herself but she's spending Christmas with her family.'

Lewis turned to Althea. 'You must know Winterborne Houghton very well to describe it so accurately to your cook, Miss Althea.'

'Well enough to draw a design, Mister Lewis.' She gestured towards the many festoons of holly, ivy and ribbons that hung about the room. 'Lady Harrier tells me this was how her father's salon was adorned each Christmastide. Do you find it as charming as I do?'

'Yes,' Lewis said, taking note of the number of tables. 'I hadn't realised Lord Granville employed so many people on his estate.'

Althea answered without hesitation. 'Lady Harrier asked him to extend his invitation to the indoor and outdoor workers at Winterborne Stickland, sir.' She looked enquiringly at the matron. 'Am I right that her friends, Sir Francis and Lady Stickland, are away from home at the moment, Elizabeth?'

Elizabeth answered judiciously, being less comfortable with blatant lies than her mistress. 'They must be, Miss Althea. The maids in the kitchen speak of nothing but their excitement at having a choice of new partners to dance with.'

Lewis was sceptical. 'Few men would be so generous to another's servants.'

'But only one has Lady Harrier for a mother, sir,' Althea responded with a smile. 'If it was she who made the request, Lord Granville will have obliged her.'

'Indeed. Have you known her long, Miss Althea?'

'All my life, Mister Lewis.'

'How so?'

'She was present at my birth, sir.'

To distract him from further questions on the matter, Althea lifted the pieces of her staff from the seat beside her and joined them together. Designed by Elias and fashioned by his carpenter and blacksmith, it doubled in length by the simple expediency of slotting one half into the other and turning a burnished iron ring around the joint to hold it firm. She placed its tip on the floor and rose elegantly to her feet, holding herself straight.

Her balance was aided both by Lady Harrier's relentless regime of exercise and by a pair of knee-high leather boots, conceived by Lord Granville and commissioned from a Blandford cobbler. The left accommodated her twisted foot and lent strength to the muscles of her calf; the right served merely to complement the other in the eyes of onlookers.

'Will you accompany me to the window, Mister Lewis? Lord Granville tells me a new moon will rise tonight.'

Without waiting for an answer, she set off past the high table, holding the staff in her right hand and moving it in time with her lame left leg. By supporting her weight on the staff as she moved her right leg forward, her limp was barely noticeable. These were movements she had practised a thousand times at home with the help of Elizabeth, Henry and Adam, and she reached the window without mishap. Her intention had been to surprise Lord Granville and Lady Harrier that night with her new-found ability to walk, but instead she had to content herself with the High Sheriff's puzzlement.

'What purpose does the chair serve?' he asked.

'Comfort,' she answered. 'I have a small weakness in my left leg which restricts how far and fast I can walk. I learnt that King Philip of Spain had wheels attached to his chair after he became crippled with gout and decided to copy the idea.' She pointed towards the eastern sky. 'The crescent should appear shortly.'

Lewis had no interest in a new moon but his curiosity about Althea Ettrick was intense. Her forthright manner reminded him of Lady Harrier, as did her easy deflection of questions that she didn't want to answer. But what was her relationship with this family, and why had he never heard mention of her? He had a strong sense that she had assumed responsibility for him in Granville's absence but was at a loss to understand why.

'The moon will be as visible in the parlour as it is here,' he said.

'Not if we wish to go outside, sir,' said Althea, nodding to the door to the terrace. 'My father is entranced by the night sky and has taught me the name of every star.'

'You surprise me,' Lewis said. 'I had occasion to stand outside with Magistrate Ettrick on a fraught evening during the Assizes and he gave attention only to his pipe.'

'I doubt that, Lewis,' said Elias's amused voice behind them. 'I recall Mister Ettrick telling me that the concern of every magistrate in Dorchester that night was why they were being kept from their beds for a riot that never happened.' He made a low bow to Althea. 'You look lovely, Miss Althea. Remind me to thank your father for allowing you to grace us with your presence.'

She bent her good leg in approximation of a curtsey, holding his gaze while she did so. 'You're very kind, sir, but the gratitude is ours. My household is deeply appreciative to have been included in your invitation, as are the Winterborne Stickland servants. Christmas is never so pleasurable when masters are absent from home.'

A flash of understanding passed between them, which wasn't missed by Lewis.

'It's the least Lady Harrier and I can do for friends, Miss Althea.'

'Nevertheless, allow me to endorse Mister Lewis's praise for your generosity when he saw how many places were laid, my lord.' She transferred her staff to her left hand, and offered her right to the High Sheriff. 'I've enjoyed our meeting, sir.'

Lewis kissed her fingers. 'The enjoyment has been mine, Miss Althea.'

'Then we are mutually advantaged,' she said with a smile, passing the staff back to her right hand and turning to walk towards Elizabeth. The woman's upward jerk of her chin was a reminder to hold her head high, and the softness in her eyes an indication that Althea was meeting Elizabeth's tyrannical demands for gracefulness.

'What afflicts her?' asked Lewis after Althea had resumed her place in the chair and left the salon with Elizabeth beside her.

'Nothing that I know of,' said Elias. 'I find her company most stimulating.'

'She spoke of a weakness in her left leg.'

'Then you know as much as I do, my friend. May I ask what you're doing here? I can't believe your charming wife and daughter are happy for you to absent yourself on Christmas Eve?'

Lewis accepted the change of topic readily, recognising that he had made his curiosity about Miss Althea too obvious. 'It's they who sent me,' he said. 'I'm tasked with escorting my mother-in-law from Blandford to Dorchester for our own celebration tomorrow.' He shook his head at Elias's expression. 'She complains less if she travels at night. Her coachman has constructed a frame that spans the seats and allows her to sleep.'

'How practical of him,' Elias said, resisting the temptation to ask how the bailiffs felt about being ordered from their homes on Christmas Eve to act as lantern carriers. 'But I can't believe you broke your journey to acquaint me with your mother-in-law's travelling arrangements.'

'No. I came with news that will intrigue you. An officer of His Majesty's guard presented himself in my office yesterday morning and demanded the return of His Majesty's letter.'

Elias's surprise was obvious. 'So soon?'

'You expected such a reaction?'

'*Hoped*, Lewis. To expect is to be disappointed. Did you give him the letter?'

'You suggested I burn it.'

'With no conviction that you would.'

'I couldn't. I am a loyal servant of His Majesty. I offered him half of what he was asking and said I'd need time to raise the amount from the parishes, explaining that further demands for money would not be popular.'

Elias gave his jaw a thoughtful stroke. 'Did the officer give an explanation for why the King wanted his letter back?'

'He claimed it was never authorised. His Majesty signs in excess of one hundred documents a day and was shocked to discover that his trust had been abused. He believes the fraudulence was perpetrated by a corrupt secretary who has since been discharged.'

'Did the officer mention whether he was continuing on to Somerset?'

'Why should he?'

'Because you weren't the only High Sheriff to receive a letter, Lewis. If your colleagues did as you did, His Majesty will have been alerted to the unrest that raised levies would generate and chose the wiser course of retraction.' Elias proffered his hand. 'Allow me to congratulate you, my friend. Your method brought quicker results than my delaying tactics would have achieved.'

Lewis accepted the handshake, but his expression was sceptical. 'We hear rumours that London's awash with pamphlets accusing His Majesty of Catholic conspiracy and corruption. Is there any truth in them?'

Everyone's favourite question, Elias thought. 'In what? The rumours or the pamphlets?'

'Both.'

An amiable shrug. 'Your guess is as good as mine, my friend.' He lifted an oil lamp from a nearby table and walked to the terrace door. 'We'll leave this way. The servants were already gathering in the entrance hall when I came to find you.' He ushered Lewis outside. 'Whatever the cause, be grateful for small mercies.'

Lewis followed him onto a paved path that ran along the house towards the driveway. 'Perhaps I should be thanking *you*,' he said.

'For what?'

'Revealing the contents of His Majesty's letter to pamphleteers,' Lewis suggested. 'You're one of the few people who knew of his demand.'

A small laugh floated back to him. 'I haven't been to London in months, Lewis. Credit yourself and your fellow High Sheriffs with the success. His Majesty will have been as disturbed by the warnings of unrest as by anything pamphleteers write.'

Their route took them past a lit window. The room was recognisable as the parlour, but the people grouped around the fire bore no resemblance to Granville's well-fed servants. Indeed, so shocking was the pallor and thinness of a seated man that Lewis paused to look. Cursing himself for not leading him across the grass, Elias, a few paces ahead, placed the lamp on the ground and turned back. Peter Dugdale was improving slowly, but illuminated faces at the window would cause him extreme anxiety.

'This man looks close to death,' said Lewis. 'Who is he?'

'One of the consumptives you released to Lady Harrier's care,' Elias answered smoothly. 'His wife and children are also afflicted, but Lady Harrier's treatments are proving more successful with them.'

'Who told her to assume responsibility for them?'

'My mother doesn't approve of disease being allowed to spread unchecked through communities, Lewis. When she realised how long your prisoners had been suffering, she insisted on visiting all their families.'

He placed a hand behind Lewis's back to urge him forward, but the attempt was thwarted by the parlour door being opened by Robert. The young footman stepped aside to let Lady Harrier and Althea enter, and the exuberance shown by Alan and his sisters to see them gave the lie to consumption. Alan took Althea's hands and turned her in her chair, mimicking a dance, while the girls wrapped their arms adoringly about Lady Harrier's legs.

'The children aren't as sick as you think,' Lewis commented dryly.

'You didn't see them when they first came here. Give praise where it's due, my friend. Without Lady Harrier's treatment, they would still be bedridden.'

'Miss Althea appears unconcerned to be in their company.'

'She has faith in Lady Harrier's long study of the disease,' said Elias, pressing Lewis into motion. 'A person has to live in close confinement with a sufferer to catch it.'

'I wouldn't permit Clarissa to consort with consumptives.'

'Miss Althea has several years on Clarissa, Lewis, and I doubt she takes instruction as readily as your daughter.' Elias lowered his arm as they stepped onto the driveway. 'The forecourt is this way.'

He held the lamp high as they negotiated the bend in the driveway, as much to make their faces visible as to light the way. Several times, the glow glanced across shadowy figures amongst the trees, but Elias saw them because he was expecting them to be there. A posse of mounted bailiffs on the forecourt would deter even the most reckless from showing themselves.

'May I offer some parting advice?' Lewis asked as they crossed the gravel.

'By all means.'

'Make your intentions clear to Miss Althea. As father to a daughter myself, I know how painful rejection can be when it is preceded by hope.'

Elias slowed, noting that in Lewis's mind 'intentions' were synonymous with 'rejection'. He introduced curiosity to his tone. 'You think she's looking for something more than friendship?'

'Of course. Every young lady longs for a husband, Granville.'

'Did you see any indication of longing in Miss Althea?'

'She made her support for you clear.'

'How?'

'By alerting you to the falsehoods she told me to explain the high number of tables and seats in the salon. I'm guessing you're harbouring rebels, Granville. You're too keen to be rid of me.'

Elias laughed. 'You're welcome to stay, my friend, though I doubt your mother-in-law will appreciate your tardiness. Miss Althea spoke honestly when she said the extra places were for Winterborne Stickland servants. If you doubt me, break your journey home and see for yourself.'

'I might do that.'

'You'd be wise to consult with your bailiffs first,' Elias muttered, nodding towards the mounted men whose impatient faces were lit by their lanterns. 'They don't look happy to have waited idly outside my house when they could have been in Blandford by now. How much are you paying them to absent themselves from their own families this night?'

'None of your business.'

'Indeed,' came the good-natured response, 'but I suggest you double the amount if you expect them to tolerate a second delay without complaint. You wouldn't want the good burghers of Dorchester learning that you use publicly funded officers as lantern bearers for your mother-in-law.'

⌒

Althea knew from Elizabeth's questioning of Sarah, the cook, and Henry's questioning of Timothy, the head groom, that Lord Granville had employed twenty indoor servants, three nurses, and forty outdoor workers before the rebellion began. Most were related to each other through marriage or birth, but some were day labourers who lived off the estate. In addition, there were fifteen children under the age of ten who received elementary schooling on the upper floor of the house while their parents worked.

This made a total of seventy-eight, but Althea's count of heads when everyone was seated in the salon came to one hundred and twenty-six. She subtracted those from Holt Lodge—Elizabeth, Henry, Adam and herself—leaving forty-four additions to the Winterborne Houghton estate in under six months, and by the clear imbalance between men and women at the tables, the additions were male.

She made these calculations while Zachariah led the salon in the singing of 'The Boar's Head' carol in Latin, and Robert and Timothy tossed a mighty yule log onto the fire in the hearth. Had Lord Granville been more approachable, she would have solicited the information from him, but he was as discreet as Lady Harrier. Together, they shared a multitude of secrets hidden behind engaging smiles, and Althea doubted that such a strong bond of trust could ever include another. She was surprised at how much the thought saddened her.

When the singing came to an end and the fire was blazing, Lord Granville welcomed his guests with warm words. He thanked them for preparing the magnificent feast they were about to enjoy, then signalled that it was time to eat by taking his seat at the high table. The room resounded with cheers and tankard bottoms being banged on tabletops as platters of roast pig, flavoursome mutton stew, suet dumplings, carrots, parsnips and turnips were passed from hand to hand.

The high table was reserved for senior members of the household, but places had been added for Althea and Elizabeth. Given the choice, Althea would have preferred a less prominent position than sitting between Lord Granville and Lady Harrier, but Elizabeth's careful placing of Bridget's cake meant she wasn't as visible to those at the other tables as she might have been.

Elias smiled as he lowered himself to his seat. 'Which deserves more praise?' he asked, gesturing to the cake. 'This remarkable edifice or your inspired invention of Winterborne Stickland servants?'

'The edifice, naturally,' Althea said with an answering smile. 'It took hours of patient baking and construction while my falsehood for Mister Lewis was momentary.'

'You did better than I would have done.'

She shook her head. 'You wouldn't have made the mistake of bringing him to the salon and allowing him to see the number of seats.'

'What was his reason for being here?' Jayne asked curiously. 'It's an odd visit to make on Christmas Eve.'

Elias repeated what Lewis had told him, adding a brief summary of what had been in the King's letter for Althea's sake. 'Lewis credits some defamatory pamphlets in London with changing His Majesty's mind.'

Althea accepted a dish of pork from Lady Harrier. The rule that evening was that every person must serve himself. 'Does Mister Lewis suspect you of writing the pamphlets?' she asked, spooning some meat onto her plate.

Elias eyed her curiously. 'Why should he?'

Althea passed him the dish and took a bowl of mutton stew from Lady Harrier. 'I've received three tracts in the post this last week and the unanimity of their message suggests a single source who resides in the West Country and has sympathy with convicted rebels. Each tract was highly defamatory of the King, particularly in regard to profiteering from the sale of slaves.'

'There are many who disapprove of the practice, Miss Althea.'

'Indeed, but few who take action to thwart it, my lord.' She added a spoonful of stew to her plate and handed him the bowl.

There was a short silence as Elias helped himself to mutton before passing the bowl to Elizabeth. 'What form do you think this thwarting takes?'

'If I've solved my equation correctly, an increase of more than fifty percent in Winterborne Houghton's population since July. Can you house and feed so many on an estate of a defined size?'

'For short periods,' he answered easily. 'Our stable block accommodated thirty of Lord Jeffreys' troops comfortably before the Assizes began, and could have taken a dozen more. Is that the only equation that's puzzling you?'

'No, but the second is more of a conundrum. The pamphlets I received lacked an author's name or a publisher's imprint and were distributed for free. That's usually done to achieve the widest audience possible in order to bring pressure to bear on the person being criticised, but I question why owners of printing presses in London were so generous in their donation of ink, time and paper for a cause which is so specific to the south-west.'

'That *is* a conundrum,' Elias agreed. 'Have you deciphered it?'

'A debt of brotherhood?' she suggested. 'I'm reminded of the witness statements from men across the Middle Shires, whose suspiciously similar testimonies resulted in the release of fifteen stonemasons in advance of the Assizes. I was curious enough at the time to search through army lists from the last decade and discovered that the named witnesses fought under you and Monmouth at the battle of Bothwell Bridge.'

'And you think the same is true of London publishers?'

Althea received a platter of buttered parsnips from Lady Harrier. 'Not precisely. London publishers tend to be a generation above you, so I imagine the debts are of longer standing. I've cross-checked the names of the better-known ones against my New Model Army lists and have discovered two who served under your father during the Civil War.'

Elias caught his mother's amused gaze above Althea's head.

'It's a mercy that only men can be High Sheriff,' he commented wryly. 'Were Miss Althea to hold the position, no secret would be safe from her.'

Once the feasting was finished, the tables were pushed against the walls and a band of farm workers struck up tunes on their fiddles. Lord Granville and Lady Harrier led the dancing, drawing everyone in the salon into a merry promenade. Long lines of laughing people weaved through each other, linking elbows to perform boisterous spins before continuing with different partners.

Althea, safely seated in her chair at the back of the room, clapped her hands when Elizabeth and Henry joined the lines. Even to her untutored eye, their steps were clumsy, but there was no doubting their enjoyment. She was blaming herself that such light-hearted fun was never had at Holt Lodge when Adam and Robert approached her with respectful bows.

Robert spoke first. 'It is the custom on Christmas Eve that male servants may request a dance with any lady they choose,

Miss Althea. Will you grant Adam and me the privilege of your company in the promenade?'

'We won't let you fall,' Adam assured her. 'You've rehearsed your walking with both of us, so you know it to be true. Robert will lend you his left arm and I will lend my right, and we will dance as a threesome.'

Althea's immediate response was a shake of her head. 'I can't. You must find young maids to partner you.'

'They're all taken,' said Robert, gesturing about the room. 'Only men are without partners.'

'We're as ignorant as you,' Adam confessed, 'but it can't be that hard if Elizabeth and Henry are doing it. Please, Miss Althea. We need a lady if we're ever to learn, and'—he produced an ingenuous smile—'you know how much you approve of learning.'

Althea was torn between praise and chastisement for the outrageous blandishment. 'We'll make fools of ourselves. My limp will trip you up, and you'll be forced to abandon me each time the couples change partners.'

'You thought you'd make a fool of yourself walking until Elizabeth and Lady Harrier persuaded you to try,' Adam said reasonably. 'And if the dancing's too difficult, we'll bring you back.'

Robert nodded agreement. 'I've not abandoned you yet, Miss Althea, and I'm certain Adam never has. Will you trust us?'

Althea looked from one eager face to the other. The idea was ridiculous and could only end in disappointment. She would fall flat on her face, they would be mortified, and the room would ring with laughter. Nevertheless, this might be the only chance she ever had to attempt a promenade, and Adam and Robert surely deserved a return for the camaraderie and consideration that, separately, they had always shown her.

She rose from her chair. 'Be it on your own heads,' she warned. 'I'll cut out your livers myself if we end up on the floor.'

Her fears were unwarranted. The boys supported her so well that she found the confidence to copy their skipping as they weaved through the other dancers. Her steps were inelegant and lopsided, with her good leg pulling her forward on a hop and her weak leg dragging behind, but every smile she received was so full of encouragement that she felt she could dance all night.

By the nature of a promenade, it was inevitable that, sooner or later, they would encounter Lord Granville. He was partnering Kitty, and by dint of Kitty linking arms with Robert and releasing Lord Granville to take Robert's place at Althea's side, Althea acquired a stronger arm to support her. With a mischievous grin, Adam spun away to twirl a young maid in a circle.

Althea slowed, forcing Elias to do likewise. 'Did you put them up to it?' she asked suspiciously.

He drew her to one side to allow other couples to pass them. 'Sadly not. My imagination doesn't stretch to ideas with such delightful results. I would guess my mother and Elizabeth are to blame.' He smiled down at her. 'Would you like me to summon Robert and Adam back, Miss Althea?'

A blush rose in her cheeks. 'I doubt they can be trusted. I only agreed to dance with them because they promised they wouldn't abandon me.'

Elias moved to her left side, holding her strongly about the waist and supporting her left arm and hand with a firm grip, removing any need for her to put weight on her palsied leg. 'Do you feel abandoned?' he asked, rejoining the line and encouraging her to skip forward on her good foot.

'Not yet,' she admitted, 'but I'm a poor partner and you'll grow tired of me very quickly.'

Elias laughed. 'I wouldn't count on it,' he said, lifting her off the ground and swinging her in an exhilarating circle.

A letter from Lady Harrier to Mistress Elizabeth Harvey, Holt Lodge, Wimborne St Giles, dated 28 March 1686:

My dear Elizabeth,

Forgive me if I am speaking out of turn, but you and I have been friends for so long that I felt the need to reassure you. Althea tells me she senses growing melancholy at Holt Lodge over her imminent departure. I have little difficulty understanding why, but will you trust me when I say that you are fretting unnecessarily?

With Granville's full support, she intends to return one day a week to assist her father with upcoming cases and continue her lessons with Adam and the Earl of Shaftesbury's son. Granville is pledged to drive her in his racing carriage, but should he be absent for any reason, his place will be taken by Timothy, our coachman.

Meanwhile, our door will always be open to you. Althea's character is too strong and independent to be changed by a title, my dear. Under your care and guidance, she is what she has made of herself—a woman so rare and unspoiled that she captured my son's heart the first time he saw her.

Take pride in her, Elizabeth, and know that she intends to hold you as close as she would her mother.

> *With my kindest regards,*
> *Your friend,*
> *Jayne*

REVOLUTION

November 1688

*. . . Unsuited for kingship, James II quickly lost the respect of
his people. In pursuit of Absolutism, he dissolved Parliament,
evoking memories of his father's inciting of a brutal Civil War;
in pursuit of unassailable authority, he doubled the size of his
army, evoking memories of Oliver Cromwell's hated military
dictatorship.*

*His Catholicism remained a point of contention throughout
his three-year reign. His people tolerated him for as long as he
continued to name his eldest child, Mary, wife to his nephew
Prince William of Orange, as his successor, but their forbearance
was tested when his second wife, Mary of Modena, a committed
papist, gave birth to a male heir on 10 June 1688.*

*Since a son must always inherit before a daughter, few
doubted that this was the beginning of a new Catholic dynasty
which would subject England once again to governance
by Rome.*

*Rioting became frequent, and the King's ability to quell the
unrest was weakened by divisions within his army. These were
caused by his purging of Protestant officers in favour of papists.
Mutinous infantrymen refused to turn on their countrymen in
obedience to Catholics, and disorder spread across the land.*

*In face of the growing dissension, seven high-ranking
politicians, including the Bishop of London, wrote in secret
to Prince William of Orange, urging him to invade England
in order to safeguard the Anglican Church and England's
Protestant faith . . .*

TWENTY-SIX

4 November 1688

ELIAS MADE HIS WAY ALONG the stone breakwater that protected Lyme Regis harbour from the sea and the weather. Begun four centuries previously, it was now a wide, imposing structure, offering an uninterrupted view of ships crossing Lyme Bay. The bay was some fifty miles wide, and on a good day vessels were easily visible against the horizon. This was a good day. The sun was shining, the air was crisp and no one doubted what they were seeing.

Word of a five-hundred-strong armada advancing down the English Channel had run like wildfire along the south coast, and Elias was one of many who had been drawn to witness it. Most of the ships had already rounded the Isle of Portland to the east, and their sails were swelling under a favourable wind. The sight was impressive. Every ship in the vast flotilla flew the banner of Prince William, Stadtholder of Holland—orange, white and blue—and to see the colours repeated on mast after mast was to understand the strength of the Dutch force.

A man beside Elias bemoaned Monmouth's naivety in coming with a paltry number of ships three years previously. 'He should've put the fear of God into King James the same way this one is doing. You don't come slinking into port with a handful of men and expect to win a crown.'

'I hear tell Prince William has sailed close to the shore all the way from Kent so that his colours and the size of his fleet can be seen and reported,' said another. 'It's enough to scare anyone.'

'Where will he land?' asked a woman.

The man beside Elias shielded his eyes with his hand and studied the lead ship's direction. 'Brixham in Devon if they stay on their present course. The harbour's a good size, and there's sheltered anchorage outside it.'

'Why didn't he choose somewhere closer to London?'

A shrug.

Elias obliged with an answer. 'There's no army this far west. The militias have been disbanded and the King's regiments are stationed around the capital. The Dutch will advance a hundred miles before His Majesty is ready to confront them.'

'How does that help them?' the woman asked.

'The more counties they cross without meeting resistance, the weaker the King will look.'

The first man nodded agreement. 'He must pray his soldiers remain loyal or there'll be no confrontation at all.'

'You doubt they will?' Elias asked.

'It depends whether they share their country's preference for a Protestant monarch.'

'Monmouth was a Protestant and he was defeated,' said the woman.

'He came too early,' murmured the man, gazing at the ships. 'The time to win a country is when the people turn against their King. If Prince William succeeds, it will be because he waited.'

⚊

Elias rode the thirty miles to Exeter, reaching the town as dusk was falling. He made his way to the Cross Inn, situated on the highway to Newton Abbot, and took his mare to the stable, where he ordered a change of horse for the morrow. He paid the ostler well to care for his mare until he returned, then took a place beside the inn's fire in order to warm himself before consuming two crabs, half a loaf, a quarter-pound of cheddar cheese and three draughts of ale.

That night, he slept the sleep of the dead. Time would tell if his recommendations for patience would bear fruit, but the omens were good that the last three years had not been wasted. He felt no guilt. King James had brought this crisis on himself through his refusal to listen to his people.

⚊

Elias's route the next morning took him through Newton Abbot and on to the fishing port of Torquay. From there, he followed the road that bordered the shores of Tor Bay, a large inlet in the Devon coastline. Rain was now falling, but the murk could not obscure the ships riding at anchor inside the bay nor the constant activity around them as barges and fishing vessels sailed in under their bows to take fresh loads of men and weaponry ashore.

Once he reached Brixham, he left his horse at a commercial stable yard on the outskirts and made his way on foot to the harbour. Small groups of people were gathered at corners, asking for news, but there were not the crowds that had lined the streets of Lyme Regis when Monmouth came ashore.

The harbour quay had been reserved for ships carrying horses, and he watched for several minutes as animals were led down gangplanks and taken to a temporary corral constructed from pre-made fencing panels lashed together by ropes. Prominent inside the corral was Prince William's fine grey stallion, which stood two hands above every other horse. Nothing had been left to chance. While horses were emerging from the stern holds, hay and fodder were being brought from the bows, and local men were being invited to assist on the promise of payment.

Payment for services rendered—whether it be in the form of porterage, board and lodging or the provision of food—had been the firmest of Elias's suggestions. He recalled his mother's stories of the ever-growing animosity towards soldiers during the Civil War, when both armies had plundered and pillaged at will, and how the tide of public opinion had turned towards Parliament when Sir Thomas Fairfax's New Model Army had paid for what it needed. Resentment grew from stealing. Goodwill came from fair remuneration.

He made his way to the New Quay Inn, where he had arranged to meet Jan Hendriksen between the hours of noon and two on the day of Prince William's arrival. The establishment was well known to both men from their regular visits to Brixham over the last six months. Posing as fishermen off foreign trawlers in the harbour, they had consumed many a pint of ale in the tavern as they debated Tor Bay's and Brixham harbour's ability to accommodate a fleet of five hundred ships.

Jan was sitting in his favourite seat in one of the bay windows, and they greeted each other with warm handshakes. Their normal custom was to speak in Dutch to thwart the curiosity of eavesdroppers, but Jan nodded to the empty bar and addressed Elias in English.

'Prince William hoped for a warmer reception,' he said, 'but we seem to have frightened the good folk of Brixham into staying at home. Would we have fared better if we had chosen Lyme Regis, as Monmouth did?'

Elias turned a chair and straddled it. 'Not with five hundred warships and twenty thousand troops. Monmouth was more of an oddity than a threat.' He called to a maid to bring him some ale. 'Are you scared of us?' he asked her in Dutch-accented English as she placed a filled tankard in front of him.

'No,' she said. 'I recognise you from when you were here before.'

'What are people saying about our ships in the harbour?'

'Some that you'll fire your guns at us . . . others that you'd have done it by now if that was your intention.'

'Listen to the others,' Elias advised her. 'We come in Princess Mary's name, and she has no wish to wage war on England. Her husband, Prince William of Orange, seeks only to persuade the King to name her as his rightful heir.'

'Will you fight if he refuses?'

'Not if we can help it. Our hope is that the people of England will side with Princess Mary so that no blood need be shed. Is that a foolish ambition?'

She wriggled her shoulders. 'I doubt my opinion counts, sir.'

'It does to me.'

'Then I wish you and Prince William well, sir, as will my father when I tell him what you said. He yearns for the happy, settled times that we had under our previous King.' She bobbed a small curtsey and left.

Jan waited until she was out of earshot. 'Those were fine words, my friend, but they were wasted on a serving wench. We need to persuade the gentry of our peaceful objectives.'

Elias grinned. 'Never underestimate serving wenches, my friend. Her father owns this inn and has a good deal of influence. Win Brixham and news of what you hope to achieve will spread throughout the county.' He took a sup of ale. 'When will Prince William come ashore?'

'At dawn tomorrow. His ship will moor against the quay this afternoon, the local dignitaries whose names you supplied will dine aboard this evening, and His Highness will lead out his army when daylight has broken.'

'I saw his grey stallion in the corral. Between them, they'll make a fine statement of princely authority.'

Jan chuckled. 'He believes in strong impressions. No one should be in any doubt as to who brought an armada to England's shores.' He drained his tankard. 'Do you plan to stay overnight? His Highness will welcome you warmly if so.'

Elias shook his head. 'I'll be of more use to him if I'm thought to be neutral.' He took some letters from his inside pocket. 'These were penned by commanders of the King's regiments and speak of wide discontent within the army. Prince William will take heart from them.'

Jan scanned one. 'This writer says that his and his troops' allegiance to the Crown has always depended on Princess Mary inheriting the throne.'

'The same theme runs through all of them. Several add that they can't vouch for their troops if a Protestant army comes against them. Did you bring a copy of the proclamation His Highness intends to make in Exeter?'

Jan removed a document from his own jacket. 'Not even King James can construe it as a declaration of war or an attempt to seize his throne.'

Elias ran his eyes over the wording. It was concise and clever, stating that Prince William had come on behalf of his wife and the Protestant religion to secure Princess Mary's right to succeed to the throne on her father's death. The tone was considered rather than bellicose, and there was no insistence that the King must abdicate in his daughter's favour, merely a request to enshrine her in law as his rightful heir.

Elias folded the page. 'I'll convey this to the commanders,' he said. 'It should give them the reassurance they need to resist any call to war.' He tucked the document away. 'King James's confidence that an enlarged army was his best protection was always misplaced. Men must believe in what they're fighting for if they're to be willing to die for it.'

'Amen to that,' said Jan, leaning forward to touch the lip of his tankard to Elias's. 'You've been a good friend to us. If all goes as planned, you and Prince William will meet in London. Will your wife be with you?'

Humour flickered in Elias's eyes. 'Do you ask for yourself or for the prince?'

'Myself,' Jan admitted with a wry smile. 'You've spoken of her so often that I need my curiosity satisfied. No man deserves to be as contented as you, Granville.'

EXTRACT FROM A SEVENTEENTH-CENTURY CHRONICLE ON
ENGLISH MONARCHS:

... *Despite heavy autumnal rain slowing his advance, William
of Orange reached Exeter on 9 November 1688, where he issued
a proclamation in the name of the Princess Royal, his Protestant
wife, Mary of Orange. This proclamation was printed and
distributed across the country, being well-received when note
was taken that Prince William made no mention of seizing the
throne for himself.*

*On 15 November three of King James's regiments defected to
the Dutch army together with growing numbers of Englishmen
who were ready to swear allegiance to Princess Mary. A week
later, the commander of the King's army, the Earl of Feversham,
advised His Majesty to order a retreat rather than engage with
the now vastly superior Dutch force.*

*Depressed in mind and spirit by the defections, and
suffering near-constant nosebleeds, James did so, leaving Prince
William free to continue his unimpeded advance. Rumours of
a bloodless revolt spread throughout the land when three of the
King's generals and his younger daughter, Princess Anne, gave
their allegiance to his son-in-law.*

*Despite Prince William's pledge that their lives would
not be forfeit, King James sent his wife and newborn son
to France on 8 December, joining them there fifteen days
later. To assuage the anger of the London Mob at the King's
flight from justice, Parliament laid charges of high treason
against his Lord Chancellor and ordered his incarceration
in the Tower of London on the night before Christmas,
24 December 1688.*

At the turn of the year, Parliament offered the throne of England to William and Mary of Orange in a peaceful transition of power that came to be known as the Glorious Revolution . . .

TWENTY-SEVEN

THE CORONATION OF ENGLAND'S NEW monarchs took place in Westminster Abbey on 11 April 1689. An hour before the service began, Elias came face to face with Viscount Lumley in the aisle as each searched for his assigned seat. Both were extravagantly clothed in ceremonial robes and ornately styled wigs, adorned with the silver coronets that denoted their ranks. With no sign of recognition, Lumley bent his knee to one of superior rank, then moved on. Elias did the same, wondering if three years of avoiding the man inside the House of Lords had been worth the effort when Lumley had clearly only ever had eyes for Monmouth.

Elias thought of his friend frequently during the ensuing hours. For all his faults, Monmouth's charm had been considerable, and with legitimacy of birth and wise advice, he could have been as loved as his father. The irony was that Argyll's prediction of a peaceful rebellion had been realised, though it was Monmouth's cousins who had reaped the reward and not him. At Princess Mary's request, her husband had been invited to reign with her, and the pair were crowned jointly as William III and Mary II in recognition of their near equal claims to the Protestant throne.

Elias's only regret was that his father wasn't alive to see this presaging of an end to division. Sir William's wish had always been that the voice of the people would be heard by those who governed them, and Elias believed that this ambition was close to fruition. There was no predicting the future, but William and Mary's endorsement of a Bill of Rights, giving primacy to Parliament over the Crown, offered hope. With power shared under a written constitution, Sir William's dream of fair government might finally be realised.

The London crowds had no reservations about their sovereigns. By evening, most were thoroughly inebriated, and drunken cries of 'Good King Will' and 'Good Queen Mary' echoed on all sides as Elias, shorn of his robes, wig and coronet, made his way back to Bow Street. He wondered if their enthusiasm would survive sobriety and had quiet faith that it would. Mary, yet to reach twenty-seven, was wiser than her father, having learnt the art of government from her husband, while William, twelve years older, had become a master of diplomacy through protecting his country from the French.

In a private audience, Elias had respectfully declined a place at court, explaining that his life was in Dorset, but he had declared himself honoured to continue as their personal envoy. He had begged a small favour on behalf of his mother, which had been granted willingly, and on his return to Bow Street he instructed Amos to help Timothy prepare the Granville coach for departure at dawn the next morning.

The elderly valet viewed him with surprise. 'Are you leaving so soon, my lord?'

Elias shook his head. 'Tell Timothy to work out the best route to the Tower. By choice, I would follow the river.'

Amos's mouth dropped open. 'The *Tower*? That's a terrible place to visit. Will Milady be going with you?'

Elias laughed. 'Of course, my old friend. Wild horses wouldn't keep her away.'

The new Constable of the Tower was Colonel Robert Lucas, who had received the keys in reward for pledging his infantry regiment to Prince William during the march from Devon. Elias had met him once or twice in the company of other officers, but their acquaintanceship was too slight for Lucas to grant Elias entry without permission.

Timothy halted the coach at the drawbridge, and Elias lowered the window to hand a letter to the sergeant of the guard. 'Please ensure that the Constable receives this without delay.'

The man glanced at the royal crest on the seal, then stared hard at Elias and his companion. 'Are you here by order of Their Majesties?'

Elias stared back. 'I doubt that's any of your business, sergeant. Deliver the letter, and Colonel Lucas will instruct you on what to do.' He nodded to an open space ahead of them. 'We will await his answer there.'

He called to Timothy to circle the gravel and halt broadside to the Thames, which was flowing some fifty yards distant. Ships were sailing in on the tide and their semblance of a convoy was reminiscent of the Dutch armada, but his companion was more interested in the facade of a high building which was visible behind the wall that bordered the moat.

'What if he's in an upper chamber?' she asked. 'I can manage one flight of stairs but not four.'

Elias followed her gaze. 'That's the White Tower. Prisoners are usually housed in the Bloody Tower. If I'm wrong, I'll carry you.'

'You will not. I have my dignity to preserve. I'll make my own way on my bottom, and you can answer to Rose when she sees the filth on the back of my gown.'

He grinned. 'You think a dirty bottom more dignified than being carried by a gentleman?'

'Infinitely so. To be taken for a frail invalid would be mortifying.' She cast him a teasing smile. 'You can hold my cloak while I make the ascent, so that no one will know I have a dirty bottom except you and Rose.'

He became serious suddenly. 'Are you sure you want to do this? You'll be left with unpleasant memories if he's as close to death as my mother believes.'

Althea tapped the leather case on her lap. 'I must. We gave her our pledge and I intend to fulfil it. She would have come herself if she could have tolerated the journey.'

—

Robert Lucas met them at the end of the drawbridge, and his expression was more resigned than welcoming. He bowed to each in turn. 'My lord, milady, I am at your command. Their Majesties have instructed me to give you every assistance. May I ask what you want of me?'

Elias responded amiably. 'An hour alone with one of your prisoners, colonel. To ensure privacy, we have no objection to being locked in his cell with him.'

'Which prisoner?'

'Lord Jeffreys.'

Lucas watched him closely. 'Am I right that your estate is in Dorset, Lord Granville?'

'You are.'

'Then I must ask the nature of your business with Lord Jeffreys.' Lucas ran suspicious eyes over Althea's staff. 'He's reviled across the land, but by none so much as the people of the West Country. I'm unwilling to grant you confidential access without knowing your reasons.'

Althea shifted her weight to her good leg and raised her staff from the ground. 'This is not a weapon, sir, merely an aid to walking.' She twisted the metal ring and handed him each component part in turn. 'Even were we inclined to harm your prisoner, which we are not, the stick, as a whole or in pieces, has too little weight to inflict meaningful damage.'

Lucas examined the pieces carefully. 'Why is it made this way?'

'Shorter lengths are more easily accommodated in the carriage. The design is Lord Granville's.'

Lucas reconstructed it. 'Clever,' he said, handing it back to her. 'Now, tell me why you and your husband wish to see Lord Jeffreys.'

Althea smiled. 'Are you hoping I'll be more truthful than Lord Granville, sir?'

Lucas was taken aback, not just by the accuracy of the question but also by her assessing stare. 'Yes, milady.'

She exchanged an enquiring glance with Elias, who nodded. 'Lord Granville's mother treated Lord Jeffreys at the time of the Dorchester Assizes for an affliction so painful that it threatened to incapacitate him. She heard recently that his condition has worsened, and since Granville was expected at the coronation she asked us to bring Lord Jeffreys some relief.'

Lucas gave a cynical grunt. 'Why should I believe you? The man was so hated, both as Chief Justice and Lord Chancellor, that he was brought here for his own safety after King James fled. Since then, he has been accused of high treason, and my guards are obliged to watch his food being prepared to ensure it's free of poison. What proof can you give me that your medicine won't kill him?'

'None at all unless you're willing to try it yourself, sir.'

'I am not.'

'Then perhaps you should allow Lord Jeffreys to decide.' Althea gestured to the leather case that Elias was carrying. 'This holder contains vials. If you show him one and tell him it comes from Lady Harrier, he will know what it is and ask you to admit us.' She paused for a reaction. 'The case also contains a letter from Lord Jeffreys which he wrote to Lady Harrier shortly after he was appointed Lord Chancellor. Lord Granville included it because he anticipated your scepticism. Will you read it?'

'Yes.'

Elias extracted the document and gave it to Lucas.

Honoured Lady,

Your son told me I would remember you when my doctor drained me of blood and money to no effect. He added that I might even agree with King Charles that licences have little value when the men who flaunt them cannot provide a cure. He was correct on both counts.

You will have learnt by now that His Majesty has elevated me to Lord Chancellor. The position carries onerous responsibilities and will exacerbate my many pains. I find myself wishing you were in London, since your ministrations were superior to anything I receive here.

Despite my often-churlish responses, I was, and am, deeply grateful for your kindness to me.

Your Servant,

Jeffreys (Lord Chancellor)

Elias retrieved the letter and tucked it inside his coat. 'Lady Harrier heard a week ago that your prisoner is close to death. She tasked us with doing what we can to make him comfortable. Is that agreeable to you?'

'Why didn't she come herself?'

'She is over seventy years old, Lucas. Her spirit is willing to journey one hundred miles for a patient, but her flesh and bones are not.'

Lucas turned to Althea. 'Are you experienced in medicine, milady?'

'Not to Lady Harrier's standard, sir, but she has taught Lord Granville and me enough to help Lord Jeffreys.'

He shook his head at her naivety. 'Two eminent London doctors have examined him and he has refused treatment from both. His mind is broken through fear of what he faces, he is in constant pain and finds eating near impossible. In addition, he is so irascible that his family refuses to visit him, and the few visitors he's had—men of the cloth—have been met with tears and melancholy. What makes you think he'll behave differently towards you?'

She fixed him with her cool blue gaze. 'Nothing, sir. I expect him to be extremely exercised about the charge of high treason that Parliament is formulating against him.'

'I suggest you don't raise that issue, milady. The subject makes him angry.'

'With reason. The charge is without merit, being a simplistic contrivance to satisfy public demand for retribution against King James. Lord Jeffreys is entitled to his anger. He's been made the whipping boy for an ungrateful monarch whose orders he fulfilled faithfully.'

Lucas turned to Elias with some urgency. 'You should speak with Lord Jeffreys alone, my lord. Your wife will annoy him if she raises matters about which she is ignorant.'

The familiar creases appeared at the corners of Elias's eyes. 'I can't do that, Lucas,' he said mildly. 'Lady Harrier insisted that Lady Granville accompany me, and my days won't be worth living if I offend both the women in my life.'

With a frown of disbelief bordering on contempt, Lucas beckoned them to follow him inside the walls and around the courtyard to the Bloody Tower. He questioned the cause of Lady Granville's limp, particularly as the odd glimpse of her feet suggested she was wearing male boots. She masked the limp well through her skilful use of the staff and her husband's supportive arm, but the drag of her left leg was very pronounced on the uneven cobbles of the courtyard.

The greater puzzle was Granville. With his status and connections, he could have picked an amenable bride, but he appeared to have saddled himself with a mouthy female whose stare was discomfiting. Suspecting that Lady Harrier was of the same ilk, Lucas felt a sneaking sympathy for the man as he instructed one of the warders outside the Bloody Tower to unlock the door.

To Althea's relief, Jeffreys' cell was on the ground floor. Wearied by her walk across the uneven cobbles, she positioned her back against the wall outside his door and placed all her weight on her good leg. 'I need a few moments to collect myself,' she told Elias. 'You should take Colonel Lucas's advice and enter alone. Lord Jeffreys may not be dressed for company.'

Elias arched an enquiring eyebrow at Lucas. 'Do I have your permission, colonel?'

'If that's what you want, my lord.'

'It is.'

Lucas inserted his key in the lock and pushed the door wide.

Elias took in the scene at a glance. A narrow, arched window. A desk, piled with papers. A gaunt, wigless figure in a nightshirt, slumped in a chair. The acid odour of suppurating sores permeated the air. He rapped gently on the door panels with his knuckles. 'My mother has sent you a gift, my friend.'

Jeffreys raised his head. 'Who is it?' he snapped.

Elias walked to the desk and placed the square leather case on top of the papers. 'Your one-time aide-de-camp and son to your favourite physician, Jeffreys. I'm here at her bidding. She would have come herself, but she shares your hatred of coach travel.'

'Dear God! *Granville?*'

'None other.' Elias unbuckled the lid of the case and removed a stoppered bottle of sweetened water, a vial and a silver cup. 'We heard a week ago that you've been suffering intolerable pain. This will relieve it.'

'Is it laudanum?'

'Yes.'

Tears of relief appeared in the sunken eyes. 'I've prayed for such a miracle.'

Elias mixed the laudanum with sweetened water in the cup, then knelt to hold it to Jeffreys' lips, taking care not to press against his ulcerated shins and unnaturally swollen ankles. 'While this takes effect, I'll select some clothes. Is your bedchamber through the archway?'

Jeffreys sucked greedily at the liquid. 'It's too much effort. I have no visitors.'

'Today, you do. I've brought an admirer who considers you the ablest jurist of the last fifty years.'

'Who?'

'All in good time,' Elias answered, rising to his feet and replacing the empty cup in the case. 'First, you must dress.' He moved to the door. 'We require ten minutes of privacy, colonel. Be kind enough to find a chair for my guest in the meantime.' He dropped an outrageous wink at his wife before shutting them both out.

Lucas drew a sharp breath. 'This is most irregular. I decide when the door is closed.'

Althea cast him a sympathetic glance. 'Irregularity is Lord Granville's forte, sir, but you needn't trouble yourself on Lord Jeffreys' account. My husband is the last person to wish him ill.'

'Why? The man is loathed even by his own family.'

'For that reason. Lord Granville feels the hatred is undeserved. As Chief Justice and then Lord Chancellor, Lord Jeffreys was duty-bound to honour King James's orders.'

'He could have declined both positions.'

'Indeed, and with hindsight I'm sure he wishes he had, though he's hardly unique in allowing ambition to cloud his judgement. The members of the House of Lords who ordered his arrest as soon as news of King James's flight became public did so only to ingratiate themselves with our new monarchs. We must hope they chose wisely.'

'Meaning what, milady?'

'They'll suffer the same fate as Lord Jeffreys if King William and Queen Mary fail to win our people's respect.' She fixed him with her startling blue eyes. 'You also, sir. Those who take rewards from unloved monarchs are rarely forgiven.'

Lucas crossed the corridor to an empty cell. He returned with a chair and placed it beside her. 'Do you require assistance to sit, milady?'

'I do not, sir, but thank you for your kindness in bringing the chair.' She stepped away from the wall with the help of her staff and lowered herself to the seat.

'What reward has Lord Granville received for the support he's given Their Majesties?' Lucas demanded bluntly. 'I have it on good authority that my fellow commanders refused to block Prince William's advance from Devon on his recommendation.'

'The letter you received an hour ago, sir.'

Lucas scowled in disbelief. 'Is that all?'

'Unless you consider Lord Granville's willingness to continue as their private envoy a reward.'

A silence followed, during which Robert Lucas pondered the implications of the word 'continue'. Had King James known that Granville was acting for his daughter and son-in-law? Almost certainly not or his lands would have been forfeit. 'Your husband's loyalties would appear to be divided,' he said.

'No more than yours,' Althea answered easily. 'I presume you acted out of principle and not self-aggrandisement when you declared for Prince William.'

Lucas could hardly miss the sharp little barb. 'What principle has brought Lord Granville to Lord Jeffreys?'

'He has sympathy for all men who are punished for the mistakes of others.'

'Did he give Their Majesties the name of the prisoner he wanted to see? Are they aware that he's offering succour to their most strident enemy?'

'I imagine they do, sir, since Lord Jeffreys is your only prisoner. Fortunately for the many others who gave their allegiance to King James, our new monarchs are more forgiving than he was. Catholics may have been removed from positions of power, but none has been incarcerated in the Tower.'

'Are you sure of that, milady?'

'Quite sure. Thanks to my father and Lord Granville, I have a large library which is added to weekly by London pamphlets, records of trials and Parliamentary business—all of which I read.'

Another silence ensued and Lucas found himself at a loss. He was used to women who were accomplished in small talk—light-hearted flattery and flirting—not one such as this, who said nothing unless asked a question. 'Who informed Lady Harrier that Lord Jeffreys was close to death?'

'John Barrett, one of the doctors you mentioned earlier. He wrote to tell her what he found when he examined Lord Jeffreys. Both he and she are agreed that he is suffering from kidney disease and is unlikely to survive the month.'

'What prompted him to write?'

'He was curious. Lord Jeffreys named her as the only physician who has ever helped him, and Doctor Barrett wondered what treatments she had used.'

Lucas couldn't contain his irritation. 'Why does that make her responsible for him now? Jeffreys ordered the deaths of thousands across your region. She should revile him.'

Althea was disinclined to be drawn into an argument on degrees of vilification. Instead, she corrected his figures. 'The numbers who were slaughtered have grown in the telling, sir. I've compiled a list from every county in the south-west, and fewer than three hundred met their deaths on the scaffold. It's harder to verify how many reached the West Indies as a result of transportation, but I believe it to be around eight hundred.'

'I was reliably informed that near on three thousand were taken prisoner at Sedgemoor. What happened to them?'

Althea gave an ingenuous shrug. 'My husband believes their ships foundered on the way to the West Indies. From the reports we've received, considerably more were listed for transportation than arrived.'

'I recall reading that men vanished off the road to Bristol. There was talk of murder and profiteering.'

'I read the same pamphlets, colonel, and decided the slur was concocted by the King's enemies to persuade him against appointing Catholics to positions of power. He might have been wise to heed the warning.'

Lucas favoured her with a grudging smile. 'On that we can agree. Are all Dorset ladies as educated and knowledgeable as you and Lady Harrier?'

'I can speak only for those who live under my father's and Lord Granville's roofs, sir, but the cleverness of our servants is inspiring. I taught my personal maid, Grace, to read in three months and am now teaching her mathematics and geometry. She's as quick to learn as my father's footman, Adam, whose fluency in Latin is the equal of mine.'

Lucas listened to Granville's footsteps approach the other side of the door. 'Not many fathers and husbands would allow such indulgence.'

'Thankfully, mine do,' said Althea as the latch scraped against the hasp. 'My life would be unbearably dull if I was forced to share it with halfwits.'

Lucas wedged his foot against the door to prevent Elias closing it, which allowed him to witness what followed. The first surprise was Lord Jeffreys. Though unshod through being unable to push his swollen feet into boots, his wigged head and clothed body softened his otherwise cadaverous appearance, and he greeted Lady Granville with something approaching a smile as her husband introduced her.

The second surprise was how easily she engaged him in conversation. She offered him her hand. 'Lady Harrier sends her regards, Lord Jeffreys, and begs you to remember that only a fool wagers money which he fears he may lose.'

He gave a husky laugh as he raised her fingers to his lips. 'What wager are you offering, milady?'

She accepted the chair that Elias brought in from the bedchamber. 'That I have a better recollection of your cases as a prosecutor than you do, sir. I have transcripts of all your trials and have re-read them many times. You were a formidable opponent.'

Jeffreys watched her dismantle her stick and place the pieces on her lap. 'Your husband told me that his mother was unusual but not unique. It seems he was right. Where did he find you,

Lady Granville?' His breathing was shallow and fast, causing him to pause between sentences.

'At my father's house, sir. Lady Harrier has been my physician since birth and Lord Granville drove her on a visit one day.' She raised her skirt six inches to show her stiff boots. 'I was born with a palsied left leg.'

'I wasn't aware that palsy could be cured.'

'It can't, but it can be ameliorated. Between Lord Granville's inventive designs and Lady Harrier's treatments, I am as you see me now.'

He narrowed his eyes and leant forward to peer at her. 'You are very striking, milady. Who is your father?'

'Magistrate Ettrick of Holt Lodge, my lord. He indulged my passion for the law, philosophy, languages and mathematics from an early age.'

Jeffreys raised his head to look at Elias, who was standing behind Althea. 'Is your mother content to have an intellectual rival under her roof?'

Elias smiled. 'Entirely content. She has even less appetite for empty-headed misses than I do. You might enjoy another stay at Winterborne Houghton, Jeffreys. The debates are spirited and informative.'

Jeffreys gave a mock shudder. 'I reserve my debates for court.' He returned his attention to Althea. 'I dislike revisiting cases and I don't suffer fools gladly, milady. Be warned that I have a biting tongue when I'm annoyed.'

'I would expect no less, Lord Jeffreys. You have not earned your reputation through kindness.'

'What is my reputation?'

'Whose view would you prefer?'

A spark of appreciation appeared in his rheumy eyes. 'The most forgiving.'

'Then that would be mine, sir. You were at your best as a prosecutor. Your oratory was the equal of Cicero's and your legal acumen extraordinary. More latterly, as Lord Chief Justice and Lord Chancellor, you surrendered judicial independence to the doctrines of absolutism and royal prerogative. I cannot fault your loyalty to King James, which was exemplary, but I question your judgement in pursuing policies that were against the will of Parliament and the people.'

His response was sharp. 'Royal prerogative demanded that the King's will took precedence.'

'Assuming one accepts the doctrine,' Althea agreed. 'But the rights and freedoms of the people were enshrined in the Magna Carta four and a half centuries ago. By proroguing and then dissolving Parliament when the members refused to approve his demands, King James rode roughshod over those rights.'

A snort of derision. 'In your opinion, milady, but you are merely aping what my critics in Dorset say.'

She gave a small laugh. 'Hardly, sir. Most of their words are unrepeatable. Your effigy dangles on gibbets in towns across the county, and youths challenge each other to spray your straw feet with urine.'

Jeffreys' mouth inverted. 'You're as free with your descriptions of bodily functions as Lady Harrier . . . *and* as outspoken. Does courtesy not demand that you show more respect to a man who was until recently Lord Chancellor?'

'My respect for you is not in doubt, sir. Were it otherwise, I would not have come. As to courtesy, it depends how you define it. For myself, I find it immensely *discourteous* when people believe me so dull and stupid that that they think flattery will content me.' She prepared to reattach her staff. 'Nevertheless, I have no wish to offend you. It has been an honour to meet you, Lord Jeffreys.'

He frowned. 'Are you leaving?'

'It would be the wisest thing to do, since I cannot promise to curb my straight speaking even for one I admire as much as you, sir. My long studies in philosophy, the law and mathematics have taught me to value truth and honesty above everything.'

'Straight speaking it is, then. Your ill-behaved youths blame me for delivering justice, milady. The south-west nurtured rebellion against a lawful king and paid the penalty for it.'

Althea shook her head. 'They blame you for delivering vengeance in accordance with the King's orders, my lord. Parliament is behaving similarly in its attempts to calm public anger by indicting you. Your committal on a charge of high treason is unfounded, but your imprisonment serves the members' purpose just as well. For a government to be seen to act bestows authority, however reprehensible those actions might be.'

'King James cited that very premise when he sent me to the south-west. The intention was to prevent further uprisings. Your husband would not accept the logic.'

'Rightly, since the logic was flawed. All King James's brutality achieved was to spark a greater uprising three years later. Parliament may have chosen to hail Prince William's advance on London as a "bloodless revolution", but it was rebellion nonetheless.'

Jeffreys brooded for several long moments. 'Will you believe that I wasn't bloody enough for King James, Lady Granville?'

'Readily, sir. You spared many lives by persuading him to commute the sentences to transportation.'

Sudden tears spilt down his gaunt cheeks and he took several gasping breaths before he spoke again. 'Not through compassion, milady. Are you aware that I profited from the sale of men into slavery?'

Althea nodded. 'Lord Granville has the names of all who were rewarded in that manner, yourself included. Will it lighten your load if I tell you that your profit was a tenth of what it might have been?'

He dashed the tears away with the back of his hand. 'Explain.'

'At its height, Monmouth's army numbered seven thousand. One-third appeared before you at trial, the other two-thirds evaded capture entirely, were assisted to escape prison or avoided prosecution before the Assizes began. Of those you tried and sentenced, some three hundred were executed, some two hundred died of gaol fever, some eight hundred were transported and some seven hundred are missing.'

Jeffreys raised baffled eyes to Elias. 'Is she teasing me?'

'No.'

'What happened to the seven hundred?'

'From what I've heard, they were shipped to France or guided north to places of safety.'

'Who was responsible?'

'No one knows, but I warned you at the time of the Assizes that for every rebel you sentenced another twenty would be created. It stood to reason that those twenty would not stand idly by while innocent men were marched in shackles along highways.'

'They were not innocent.'

'Most in the south-west would disagree, my friend. They say you used trickery to entice men into incriminating themselves.'

Jeffreys turned to Althea again. 'You claim to have some knowledge of the law, milady. What is your opinion?'

'That the wording of your inducement was deliberately imprecise, sir. A man on trial for his life would always interpret "leniency" to mean a lighter sentence. Were you and I to dispute the matter in court, I would argue that to encourage guilty pleas on the promise of a more lenient punishment—only to impose the full penalty by virtue of those pleas—was fraudulent.'

'We hadn't time to hear each case individually.'

'Perhaps so, but that's no excuse in law, sir. The relevant clauses in the Magna Carta state that a freeman shall not be seized or imprisoned except by the judgement of his equals or by the law of the land . . . nor be denied or suffer a delay in his right to justice. I've abridged the wording, but that is the thrust of the meaning.'

'You're a purist.'

'The law is pure, Lord Jeffreys. To force it to bend to circumstance is to corrupt it.'

Another rush of tears. 'You think I haven't considered this? I am fully aware that I am now accused of the same crime as the men I condemned.'

Althea pulled a kerchief from her pocket and offered it to him. 'The charge would have been formalised by now if Parliament had any serious intention of trying you, sir. They, too, are bound by the injunction not to thwart or delay justice.'

He dabbed at his eyes. 'Crowds bay for my blood. I hear them from inside these walls.'

She rested her elbows on her knees and leant forward to shorten the distance between them. 'Mobs are notoriously fickle, sir. The cause they espoused a month ago will have been forgotten in their celebration of King William and Queen Mary's coronation.'

'Did Granville attend?'

Althea nodded. 'He did, and said it was deeply moving to see the crowning of joint monarchs.'

'It won't happen again. The circumstances of Their Majesties' accession—married cousins, both with legitimate claims to the throne—are too unusual to be repeated. Will they reign well?'

'They've made a good start, my lord. Their acceptance of the Declaration of Rights has been welcomed across the country.'

'Only a foolish monarch signs away his authority.'

Althea reached for his hand. 'Or two wise ones who seek to end the division that has riven this country for half a century. Shall we take a wager on how well they fare during the next five years?'

Jeffreys clasped her fingers in his. 'Not if you expect the bet to be honoured. What little health I had is abandoning me by the day.'

'But your mood is lighter, sir. Has the laudanum lessened your pain?'

He eyed her with surprise. 'Why, yes!' he exclaimed. 'How strange. I hadn't realised it had gone.'

Althea smiled. 'Lady Harrier asked me to tell you that she hopes you sleep well this night and that your dreams will be pleasant ones.'

The remark was greeted with a delighted chuckle. 'She said that once before.'

'She also pledged me to be at your service for as long as Lord Granville and I remain in London. I clerked for my father from the time I was ten, taking dictation for letters, collating information for cases and writing reports. Will you allow me to perform similar tasks for you?'

His brief happiness turned to melancholy. 'I have no such tasks, milady. I am persona non grata. My friends and family have deserted me.'

'Not all, Lord Jeffreys.' She nodded to the papers on the desk. 'Two of those pages will be from Lord Granville and Lady Harrier.'

'I cannot read them. My sight is failing.'

'Your vision is blurred by cataracts, sir. Lady Harrier asked me to look for cloudy films across your lenses and to offer my help if I saw them. I do so willingly. If you permit me to be your eyes for the next few days, you may find you are not as friendless as you think.'

From his place in the corridor, Robert Lucas watched sobs rack Jeffreys' frail frame as he confessed to unbearable loneliness. With brusque sympathy, Granville stepped forward to place a hand on his shoulder before removing the leather case from the desk and lifting a sheaf of papers, which he offered to his wife. With a gentle squeeze, she slipped her hand from Lord Jeffreys' grasp and took the stack. Sunlight was shafting through the narrow window and she turned on her chair so that the beam shone on the pages. A reflected glow played across her face, and Lucas thought Jeffreys had been right to describe her as striking.

As he listened to her read a letter aloud, Lucas examined his conscience in his dealings with Jeffreys. His view of the man had been formed by what he had heard from others—*a vicious, arrogant drunk with the manners of a brute*—and his visits with him had been ill-tempered and brief. He had paid lip service to Jeffreys' infirmity by providing doctors, but both had received short shrift when they recommended leeches and purges, and Lucas's meagre sympathy had turned to irritation. Yet he realised now that whatever afflicted Jeffreys was of long duration, and he questioned why he had allowed prejudice to colour his judgement.

In the company of people who engaged with him frankly and without artifice, a lighter side to Lord Jeffreys emerged. He chuckled frequently and gave way to sudden flights of fantasy, using the commanding oratory for which Lady Granville had complimented him. On the occasion when he quoted Cicero, she laid the papers aside and answered him in Latin, laughing when he replied in the same language. Thereafter, they mixed the tongues indiscriminately, teasing one another with their fluency.

Inevitably, Jeffreys tired. Lucas estimated an hour passed before his shoulders slumped and he raised pleading eyes to Granville. 'I am done,' he said. 'By some miracle, you have found a wife as delightful and intelligent as your mother, but I am too weary to spar with her further. Will you help me to my bed?'

'Consider it done, my friend.'

'And will you stay with me while I sleep?'

'I will, but first I must escort Lady Granville to our house in Bow Street. I shall return in time to give you more laudanum and sit with you through the night. Is that acceptable to you?'

'Yes.'

'As *quid pro quo*, will you allow Lady Granville to take your papers away and compose suitable replies to all those who have written to you? She will come again tomorrow morning to seek your approval for what she has penned. Is that also acceptable to you?'

Jeffreys only answer was an eruption of weeping and an extension of his hands in gratitude to them both. Without fuss, Granville stepped forward and lifted him bodily from his chair before carrying him through the archway to his bedchamber. Similarly unfussed, Lady Granville reattached the pieces of her staff and rose to her feet. Shifting her weight to her good leg, she leant the staff against the edge of the desk and began gathering the pages into manageable piles.

'May I help you, milady?' Lucas asked from the doorway.

'Please, sir,' she answered. 'You'll carry these more easily with two hands than I can with one.'

He moved to her side and she placed the stacks on his open palms. Thanking him, she used her stick to walk to the door and then stood aside to let him exit ahead of her, drawing the door closed behind them without affixing the latch.

'The rattle of metal may disturb Lord Jeffreys if he's asleep before my husband leaves,' she said, resuming her place on the chair and propping her staff against the wall. She tapped her lap. 'Allow me to relieve you of your burden, colonel. Your arms will tire very quickly under that weight of correspondence.'

He handed her the bundle. 'I hadn't realised he couldn't read, milady.'

'I wouldn't have known either had Lady Harrier not told me to look for cataracts.' Althea rested her hands on the topmost page. 'Consider it a blessing. The letters I scanned earlier were very brutal.'

'The two you read aloud were laudatory.'

'I have an inventive mind,' she confessed. 'He's much weaker than I was expecting and I saw no point in adding to his melancholy.'

Lucas marvelled at her quickness of thought. 'Your kindness has improved his mood, milady. Laughter has been unheard in that room until today.'

Althea toyed with telling him about the euphoric effects of laudanum, but instead adopted Lady Harrier's discretion on matters relating to patients. 'To free him of pain was bound to raise his spirits, colonel.'

Lucas made a confession of his own. 'I feel I should have tried harder to engage with him. He showed you a pleasant side to his nature which I haven't seen. I am now wondering who is the real Lord Jeffreys.'

She responded with amusement. 'That's a philosophical question, sir. Are you sure you want to indulge in scholarly debate at this time of day? What is any man other than the sum of his parts? We are all a mass of contradictions.'

'I suspect you're alone in seeing contradictions in him, milady. To men such as me, he presents himself as an arrogant bully who dislikes having his judgements questioned.'

'You're shockingly indecisive, sir,' she teased. 'It's a bare ten seconds since you acknowledged he has a lighter side. What is that if not a contradiction?'

A smile lifted the corners of Lucas's mouth. 'Can you name others?'

'Not without divulging confidences, but I can attempt to explain why you have such an unfavourable impression of him. Do you wish me to try?'

'Yes.'

'Constant pain gives rise to irritability . . . superior intellect leads to impatience when contradicted . . . an inability to admit that ambition blinded him to King James's flaws demands that he attack first.' A small shrug. 'All men who reach positions of power fear having their inadequacies exposed.'

Lucas thought of his own self-doubts. 'How long has he been in pain?'

'Most of his adult life, I imagine. Lady Harrier tells me he was in agony during the Western Assizes three and a half years ago.'

'Are she and Doctor Barrett right to say he's unlikely to survive the month?'

Althea recalled the symptoms that Jayne had instructed her and Elias to look for: cataracts, extreme fatigue, shortness of breath, swollen legs and ankles, ulcerated skin—all of which were present. 'I'm afraid his time may be shorter, sir. His wife should be informed. It may be that her desertion of him has more to do with fear of baying crowds than lack of affection.'

'You can't assume that, milady. Their marriage was known to be stormy.'

'"Stormy" is a common synonym for "passionate", colonel, and I for one would hesitate to define what form their passion took, since I'm told she's had several pregnancies. With your permission, I'll write to her tonight and offer her my husband's protection if she's willing to come. Would you care to make a wager on whether she'll accept?'

With a wry smile, Lucas retreated to the opposite wall. 'No, thank you, milady. I'm a quick learner and will follow Lord Jeffreys' example by refusing. May I ask you a personal question?'

'By all means, though I reserve the right not to answer.'

'Do you and Lord Granville have a daughter?'

A laugh of genuine amusement issued from Althea's mouth. 'Will it alarm you if I say that we do, sir, and that she is the apple of her father's eye?'

Lucas responded with a laugh of his own. 'Not at all. It would persuade me to beg an introduction for my son should I ever have one.'

'I shall look forward to meeting him, though I make no promises on behalf of my daughter. If she follows the same path as her mother and grandmother, she will bide her time and choose for herself. Do you have a wife, sir?'

He shook his head. 'I've not shared your husband's good fortune, milady.'

The door eased open and Elias stepped into the corridor. 'You'll have to wait in the queue if you want mine, Lucas,' he murmured, lowering the latch without a sound. 'Jeffreys is even more enamoured of her than he is of Lady Harrier.' He shook his head at Althea's enquiring look. 'Days at the most,' he said. 'He can't produce urine, his lower legs are bloated and the skin covered with suppurating ulcers. I'll cleanse them with brine and bandage them on my return.'

Lucas protested. 'Such tasks are beneath you, Lord Granville. I'll send maids to clean and bandage the wounds.'

Elias suppressed a sharp retort that Lucas should have done so sooner. 'Your maids aren't trained to Lady Harrier's high standards, colonel.'

'Even so, my lord, it's hardly a task for a duke.'

'Why not?' Elias asked, removing his embroidered jacket and laying it on the floor. 'My mother has been treating open sores for half a century and her rank is the same as mine.'

Lucas watched him lift the papers from Lady Granville's lap and kneel to place them in the centre of the silk lining. 'Allow me to send for a bag, sir.'

Elias shook his head, folding the collar and tails across the pile and drawing the sleeves together in a tight knot. 'There's no need. This serves just as well.' He stood, holding the makeshift knapsack in his left hand, looking more impressive in a simple waistcoat, shirt and britches, with his hair falling naturally, than Lucas in his extravagant uniform and tightly curled wig.

Althea watched the colonel stiffen with irritation and wondered why men who conformed to social convention found Elias's unorthodoxy so threatening. Lady Harrier put it down to envy—a wish to enjoy the same freedoms that Elias exercised—but Althea saw lack of confidence. Lucas had believed himself to be in control of his Tower and was floundering in the face of a royal request and his prisoner's joyful reception of a rakish duke and his crippled wife.

'What time will you return, my lord?' he demanded. 'I have duties to perform and cannot promise to be available.'

'I wouldn't expect it,' Elias answered without rancour. 'All I require is that you instruct your warders to allow me entry.'

Althea reached for her staff. 'You've been more patient with us than we deserve, colonel,' she said, rising to her feet and offering her hand. 'I have enjoyed my conversations with you and, though you rejected my wager, may I have your permission to write to Lady Jeffreys?'

He stooped over her fingers. 'You may, milady. Will you count it as a win if she comes?'

She smiled. 'Not unless Lord Jeffreys agrees to see her, sir. If he refuses, I shall admit defeat and accept that your definition of stormy is correct.'

Amusement lifted his lips as he released her hand. 'I'm inclined to hope that the defeat is mine, milady. I'm intrigued by your theory that Lord Jeffreys is a mass of contradictions.'

'Are you curious enough to help me prove it?'

Lucas ducked his head in a bow. 'I am, milady. I shall instruct my yeomen to grant you and Lord Granville admittance for as long as is needed.'

EPILOGUE

ROBERT LUCAS NOTED IN HIS ledger that Lord Jeffreys died peacefully in the early hours of 18 April, having made his farewells to his wife and children the previous day. He recorded the deceased man's age as forty-three and wrote that he kept his wits and speech to the end. Beneath the entry, he inscribed in stylised script: *Lord Chancellor of England 1685–1688. God rest his soul.*

'He achieved a great deal for one so young,' he said, laying aside his quill.

Elias turned from the window, where he had been watching uniformed yeoman carry Jeffreys' shrouded body to the Tower chapel. 'He was born two years before me, almost to the day, yet our lives could not have been more different. I gained a title through an accident of birth. He did not. Every advancement he made was through his own efforts.'

'At a high price. Few men have attracted as much hatred as he did.'

They were in Lucas's office in the White Tower, having sat with Jeffreys through the night. A friendship had developed between them over the last six days, and Elias placed a chair on the other side of the desk and lowered himself to the seat. 'His misfortune was King Charles's death. The events that cost him his reputation were King James's accession and Monmouth's rebellion. He was a better Chief Justice under the more benign brother.'

'King Charles never faced an uprising.'

'And would have handled the aftermath better if he had. He certainly wouldn't have encouraged Jeffreys to deepen the enmity between a king and his subjects.'

There was a long silence.

'You puzzle me, Granville,' Lucas said finally. 'Even after a week in your company, I still don't understand your sympathy for Jeffreys. You disagreed with everything he did, yet you showed him kindness. Why?'

Elias propped his elbows on the desk and folded his hands beneath his chin. 'Did Lady Granville not explain it to you? She told me you questioned her on the matter.'

'Briefly, but her answer was hardly enlightening. She said you had sympathy for all men who are blamed for the mistakes of others.'

'I do.'

'Except I have the impression that your feelings are of longer standing than the events of the last four months. Did you sympathise with Jeffreys at the time of the Assizes?'

'It was hard not to,' Elias answered. 'He was in a difficult position—to obey his instructions or make an enemy of the King by rejecting them.'

'Did he show an inclination to refuse?'

'None at all.'

'That must have tempered your sympathy.'

A faint smile twisted Elias's mouth. 'The opposite. I pitied him more. For an intelligent man, he had a shockingly closed mind to the possible consequence of delivering a Catholic king's vengeance.'

'Which was?'

'King James's fall.'

Lucas studied him. 'Was Jeffreys aware that your allegiance lay with the House of Orange?'

'No. His single suspicion was that I was trying to win mercy for rebels.'

'Were you?'

Elias nodded. 'They weighed on my conscience. I could have prevented the rebellion had I been willing to end Monmouth's life. I visited him in the Hague two months before his departure and had the means to do it in my waistcoat pocket.'

'What means?' Lucas asked curiously.

'A packet of white arsenic. He was living on brandy, and there was a good chance his valet and physicians would blame a vomiting death on excessive drinking.'

'Did Lady Harrier know of your intentions?'

Elias shook his head. 'My mother doesn't approve of murder, Lucas. I acquired the arsenic in London.'

'What persuaded you to stay your hand?'

Elias thought back to the evening in Monmouth's cell-like parlour. 'I wasn't confident that his death would be deemed natural. He was of royal blood, and greater damage would be done if unlawful killing was suspected. The Dutch would have blamed the English, the English the Dutch, and the fragile peace between the two countries would have been broken.'

'You must have foreseen that before you visited him.'

Another shake of the head. 'At the time, I could only guess at how events would unfold. My real target was Argyll but I couldn't get close to him. His was the mind behind the plot. Without him, Monmouth would not have proceeded.'

The idea elicited a low laugh from Lucas. 'Few would have mourned Argyll's passing. He wasn't much liked, even in Scotland.' He paused. 'How was any of it your responsibility? The blame for what happened lay entirely with Monmouth.'

'I was told by a source in Holland that he intended to land in Lyme Regis, and I took exception to him choosing a Dorset port to start his uprising. King James was bound to make an example of the county that welcomed him ashore.' Sudden amusement lit Elias's eyes. 'I have less affection for London. Had Monmouth sailed up the Thames, we would not be having this conversation.'

'Londoners wouldn't have flocked to his standard.'

'Jeffreys thought the same. Eagerness to align with a usurper could never happen in the capital.'

Lucas smiled at the dryness of his tone. 'Until four months ago.'

'Indeed. Even London despairs of bad government eventually.'

'You think it was despair that drove the rebellion?'

Elias thought of the poverty that so many of the rebels had endured. 'Or hope. The two emotions are closely linked.'

'Hope for what?'

'To be heard. Their voices resounded loudly when they fought at Sedgemoor. Even Feversham admired their spirit, reporting that it had taken his professional army three hours to overcome an untrained peasant force armed only with pitchforks. Had the King addressed their grievances, he might still be in power. Instead, he sent Jeffreys to silence them permanently.'

'With limited effect, if your wife's calculations are correct.'

Humour twitched at the corner of Elias's mouth. 'My wife's calculations are always correct, Lucas.'

He received an answering twitch.

'It was a foolish policy from the outset,' Elias continued. 'Grievances endure, however brutal the attempt to suppress them. Monmouth set a fire and King James stoked the blaze, a truth acknowledged by Lord Jeffreys in the last few days.'

'With regret?'

'For himself but not for the King. He wanted to be remembered for a lifetime of achievement, not a few wretched weeks in the autumn of 1685. He asked Lady Granville if she thought his epitaph would be "The Hanging Judge" and she said she feared it would.'

'She wasn't usually so unkind,' Lucas said in surprise. 'Most of the letters she read to him were contrived, as were the answers she composed and never sent. He died believing he still had friends and admirers. Why didn't she suggest a different epitaph?'

'He wouldn't have believed her. For all his faults, he never shied away from the truth. He accepted her assurance that he had secured his place in history. In the long list of unremarkable Chief Justices, one name—Judge Jeffreys—will be remembered. The idea appealed to him.'

'He'll be depicted unkindly.'

Elias nodded again. 'As Oliver Cromwell is, but he and his failed republic are not forgotten. You and I will shrivel to dust whatever our small successes, Lucas, while those who make their marks on history—good or bad—live on.'

'Monmouth also?'

'Monmouth also,' Elias agreed. 'He and Jeffreys will be forever linked.'

'Did they meet in life?'

Elias shook his head. 'If they had, they would have detested each other. They shared a yearning to be admired, but in every other respect their characters could not have been more different.'

'Which did you prefer?'

Elias pushed back his chair. 'The same that my wife admired for his mind and my mother for his stoicism in the face of illness.' He rose to his feet. 'Lord Jeffreys. He was a man of principle. He stood by his oath of loyalty to his king to the end, regardless of the consequences to himself.'

'Will history see it that way?'

Elias retrieved his coat from where he had placed it on a coffer. 'Unlikely. He was dealt a poor hand and played it badly.'

'You think Monmouth played his better?'

'Not at all, but he was pretty and had charm, neither of which were qualities possessed by Jeffreys. Lady Granville predicts Monmouth will be romanticised as a Protestant martyr, while "Bloody Jeffreys" will be demonised as a vengeful king's cat's paw.'

Lucas watched him shrug his arms into the sleeves. 'He asked me two days ago if I thought you were responsible for the seven hundred men who went missing. I said I believed you were. Was I right?'

Elias threaded his buttons. 'How did he respond?'

'He agreed with me. He said you have a way with the lower classes. If anyone could spur rebel sympathisers to action, it would be you. He told me, too, that your mother made regular visits to Dorchester gaol. He suspected her of collusion in your enterprises.'

'My wife also?'

Lucas nodded. 'She's too knowledgeable about the law not to have assisted rebels to avoid prosecution. Jeffreys said your family

468

delights in nonconformism, and he envied you for it. Were he to have his life over again, he would live as you do and not as he did.'

Elias took a moment to answer. 'Thank you. You didn't have to tell me that.'

'He wanted you to know. He had only gratitude for the kindness you and your family showed him, and it lightened his conscience to think that seven hundred of the men he condemned escaped.'

But if Lucas hoped to tease a confession, he was disappointed. Elias pulled his gauntlets from his pocket. 'I must take my leave. Lady Granville will want to know the sad news.'

Lucas stood and moved around his desk. 'Will I see you again?' he asked, offering his hand.

Elias clasped it warmly. 'Not for some time. We'll leave for Dorset as soon as our carriage is ready.'

'Then give my regards to your wife. I envy you, Granville. She's a remarkable lady.'

'I know. I thank Monmouth for her every day.'

Lucas frowned. 'Why Monmouth?'

Elias pulled on his gauntlets with a laugh. 'Without him, I would never have met her.' He turned towards the door. 'May fate smile as kindly on you, my friend, but be sure to recognise when it does. Telling gold from dross is not always easy.'

ACKNOWLEDGEMENTS

WITH THANKS TO ALLEN & Unwin's editorial teams in Australia and Britain who gave me invaluable assistance in the making of this book.

Also to Robert Milne-Tyte for his immensely readable history *Bloody Jeffreys, The Hanging Judge*; and G.W. Keeton for *Lord Chancellor Jeffreys and The Stuart Cause*.

My special thanks go to the ordinary men and women of seventeenth-century England who endured a brutal Civil War, a failed republic, a rebellion and a revolution to make their voices heard.

When we take democracy for granted, we forget how many lives were sacrificed to win it for us.

By accepting their roles as constitutional monarchs, William and Mary ended fifty years of political turmoil and gave the British Isles a stable form of government that has lasted for three and a half centuries.

The Swift and The Harrier

MINETTE WALTERS

'A cleverly crafted combination of romance and
adventure story.'
The Sunday Times

Dorset, 1642: When bloody civil war breaks out between the King
and Parliament, families and communities across England are
riven by different allegiances.

A rare few choose neutrality.

One such is Jayne Swift, a Dorset physician from a Royalist
family, who offers her services to both sides in the conflict.
Through her dedication to treating the sick and wounded, regardless of belief, Jayne becomes a witness to the brutality of war and
the devastation it wreaks.

Yet her recurring companion at every event is a man she should
despise because he embraces civil war as the means to an end. She
knows him as William Harrier, but is ignorant about every other
aspect of his life. His past is a mystery and his future uncertain.

The Swift and the Harrier is a sweeping tale of adventure and
loss, sacrifice and love, with a unique and unforgettable heroine
at its heart.

The Last Hours

MINETTE WALTERS

When the Black Death enters England through the port of Melcombe in Dorseteshire in June 1348, no one knows what manner of sickness it is or how it spreads and kills so quickly.

The Church proclaims it a punishment from God but Lady Anne of Develish has different ideas. With her brutal husband absent, she decides on more sensible ways to protect her people than the daily confessions of sin recommended by the Bishop. Anne gathers her serfs within the gates of Develish and refuses entry to outsiders, even to her husband.

She makes an enemy of her daughter by doing so, but her resolve is strengthened by the support of her leading serfs . . . until food stocks run low and the nerves of all are tested by their ignorance of what is happening in the world outside. The people of Develish are alive. But for how long? And what will they discover when the time comes for them to cross the moat?

Compelling and suspenseful, *The Last Hours* is a riveting tale of human ingenuity and endurance against the worst pandemic known to history. In Lady Anne of Develish—leader, saviour, heretic—Walters has created her most memorable heroine to date.

The Turn of Midnight

MINETTE WALTERS

'If you enjoy C.J. Sansom or Philippa Gregory, pick up
this masterfully woven tale.'
Better Reading

As the year 1349 approaches, the Black Death continues its devastating course across England. In Dorseteshire, the quarantined people of Develish question whether they are the only survivors.

Guided by their beloved young mistress, Lady Anne, they wait, knowing that when their dwindling stores are finally gone they will have no choice but to leave. But where will they find safety in the desolate wasteland outside?

One man has the courage to find out.

Thaddeus Thurkell, a free-thinking, educated serf, strikes out in search of supplies and news. A compelling leader, he and his companions quickly throw off the shackles of serfdom and set their minds to ensuring Develish's future—and freedom for its people.

But what use is freedom that cannot be gained lawfully? When Lady Anne and Thaddeus conceive an audacious plan to secure her people's independence, neither foresees the life-threatening struggle over power, money and religion that follows . . .